# The Journey
# of Love and Hope

IVF From a Bloke's Point of View

## Robert Forde

authorHOUSE®

AuthorHouse™ UK Ltd.
500 Avebury Boulevard
Central Milton Keynes, MK9 2BE
www.authorhouse.co.uk
Phone: 08001974150

This is a work of fiction. All of the characters, organizations,
and events portrayed in this novel are either products of the
author's imagination or are used fictitiously. Any resemblance
to actual persons, living or dead is purely coincidental.

Published by AuthorHouse     08/13/2012

ISBN: 978-1-4772-1948-5 (sc)
ISBN: 978-1-4772-1949-2 (e)

# Foreword
## by Colin Litten-Brown

I have known Robert and Iona Forde for a few years now. Rob and I gravitated together inevitably due to the many things we have in common, not least of which being that we have both experienced the process of IVF first-hand and indeed it was through mutual friends at Infertility Network UK that we became acquainted.

Even so we would have probably become friends anyway as we both like science fiction, hate sport and are rather too fond of our food and drink. By strange coincidence we also both work in the FMCG industry (fast moving consumer goods, for those of you not familiar with the acronym or, to put it another way, pretty much everything you will find on the shelf at your local supermarket).

While Rob is a packaging engineer and I a lowly chemist we have both experienced the weirdness that is corporate life and spent many a happy evening swapping "war stories" from our respective companies. Fortunately, Iona and Jennie also share similar interests and background so when Rob and I were in full flow they would simply leave us too it and have their own far more intelligent conversation.

I can therefore fully relate to some of the anecdotes which Rob liberally sews throughout "The Journey of Love and Hope" and, indeed, one or two are very familiar as they are based on my own experiences and were happily donated to the cause. This is not to say that Rob's tale is not generally factual but as a writer I do appreciate the need for poetic license here and there to make the story flow better.

It was, however, the assisted fertility that drew us all close as we found ourselves foundering on the same rocks of despair in the stormy seas of IVF, not knowing where to turn to or who to trust. It was at the point that we had both been fortunate enough to encounter Dawn and Andrew who were truly invaluable when it came to straight advice that we realised that there was succour to be had in others.

I take some pride in sowing the seeds that sent Robert on his mission to write not only this book but more importantly the real version that became so much part of his life for over a year. Having shown him the articles I had written for the local NCT newsletter and the INUK magazine and also confessed that I lacked both the time and inclination to pen a public book on the subject, I suggested that he might consider such an undertaking and he jumped at it with enthusiasm.

My intention in writing the articles had always been to try and give something back, to impart even a few nuggets of good advice to anyone facing the same uncertainty as Jennie and I had. The help and advice we had received from others had made all the difference to us so it was inconceivable that we would not give the benefit of our experience to others.

Regrettably there was little I could write in such a small number of words but whatever I did this book goes so much further.

It does not matter whether you are about to undertake the process yourself, are considering it for the future or are simply an interested if impartial party. The Journey of Love and Hope is a treasure chest of good tips and advice but written in a way that is easy to the eye. It gives a good account of what you might encounter while, at the same time, being an interesting read.

It has been a pleasure and a privilege to read the manuscript and make suggestions here and there but while a keen amateur author myself I do not claim to be the world's best proof-reader. I am sure there are mistakes in the book so please make allowances. Rob has started proof-reading my novels, mostly so he can sponge a free copy from me but at least we are now mutually helping each other in this way.

I do hope that you enjoy this book. For me it was fascinating to read and compare to my own experiences some of which naturally differ significantly from Rob and Iona's journey but the feelings and anxieties are the same. If, as I hope, you read this with a greater appreciation as to what people in our situation have to go through then I am glad but if you are about to embark on assisted fertility yourself and even one gem of knowledge that Rob imparts makes your journey that bit easier, well, then his job is done.

Either way, may your own journey take you to a better place.

Colin Litten-Brown, Kent, July 2012.

# Introduction:
## A few confessions...

This is a work of fiction. There, I've said it though in my defence the key elements of the story *are* based on true events. I am sure as you read my tale that you will realise that my decision to change the names, places and dates throughout the story was done to protect both the innocent and the guilty. I am not going out to either judge or embarrass anybody and therefore any connection with anyone living or dead or any organisations is purely coincidental and unintentional. Where I have used real companies or people I have done so in the context of historical events.

It's a bit like the movies where the film starts and the phrase "this is a true story" flashes across the screen. You may not be aware but once the film starts, everything can be regarded as fiction and often the fact that it is based on a true story is itself part of the subterfuge. This is, of course, not always the case but where they do follow historical events it is rare that they do so religiously. History is normally a bit dull for Hollywood.

To that end I hope you appreciate that I do not feel too guilty altering the basic details.

This first confession, of course, includes me. Robert Forde is a fiction just as much as everyone else in this book. This again is purely to protect the identities of those involved to ensure that their privacy is maintained. If anyone wants to waste their time making anagrams or looking for any other form of significance in the name then I can stop you now. He has no connection to me whatsoever with the exception that like Robert Forde my real name and that of my wife have unfortunate comic associations so as I have been cursed in this way all my life, I am quite happy to lumber Rob Forde with the same handicap.

My second confession is that not everything that you will read happened to me personally, though most of it comes from the first-hand experience of one reliable chap or another. It is a sad fact that life is often not helpful when it comes to good narrative practice and where I felt the story was "lacking" I have taken the liberty of embellishing it with anecdotes from friends and associates.

This is not to say that these anecdotes are not also based on truth and I have been careful to only include events that I am pretty sure really happened. The originators of these anecdotes have all given their anonymous blessing to use them as again there is nothing to connect these tales back to any real people or places.

Most importantly, where I have used second-hand events they are not at the "crucial" parts of the tale.

My third confession somewhat links to the second in that I have used a modicum of poetic license here and there to dress up events, partly to make them more interesting to read but often to obfuscate and provide misdirection so that anyone reading this who knows me is less likely to recognise these parts as relating to my wife and I.

It is very easy to write what you know and that often includes very personal moments that any member of the family or close friends would instantly recognise so some of these "in-jokes" actually relate to other people's families and not my own. If you do happen to recognise something then don't worry, your identity is safe!

Finally, more of an acknowledgement than a confession, I would like to thank the science fiction author Colin (Bob) Litten-Brown not only for sharing his own experiences but for his assistance in the preparation of this manuscript, especially his help with some of the larger words of two syllables or more and those wiggly things and dots that I think are called punctuation, something my brain seems curiously blind to.

Colin also gave me some good tips in terms of structure and flow as well as giving me a pretty good overview of the murky waters of the publishing world, something I have to say I was somewhat naive about. In thanks for everything he did for me I am pleased to provide him with a shameless plug, especially as in all seriousness having read the (free) copies of his books in my possession they are actually quite good. Thus, having never bought one, here I am recommending you to go and do so, but hopefully you will not be disappointed. If you are, remember who wrote it and don't shoot the messenger!

While we are on the subject of recognition, I would like to extend my most grateful thanks to all of those who helped my wife and I through this most difficult period of our lives as well as the contributors who donated stories and anecdotes for me to adapt. In deference to their wish to remain anonymous I will not name them here but they know who they are and my best-felt thanks go out to them all.

I had never expected to find myself writing a book. I

had always felt that the old adage that everyone has a book within them was utter rot, especially as I have met many people in my life that if they do have a book inside them it probably got there through ill-advised ingestion.

It was interesting how I felt moved to put pen to paper, or at least finger to keyboard and all I can say is that it was an experience that I will never forget and I would recommend to anyone. As a form of therapy it was most excellent but once I had managed to write the first sentence (not as easy as you would expect) the flow of creativity was quite a buzz.

With all this in mind, I do hope you enjoy this book. I enjoyed writing it although experiencing the events that form the basis of the story was for both my wife and I a real emotional rollercoaster and if you want to know whether we ended on a high or a low, well you will simply have to read to the end.

If there are any pearls of wisdom that can help others who find themselves in our situation then that would make me feel particularly good. I only managed to get to where I am through the kindness and advice of others who had already been through the same issues that my wife and I faced, advice that was sadly lacking from the official services that I felt should have stepped up to the plate.

Whatever you take from this book, I hope it is positive.

With very best wishes, Robert Forde.

Okay, let the journey begin.....

# Chapter 1:
## Sorry, who are you..?

This is a book about a book. In that respect, this story is not in the least unique but the book in question, well that *is*. You will not find this particular work on any bookshop shelf, it graces the stacks of no library and nowhere on its cover will you find even the hint of an ISBN. It is a book of which but a single copy exists, a volume which was aimed at a readership of one, very particular person who, as you will realise as you read on, may not even exist.

What could this book be, you may well ask? At this stage, all I will tell you is the title which by now you have probably guessed is "The Journey of Love and Hope".

This is the story of the events that lead to the inception of this unique work of literature, a tale of true events but with one very specific aim. It is the story of the journey that my wife and I undertook over the last few years but that journey was an emotional rather than a physical one.

I am, however, getting far ahead of myself for in order to tell the story of the book I should give you at least some idea of who I am so as to put things in context.

My name is Robert Forde. Again that should not be a great surprise to you as it is written all over the cover and thus a bit of a give-away. To be literally correct my name is Robert David Forde and it has been pointed out to me on numerous occasions that this shortens to Rob Da Forde and would make a particularly good rap name, especially in Detroit.

If you could meet me you would realise that I am about as likely to grab a microphone and start talking quickly in that monotone common amongst stars of that particular genre of music as I am to become an Olympic high jumper. Haling as I do from Oxfordshire I was blessed (or cursed) with a slightly posh voice despite the fact that I am, like my parents before me, devoutly middle-class.

Robert Forde was not blessed with the physique of a Greek god and the only six-pack I possess is the metallic form filled with Belgian lager, one of which is providing moral support as we speak. If it is true that within every fat person there is a thin person trying to escape then I have been guilty of false imprisonment for many years. Robert Forde was built for comfort, not for speed. I don't use the excuse that I am "big boned" or have a stocky build. I just eat too much. At least I am not self-deluded like many others I have met.

Fortunately, Rob Da Forde is not a moniker I have been endowed with, though there are those that call me Harry for equally unlikely reasons.

It was one of those passing moments, back in my student days, that were in hindsight, inevitably going to follow me for the rest of my life. It was the day of the last of my final exams; fortunately a morning affair and a group of my fellow packaging students had decided to undertake the "eight pint challenge" at the Brewer's Arms, our local watering hole.

The lounge bar of this classic student haunt is equipped

with eight pumps. On the left there is a popular brand of stout, followed by three real ales that are staples of the pub's drinks menu followed by two "guest" ales that vary on a monthly basis, a strong foreign lager and finally a good old-fashioned scrumpy cider of the sort that long-term exposure to will impair your eyesight.

As challenges go it was not a particularly difficult one, the rules as far as there were any were very simple, you started at one end of the bar and had a pint from each pump in order until you reached the other end and you had to do so by the end of lunchtime drinking.

This was, of course, back in the days prior to all-day opening when some pubs actually closed for a few hours in the afternoon to wring out the carpets so that you were forced to down your eight pints in, by the time the exam was over, what amounted to around ninety minutes (just over eleven minutes per pint).

You only had one choice and that was simple: which end of the bar did you start i.e. did you go left to right or right to left or, more importantly, did you start on the stout and finish on the scrumpy or vice-versa?

I will not bore you with the aftermath of this session which, by the way, did not include anything sensible like lunch but the drinking was interspersed with such imaginative games as "who can belly dance the quickest", "who can belch the word 'bollocks' in the most convincing way" and, pertinent to my good self, "who is the person least likely to be mistaken for Harrison Ford?"

Needless to say I won both by virtue of physically being the person most suited to the role but also with my surname the result was inevitable. By the back-straight of the bar "Harrison" had been shortened to "Harry" and by last orders the nick-name had stuck.

People still call me that today though few either know

or remember why. I just hope the actor who I hold in high regard never finds out he has been compared to someone with the appearance (but not the strength) of a moderately bored mountain gorilla.

I am not putting myself down, the fact was and to an extent remains that I am on the larger side but I blame nobody but myself. I love my food and detest exercise which is a recipe for disaster or at least obesity. Boredom and loneliness paid more than their part to result in the portly person I now am.

The only reason I mention it as I wanted to begin to paint a picture of Rob Da Forde, rapper to the rotund.

I have alluded to the fact that I went to university and in that respect regard myself as fortunate, especially in the economic climate of the twenty-first century where jobs are scarce and every educational advantage is worth its weight in gold.

My chosen subject was packaging engineering which you may frown at, this not being one of the regular degree subjects that most people seek but is perhaps one of the most crucial.

If you consider just about everything you purchase, from food to furniture, it usually comes packaged in some kind of outer carton, bag, box or blister pack. These things don't grow on trees (okay, technically the wood pulp in the cardboard *does* grow on trees but the finished folding corrugated carton does not) and it is the job of the unsung packaging engineers and packaging designers to come up with that mountain of surplus material that you so casually throw into the recycling bin.

To put it another way, I design boxes. This is a terribly simplistic view but I have found myself in all too many social occasions where I begin to explain what it is that I do only to be faced with what is becoming a familiar glazed expression. Rather than bore the pants off of whichever unfortunate soul had asked the question I usually revert to "I design boxes" as a quick summary of what is in fact a very complex and interesting (at least to me) subject.

As careers go, it is okay if you like that sort of thing and certainly beats hearing the continual beep of the bar code scanner or having to constantly utter the mantra "do you want fries with that?". This is not that either is a bad thing, you understand, but packaging engineering certainly pays better and you don't have to work weekends.

On the flip side, I am not curing cancer and arguably rather than saving the world I am contributing to its accelerated demise though in my opinion it is not the world that is in trouble, it is just us! Planet Earth will get along just fine with or without us. In my defence a lot of my undergraduate dissertation work was looking at the subject of secondary uses for primary packaging – finding some other function for it rather than just throwing it away – something that is still close to my heart.

So what does this have to do with anything? Honestly, not much but that is precisely the point. If you wind back the clock twenty years you will see that long-departed younger version of me embracing life at a moderate pace but wallowing in a sea of loneliness, longing and lager, unaware of just how long he would have to wait until that side of his life began to sort itself out.

Robert Forde was, as now, totally unremarkable, one of the millions of anonymous faces in the crowd. Where I had glances at all it was usually from women looking at me with mild but passing revulsion that I was on the portly side but I knew that the memory of me would be as transient in their minds as a snowflake on a sunny day.

Despite attempts to the contrary I find that I cannot generate much of an interest in sport and while I am not particularly into computer games I do like science fiction, a social Achilles heel that probably did not do me any favours (sorry Colin!).

While at the time I felt a sense of great isolation, looking back I realise that the problems I felt were uniquely mine, an inability to find a girlfriend being top of the list, were sadly all too common in society, not that I could see this as I wallowed in the warm mud of self-pity.

It is like the check-out queue at the supermarket. You always feel as if you manage to pick the line that moves slowest only because you only remember those annoying times when the queues either side of you race past as the little old lady in front of you helpfully finds the correct change for her shopping from the deepest recesses of her handbag while telling the check-out girl her entire family history.

Major economies have risen and fallen faster than people like her can find that last elusive penny, made more annoying as they are genuinely doing it to be helpful when in fact simply handing over a tenner and getting the change would have been much faster and the store probably counts its change by the tonne.

The human brain doesn't record those times when you stood in line and were served in good time while lost in your own thoughts.

It is the same with friends. You always dwell on those smug men into whose arms women seem to throw themselves no matter how badly they behave, not recognising that for every one of those you probably know half a dozen others who are finding the whole process of attracting a mate as baffling as yourself.

And so it was. Robert Forde or Robert the not-so-great as I used to call myself entered the world of men with a relatively good education (a scraped upper second class degree) a fair bit of excess weight and near-terminal loneliness. It passed almost unnoticed that I managed to walk into a good job in a multinational company – let's just put it this way, at some point you have unwrapped and eaten something that was made by my former employees unless you have *serious* dietary restrictions.

Even in those days, the beginning of the 1990's, the job market was in decline but it was a measure of my self-absorbed and self-indulgent moaning that I did not appreciate that in fact I was fortunate that at least the employment side of things was ticking along nicely. This was only partly due to my natural abilities, it has to be said. Where I was fortunate was to work with a very select group of mentors who had far more belief in my abilities than I did and kept my career on the straight and narrow while I was nowhere near the tiller of my own boat.

Friends and family alike gave me the same condescending (if annoyingly true) advice that there was someone out there for me and that "it" would happen someday. This advice normally came from people within relationships rather than single guys so I rarely gave it credence and as to the advice that I should lose weight, well that went in one ear and out the other. Eating was pretty much all I had.

It was not that I was self-deluded in terms of my size but simply that eating is an addiction just like smoking and was something I had to deal with in my own way but that is another story.

And so it was that Robert Forde plodded along, living from one year to the next in the increasingly forlorn hope that "Miss Right" would sweep into his life.

Do not, by the way, feel in any way sorry for Rob the younger. I look back on that period of life with little more than acute embarrassment and I have nothing but heartfelt thanks for my friends and family who put up with my eternal whinging for so long.

Little did I know, however, that not a million miles away, a rather attractive young lady was herself just emerging from teaching college and feeing just the same as me.

The years rolled by as did some of the most pivotal decisions in my career, not that I realised at the time just what the significance of my choices were. We all follow a path in life and every now and then meet a crossroads where a simple decision will decide the whole course of our future destinies.

Some people reach these junctions and pause, deliberating carefully what they should do while others stride confidently down their chosen route, comfortable with their ability to always know what is best.

I think I managed to pass just about all of my crossroad markers with my head down (or up my own arse as some might suggest) such that I probably even now could not tell you when they all happened. I treated them in the same way as I would selecting a menu choice at my local curry house, it depended on what I fancied on the spot regardless of the effect it would have on me in the morning.

In some respects it was the joy of being a bachelor, with only myself to look after, not that I was doing such a grand job of that, it really didn't matter too much what I did so long as I stayed employed and was able to fund my sedentary lifestyle.

For that reason, my career was something that seemed to happen despite me and around me rather than with any conscious effort on my part. Looking back I realise what happy carefree times they were but more on that later. If I knew then what I know now about what a nasty place the world really is I might have taken my choices more seriously.

Needless to say, after a decade of wrapping the kind of snack products I liked to consume (and having access to a company store which was really not conducive to dieting) I jumped ship to a packaging consultancy more so I could move back to my native Oxford than any other reason. Living up north as my first job had required really did not suit me, being the devout "southern shandy" that I am as my old colleagues fondly called me.

There is one thing to be said about most multinational companies, they are not based in exciting places whereas being back among the alleys and spires of Oxford was a breath of fresh air.

The pivotal first job I had landed had been placed in what is often noted as one of the most built-up places in the country where you were never more than a few miles from a motorway and the constant buzz of traffic was unavoidable.

My undergraduate days had been spent at a much lesser university far from the comfort zone of home but the fact was there was never any real danger of my qualifying for Oxford. When it comes to academia I was always economical with my time and effort, doing just enough to pass relatively well rather than excel. I was not Oxford material even though Oxford ran through my veins.

With my thirtieth birthday long gone the deeply gnawing angst that I was going to remain single had subsided to a bitter inevitability. All of my friends by now were happily wed and progressing to the stinky nappy stage whereas I had been left far behind and nobody really thought that I would sort myself out.

I was neither surprised or in any way hurt when this resulted in my once best buddies suddenly becoming rather vague and distant as the focus of their life shifted to their new family commitments.

I could not understand what they were doing but I did accept it, all the while my heart fracturing even further at the sense of loss that I was not going to experience even the smallest part of what they were now enjoying every day.

In twenty years the longest I had managed to go out with anybody was three months and that was only because when I asked her out she had been too embarrassed to say no and it had taken me that long to realise.

Worse was the fact that I had wasted six years in a futile attempt to attract someone who I thought I loved but who clearly had no reciprocal feelings for me which I have no doubt psychologists would have a field day with but at the time was the most important thing in my life.

I know I am not alone as I have met others who have done the same thing, butting their heads against a barrier like goldfish in a tank, constantly in denial and yet carrying on as if giving the woman in question yet another present would in some way bring her around. That is another story (part of the same "another story" alluded to earlier and which I may one day write).

For whatever reason, things simply did not work out but largely it was down to the fact that not going out much or being particularly social, especially with all my mates married off and long gone, I was not really in a position to meet anyone.

There was also the question of my appearance. I cannot tell you when or why it happened but one day I looked in the mirror and had the curious thought "Well, I wouldn't go out with you so why should I expect anyone else to do so?" This is not some weird homosexual thing, before you ask, but there comes a point where you have to admit that if your target is beautiful, attractive and intelligent then you ought to at least attempt to offer the same in return.

Talk about stating the bleedin' obvious. It was sad that it

took me nearly fifteen years to realise what people had been telling me all along.

Now, I am not suggesting that fat people cannot be sexy or in any way nice people, just look around you and it will not take long to find many who are both happy in life and, more importantly, married to someone who loves them.

It was the former of these that was the problem. Fundamentally I was not happy in life and whether correct or not my weight was a large part of the problem, if you will excuse the pun.

Again I will not dwell on the details but in 2004 for whatever reason I found the strength to drop seven stone in weight. My friends and family were as stunned as I was at the result. The new Harry Forde was still overweight but it was the psychological impact that was most critical.

For the first time in nearly two decades, I was finally at peace with myself.

Okay, all very Zen but the fact was I was still just another face in the crowd, I had not changed my lifestyle all that much beyond dropping the odd few thousand calories every day from my dietary intake and my contentment was as much the final resignation that I would remain a bachelor than anything else.

It was during the spring of 2005 that an old college friend of mine announced her wedding. I had always counted her among the seriously attached crowd although her engagement had in fact lasted fifteen years and her kids were teenagers.

One thing after another had at first delayed their marriage until it had reached the point where not being married had become habitual. To this day I don't know what triggered their decision to wed, whether it was out of a sheer whim or something more personal but whatever the reason the small white envelope popped through my letterbox sometime around Easter.

I will be perfectly honest my first inclination was to decline the invitation. By now I had spent my entire adult life going to parties, weddings and other social occasions alone. At first this had been no problem but as friends became couples I rapidly became the odd number. There is something frightfully British about the need for symmetry at a dinner party and as fewer and fewer single people remained it became more and more difficult to pair me up.

I did not notice when I stopped being invited to dinner parties due to my acute asymmetry but eventually it did occur to me.

Weddings were less of a problem; there were always odd numbers of distant relatives around which I could fill a gap even though it was worse to be on your own among weird strangers than to be single around people you knew.

Having never been a proficient gooseberry, I found myself more and more declining the few offers that came my way, gracefully doing the right thing (as I felt) and just keeping out of the way and not making a fuss.

So it would have been with Sandra's wedding had I not bumped into her on the train and been embarrassed into saying I would go – well you can hardly say no to someone's face especially when they are devastatingly attractive and you cannot think of a reasonable lie on the spot.

Committed as I was I sullenly put the date in my diary and returned the obligatory RSVP, grudgingly ticking the box to say that I would not be bringing a partner.

My only consolation was that the reception was to be held at the Malmaison Hotel in Oxford which is sited in the old Oxford prison – for those of you who remember the classic Ronnie Barker series "Porridge" it is the location used for Slade Prison prior to its conversion into a classy hotel.

I had wanted an excuse to go there for a long time so in some respects here was one handed to me on a plate. Had I not been so petulant I would have probably accepted on that basis alone though I know what you are thinking, I should have been going because she was a friend. I know and I can only apologise profusely for the way I was back then.

Sandra had not been on my course but had studied education. I only knew her as she had for a while gone out with one of my friends and we had oddly kept in touch where he had dropped off my radar years previously. Sandra had become used to using me as a sounding board and regarded me as "safe", probably as she knew I knew she was well out of my league so would never dream of making a pass at her despite the effect she always had on my hormones.

More recently we had drifted apart as often happens with age but she had kept sufficient fondness for me and appreciation of the moral support I had given her to eventually invite me to her big day.

Luckily, I committed myself to going early enough to book a cell room at the hotel. If you have never encountered this place on the TV (I believe it was used in an episode of Inspector Morse), some of the rooms are in the cells in the old cell block and still maintain the thick metal doors, though the decor has vastly improved from its original purpose.

The big day arrived and fortunately the weather, forecast to be horrible, held during the service and the rain only arrived once we were safely ensconced in the hotel.

It is surprisingly cramped in the Malmaison and you appreciate, standing there with a glass of champagne and some indescribable canapé, what the conditions must have been like for the inmates. Despite the renovations, the wind still whistled under the doors and the whole place felt decidedly claustrophobic yet chilly at the same time.

I knew very few people. That is to say, I theoretically knew many of the guests but most of my friends I had not seen for many years and we had all changed markedly in that time. Conversation was stunted and dwelled for the most part on "old times" with the inevitable "so what are you doing now" ploy to compare yourself to your fellow students to measure your level of success.

For me it was quite a surprise to find that despite their success in the marriage department I was actually faring particularly well on the employment stakes and to my estimation ranked in the top five for salary. It gave me a small but satisfactory moment of smugness that was soon dissipated by the ever-present awareness of my single status.

The friend who Sandra had once dated was also there and I was pleased to discover that he had become a total arse. All guilt I harboured at having lost touch with him dissipated in an instant.

I stood, glass in hand, with the appropriate look of congratulations as the newly-weds made a few speeches, thanking us for coming and that sort of thing before explaining the arrangements for the rest of the evening.

With horror I listened as they described the inevitable disco. I dance about as well as a Manatee hang-glides so the moment the strains of "Ebenezer Good" piped up I was heading for anywhere but the dance floor.

The Malmaison is furnished with a number of outdoor places and in anticipation of the cold they had erected paraffin heaters. Despite this, few hardy souls ventured into the frigid night air and indeed the bulk of the party had seemingly embraced the booming noise, having all crammed into an area far too small to accommodate them all.

I found myself wandering through the nearly empty cell block with the words *"Norman Stanley Fletcher"* echoing

already made the connection and would make much hilarity of the fact at some more appropriate time. At least her middle name was Olivia, not Rusty which would have sealed her doom.

Nothing mattered that night. As tired as we were it was so nice just to be with each other and to revel in the fact that our most cherished hope had finally come true. With the exception of my cousin Dave and his wife having a most spectacular and, it has to be said, entertaining bust-up in the car park for reasons I doubt either of them would remember when they sobered up, the day had been faultless.

All our years of waiting had been rewarded with the perfect day.

This was followed by a perfect honeymoon, island-hopping around the Caribbean for two weeks, not that we really appreciated the place much, spending most of our time languishing on the beach, wallowing in the sea or the pool or engaging in those private activities that honeymoon couples are accustomed to do.

We came back to a drizzly England with seriously deep tans that were totally inappropriate for the weather and in my case the same cheesy smug grin on my face that had probably not moved since she had said "I do."

Our return had been timed to bring us home just in time for Christmas, made even more special that year as we spent the whole of Christmas Eve unwrapping wedding presents only to follow it the next day with the traditional festive gifts.

I really felt as if I knew exactly what wedded bliss really meant.

With the bitter winter blast of January came the inevitability of the return to work and that sense of regret that our special time was well and truly over. Still, we now had the rest of our lives together to plan things and do things.

Not long after we had set up home together, Iona having found a teaching position not too distant to Oxford, I found myself looking in the mirror one day and was somewhat amazed at the stranger who stared back.

I had barely known Iona for two years but here we were now happily married and for the first time I realised just how much I had changed. That scared, lonely, neurotic person I had once been was gone, replaced by the happy, confident fellow who now admired his own appearance.

Something in my face had changed. I could not put my finger on what precisely but there was an edge to the features that I had not noticed before. It could have been a simple symptom of the fact that I was not getting any younger or a touch of maturity that had so long been absent. Either way, the sad old Robert Forde of before had quietly died and nobody had mourned his passing, least of all me.

Gradually, the grind of everyday life descended around us and we soon went from newly-weds to the point where our first anniversary was looming on the horizon.

We had the conversation.

Whether it had been on her mind for a while she would not say and nothing about the evening in which it occurred seemed to be any different from all the other evenings we had spent together.

For sure she was well-informed and knew precisely what would happen if she were to come off the pill and perhaps it was time to start thinking about the possibility of children.

Luckily, it had been on my mind for a while as well. By this stage I was rolling rapidly down the hill of my thirties to the point where turning forty was not as far away as I cared to admit. As nice as enjoying each other's company had been after the wedding it was in truth no different than before we were married.

I am not quite sure what I had expected to be different but clearly something was as my thoughts turned more and more to how nice it would be to have little ones running around the place.

Iona had clearly built herself up for the conversation so when she realised that I was very open to the concept the look of sheer relief on her face was a picture. In far shorter time than I am sure she had anticipated the decision was made. She would cease the contraception and we would allow nature to take its course.

It was a terribly exciting moment. I did not really have any idea how long it would take the pill to flush out of her system but as the weeks went on I knew that the chances of her conceiving were becoming greater and greater.

Life was so perfect, I had met the woman of my dreams, we had married and now we were busy working on the new model Forde. What could possibly go wrong?

I am not particularly religious though in some irrational ways I am superstitious and I should have known better. Even as the thought had crossed my mind, somewhere up in the clouds, the ancient, malevolent figure that was Fate looked up from his multi-dimensional chess game and smiled. Someone had made a statement that he simply could not ignore.

"What could possibly go wrong?" Fate shook his head. "Well, my friend, allow me to demonstrate..."

From his pocket he took the pair of dice, perfect solids impossibly based on nonagons that would have made Pythagoras weep at the inadequacy of his dodecahedron.

Casting the dice across one surface of the chess board,

Fate peered down at the result and smiled, pleased with what he saw. With a gentle wave of his hand, destiny was sent forth to deliver the consequence.

I don't know what they teach at school these days. I did read somewhere that the three "r's" have been replaced by the three "t's", texting, typing and something else beginning with "t" that escapes my memory. Whatever it is, the principle is similar in that the idea is to try and impart the basic skills required to survive in society (again, without needing the phrase "do you want fries with that").

During my rather economically-approached academic career while I did not excel I did do more than adequately given my general lack of effort when it came to homework and, by the time I reached university, well-honed exam question spotting skills.

Like many people I entered the big, nasty world of adulthood in the assumption that I was now ready to function and deal with most problems but the fact is that school only prepares you for the "model" life.

Careers officers' true role is not to suggest a job for which you might be suited but to manage expectations of your ultimate destiny. For those with delusions of adequacy the incessant beep of the supermarket check-out awaited while others with at least a passing degree of talent were shepherded into the middle class line with the rest of the wage slaves. Only the ones they had already given up any hope of became entrepreneurs or rock stars.

I do recall a rather bizarre "general studies" subject which had useful things like how to write a cheque which in hindsight was somewhat of a slur on not only my intelligence but also my fellow grammar school pupils who were theoretically in the top twelve and a half percent in terms of intelligence. Lessons on how to sign your name on a small piece of paper indeed! I could only imagine what they were teaching in general studies for the other eighty seven and a half percent of the population – probably "left" and "right" on their shoes.

The fact was, of course, that school really does not prepare you for real life. University is little better and in many ways a lot worse. You can make mistakes there with at least some buffer between you and the harsh reality of life.

Most of my tutors were so detached from reality that I would have not been surprised if they were not in fact aliens. It felt strange being taught what aspects of a subject would be useful to us in our chosen profession by people who had never had a job in industry themselves.

Most of what we generally learn that really keeps us on the straight and narrow when we fly the nest we pick up in the playground, down the pub or any one of a hundred other social interactions with our friends. There are very few kids who do not have a detailed vocabulary of popular slang and swear words by the time they reach ten but who know absolutely bugger all about the subjects their teachers futilely try and drill into them during school.

Armed as I was with a particularly good selection of ways of describing the male and female genitalia I naively felt that I was ready to face whatever it was the world had in store for me.

Of course that was my first mistake. Had I realised that on turning eighteen I was about to embark on nearly as long a period of loneliness and heartache I would have probably drunk far more than I actually did on that most disappointing of birthdays.

There was nothing in that long academic preparation to tell me how to attract a girlfriend and as you have already read it took me rather too long to pick up the knack.

Simultaneously, there were yet other things lurking in the background, little time bombs of the unexpected that many of us have at some point in our lives and which changes us forever.

For some it is a horrible disease, for others their future holds some nexus point of tragedy, the early loss of a loved one, for example or an untimely death under the wheels of a mobility scooter. Other more lucky souls have a lottery win or find unexpected fame and success though I doubt if the good ever fully balances the bad.

Fate had just set the timer on one such explosive for Iona and I.

The months went by and, without going into graphic detail, we were at it like rabbits. This of course was by no means a problem for either of us. They do say that practice makes perfect and I am a true perfectionist! It was not that I was making up for the barren wilderness that my sex life had been for the bulk of my adult life but we were now on a mission and an enjoyable one at that.

While I sensed Iona was impatient my guess was that with the effects of the pill still wearing off that it would take a while and there was still part of me that enjoyed us being a carefree couple so when nothing happened at first I was not in the least worried. There was no immediate panic and besides it gave us more opportunity to keep practicing!

I suspect in hindsight that she was not quite so relaxed about it and I am sure the doubt crossed her mind far earlier than it did mine. For me I only had to look at the friends who had either had kids before they married or been too enthusiastic on honeymoon to realise that we had that special time – wedded yet untied.

A few months became several months and excitement became tinged with an edge of anticipation. An unspoken point was reached and the mood began to change. It is so easy to be "not trying but not trying to prevent it", coming off of contraception and allowing nature to take its course.

It's a bit like playing roulette in a casino but where the odds are stacked in your favour – sooner or later you expect to hit the jackpot. It isn't a matter of 'if' it is simply a matter of 'when'.

We had passed the point of "not trying to prevent it" and were well and truly trying but nothing was happening.

By this time we were rapidly developing a circle of friends and family with babies and small children so it was inevitable that they were sooner or later going to come and visit. What would be more logical therefore than to buy the odd toy here and there for them to play with while they were here (and, of course, when ours came along we would already have them)? Books would be bought as presents, duplicates purchased and stored away "just in case".

Were we tempting fate? I have already mentioned that I am somewhat superstitious but I have heard far more rational people than I turn all astrological at times like this. It is nonsense of course, whatever was going to happen had nothing to do with any mythological figure but we all have some throwback to our ancestral fear of the unknown and worship of the natural gods that break the surface at such times of stress.

Things became serious when we had the conversation about names. This is perfectly natural but it is like naming a pig you intend eventually to eat – always a bad move. As soon as you have put a name on a potential baby it suddenly adopts a pseudo-existence, becoming a virtual entity that only requires the actual physical process of manufacture to realise. This, of course, also weaves a web of emotional connections that lays a potential trap for the future should things not happen according to plan.

We talked about names at length and picked ones we liked, hedging our bets between a boy and a girl; gazing with starry eyes across the expanse of time to all those moments we would share with the children-to-come. I was the big hairy hunter, standing at the entrance to his cave beating his chest with not a care in the world and not a thought to the fact that we were anything but perfect.

We were ready to populate the world with the new Forde dynasty, it would be a great and terrible lineage, lasting for generations as our descendants roamed their way around the world undertaking great feats and achieving incredible things.

Meanwhile back on planet Earth, the months continued to pass and absolutely nothing continued to happen. The oracle of all information, the internet was again consulted for foods and healthy living regimes that could improve the chances of conception. Old wives tales abounded and were tried. They all failed with a crushing inevitability.

You know things are beginning to change when a diary becomes involved. Dates are logged, learned texts scrutinised for the optimum times to have intercourse. While still pleasurable, there is an undercurrent of something more urgent, more clinical. Nature isn't taking its course but that is just luck, all it needs is a bit of a nudge in the right direction, surely?

Even at this point you justify it in your head. It is not that there is anything wrong it is just taking a bit of time that is all.

It was also around this time that I became familiar with a particular aisle in the chemists, that aisle that sells certain self-test kits that should have a health warning on the side "warning, use of this kit is likely to bring a hell of a lot of anxiety and disappointment". At first I felt like I was buying a top-shelf example of gentlemen's literature, wandering around that famous high-street Chemist as if I were browsing for chewy bars or toothpaste and just

the oddities of men that women sometimes forget. Unlike the fairer sex we have a rather schizophrenic approach to the discussion of such subjects. In the right situation and appropriate company (okay, down the pub with our male mates), most men will wax lyrical about sexual organs, our prowess in the bedroom and volunteer the most intimate details at slightest opportunity, some even revealing their genitalia with some pride under the right conditions (put another way the right amount of alcohol).

Stick us in a doctor's surgery in a room devoid of male support and suddenly we revert back to shy six year olds and the whole subject becomes taboo. This is only heightened when the women present show their vast superiority over us weak men by discussing their own problems as if they were chatting about the most mundane of subjects. I am sure it is not like this but it reminds me of travelling on business in Japan.

There is, or certainly used to be, a certain business ethic in Japan where after a long and hard negotiation both parties would then go out and party to considerable excess. This would, depending on the importance of the meeting and those present, involve at least three bars, a good meal and then either Karaoke, gambling or, most frequently, yet more drinking.

I will hand it to the Japanese that I have had the sincere pleasure to meet over the years, as well as being perhaps the most polite people I have ever met they can certainly pack it away! There was one particular gentleman whom will forever remain nameless who earned the nickname of 'hollow legs' from my American colleagues due to his ability to sink a bottle of whiskey without any outward affects.

This, however, is the point. If you had a meeting the next morning, the differences in cultures were obvious. The Americans and Europeans in the room would all be reaching bleary-eyed for the coffee, groaning and generally admitting by their body language that their internal organs were still in deep trauma. The Japanese, however, would all be sat stiffly upright, immaculate in dress and other than the fact that you could see it in their eyes, showing no sign of weakness whatsoever. How they must have been suffering inside!

The moral of this story, never judge a book by its cover, I think suits my purpose nicely. Men and women just accept that we have our own ways of dealing with these sorts of situations on the outside; it does not mean that we are feeling anything different on the inside.

I am probably being terribly unfair to Iona and I am sure she felt as self-conscious as I but it was just that she was being far more mature about it.

Inevitably, the subject came up but it was at that moment that I reached an epiphany in that there was a much bigger picture here. My desire to have children is very strong but it was only then that I appreciated the sheer deep-seated instinct that drove my wife. I could see it in her face that this was a far more momentous occasion than I had given credence.

A decision had to be made and quickly. Did I want to carry on being an insensitive selfish bloke or was I going to grow up and talk like a rational adult. Bit of a no-brainer really.

With the cold shower of reality now over, I felt the blood seeping away from my glowing cheeks and with a new sense of confidence and purpose, engaged with the good doctor to lay out our situation.

*How long had we been trying?* Ah, a nice easy one to start. *Any relevant medical history?* Well, nothing serious in a long time though I could still see her eyeing up my generous physique with acute suspicion. References were made to the blood work she had proposed and she was evidently not convinced at my own optimistic self-diagnosis. *How long had Iona been off the pill?* Again, the answer to this was simple indeed.

*How often did we have sex?* In hindsight we should probably have rehearsed this one rather than doing what I am sure every couple in the country does which was to look at each other, open mouthed in the hope that the other would answer or that if we did speak at the same time we would say the same thing. Telepathy would be really handy in this sort of situation and if the Human species ever evolves this faculty, it will be largely as a result of moments like this.

We gave an answer that seemed about right and which, judging by her expression, the Dr Armstrong probably took with the same pinch of salt that she needed for my estimation of the number of units of alcohol I drank in the average week. I wonder if anyone has ever done a survey about what people actually do compared to what they say to a doctor?

With my blood tests ordered, attention focused on Iona and it was here that our GP decided to start her real investigation. In hindsight, this felt a little unfair to me. Surely with my A-level biology knowledge it takes two to tango when it comes to making babies? Given this, therefore, there is equal chance of either side having a problem?

This brings me onto a very sticky subject and one that I will probably touch on several times, that of 'blame'. I cannot imagine what goes on behind closed doors between some couples that have fertility issues but as my friend Colin suggests in one of his published articles (which I reproduce here with his blessing) you will end up falling into one of three camps:

1. "It's your fault". Uttered I would imagine

predominantly by men and history is replete with Kings who have used this very line as a convenient way of annulling marriages (usually by means of a sharp axe). Anecdotally I have heard of more men blaming the wife for any problems, whether they are biologically hers or not. My advice is just not to go there. Discovering you are infertile is hard enough without some drunken plonker assuming you have done it just to annoy him.

2. "It's my fault". The swingometer has now buried itself over to the other side of the scale. What is most dangerous about this is that it is probably well-meant and designed with the intention of reducing hurt for the other person. Do not for a second assume that this is true. Tell yourself one thing, "It is not all about me!" You might think that you are being helpful but you could easily come across as taking all the attention onto yourself and martyring yourself for the cause. I suspect a lot of couples start out in this area.

3. "Shit happens". As my wife's family are fond of saying, "Life is as fair as Digger's bottom" and given that Digger is a jet-black Labrador dog, you get the picture. On the great bell curve of life you have found yourself several standard deviations from the norm. To put it another way, you just got shit out of luck, buddy!

The fact of the matter is that unless you did something particularly stupid earlier in life, like sliding down a banisters and using a razor blade as a brake, you will have to accept sooner or later that it is just one of those things and with over six billion people on the planet, not everyone is going to get an easy ride.

It is interesting that faith creeps in at this point but in a slightly tangential way. People tend to do a lot of praying when there is something important they want which is odd as anyone of true faith will know that God isn't some omnipresent concierge service and certainly does not perform on request. However, this I can understand. We all have the need for something higher in our life, whether it is the one Christian God, a host of minor deities controlling the natural forces of life or that wayward spirit to whom tens of thousands of men pray to each week to ensure their football team wins on a Saturday afternoon. It is human nature to seek guidance and to pray for good fortune.

What is odd however, are the bargains that are made. I know for I have caught myself doing it with particularly spooky results. Some years ago in the depths of my sad lonely existence I would have done anything to be in a steady relationship. My life was filled with all kinds of excuses and surrogates (such as food, booze and concerts, the latter reaching over one a week on average at one stage). I often asked God why everyone else had a girlfriend but not me, though I am sure if he had been inclined to answer he would have probably said something along the lines of "take a look in a mirror, stop whining and get a grip on yourself".

I have never been a particularly spiritual person, preferring cosmology to theology but the idea of an all-powerful being is not something to which I am totally closed, I just think that all the descriptions of God I have ever heard are somewhat belittling. However, it came to pass (so to speak) that with nowhere else to turn to I made a bargain with God. I was in a very good job but if it was a choice between a career and a wife I would choose the latter.

A month later I met Iona. You will read later about the rest of the bargain. Okay, so in fact it was pure coincidence but it is very easy to prescribe divine intervention even if it is retrospective and this is what I often hear in these sorts of situations. Have you ever heard the expression "God must be punishing me for something I did in a past life?" Yes? Then you know exactly what I mean.

If that is the way God keeps tally then I really wish one of the disciples had remembered to mention it at the time. If we are being punished for deeds in our previous incarnations then at least let us have a flash-back so we can remember what the hell it was we were supposed to have done so we can feel properly guilty about it.

We went through this and to some extent we are still doing it to this day. It is very hard to divorce yourself from the idea that there must be a reason why things are happening. Iona and I both have a very empirical view of life. Everything must happen for a reason. Of course, there is a reason why things are happening but it is a natural one, a biological one and almost certainly just a random act of bad luck on our part that could never have been anticipated or prevented.

Let that be a lesson to you all!

Well, there was not much else to do at that point so leaving with the professional advice I had suspected which pretty much amounted to 'don't worry and keep trying' we headed off with our forms for the phlebotomist, more so the doctor could justify her nagging about my weight than anything else.

Somehow, neither of us felt totally satisfied or reassured.

# Chapter 4:
## Testing times...

Iona hates needles with a vengeance to the point that her body conspires against even the most skilled of phlebotomists. Even before this little episode in our life I recall her going for tests for some other minor ailment and telling the nurse about to take the sample that she would have difficulty finding a vein. The nurse, confident at her own abilities and like many medical practitioners unwilling to accept the word of a member of the general public confidently took out her equipment and started jabbing around. Five minutes later she had a very sheepish look on her face as she sent Iona home covered in plasters masking her several failed attempts.

I do not mind them myself having had loads of blood tests as an asthmatic youngster though I still could not bear to inject myself. My tolerance of pain is, like many men not accustomed to playing rugby, pitifully low.

Giving blood for samples is, as I am sure many of you will know, a bit like going to the post office. Whether you go to see the nurse at your local surgery or the phlebotomist at the hospital, the place is full of old aged pensioners and you often simply take a number and wait your turn. The posters and magazines are the same old stuff you find in hospitals around the country so you always end up simply sitting there, waiting as the minutes trudge by, wishing you had brought something to read.

For sure there are magazines there that kind folk have donated but they tend to be along the women's interest line with a few token golf publications for the men and I have long since given up the optimism of trying to find anything even remotely interesting in the dog-eared pile. I am also fed up of picking up Cosmopolitan just to get some old bag staring at me as if I were some sort of pervert just looking for the pictures of women in underwear which, of course, like any other bloke I was.

I have found from experience that the most needed object after Iona has been in to give blood is a chocolate bar. Technically I am guessing that a glass of water would be more medically beneficial but chocolate seems to be far better received by her.

This was particularly true on the day we went for the required blood-letting as ordered by Dr Armstrong. We had both been furnished with the appropriate sample request forms and it was clear from the plethora of ticks on hers and the meagre scattering on mine that she was going to get the worst deal out of the morning and would come out like the victim of a Hammer horror movie.

In anticipation of this I had foresightedly purchased an appropriate item of confectionary which I had intended to use as a reward after the deed was done but when I saw the look of anxiety on her face and realised it was far more than her instinctive fear of the needle, I caved in and gave it to her in the waiting room. A lot was riding on the results of these tests.

The clinic was of the drop-in kind and opened early. We had worked out that if we arrived for one of the first appointments there was a good chance we could make a swift exit and still both get to work at a decent time. Iona's teaching schedule was such that her first lesson was not until late in the morning and my job was sufficiently flexible that I could pretty much roll in at any time so long as the job was done.

As the department officially opened at seven thirty in the morning we guessed that arriving at seven would be more than plenty enough to secure us pole position. How wrong were we?

I was quite staggered when we stepped into the waiting room that the next laminated number hanging from the hook was not one but five! Dotted around the room were four old aged pensioners who had the look that they had possibly spent half the night there. Nowhere in sight was there any sign of family members or anyone else who could have dropped them off and there was a sense of abandonment about them.

It was only later that I realised they were probably patients in the hospital and given most old wrinklies are pretty nocturnal they had come down early for their blood sample merely to get a change of scene.

I let Iona take number five and I took six. At least that way she was one person fewer in the queue which would take away some of the anticipation and she would have time to recover and eat the other half of her chocolate bar before we left.

She emerged after a few minutes looking pale and drawn and when I took her place the phlebotomist was still packing up the various vacuum tubes of blood, each destined for a different assay. There were a lot of them, far more than in the kidney bowl laid out for me.

Phlebotomists or nurses who take blood on a regular basis all seem to have a different approach or technique. Some are very chatty, putting you at ease while they surreptitiously prepare the needle while others are very clinical but efficient, simply getting on with the job in hand methodically and without fuss.

This one very much tended to the latter. It is a bit like taxi drivers. I have hailed cabs all over the world and the same is true wherever you go, you either get one who wants to talk for the entire trip or alternatively the silent type that give you the mild impression they are going to drive you down some quiet side street and murder you.

To be honest I always prefer the quiet types (until we reach that quiet side street). I find small talk about as easy as reading ancient Greek, partly due to my strange phobia of looking daft and partly to a natural shyness which also never helped in the whole "attract a girlfriend" episode of my life.

Even so, there are limits and apart from confirming my name, this chap did not even look at me let alone speak and when he did glance in my direction it was only to stare at the offered arm to seek his target. I am blessed with very big and throbbing veins and have never had a problem with needles so his job was easy.

I remember long ago at school when we were being given our booster jabs we were all lined up along the corridor by class with the end of the line peering nervously around the corner into the sick room (I doubt it is called that in these politically correct days but I have no doubt it still smells mildly of sick). As one pupil emerged, hand clasped over the freshly-applied sticking plaster another would shuffle in.

By quirk of my place in the register alphabetically I was behind Stephen Farmer, the class bully but for the first time I noticed that he was not his usual loud, brash self and had not even attempted to give me a shove or call me any one of his dozens of pet offensive names.

The evil but pleasant thought crossed my mind that he was in fact terrified of the prospect of receiving his immunisation. For the first time in my life I had something over him as for me the process was relatively mundane.

As the line shuffled ever nearer and Brown emerged followed by Chester, Corrall and Dimmock our turn grew steadily nearer.

Finally, Farmer was at the head of the queue and by now white as a sheet and panting. This is back in the days before the nanny state really kicked in so teachers were not quite so attuned to any potential damage to their charges (and indeed would beat them with a cane at the drop of a hat).

I certainly doubt that they would allow what happened next to occur in the modern litigious society.

Farmer stood for a moment and then turned to peer into the medical room but his fear overcame him totally and in one fluid motion he fell flat on his face as he passed out. It was a priceless image that has remained crystal clear in my memory ever since.

The teachers were completely non-phased by this and, once the previous victim had departed, hauled Farmer into the seat, stuck him with the inoculation gun, and then hoisted him away to somewhere relatively comfortable where he could recover.

While he did indeed recover in no time medically, emotionally his position as head honcho in the class was well and truly over.

The last I saw of him he was serving in Burger King where I took some pleasure in telling him that I did *not* want fries with my bacon double cheeseburger but I did think of him as I watched the vacutainers fill with my dark crimson fluid.

Iona was riding on a sufficiently high sugar and endorphin rush by the time I had emerged that it was safe to go and that, as they say, was that. With the tests underway there was nothing we could do but wait for the results.

Life went on as normal and to some extent we both switched off. There was a sense of progress in that we were at least doing something, even if we had no idea which direction that something would take us and it would be at least a week before the tests were complete and we could make an appointment with Dr Armstrong to discuss the results.

It happened that I was in Europe for two days during that period. My position in the packaging industry took me all over the place which was great in terms of experience but inevitably such trips were a nightmare of preparation. It did mean that I put the whole subject of the blood tests out of my mind as I immersed myself in the complex subject of breathable packaging (the sort used to wrap food that allows some gases to permeate through but not others for reasons that are very important but of no relevance here whatsoever).

Samples and presentation in hand I drove down to Heathrow to catch the stupid o'clock in the morning flight to Paris while Iona plodded along with her daily routine and her own simmering thoughts.

You may think that travelling abroad for business is very exotic and exciting but those of you reading this who do this on a regular basis will know that it is anything of the sort. In my case the trip consisted of drive to car park, courtesy bus to terminal, sit around terminal, fly to Paris, taxi to customer, all day meeting with customer, taxi to hotel, nasty dinner in hotel, restless night, nasty breakfast in hotel, taxi to customer (again), all day meeting with customer (again), taxi back to airport, flight home to Heathrow, courtesy bus back to car park and then drive home.

It is not exactly what you would call stimulating travel. What is even worse is that the customer in question is in one of the industrial areas on the north of the city and to keep costs down my colleagues and I stayed in a low-rate hotel nearby surrounded by nothing but roads and pylons.

These trips are, to be honest, exhausting and by the time I stepped back through my front door I felt as if I had been constantly on the go for nearly forty eight hours. Conscious that I was still woozy the next morning Iona kindly drove to the surgery.

I do remember a sense of anticipation going back to the doctor to discuss the results. I had been somewhat incensed by her snap assumption that just because I was big that I was one breath away from a coronary so was dreading what the blood work was going to tell me.

In hindsight I should probably have been trying to score fewer points against Dr Armstrong and focusing more on the issue at hand but I have to admit the sense of satisfaction I had when my blood tests all came back okay. Fasting glucose, cholesterol, blood pressure, all were within normal limits. The frustration on her face was a picture! This of course did not stop her giving me a lecture, especially as she had already built herself up for one before looking at the results. With obvious irritation she informed me that I did not have diabetes, adding "but you might in the future!" True, but I didn't at that precise moment in time! Strike one for the home team.

She is, of course, completely right and I realised afterwards that I should not tempt fate by being blasé about my condition. With my size, eating habits and sedentary lifestyle it was actually a miracle I was in as good a shape as I was.

Iona's blood work was also normal or at least that is what we were told at the time. The good doctor was simply looking at the results on the screen against which the technician reporting the data had kindly put a high and low limit to indicate the normal range.

One particular hormonal test, however, for follicle stimulating hormone (FSH) came back with a result of 29.7 but no more was said about that at the time. Armstrong only raised it as the figure was outside of the quoted range though she was not in the least concerned. Keep this fact in mind for we will return to it later. More as a box-ticking exercise, a repeat hormonal test was ordered.

It was back to the phlebotomist again. This time, we arrived even earlier but despite showing up just after seven Iona was *still* fourth in the queue, the three ancient crones huddling in the corner like Shakespearean witches staring at us with the mild suspicion that only pensioners seem to be able to express.

We had not learned from our previous experience and brought anything to read even though we knew we had at least an hour's wait ahead of us. The time dragged by and Iona's reward chocolate was long gone by the time she was called in.

Fortunately for her, the bubbly young woman taking the blood was far more into the chatty, put-you-at-ease crowd and actually managed to draw a sample with the minimum of digging around. Experience would show that she was the exception to the rule.

Yet again we had to wait another week for the result before being able to make an appointment and it was beginning to dawn on me that this was not going to be a quick process. Already it had been nearly three weeks since we had made the first visit and we were barely scratching the surface.

Finally, we were back in Dr Armstrong's office to be told that the FSH level was 26.4. That was all she told us, not what the significance of the number was, just that it was 26.4. She dismissed it as nothing and pondered her next move.

Something I have to say about our doctor was that she had the strange habit of thinking aloud sometimes and the most common example of this, which she demonstrated for the first time that day, was to turn to us and ask "what do you want to do next?" It was only much later that I realised that she was simply articulating the thoughts in her head but I must say that at the time I really felt like replying "you're the bloody doctor, you tell us!"

With nothing particularly indicative in the blood results, the doctor moved on to the next test in her arsenal and suggested that Iona go for an ultrasound test to have a good look at her ovaries.

Here I have to beg ignorance and whilst I know what an ultrasound test is I was not present for the procedure itself having been called for a repeat visit to Paris on the day in question.

It was only an out and back trip so I was home by nine in the evening and Iona explained what had happened.

She had been instructed to drink loads of water in the two hours before the scan to fill her bladder and make the scan easier but as the clinic was inevitably running late, by the time Iona was called in it was nearly three hours and she was busting for a wee.

The technician went through the motions of performing the scan to look at the state of Iona's ovaries but gave an expression which told my wife that something was not right. This was a most unprofessional thing to do, especially as she then went on to say when Iona queried her expression that she could not discuss the case but that the doctor would explain the results when Iona saw her.

When asked how long she would have to wait to make the appointment with Dr Armstrong Iona was a bit shocked to be told ten days. The outpatients clinic where the scan was taken was only across the car park from the surgery – how were they going to deliver the report, by carrier snail?

Thus, in the blink of an eye, another fortnight was lost.

At home, our conversations were becoming more cautious. Time was quite definitely marching on now and despite our continual attempts, nothing continued to happen. There had still been this sense of anticipation that all our visits to the surgery would prove to be for nothing and that Iona would suddenly fall pregnant and we would laugh about the whole thing. As winter descended we found ourselves not laughing.

The sense of dread heading to the surgery towards the end of November hung heavy in the air. Even a dullard like me could not help but detect how frightened Iona was. Whatever was said that day, we both knew that we were going to learn something that would change everything.

Were we ever right!

I had never really been cognisant of the term 'polycystic ovaries' until that day and even now my understanding of the condition is only scant. Like a lot of men, I sort of jumped to the bottom line which I pretty much understood as "so that's bad, isn't it?" Okay so I am not that stupid but for those of you out there in blissful ignorance, here is my shaky understanding of polycystic ovary syndrome (PCOS).

In PCOS, as the name implies, the woman has a number of small cysts around the edge of their ovaries. These cysts are actually under-developed egg-containing follicles and it is usually a hormone imbalance that has resulted in their formation. It is actually relatively common and can be caused by lifestyle effects such as being overweight. While incurable, the symptoms can be treated. Of most importance, however, is that PCOS can result in problems for women trying to become pregnant.

Bombshell!

I could see it in her face. We had skirted this issue for so long, playing the blame game I have described above but now it was in black and white. While not definitely the cause of all our woes, Iona had a condition that was certainly contributing. I felt absolutely terrible, knowing how she was going to feel just at that moment. The scant medical facts we had at our disposal were now stacked against her.

Was our doctor sympathetic? Not entirely. It was becoming very evident by now that Dr Armstrong was a true optimist but there are times when you really just want to be given a straight answer. Still, we were clutching onto the hope that she was the medic here and ought to know what she was talking about, a natural assumption I would have thought.

To her credit, going through the motions, Dr Armstrong's attention now settled on me. We had a fair idea of Iona's situation which while not fundamental to our plight was certainly cause for some concern but before she could recommend a course of treatment to counter the PCOS she would need to know more about my situation.

A large spotlight was suddenly shone into the very depths of my soul. This was the one thing that most men dread more than anything else.

The spermiogram! Core to our very being is the thought that our seed is strong and true, a host of mighty warriors ready to shoot out and perpetuate our noble line. For heaven's sake, it is only understandable, the only thing us men have to do is that so it is really important to us that everything is working fine. The concept of 'firing blanks' as the phrase goes brings terror to most men. What use are we if not for that?

I had never done one before and the thought filled me with a cold dread but what choice did I have. Iona had already undergone her investigations and all the associated heartache so what right did I have to baulk at the thought of what I had to do.

The doctor presented me with the analysis request form and, yes, you guessed it, a small pot and told me to go forth and deliver.

I had never seen one of those forms before so would not have recognised it for what it was until then. Why, therefore, did I walk out assuming that everyone else on the planet knew exactly what it was and what I was about to do? You would have thought I had a pornographic DVD under my coat the way I was behaving.

Men, note to self, this is where your wife's handbag comes in really useful!

Giving a sperm sample can be I was to find, a very lonely activity. There are certain logistical problems around the actual process, most importantly that the lab has to receive and analyse the sample within two hours of issue and that preferably the sample is kept warm once it has left the body.

This being the case, many men prefer to complete the required process in the comfort of their own homes, perhaps with the assistance of their wives but at least in safe and familiar surroundings. The size of the pot allows for transportation in a trouser pocket to keep sufficient warmth in it in the short-term.

Of course, this assumes that you are a stone's throw away from the laboratory and that they have not assigned you one in a run-down hospital twenty miles away requiring navigation through terrible roads in rush hour.

My satellite navigation system which is normally pretty good when it comes to estimated arrival times simply cannot get it right when it comes to this particular medical facility. At the beginning of the journey the e.t.a. will be in the order of twenty five minutes and an hour or so later it will happily inform me that we are 'arriving at destination on the right".

It is very fortunate that I am a control freak and naturally distrusting of most things. I am almost bordering on obsessive compulsive disorder when it comes to being late for anything to the point that I am usually disgustingly early.

Given the situation where I had to produce a sample and then get it to a lab at least a half-hour away, find the lab in a hospital I had never visited and then assume they would be able to analyse it straight away for me negated the option of home sampling. At least by waiting until I got there, I would have plenty of time to undertake the task in hand (literally) and deliver it proudly to the appropriate technicians.

The journey was a nightmare but at least the parking was good, much to my surprise. When I got there the road outside was lined with cars which filled me with dread yet the car park itself (which was free for the first fifteen minutes) had plenty of spaces. Bonus!

Now all I had to do was to locate the appropriate department and ascertain where the nearest gentleman's toilet could be found. There was a map on the wall with a labyrinthine plan of the hospital but nowhere could I find the department I was looking for. In horror I began to think that I had come to the wrong place.

It is a guy thing never to admit failure and have to ask for directions but in this case the clock was ticking on my car park ticket and I really did not want to have to pay for want of a few minutes.

I regretted my decision the moment I stepped up to the reception desk and the woman sat staring at me gave me a look of total disdain. When I showed her the form I had been given you would have thought I had just handed her something revolting but with an impatient sigh she took her laminated map and pointed out where my destination could be found – as it was, the phlebotomy department.

There was no point in arguing that the legend on the map had nothing to do with what was written on my letter and therefore how was I supposed to know that was the right place but apparently she thought it would be obvious.

Feeling irritated and slightly flustered I followed the appropriate colours on the wall – helpfully put in place to guide you to certain areas of the complex but I wondered if anyone had considered those unfortunate souls who are colour-blind. I had visions of people going in to have a broken wrist put in plaster only to end up in the morgue!

There was a men's toilet but with some alarm I realised it was accessed from the waiting room – predictably filled with old aged pensioners who glared at me as if I were about to mug them.

I stepped through the suspiciously thin door into the disinfectant smell of the lavatory.

If you will permit me to digress again at this stage, I have alluded to the fact that I often travelled abroad on business and among the many destinations I have chalked up I have been fortunate to spend some time in Amsterdam.

The red light district, while appealing to me only in the detached terms of a tourist did have a thing or two to say about eroticism. One of the funniest things I have ever seen is a colleague of mine walking into one of the sex shops and hitting his head on an enormous black rubber double-ender hanging from the ceiling. I am reliably informed that the aforementioned implement is designed for two ladies who are similarly minded to find alternative entertainment to online bingo.

This is, of course, not important, I only mention it as it was one of those "you had to be there" moments that will live with me for the rest of my life. I cried so much with laughter that we had to leave the shop and return later to satisfy the needs of the anecdote I am really trying to get to.

The particular establishment in question specialised in video entertainment and there seemed to be a rule of thumb that the deeper into the shop you went the more "specialised" the subject material became. By the entrance the videos tended to be low budget soft porn affairs where, if the covers were anything to go by, a range of moderately disinterested Eastern European ladies would parade around in their underwear. Nothing particularly risqué there, you may say and you would be right.

Further in the titles become more exotic and the underwear more transitory. Beyond that the shelves started to adopt a level of categorisation, depending on your personal peccadillo. Nurses, no problem. Schoolgirls, third shelf on the left. Large ladies, take your pick.

Now, I must point out at this stage that beyond the usual juvenile interest video porn really does not interest me much. When I was a teenager, back in the days that the Betamax war was still raging and there was even the long-lost third format of Video 2000 my father used to rent a sexually explicit movie from the only video shop in town of a Friday night.

He would not watch it immediately, the aforementioned cinematographic classic would be secreted in the airing cupboard while he went to the pub but he forgot the golden rule that he had sons and we were not stupid. We'd discovered the first video some months previously so while he was out, my brothers and I would happily view whatever offering there was, carefully rewinding the video and replacing it long before he returned.

After a few weeks even us in our pubescent adolescent state with our hormones oozing out of every pore realised that the quality of the videos both in terms of content and physical recording were awful so the game changed to one of winding our father up.

At first we would leave the tape at the end so he would have to rewind it but as this was often the case with rented videos we soon realised that this was not subtle enough so started putting the tape back in a slightly different place than we had found it.

Still the tapes were rented so eventually we left a note on one stating "Don't bother, its rubbish!" No further tapes were ever rented and the subject was never raised in conversation.

It has to be said that my experience of these rather lame and low budget creations could not prepare me for such classic titles as the masterpiece "Park it in my Ass" which is one that for reasons I cannot explain seems to have stuck indelibly in my mind.

The middle of the shop allowed for another moment of hilarity as my colleague and I sought for the most ridiculous movie title.

Beyond this point the game changed and became one of see at which point towards the back of the shop you reached your comfort zone.

I will not go into details but once you have catered for all of the regular fetishes you start to get into the murky waters of the bizarre and, it has to be said, downright wrong.

For my part I usually bottled out around three quarters

of the way to the ominous back shelves of the shop and to this day could not tell you what was there. Frankly, I don't want to know.

The point is that all tastes were catered for, so long as you were prepared to part with good money (which I never was) but the gents toilet at the hospital reminded me of the many and varied delights of Amsterdam in no way whatsoever. As experiences go, it was about as erotic as a lamp-post.

It has to be said that the hospital in question was not what could be called a jewel of the National Health Service. The buildings looked as if they had been temporary pre-fabricated sections that had been erected while the real hospital was being built but that the latter event had never happened. They also looked about thirty years old and that no attempt to decorate them had been made in all that time.

The gents were no exception and had the sort of decor that made one crave for utilitarian. The water pressure in the taps was like a Dachshund having a pee and the "Extreme Thrust" hand dryer had the same burst of air as an asthmatic pensioner's breath.

I stood in the small white room and stared at the three cubicles ahead of me. The first was occupied which somewhat ruled it out and in classic male fashion that immediately meant that I should select the third and leave a "one dunnie" gap between myself and the current occupant of the first.

Feeling infinitely uninspired I took my place in the end cubicle and shut the door. Apparently, according to the noticed scrawled in marker pen on the door, "Troy is a rent boy". I wondered what had caused the author to announce this fact in such a way.

There was nowhere to put my little pot, the top of the toilet paper dispenser being sloped at an annoyingly sharp angle. My only recourse was to stuff it open in my shirt pocket until it was required, the sample bag being stuffed in my trouser pocket where it hopefully would be out of harm's way.

I doubt there is a man on the planet who would freely admit to the level of self-gratification they have enjoyed throughout their life and I am certainly not going to elucidate on that particular fact here but needless to say I was aware of the mechanics of what was required.

The problem was, I was now in a very quiet room with a complete stranger and had not made any obvious lavatorial noises. A flush of self-consciousness came over me but only for a moment as a terrible dread descended.

I must have caught the other man just at the point where he was going to enjoy the fulfilment of a "number 2" but another of the great unspoken rules is that you do not let other people hear you at the moment of release.

The poor bugger must have been clenching in the hope that I would just pee and piddle-off but now I had locked us in a waiting game.

For several seconds the impasse held but nature was against him. I had not even unzipped my trousers so was in no particular hurry but his biological needs had clearly been urgent enough to encourage him to bare his unwary buttocks to the cold evil that was the hospital porcelain.

I felt like a complete pervert, standing in a toilet waiting for someone I had never met to drop his load so decided to at least try and get on with my mission.

Don't panic, I am not going to provide an explanation of the act apart from to say that having reluctantly adopted the position and entered that meditative state where I was trying to find inspiration from even the remotest part of my fortunately fertile imagination, the other guy let slip a fart that hailed the avalanche that quickly followed.

Several of my family use the expression "better out than in" when they blow off but this was one of those moments when that saying was very doubtful or at least depended heavily on your point of view.

For his part, given the explosive nature of the event I am sure that he felt infinitely better for the release, sufficiently so to cover his acute embarrassment at having so loudly trumpeted in front of a stranger.

Regrettably I had no such sense of pleasure. All even remotely sexy thoughts went out of the window as my ears were assaulted by the incredibly prolonged discharge followed, as it was after a slight pause, by a sigh that could only be described as heartfelt relief. It was also followed a moment later by the most incredible smell. The blockage that had just shifted had evidently been there for a while.

That I provided a sample at all was a miracle but when I emerged from the toilet a few minutes later I simply felt dirty. I was so dejected that I no longer worried that I had the sample pot with its pitifully scant contents hanging inside the clear sample bag as I walked up to the reception desk.

I have never quite got to the bottom of what was going on at the hospital but the depressed appearance of the buildings carried on with those that worked there. I would subsequently visit the place a number of times but in all the occasions combined I do not recall any member of staff ever smiling.

The woman behind the desk was no exception and regarded me as if I had just dropped out of a dog's bum. I was in no mood for conversation and really did not care what she thought of me so proudly held up the sample bag and gave it to her.

She stared at the contents, then at me with a fixed look of disdain before turning to drop it into a basket to one side.

My presence was no longer required and we had managed to undertake the entire exchange without a single word. Her role did not, it seemed, extend to customer relations.

My next action was going to get me into a load of trouble but only because I confessed to it as soon as I got home. Between the phlebotomist and the reception is a small café run by the WRVS, that stalwart bunch of volunteers who I think are greatly under-rated in terms of what they do for this country. At the time, they looked like a heavenly host as I headed back to the car, sullied and glum.

What could possibly cheer me up at a time like this? What else but a large bacon butty of course!

That confession earned me an extra half-hour on the cross-trainer for sure but you cannot imagine how soul-soothing it was at the time. Forget endorphins and chocolate, that thin salty, fatty lump really did the trick.

I had the good fortune of working for a company that was very relaxed and laid back about time keeping so long as the job was done. I had told them that I was going for a hospital check-up but there was an underlying feeling that I was being somewhat dishonest in not telling them what the check-up was for.

Frankly, it was none of their business but I did realise then that Iona and I had entered an underground, clandestine world of secrets.

One of the many difficult things when you have realised that pregnancy is not going to be as simple as all that is the fact that pretty much everyone around you happily gets on with it without any apparent problems. Friends and family spit out babies in an almost offhand and casual manner but then comes the crunch. The conversation, backed by a huge spotlight, focuses on you and the inevitable "not long for you two, then" or "so are you trying?" phrases drift over the dinner table.

I wonder if anyone really believes the off-the-cuff responses, vague mutterings about being really busy, about concentrating on careers or just enjoying being married for a bit before starting families. The comments are, I know, well meant though with an edge of probing (everyone loves to be the first to know good news) and you immediately feel like you have been caught in the lie.

This is also true at work, especially if, like me, you share an office with people you get on with and regard as friends. They only have your best interests at heart and it is very difficult indeed not to be lulled into a false sense of security and inadvertently make a slip, alluding to what was central to your life. I found this part very tough indeed.

We have found ourselves over the process putting words into other people's mouths, making the assumption that they are talking about us and coming up with all sorts of theories as to why we haven't propagated yet.

I got quite skilful at the art of changing the subject or answering with a glib reply that was totally meaningless (something men are amazingly skilled at – we can hold entire conversations with no factual content whatsoever).

There is also the competitive aspect to babies that I had never really considered. Sibling rivalry can be very strong and there seems in a lot of families to be that unspoken race to have the cherished "first grandchild", closely followed by the first girl/boy depending on what the first grandchild was. When you have fertility problems, the gates have opened but your horse is standing defiantly refusing to run. Without wishing to sound sexist (and I apologise if at any point in this book that I do) I think this is more of a woman thing than a man thing.

Needless to say, whatever the race, we lost it.

Job done there was not much else to do but sit and wait for the results. By this time I was well into the dodgy waters of trying to divert attention from Iona by saying that although we knew her situation, there was still every chance that the fault was primarily mine. Many women with PCOS conceive naturally, let alone with treatment so her condition could well have been coincidental. You will probably recall my previous advice on this which I was well and truly ignoring.

I guess I meant well but in hindsight I'm not sure I was helping the situation very much.

It was, however, with that sense of bravado that we returned to the doctor about a week later to get the results.

There have been many situations in my life where I have felt my heart sink but none quite like this. Our doctor was her usual chatty self as she delivered our second bombshell, the news that I had a very low sperm count, poor motility and insufficient sample to even measure the morphology.

Bugger!

Even as the news was sinking in I felt like screaming at her "do you have the slightest idea what I had to go through to even produce that?" How on Earth was I supposed to provide a copious and energetic sample while performing the five-fingered shuffle in a gent's convenience with someone suffering diarrhoea while I did?

It did not really strike me at the time but a theme was underway by this time. The theme was quite simply a complete and utter lack of any form of emotional support from our doctor. For me, this news was quite devastating, it was one thing swaggering around being all supportive and reassuring to my wife, it was quite another being bluntly told that my seed was rubbish.

Another theme did become apparent. Our doctor decided that the best thing to do would be to send me for another test. This would become her answer to everything over the next year or so!

Tired, dejected and with no prospect whatsoever of a bacon butty, we left the surgery in the knowledge that there were issues on both sides, compounding to make what was now clearly a very serious problem. Our doctor had been quite oblivious to our mood, unconcerned as to the emotional effect that it would have on us and had simply send us out with her usual optimistic "don't worry, it will be alright".

It was now Iona's turn to try and console me but she was clearly in a bad place herself.

It was with far less enthusiasm that I made the second journey to the hospital but needs must as they say. Once again, the jostle of cars parked out on the road belied the fact that parking was not an issue. It seemed clear that people were simply trying to avoid the cost of the ticket when a perfectly free alternative was right on the doorstep. As I was not going to be more than ten minutes it was not a problem for me.

All too soon I found myself in the familiar cubicle. I had thought that my first experience was about as low as it got but this time I faced the added problem that no sooner had I locked the door when another man entered the room, taking up position in the second cubicle and then demonstrating the fact that he was undertaking the same mission as I but with infinitely more and quite vocal enthusiasm. By the gentle rustling of paper he had evidently also brought his own inspirational literature.

I'm sorry but there are some situations that I really think are above and beyond the call of duty and this was one of them. It was only my drive for the end result that stopped me from simply walking out and going home. He had clearly known that I had just occupied my own cubicle so I was back in that dilemma of what to do next. Did I pretend to go, flush the toilet and leave, hanging around until he exited the gents so I could go back or did I simply stand there like a gormless idiot until he cleared off?

I opted for gormless idiot routine and fortunately my lavatorial companion was quick about his business. The sounds he made will haunt me for the rest of my life and I suspected that in Amsterdam he would have been able to happily peruse the most extreme video nasties without batting an eyelid.

The contents of my sample pot did not, to my inexperienced eyes, look much different in volume or appearance than the first which depressed me no end.

My previous experience had somewhat hardened me to the post traumatic stress such that I was able to resist the delights of the hot food counter on the way back to the car. Okay, that is not entirely true, they were for some reason closed but I *would* have resisted had they been open, honest!

This was a very surreal time and it felt like swimming through treacle. Although we were doing things it did not feel like we were actually making any headway. There was a pretty good reason for this…we were not!

The news on our return to the surgery was not good. My second results had come back as equally depressing as the first, simply reinforcing the utter sense of uselessness and failure that I had, even though the voice of reason (and desperate hope) in my head still told me that I didn't have a problem, I was simply a victim of circumstance i.e. having to deliver my sample in the worst place possible.

Still, our ever-optimistic doctor had the answer to that…she sent me for another test! It was as if she were trying to make me produce a good sample or go blind in the attempt.

Packed out of the door with yet another plastic pot and the usual absence of emotional support I resigned myself to a third trip to what was easily my least favourite place on the planet.

This time I had a bit of a shock. Cruising into the car park I suddenly discovered that my previous two visits must have been during a bomb scare or something. Far from the wide expanse of empty car park I joined the back of the queue to bedlam. The car park is laid out as a series of small areas linked with some narrow roads which basically means as soon as it fills up there is no room to manoeuvre. This linked with a bunch of people who were clearly both in a hurry and totally incapable of driving properly, I had no chance. It took nearly fifteen minutes to simply bypass the carnage and get to the exit so that I could drive a half a mile down the road to the next available space.

It was, of course, raining in that way that is by some higher natural law compulsory in such situations. It was December so not exactly a huge surprise.

My experience this time was even more oppressive than the last. As I was entering the toilet I helped a disabled man who was negotiating the tight turn that was required to get to the cubicles (the disabled toilet being literally and, for him, very unhelpfully disabled at the time). Broken cubicles seemed to be a theme as my "usual" number three stall was also locked with an "out of order" sign.

He was clearly going to take some time so when I locked myself into the cubicle next to him I had resigned myself, as probably had he, that we both simply had to just get on with it.

Then another man came in. The whole dynamic changed. In box number one was the very nice disabled man who through no fault of his own was going to be a while. In box number two was yours truly with his small plastic pot. Box number three was out of bounds which meant that there was nowhere to go for Man number three.

He obviously had intentions of visiting either box number one or box number two rather than facing the aluminium trough against the wall and he wasn't bothered which but judging by his very loud and obvious tutting, sighing and other "look, I'm here and I'm vastly more important than either of you" noises, was not a man accustomed to waiting.

Being in a gent's toilet is remarkably non-erotic. Listening to someone emptying his bowels even less but when there is someone standing outside the door making his presence acutely felt, it is no wonder my latest sample was not very good.

I was feeling in a particularly mean mood, mostly because the third man had been so utterly rude himself by his attitude so I took my time. Needless to say, the old man was also taking his time but not for the same vindictive reasons as myself.

The tutting man left with an angry sigh just before I was finished which is just as well as I had been practicing my best withering stare in the privacy of my cubicle.

The butty shop was open when I came back from delivering the sample but I did not even consider going in as I just wanted to get the hell out of there.

# Chapter 5:
## New year, new hope..?

The year ended, Christmas was spent with family with small babies and, although we had been technically trying for less than twelve months and only under the care of our doctor for a mere few, it felt like a lifetime.

Oddly, with the emphasis shifted somewhat on my results, Iona was left in limbo at this stage.

She kept pushing the GP for answers or even ways forward – options for us to consider but Dr Armstrong wouldn't budge so we spent our time being glad for everyone else and wondering what we had done so wrong, why we were being punished and therefore punishing each other.

Emotionally we were both frazzled but we propped each other up and bolstered ourselves with the thought that 2009 would be a better year and that things would move forward.

There was of course one flaw with this plan…

I love Christmas, always have. There is something warm and soul-refreshing about the whole festive period. A lot of is it that I love giving presents. Don't get me wrong, I like receiving them as well but I love buying and wrapping things throughout the year and the thrill of anticipation when the recipient opens what I have bought.

The end of 2008 was no exception as I had bought Iona a Nintendo Wii and Wii Fit. Partly, this was due to the fact that I fancied having a go on it myself. Blokes are notorious for buying presents that they actually want to play with themselves. Look how many sons end up with train sets, Play Stations or Scalextric when they are clearly too young to appreciate them fully. How lucky that Dad is always there to step in and show them how to do it...

The main reason for getting the Wii, however, was that we were both heavier than we should be, a fact that could not be helping our cause in all honesty. I normally have a particular aversion to exercise, I've never been particularly keen on sport either as a participant or a spectator and my job has resulted in my leading a relatively sedentary lifestyle. That really had to change for multiple reasons.

Iona was suitably pleased and we were very quickly in the New Year tracking the progress of our weight loss and fitness regime on the aforementioned machine. We had also purchased a rowing machine a couple of years before which was dusted off and put to good use as a supplement to our exercise and that was without considering the necessary dog walking every day.

I like to cook so our food intake was controlled and healthy and we began 2009 with a sense of trepidation but at the same time hopeful anticipation.

Our doctor managed to dash my mood within a week. The latest test results were abysmal and the sample size small to the point that she actually questioned me whether I was 'doing it right'. What did she think I was doing? I did at that stage begin to wonder whether the romantic setting of the gents toilets was having more of an effect than I had thought.

Whatever the reason, I was three for three in terms of poor results and whatever she could say (which was not much in terms of medical advice but plenty in mindless optimism) the results were what they were.

By this time, Iona was starting to get more than a little impatient with the good doctor. We had spent months going through round after round of tests and really did not have a huge amount to show for it when it came to an action plan.

Even so, we did not question her judgment even though it should have been obvious that she was simply clutching at straws and not following any kind of logical plan.

Iona had spent a lot of time on the internet by now. Being a biology teacher she knew more than the average laywoman about reproductive matters and had been swatting up on the subject. It was depressing the number of times she had to make suggestions to the doctor at these moments and actually start answering the "what do you want to do?" question.

Our doctor's inability to use her computer was also becoming annoying to me. Often, she would blunder around the screen trying to bring things up and either access the wrong results or not press the one button that was clearly the one she needed. I would sit there, smiling sweetly as I ground my teeth down and storm clouds rumbled in my head.

As you can tell by now, we were not really gelling with our doctor by this stage. My faith in her was very much starting to crumble.

Iona had reached the same end of her tether and was not taking any prisoners. She was certainly not going to leave the surgery without an action plan. Well, a plan is what we got.

In order to try and counter the polycystic ovary syndrome, the doctor prescribed her on a three month course of clomiphene citrate which was supposed to increase the chance of her becoming pregnant, I think by encouraging the release of an egg or something like that.

Whoopee, a magic pill that would solve all of our problems. Surely this would do the trick? It stood to reason that if Iona's ovaries were a bit iffy and my sperm a bit on the lazy side (not a huge surprise given the individual they were coming from), all we both needed was a bit of a prod in the right direction.

It was a plan and it sounded like a good one. Just for good measure I was sent off to do yet more tests, fortunately this time back to the good old phlebotomist down the road which was far easier and this time to look at my hormones which, as it happened, turned out to be all okay but that was another test checked off of our doctor's list.

Like all miracle cures, there is always a potential price to pay. When you look at the list of potential side effects of clomiphene citrate they are quite scary (especially as a man when you see the words 'mood swings'). What is even scarier is that prolonged use of the drug has been to my understanding linked with an increased prevalence of certain cancers which can never be good.

The risks were in fact such that Iona could only go on the drug for a total of six months so Dr Armstrong gave her an initial three-month course so we could "see what happened".

There was a brooding suspicion hanging over the pair of us that we knew exactly what was going to happen.

Now I am probably being very unfair to our doctor and someone better versed in medical matters than I will no doubt read this and say that she was acting properly and undertaking a normal sequence of investigation. The problem was that she did not come across as following a logical sequence and each time it was as if she were grasping at straws and really not fully comprehending of exactly what she was doing.

This was not a time we wanted nice. This was a time when we wanted straight talking and practical. Nice would have been a happy bonus to this but on its own it was simply not enough.

When I was a child one of my GP's was an ex-army doctor and he did not do nice. I remember that he was tall, short-haired and to my knowledge had facial muscles that were incapable of smiling.

Given that I used to find every excuse under the sun to skive out of "games" or "P.E." at school, I was a grand master of the unexpected and near-terminal illness that would inexplicably coincide with circuit training. As I have mentioned in the past, other doctors would prescribe the dreaded pink gloop if they thought I was making it up but Dr Brett was quite another matter.

Dr Brett had spent most of his medical life dealing with malingering cadets so had seen every trick in the book. When I was older, he told me a story of one particular individual who would develop the most incredible symptoms whenever it came to a particularly long cross-country run, especially if in full kit until one day he sent the poor lad back to his sergeant with a note explaining his condition.

The sergeant eyed the beaming cadet as he handed over what he thought was his sick note and eyed the diagnosis… "malingering". It was compounded by the fact that the poor recruit decided at that moment to cheerfully pipe up…

"Doc says I have that and that it is a very bad case."

I have never entertained thought of a military career but

even I know that this is the kind of ammunition that you simply do not give to a sergeant.

Dr Brett claimed that he never found out what the sergeant did to the hapless cadet but whatever it was had cured his ailment. The cadet never came back to the infirmary.

Even at the tender age of nine I knew better than to try and fool Dr Brett though it took my mother a lot longer to realise that his success rate at curing me was far better than his practice colleagues. Had she done so, my skiving days would have been curtailed at a much younger age than they eventually were.

Looking back, I doubt if Dr Brett has any idea on the effect he had on me! However, the one thing that was never in question was his professionalism. On the rare occasion that I was presented before him with a genuine ailment his diagnosis and choice of treatment was fast, decisive and effective.

Dr Armstrong was failing pretty badly at being fast or decisive but even then I was not totally questioning her effectiveness.

Unbeknownst to me at the time, Iona's desperation was such that she would have risked far more dangerous drugs as those being offered if there was a guarantee that something would happen. At the time, however, I did not think of this. We had a medical treatment, positive action for a change and all we had to do now was to wait for the drugs to do their thing.

In my head I tried to rationalise things. The tests had not stated that either of us were actually infertile so theoretically things could still happen naturally. The medication that Iona had been given would simply facilitate this process so all we had to do was go back and make like the rabbits.

So, there we were, Iona happily (I thought) popping

the fertility pills and us back to our cycle of checking dates, planning our naughty nights and generally doing whatever we could to increase the chances.

The intensity by which we followed every old wives tale in the book (and, I am sure, invented a few of our own) increased. For sure I was beginning to lose track of what I was supposed to be eating, which cracks in the pavement I could and could not walk on and what the significance of five magpies is.

I don't know about you but there are some pretty strange superstitions out there and it is not helped by the fact that regional variation can create a lot of marital strife. Take, for example, the aforementioned magpies. Now I am not hugely superstitious but I do on occasion spot one of the black and white scavengers and start manically seeking for a second along the whole "one for sorrow, two for joy" illogic.

When you are facing fertility issues, it is the third and fourth of the bloody birds that often causes issues…three for a girl and four for a boy. Frankly, neither of us was fussy and three or four was fine by us.

It is when we get to five that the argument starts. In my version of the rhyme, it is five for silver six for gold but for Iona it is five for a letter and six for something better.

Now, call me silly but I would rather have silver or gold over a letter any day (unless the letter was from the Premium Bonds or the National Lottery to say I had won a six-figure sum). The trouble was, the rhyme was one of those totally trivial things that could turn into a full-blown argument as soon as we spotted the fifth magpie.

Iona was obsessed by the bloody things and would start reciting her version of the rhyme as soon as the birds appeared so unconsciously I started doing the same but the moment I inadvertently said "five for silver" I would get sharply rebuked for getting it wrong.

The fact was, she was already narked that the fifth had appeared and we were getting neither a girl nor a boy but she would simply not accept that like many expressions, the magpie rhyme was subject to significant regional variation.

I sensibly decided never to raise the question as to at what point the rhyme would re-set. For example, if you saw a magpie (thus "one for sorrow"), how soon would you have to spot a second before being in a situation for "joy"? If you didn't see another one for an hour, did that still count or was that just double sorrow?

Why are rhymes never clear on points like this (or is it simply a case that I should stop analysing them so closely)?

Still, magpies aside, we ran our lives in such a way that no devil, imp, minor deity or other ethereal being could take offence and should have smiled fondly on us. Iona dutifully took the pills and we went about our nocturnal activities with gusto.

What could *possibly* go wrong?

# Chapter 6:
## Thanks for playing; here are some nice parting gifts...

With impeccable timing my company decided in its impudent wisdom to pick the end of February to announce to me that my entire department was being made redundant. Glad I wasn't undertaking any blood pressure tests right around that time as a huge rug was whipped out from under my feet.

I remembered the bargain with God that I have mentioned before where I had traded my career for a wife which just goes to prove that you should be really careful what you wish for! I hadn't taken into account that once you had a wife and were seeking to have children, it would be a really good idea to have the means to support them.

Here we were doing everything we could to produce a child and suddenly not only did I have the dent in my manhood that crappy sperm delivered but now I was going to be in the position where I could not provide either.

If ever I get this published I will write a separate book

about my experiences of being made redundant but suffice to say I fell into a very dark place full of anger, rejection and betrayal. Fortunately thanks to Iona that dark hole was not laced with alcohol that it could so easily have been a few years previously.

It was a serious emotional kick in my poorly-functioning knackers. Once again this is very much a man thing and probably comes across as terribly male-chauvinistic but I am still of the mind-set that I want to do my part, as much as I would love to lounge about the house all day watching movies given half a chance.

We were, by now, in the aftermath of the credit crunch and the markets were still spiralling into the abyss. Companies all around the world frantically tried to cut costs as they realised that their cash-flow was almost nonexistent and that most lines of credit had suddenly and sharply dried up.

I haven't really gone into much detail as to my job, largely because it bears little relevance to this story but in essence I worked at this time for a consultancy that went around solving problems for major packaged goods companies, the sort of people who make everything from ready-meals to rug shampoo, tomato sauce to toilet cleaner. If it comes in a bottle, box, bag, can or carton then my company has probably, at some time, looked at it.

We would approach the multinational companies or in some cases be invited in to look at specific problems, for example child-resistant closures, biodegradable packaging, smart packaging…you name it, we worked on it.

The critical fact, however, was that we were *consultants*. Every industry has its consultants but I believe it is only the medical profession where they are a full-time function. In every other sector, the consultant can basically be seen as someone who does not work for your company who is brought in to tell you what you already know and who is paid twice what you pay your own staff for the privilege.

When I worked for a multinational we used to regard consultants as a total waste of space. Management consultants are the worst and I met a few, concluding that they all seemed to work in the same way. They would start by questioning a cross-section of the employees including upper management and the CEO. The lesser members of the workforce were, of course, irrelevant. What they were really trying to do was ask the CEO what he wanted to do and then spend the rest of their time coming to the same conclusions only with a wealth of carefully filtered evidence.

The CEO would go away happy with the justification that he (or she) was not only doing the right thing but had thought of it independently and the consultants would go away happy (and a lot wealthier). It was only those on the factory floor who ever really seemed to see what was going on.

My attitude changed, of course, when I was offered a place at a consultancy. If nothing else, the money was so much better than being that poor grunt on the factory floor who I was now interviewing.

Of course, my justification is that *technical* consultants offer a lot more than management consultants. We are able to specialise in our subject and spend a far greater time keeping abreast of new developments, interfacing with universities, research groups and manufacturers as well as having the time to work on specific problems or new concepts.

It is a lamentable fact that when I worked for the multinational corporation, I spent far more of my time sat in meetings talking about projects than actually working on them. Like all big companies, those involved in fast moving consumer goods are as bogged down in bureaucracy and process than any civil service department.

As a consultant, while we had our fair share of meetings I had so much more freedom to actually work on technologies that the job was infinitely more interesting than anything I had done before.

What was even better was that we had money pouring out of our ears. The sort of company we were employed by had very deep projects and only brought the likes of us in when they had a particularly big technical problem to solve. It did not seem to matter to them that they were at the same time employing a whole host of their own scientists who were fully capable of solving the issue and already on the payroll.

The credit crunch brought this gravy train to a rather nasty halt, indeed it was a derailment of monumental proportions.

Whereas before consultants were brought in at the drop of a hat to solve even the simplest of problems, the dearth of cash suddenly made accountants sit up and review just what they were spending their precious research and development budgets on and it did not take them long to realise just how much consultants were really costing.

I had heard much on the news about "boom and bust" but had not really given it any heed until this moment when we were well and truly bust!

The company's contracts had almost overnight dropped by eighty percent and there was nothing else they could do but to contract to accommodate. As the owners' skills lay in design it meant that all the additional branches they had grown into over the years, engineering, formulation and, most importantly, packaging, were shed to ensure the survival of the core business.

With the benefit of hindsight and calm I can appreciate why they did what they did. Like a lot of industries, they had to do what was necessary to survive and unfortunately this did not include retaining my services.

At the time, however, I thought they were a bunch of total bastards.

What is totally scary is that I had a premonition that something terrible was going to happen the night before. Sadly this moment of precognition was fuelled by a few too many glasses of cabernet sauvignon.

I am a firm believer that the modern human has almost totally suppressed those natural instincts that most of the rest of the natural world rely on. In the case of a forest fire, most sensible animals would have long since buggered off before any humans present would have sniffed the air and said "someone having a barbeque?"

Similarly with earthquakes where mankind spend millions of pounds funding a host of scientists with precision instruments (supported by less than precise theories) but all we need to do is watch the birds and wait for them to all leg it (or, at least, wing it) hours before the tremor hits.

All I can imagine is that the signals were there and that my brain had captured them but starved of the mechanism to process that information. This inhibition, the sensual numbness caused by generations of modern living were smashed asunder as the second bottle of Auzzie red chased the first down.

I was not drinking alone, I hasten to add. While Iona does not usually partake and anyway hates red wine, her brother is another matter and while our drinking sessions are infrequent they usually make up for lost time. It is not unusual for us to drink a wine box between us (and I do mean the three-litre jobs, not the two and a quarter litre ones that the supermarkets have recently snuck on the shelf) and still be looking for more.

At a weekend this is excess enough but on a school

night, as Iona calls any evening preceding work…well it is of course plain stupidity.

My reaction to alcohol is generally confidence followed by bullshit (confidently talking crap) followed by mild depression (general lack of confidence) and then sleep (confidence returning so much that I will pass out anywhere). Often stage three is skipped entirely and I simply go from the bullshit stage to happy sleep and snore the entire house down.

This night, however, I was overcome with the absolute certainty that something terrible was going to happen the following day and indeed that I was going to be fired. Iona tried to reassure me in that patient way that only a sober wife can do while talking to a drunk husband. In her case it was annoyed pity, desperately trying to be a loving wife and listen to my ranting while knowing that having kept her up I would then continue to keep her awake once I dropped off.

She must have thought I was mad or at least more pissed than usual.

Of course, by the morning the whole incident while not forgotten was at least buried under the throbbing haze of the inevitable hangover. Not for the first time I was glad that I had the option of taking the train to work. There was no way I was legal to drive! Iona's normally strict "not on a school night" rule was a wise one.

Again, I don't want to dwell on the moment of being told my services were no longer required but in my defence it was not handled in the best possible way. I had a meeting booked to go through my mid-year review and given lots of forms to fill out in anticipation of this. The reason, it transpired, was that my boss at the time, Desmond, was a total coward and knowing he had to break the news had decided to do so under the mask of the mid-year reviews so that we did not suspect that anything was wrong and come prepared to challenge him.

The meeting time came and I entered his office pleased with myself that I had put together a good plan for the rest of the year as well as having more than achieved my objectives to date.

I could tell from his furtive expression that all was not well and I was not to be disappointed. Desmond had probably been stewing about the prospect for a while but when it came to it the announcement was somewhat blunt. Putting a nasty twist on the whole thing, he tried to justify the closure of my department by reference to a report I had recently written in which I had made recommendations as to how to make it more efficient.

Still in a state of shock I did not know how to react. The actual fact of being made redundant was tempered partly by the knowledge that I had predicted it and partly by the growing annoyance that my report had been perverted to suit their needs.

When he asked me if he wanted him to tell my team I nearly swore at him, growling through gritted teeth that I would do it. There was no way I was going to let him do to them what he had just done to me.

It was only as I was leaving the office and bumped into Desmond's boss that I had a glimmer of relief.

"If it makes you feel any better, he's gone as well." Mark shrugged and I could tell by his face that he was also on the list.

We headed down the pub to drown our sorrows and also to come to terms with the situation as well as discussing our next steps. There had been no discussion about alternative employment options, redundancy payments or anything else and I wanted to brief my team to keep a steady head until we had negotiated properly.

The truth was that I wanted a distraction from the sheer panic that was raging through my head. We had spent so long it had seemed going through the emotional turmoil of trying to have a family and now I had let the side down by losing my job.

I felt sick to the pit of my stomach and this time I knew it was not the alcohol. I called Iona and she jokingly asked me if I had been fired. When I told her I had she went very quiet, recognising immediately that I was not joking. I felt terrible, knowing that she was rapidly going through the same thought process that had gripped me for the last few minutes.

Typically, she took it bravely and said that we would get through it. I knew then and there that even this was not going to stop her resolve and I regretted my own weakness for having even thought about it.

She was, of course, right. As long as any children were fed, clothed and above all loved, what else mattered? I tried to emulate her and look on the bright side I did have a potential new career as a house-husband if all went well.

On a very practical point of view, I was on good money without which our lifestyle would be drastically different. Fortunately, Iona is extremely sensible when it comes to money, just as well as I am in the proverbial camp of "money talks – it says 'goodbye'" and had a large collection of CD's & DVD's to prove it. She, on the other hand, had been saving hard before meeting me in the expectation that she was going to live alone and thus would need the deposit for a house.

I was very glad that I had let Iona's approach to money override mine. We had for the last couple of years been planning to try and move out of our mid-terrace house, not that there was anything particularly wrong with it apart from a few mildly-irritating things but mostly as we both hankered to live in the country. A long-term plan had been put in place which was just as well as when the axe fell it meant that we were not enslaved to the crumbling banks with heaps of debt.

The more I thought about it the more I saw the dreams we'd made for our life together crumbling around our ears. My company had taken the job, my livelihood and our dream of a lovely house. They were not going to take the dream of a child.

Being made redundant gave me yet another thing to wallow in self-pity about and I am afraid I did a lot of that. It was around then that a lot of friends started to drift away which was sad but I let them go. The few that remained joined the close ranks of family who proved to be so supportive to us.

You cannot imagine how difficult it is when people are being sympathetic to you about one thing and yet oblivious to the fact that the overall situation is far worse. The temptation to tell people was very strong but had to be resisted. We had decided to keep our situation secret but the more time went on the more difficult it was to tell anyone yet at the same time it burned inside me to share our troubles.

I managed to negotiate four months redundancy notice on time and a half, mostly as I pointed out that they still had a couple of major projects on the go and if they didn't play ball we would down tools and walk that day, leaving them well and truly in the lurch. They also offered a good compromise package which meant that I was in the fortunate position of leaving the company with a redundancy cheque equivalent to nearly a year's salary.

Every time I turned on the television and caught the news of one factory closure or another, I realised that I was lucky to get such a good payout. It also meant that the pressure to find another job was not immediate which was just as well as the job market was pretty much nonexistent!

What worried me most was that the added stress of the imminent end of my job would lessen my already diminished performance, negating any benefit of the fertility drugs that Iona was on. As the months flew by, inevitably nothing happened. Pregnancy test kits were joined now by ovulation kits in a desperate attempt to get the timing spot on but to no avail.

Slowly but surely, our action plan crumbled to dust. More was unsaid between us than was said but there was no longer any need for words. We both shared exactly the same dread.

Finally, the course of tablets was over and the empty box meant that it was time to return to Dr Armstrong.

Once again we found ourselves in the all-too familiar surroundings of the doctor's surgery, depressed, dejected and struggling to make sense of it all. I for sure was pretty fed up of the endless cycle of tests but deep down I knew that there were steps that we had to take in order to get to the root of the problem. Nagging just below the surface was the very real thought that a natural pregnancy might not be possible.

Please, not more tests!

# Chapter 7:
## A second opinion, and a third...

Well, I didn't have to go back to the phlebotomist nor was I being expected to run the gauntlet of the hospital gents. This time I was sent to see the urologist. For the first time I felt as if Dr Armstrong was actually admitting that she didn't have a clue what was wrong and was therefore finally referring us to someone more specialised who might.

Although I didn't have to experience the pleasure of the toilets I still had the fun and games of the car park at the hospital, once again stuffed to the gills which meant I had to park halfway across town and was nearly late for my appointment.

My timekeeping was not helped by the fact that I had no idea where the urology department was, my geography being limited to the phlebotomy department and its conveniences (and, of course, the snack bar).

Once again, the map of the site was devoid of any section bearing the word "urology" and I had to ask the mildly bored receptionist where I needed to go. Grudgingly she gave me directions and sent me on my way.

I needn't have worried. Being a stickler for timekeeping I tend to forget that other people are not and in the case of hospitals, appointments rarely stay on track and today was no exception.

It was one of those depressing waiting rooms with hard, uncomfortable chairs, the obligatory dull reading materials and the long line of patients in the queue ahead of you no matter what time you arrive. In my case I turned up only a few minutes before my prescribed time but there were still five people ahead of me.

Not for the first time I kicked myself that despite previous experience I had still not brought anything constructive to read or do and the dull time dilation set in again. Gradually the queue of people ahead of me shrank until I was sat alone but it was not until then that I noticed that no further patients had arrived. Clearly I was the last on the list.

The previous patient emerged and headed home and I sat in anticipation for my turn.

It would be an interesting experiment to perform on people to see how long in such situations they would wait until it became obvious that they had been forgotten. Some folk might wait patiently for a few minutes, others possibly as much as half an hour.

In hindsight, the fact that I lasted about two minutes was probably a good thing. When I went up to the desk I saw my notes still there and the look on the nurse's face as I appeared was a picture. She had completely forgotten about me but my reminder meant that the nurse managed to catch the urologist before he went home. Had I left it any longer I would have been stuffed.

We were both a bit flustered during the appointment. I for the obvious reason that I had nearly had to go home without seeing the specialist, he as running as late as he was, the urologist had evidently planned his escape only to be dragged back for another pesky patient.

My appointment was short, something we were both glad about. As it was, there was little he could say. Once I'd undergone the inevitable dropping of the trousers and he had made a cursory examination he decided it was time for an ultrasound scan on those articles most precious to me. This was getting serious! The thought that there might be something structurally wrong with the old two veg was inconsiderable!

The fact that I was now in the hands (so to speak) of an expert, someone a rung or two up the medical food chain was also concerning. No longer was I just another case of man-flu at the local surgery, this required specialist knowledge. I asked what it was they were looking for and while he gave me a whole list of symptoms ranging from the trivial to the terminal, there was only one that stuck in my mind.

Testicular cancer is a very serious thing. I know as a close member of my family suffered it whilst in his twenties which was a very shocking occurrence. Cancer scares the hell out of most people but cancer of the knackers? It makes me shudder even now to think about it. Anyone reading this that has had the bad fortune of suffering from testicular cancer, you have my utmost sympathy. Even the fact that I was going in to be tested for it was enough to put me into a cold sweat.

I had to wait for the appointment and being a total control freak I hated this part. Inevitably, waiting for the ultrasound scan meant another few weeks delay, partly to get the procedure done and partly to then wait for the official results. Yet more delays, yet more time passing.

Work was no longer the escape that I had not appreciated it had once been. The atmosphere was understandably tense as the last day approached, not helped by the fact that I was already on edge.

In some respects, it did me a favour in that nobody at work suspected there was anything wrong in my personal life, putting my mood down to the fact that I was losing my job. Despite this, I managed to stay focused and professional though heaven only knows how.

What was more difficult was the fact that I had to start the process of finding a new job and there was no way I was in the right emotional place for this. I signed up for all the careers counselling that was offer but knew in my heart that it would be mostly wasted.

The appointment finally came and I dutifully trotted off, not really knowing what I was getting into.

This time, I allowed plenty of time to get parked. It was just as well as the space I found was even further from the hospital than before. Luckily, however, I had downloaded a map of the hospital on the internet and for the first time I had a pretty good idea where I was going, finding the correct department without having to bother the Rottweiler on reception.

I sat meekly in the waiting room, well, okay, the recess in the corridor that they laughingly called the waiting room, until it was my turn which remarkably came slightly earlier than the appointed time. The one thing I will say for the staff who undertook my ultrasound scan, they were efficient. Utterly devoid of personality but efficient!

I'm not saying that I expected huge discourse or any exuberant in-depth conversation but they must have realised that I was in a very embarrassing and vulnerable position so a bit of chat would have been nice.

Girls, I am sure you are shouting at me again now along the lines that I think I had it bad. Trust me I know you have to go through a lot worse. Iona was sent for a cervical smear around this time and while not really understanding what you go through I appreciate it is highly unpleasant on so many levels.

To be honest, it was a doddle physically. All I had to do was 'drop 'em' and lie on the table while the ultrasound operator put on her glove. She looked at me with one of the blankest expressions I have ever seen which really put me in my place. I was evidently not the first cock of the day and definitely not the most impressive. At least that is what her expression communicated. Conversation not being an option, I had to stare at the ceiling while she produced the big jar of lubricant.

Bugger me that stuff is cold!

With my gentleman vegetables nicely lubricated, she rammed the head of the ultrasound scanner into them to get a real good look. There were times when I am sure she almost forgot she was doing an external examination!

There was no bedside manner with this one. She came right out and asked me if I knew what varicose veins were. Oh great, why not just tell me I have an alien implant in the left one just for good measure.

I knew what they were, sort of, but thought it was what you get on legs when you are old and lose all residual fashion sense. It hadn't really occurred to me that as you get veins in the rest of your body, blood having to go somewhere after all, that you could also get the same problems elsewhere. I was a bit surprised as I didn't think they would tell me the results of the scan immediately, I thought they had to go through the doctor first.

The good news was that it did not appear to be cancer. The bad news was that I was pumping too much blood down there and cooking the little fellas. This combined with my rotund physique meant that poor old Percy and the twins were permanently at a temperature that was not conducive to sperm production.

Depressing as it first seemed to be, this was good news. It was a symptom that could indeed result in male infertility but was at the same time potentially treatable. I had also fortunately not had any of the other side-effects of varicocele such as atrophy (shudder) or an ache in the groin (shudder again).

Having delivered the verdict she started packing up and I assumed that my presence was no longer required.

I noticed that she only gave me one sheet of paper towel to wipe myself down with. Oh, very bloody funny I'm sure! What's worse was that the paper she gave me was super-absorbent…towards water but seemingly greasy lubricant-repellent. Rather than cleanly wipe it off it more sort of smeared it around so I just gave up and resigned myself to a squelchy drive home where a hot shower waited for me.

The question now was what exactly was going to be done about it? I could spend the rest of my life wearing loose-fitting trousers, going around 'commando' I believe it is called and walking with a certain wide-legged swagger but that was somewhat impractical.

No, the answer was much simpler than that.

Once again I was back to see the urologist and this time the nurse managed to pass my notes along so that he was actually expecting me. He was a bit surprised that I knew the results, confirming what I had suspected in that the sonographer probably shouldn't have said anything.

Even so, the results seemed to give him some confidence and he decided that I had to go for what he described as embolization which meant a trip to the radiologist. Radiologist? That's even more specialised than an urologist isn't it? Still, if it meant improving my sperm count and everything else then of course I would do it.

I was packed away to make yet another appointment, indeed two of them. What made the whole process even more tedious was that at every stage we still had to go back to Dr Armstrong to track the progress, even though she was not actually providing the advice any more, at least on my side.

Sensing our frustration at the speed at which things were happening, she once again focused on Iona and after another lengthy and slightly confusing consultation I was not the only one going to an '-ologist'. Our doctor, no doubt fed up of us making her office untidy all the time, had finally given up pretending she even remotely knew what she was talking about and referred Iona to a gynaecologist.

One of the good things about galloping towards redundancy was that I got a lot of time off for job hunting and general farting around so it was no issue for me to disappear to go with Iona for her appointment which was luckily in one of the local clinics so we didn't have the joys of the parking situation at the hospital.

The gynaecologist really went to town on Iona, ordering up a whole bunch of tests, performing a speculum examination and ordering repeats of the FSH test as she realised that we had been misinformed and it had not done on the right day. This was really annoying as we had hinged months of treatment on test results that were, it seemed, fundamentally flawed. She also ordered a hysterosalpingogram (HSG – oh the joys of acronyms), a word that the spell-checker on my computer had no chance of getting right!

It was critical that the tests were performed on a particular day in Iona's menstrual cycle which put her a bit on edge and she had to plan time off to accommodate it while being vague at work precisely what medical reasons she had to take time out.

The procedure was, I know, horrible for her. Well, that

is not exactly true, while she was apprehensive about the procedure she was more scared about what it would find.

By this time, however, although I was undergoing separate investigations the gynaecologist was understandably taking both of our situations into account and whatever the results of Iona's tests was not going to discuss further options until all results were back in.

For me life went quiet for a bit while I awaited my appointment at the radiology department, not without a little dread, I might add. There had been lots of talk about the fact that it might not work, some talk about the benefits in terms of improved sperm count and motility but just as a post-script an off-the-cuff comment about the fact that it could all go horribly wrong with somewhat dire consequences. That's always the bit you don't want to hear, especially when it comes to such treasured parts of your anatomy!

The day came and like a lamb to the slaughter (well, not quite) we went back to the hospital. Iona came with me as it was the kind of procedure from which you are not allowed to drive back from for obvious reasons. I had done some reading up on the subject and knew that to get to the offending vein they had to go in via my groin somewhere and poke something in (okay, a very non-medical overview but you get the picture).

From what I could tell the procedure was supposed to regulate blood flow to the important parts as far as sperm generation was concerned but whether that was opening veins, shutting parts off I, to be honest, was really not sure. It had been explained to me but as I headed to the hospital I realised that I didn't actually have a clue.

I did have an idea of the process which basically meant that I would have a local anaesthetic in the downstairs area while they did what they had to, a quick stitch up and then after a few minutes to make sure I wasn't having a major wobbler, I would be packed back out of the door.

The nurses attending me that day were really nice, very friendly and ready to answer whatever questions I might have. The consultant radiologist or whatever he was had evidently gone to the same finishing school as the ultrasound operator as he had almost no conversation whatsoever, leaving the whole annoying "dealing with the patient" bit to the nurses.

Like a lot of these sorts of minor procedures, most of it involves from the part of the patient lying about in a state of undress. In my case, it was only half a state of undress as they were really not bothered what I did on the top half of my body. With a small towel over me for modesty, I lay on the bed while the nurse went through the consent form with me, which pretty much sounded like "if we screw up you agree not to sue us". There was not that I could see a "I'd rather you didn't screw up if it is all the same to you" box to tick so I resorted to signing my usual squiggle of a signature and hoping that I was not among that tiny percent of unfortunate buggers for whom things turn out badly.

Just as boredom was setting in, realising that it must be equally dull for poor Iona sat outside, I was wheeled into what for want of a better phrase I will call the operating theatre. It consisted of a motorised bed that would allow the patient to be held in pretty much any position and the most enormous piece of equipment you have ever seen that consisted of a huge arm that came over and lots of TV screens. This was the business end that the radiologist was going to drive but frustratingly I could not see what he was doing.

Being a bit of a technology fan, I love visiting factories, going round museums and all that sort of thing so I was perfectly happy lying there gawping around at the big shiny toys. The power leads snaked out of the top and through a complex series of pulleys and clips was held overhead before entering the junction box on the wall. It was while I was staring around following the path of the cables that the nurse almost had a heart attack thinking I was lapsing into a coma or something. She asked me with a very worried expression whether I was okay and didn't seem all that impressed when she found out I was just being nosey.

I really cannot tell you what they actually did. Once the anaesthetic kicked in I couldn't feel a thing apart from the mild and lingering embarrassment that one would naturally have while a bunch of people are messing around with their plumbing.

With some relief I was told that it was all over and was wheeled back into the recuperation room to get bored again. I wondered if I would be allowed a bacon butty but decided that the answer was more than likely going to be no, although as Iona points out, I never actually asked. Trust me, however, the answer would have been no!

I had to wait a bit in case the wound leaked or there was any adverse reaction (I didn't get to the bottom of this but there was some mention of things swelling up or turning blue, neither of which sounded good). There was a clock on the wall which was a very bad thing as I spent the next hour or so glowering at it until the nurse finally remembered I was there and, once she was happy that I wasn't leaking and knew which direction gravity operated in sufficiently to walk, told me I could go.

Sensation gradually returned and to be honest, they felt just like they had before the operation (which was a huge relief as at least I *could* feel them).

The only downside of the operation was that I was instructed to go back six weeks later to do a repeat sperm test. The delights of the gentleman's toilet beckoned! What was more annoying was that I could not go back to the urologist until after this which meant another two months before anything would happen.

When I got home and checked my diary I realised that my next sperm test was due the day after I became officially unemployed. Typical!

Despite searching far and wide it was pretty evident that there was nothing in the job market for someone with my skills so I pulled in a few favours and decided to go freelance.

This was, of course, the same calibre of decision as the one to be a bachelor for eighteen years of my adult life – something I really had no choice in. I could of course have signed on but something in me realised that if I did this it would be the end of my professional career.

As it was, I had a few contacts from my previous life and a couple of them brought in sufficient work to keep me at least partially occupied and to bring in more money, barely, than I would on the dole. It wasn't much but I knew that if I were to make it as an independent consultant then I would inevitably have to start small and build up gradually.

I know what you are thinking; I was starting up as a consultant in a market that was dumping consultants on a daily basis. Not the greatest business plan but at the time it felt like a great idea.

For sure, with all the medial procedures and everything else the freedom was very appealing and there was always the optimistic dream that I would make a success of it.

There was of course only one slight problem. While technically I am very good and have always done a great job, an entrepreneur I am not and I am about as good at business as I am at breathing underwater without an aqualung.

At this stage I had not encountered all the problems that self-employment brought and I did keep a close eye on the job market with the desperate hope that the perfect job would appear.

Iona was fortunately still in gainful employment and got on with her life about as normally as possible. We talked often about our situation but mostly when one or the other wanted to vent our frustration as to how long everything was taking. She was very, very supportive of my going freelance, once again taking the practical approach that my redundancy effectively paid my salary for the next year and anything I earned in the meantime was a bonus. It meant that I had a year or so to make a go of it.

What was scary was that we had probably spent that long already in our pursuit of a baby and really did not have a lot to show for it.

For the first time in my life I noticed the constant, background angst that never seemed to fully go away. My brain would never totally switch off, whether it was chewing over the consultancy or our fertility issues. I began to get very tired.

The day arrived when I had to go back to the hospital for the dreaded sperm sample. I will not bore you with the details as I am sure by now you have a far more graphic image of the gentlemen's conveniences than you had ever really wanted to have. Needless to say it was another pantomime of parking on the way there and the usual soul-destroying process to produce the sample.

What was interesting, however, was that I remembered the time that I handed the sample into the lab. It was nine in the morning and I knew this as I had planned to get there early so I could get home and work on some things I was involved in at the time.

I had an appointment with the urologist booked for the week later but this was cancelled and put back another week for reasons that were never really explained to me. This was not a major problem apart from the nuisance that yet another week of inactivity had passed and from the beginning of the whole process, time was marching relentlessly on.

In the mean time, Iona had the results of her latest set of blood work. This time her FSH was 37.8 although we were not actually given the number at the time. When Iona was given the results she was simply told that they were "fine". When we pushed as to what this really meant we were simply told that if the numbers were of concern then it would imply that Iona was, despite her age, pre-menopausal.

Beyond this, the gynaecologist would not propose any further treatment as I was still awaiting my results so we were packed off yet again.

The day came for my next urology appointment and, getting used to the rubbish parking at the hospital now I left in my usual ridiculously early time to ensure I was there. I had an hour and a half to make the twenty-five minute journey and get to my appointment. That should be plenty, I thought.

I hit the back of the queue just after leaving home. I never found out what the problem was but it would have been almost quicker to walk. Realising that the motorway was kaput, I decided to go the back way, only to discover that everyone else in Oxfordshire had made the same decision!

As I crawled through town, the time ticked away until the point where I was racing towards the hospital with only five minutes to go before my appointment.

It was, of course, the worst ever day for parking. The nearest spot I could find was literally a half-mile away and I legged it to the hospital and down to where I had gone before, arriving bang on time – only to find that the urology department was not there anymore but in a completely different part of the building! The buggers had moved it without telling me.

I checked the letter I had been sent but it didn't provide any further clues.

At this point I gave up. I was going to be late anyway so I may as well arrive later and composed than slightly late and knackered.

I needn't have bothered. Everyone else was late as well having undoubtedly suffered the same problem as us and the urologist was running approximately fifty minutes behind schedule yet again, which at least gave my heart rate time to settle back to normal before I saw him.

His first question threw me completely. He had received the latest sperm test results but questioned why I had performed the test only six weeks after the operation, testicles taking something like seventy two days to make new sperm so I had not waited anywhere near long enough. I was completely exasperated! Why had I gone so early, because the stupid bugger now asking the question had told me to! I knew I had not been mistaken as I had written down the instruction at the earlier appointment and even double-checked it with him.

Without the "stupid bugger" bit I told him as much as my blood boiled with anger.

There is a look that I am becoming quite accustomed to now. It is that look given to you by a medical professional when you have pointed out to them that they are wrong but they simply stare at you as if you had spoken to them in Martian. The matter was not pursued indeed it was simply ignored by him. We have a dog and take her to an extremely good local veterinary hospital whenever she needs treatment. There we see a most excellent vet who whilst very experienced, is quite happy to admit when she does not know something and either consult a colleague or look it up on her medical database. This I find incredible, my dog gets better medical care and professional advice than I do! There is something fundamentally wrong about that.

I then noticed something deeper and more sinister about the results. As I have mentioned above, I clearly remember handing the sample in almost bang-on nine in the morning. It was with some shock therefore that I noticed that the sperm test had been received by the lab at one fifty-eight in the afternoon, almost five hours after I had given it to them.

Time and time again I had been told the importance of measuring the sample within two hours of production and that it should be kept warm in that time. This measurement was way beyond that and it suddenly brought into serious question all the other results. If the lab were that slow at investigating the sample how could any of the results be trusted?

As with the previous ones, the count, motility and morphology were low, nearly as low as my mood. He then dropped another bombshell by telling me that the procedure would probably not increase my sperm count anyway.

Excuse me?

If that was the case, why the hell did I go through it in the first place? I now didn't know whether I was coming or going as everything he was telling me seemed to be contradictory to what had been said before. Which was right?

It was then that he uttered the acronym I had been dreading. In his opinion, if my results did not improve then his recommendation would be that we would need to consider in-vitro fertilisation, IVF.

I left there utterly bewildered but with another pot to do a further semen sample, this time after the correct period from the embolization.

After the appointment I checked the notes I had taken

in our previous meetings and he had clearly told me prior to the embolization that it would increase my sperm count by not killing them off. I was not imagining it, he was giving me a mixed message.

Not only had I wasted my time doing the sperm test it now seemed that the operation had been pointless and all my previous sperm tests were questionable. After months of soul-crushing procedures I was no better off than when I had started.

That afternoon we saw the gynaecologist and she went through Iona's hysterosalpingogram results showing that she had patent ('open' to us laymen) tubes and day 21 serum progesterone indicating ovulation. No real discussion as to the significance of the FSH levels was had at that time and indeed these seemed to have been forgotten.

She told us to wait for my next sperm test results and depending on how high or low they were she would see us sooner or later for next steps.

We left even more frustrated than before. It was like Groundhog Day; we would have a test, go and see an expert only to be told to go for another test and come back when the results were ready, only to be sent for another test...

It dawned on me around then that counselling was still nowhere to be seen. Iona and I were both clearly suffering emotionally and struggling to come to terms with the incessant sequence of tests and inconclusive results but none of the experts we had seen had even suggested any help groups or counselling services.

We decided therefore to find one for ourselves.

# Chapter 8:
## Help! We need somebody...

It was towards the end of 2009 that something else happened, something that would take our journey in a whole new direction (and fortunately, for us, forwards rather than backwards and round and round in circles thanks to the medical profession).

Through one of Iona's colleagues at a random party we were introduced to a couple, Dawn and Andrew, who had coincidentally been through multiple rounds of IVF, been messed around far worse than us, dabbled with the idea of adoption and had finally had two charming daughters using both donor eggs and sperm. They were both actively involved in the one of the leading UK infertility charities and even more conveniently lived just down the road.

I do not know how the conversation came around to IVF but most likely it was them volunteering the subject. Dawn and Andrew are the sort of people who love to share their experience in the hope that it will help others but little did they know as we chatted over the canapé's at the party that they were describing our own problem.

Iona and I had a quick chat in private and took them to one side, explaining that we were undergoing investigations for infertility and that IVF had been mentioned but that we were keeping the whole thing secret. They were more than happy to talk to us and a follow-up dinner was planned.

Armed with a box of chocolate nibbles and a bottle of wine, we headed over to their place, both a bit unsure as to what to expect. What we found was most unexpected but in a very pleasant way. Dawn and Andrew were not only exceptionally nice people but incredibly open about their own experiences and happy to discuss them with us and answer any questions we had. They were a breath of fresh air! For the first time, someone was giving us a straight answer, even if it was not an easy answer to give.

For me it was a revelation having another bloke to talk to who seemed to understand entirely what I was going through and indeed even worse, being himself totally infertile.

In the course of one evening they told us more than we had discovered after nearly a year of treatment and desperate searching on the internet.

What was scary was the fact that if what they were telling us was true, the medical experts had misdiagnosed so much for them and far more seriously than the apparent errors in our case and my faith in doctors crumbled even further.

Their experience was that while GP's have a good grounding in basic medicine, they generally know very little about fertility but were often not willing to admit that fact. Given that one of the main things people will go to the doctor about are matters involving childbirth or infertility I found this astounding but it tallied with our own experiences.

They gave us the low-down on IVF, pointing us in the right direction for all the information we could possibly need on the subject, something our various doctors and consultants had utterly failed to do. From my point of view it was incredible, speaking to a man who had found he was infertile but was clearly happy with the fact that he had children, even if he was not the genetic father.

I admired his strength but at the same time I could see on both Andrew and Dawn's faces the memory of their own frustrations. I understood why they were so keen to help others in that they were desperate to stop couples like us going through the same hell they had suffered. Considering my own relief at having spent just a couple of hours in their presence and the wealth of information they had passed on, I realised just how terrible it would have been carrying on practically blind as they must have done.

I can only describe it like buying a flat-pack chest of drawers but discovering the instructions were missing. You are faced with the dilemma of carrying on regardless and inevitably making a total hash of it or trying to find someone who can explain how it is supposed to go together.

In Dawn and Andrew's case they had been forced to carry on regardless with no information and had nearly divorced as a result of the stress they had undergone.

As I have alluded to before I do have a habit of becoming somewhat self-absorbed and it was as a result of this that I had not until that moment considered the effect that the ongoing situation was having on my own marriage. It was scary to take a step back and look at it with different eyes and see that we were under a lot of stress.

Our only saving grace was that we do talk more than I think some couples do. Lack of communication seems to me to be one of the biggest killers of marriages.

It was a strange evening and as the wine coursed through my veins and produced the inevitable stage one confidence we were invited to simply fire away with questions as they did their best to answer and we took up their offer.

A very large can of worms was, for me, opening at this time. With my semen results poor and at best spurious and with Iona's results equally suspicious, the looming fact that we were going to need IVF was being rapidly followed by a darker thought lurking in the shadows behind. We might need donor treatment.

The evening ended and our heads were reeling with the new information that we had learned but also the knowledge that there were people out there who were more than happy to give their time to help people like us. Dawn and Andrew promised to put us in touch with other people in the area who they knew whose experiences we might find useful and who were more than happy to share as they had.

Armed with all the information we had been given it was time we realised to start gathering it all together and the "purple file" as it became know was created, already bulging with information, test results, letters from the various medical experts and everything else relevant to the case. It was depressing how much paperwork we had already amassed.

When collated like that it was scary just how much information we had, especially as the medial experts did not seem capable of doing anything constructive with it.

More and more we found ourselves on the Internet looking up information though this time from sites that had been recommended to us and the more we looked the more depressing it got.

As the year drew to a close, we faced another Christmas of uncertainty. Were we ever going to have kids and, more importantly, were they going to be ours? Dark thoughts were brewing in my mind.

When it comes down to it I am basically a huge child

at heart and as such as I have said before I love Christmas. Our family tradition has been honed and developed over the years to such a state that we are the grand masters of excess.

What has helped is the fact that circumstances have meant that the immediate family were all, until recently, adult with no small children involved. My siblings and I were growing up but for one reason or another none of us had propagated.

This did not prevent us from having a very childish approach to the festive season but we had managed to come up with a formula that made the day last.

For me it all started on Christmas Eve. I love cooking so usually take over the chef's role for the big day, much to the relief of my mother who while a good cook secretly hates being a slave to the rest of us. I always saw it as my way of taking the domestic pressure from her for at least one day but actually I enjoy it so much I would hate to give up the responsibility.

This does not mean that I want to spend my entire day in the kitchen so my habit is to cook all the meats on Christmas Eve, assisted by a bottle or two of spectacularly nice wine. This means that on December 25th all I have to do is vegetables and potatoes as well as steam the Christmas pudding.

That, of course, does not happen until later. First there is the matter of the full-English breakfast that none of us actually need but we all seem to partake in and the opening of a few small presents. There is also a morning glass of bucks fizz or something else "light" before we all trudge down to church for the morning service (which, having just been to midnight mass, is always odd as we have only said Happy Christmas to most of the congregation a few hours previously).

Back to the house we then engage in the full orgy that is Christmas Dinner and which, by the time we have farted around and got everything ready, tends to happen just in time to miss the Queen's speech. Dinner usually involves a few table presents and lashings of the booze of your choice.

Late afternoon is usually consumed with a bit of a doze and whatever film happens to be on the telly before we get to early evening where everyone tucks into leftovers before the serious business of tree presents begins.

On a good year we can keep it going until ten in the evening by which time everyone is so stuffed and drunk that we all fall into bed.

Iona's family, while a bit more reserved had their own family traditions that still involved good food, fine wine and lots of present-giving.

This year was different. There were four babies on the scene, two on each side of our families and all born within the last nine months. It had already been a busy season of christenings, something that Iona and I had both found quite hard but now we were in that most personal of family times.

For the first year the families had not all come together. This year, the siblings were enjoying their first year with their new children and not only did we not have the great gatherings of old but we found ourselves driving halfway around the country during the fortnight before Christmas visiting them to distribute presents as we could hardly expect them to come to us when they were the ones carting a small baby around.

Even our immediate world was leaving us behind, it seemed. What was worse, there were four newborn's to buy for which meant we were shopping in the very stores we dreaded walking into, making multiple purchases for children that were not our own.

It was agony spotting things that we really liked but for babies we didn't have.

For me Christmas was doubly-depressing. The consultancy was already proving to be a lot more difficult than I had envisaged and once I had exhausted my initial contacts, finding new ones seemed to be an impossible task. The fundamental problem was that I was totally useless at selling myself and to be honest my heart really wasn't in it.

Christmas was a great excuse to stop and take stock. All of the companies I was dealing with had shut down for the festive season and when it came to our doctor there were no results we were desperately waiting for. There was nothing to do but simply stop and reflect on the situation. It didn't take long for this reflection to include a stiff drink!

Iona took a less alcoholic stance but I knew she was spending just as long as I was contemplating and in her mind our circumstances were as mulled as the wine we had in the village square on New Year's Eve.

Somewhere along the line we compared notes and it seemed that a week of chewing over the problem had done us both the world of good.

Unanimously we started 2010 with the same unspoken resolution. We were going to damn well get something sorted out once and for all. Certainly I was getting both tired and pretty brassed-off with the whole process and craved that once and for all someone somewhere would just give us a straight answer.

I had also personally resolved that I wasn't going to take any more crap from anybody. It was now pretty clear that the system was on the whole failing us and while I was not actively seeking to enter any formal complaints, doing so was still a possibility and something I was becoming more and more willing to use as a threat.

The purple file had allowed me to keep track of what had been done and said, augmented as it was with my own notes. While it did not actually point to malpractice there was certainly no sign of any hurry in the course of treatment we had been offered, as if everyone involved simply expected Iona to fall pregnant naturally and get out of their hair.

My first task in the New Year was to head to the hospital. My latest sperm test was due but this time I had been careful to make a precise note of the time when I had submitted the sample given how long it had taken them to analyse the previous one.

By this stage I was becoming numb to the surroundings of the lavatory and whatever sample I was able to provide was the best that was going to be available under the circumstances. My previous experiences were burned into my very soul such that I knew it could not possibly get any worse and for once it did not. While I did not have total privacy I was at least able to filter out the strained farting from the next cubicle while I robotically did what was necessary.

I had, as I said, resolved to take a firm hand with the medical system and they did not take long to afford me the first opportunity to complain. Despite the fact that every one of my previous tests had been available within the week, this set took nearly three and allowed me several irate phone calls before they finally surfaced.

On the principle that we were going to take the bull by the horns, we had by this time done a lot of research on the Internet regarding IVF and through this and conversations with Dawn and Andrew there were two quite blunt facts that had emerged.

Fact number one: the NHS had recently changed their

criteria for IVF treatment, one of which most critically was that they would only offer treatment to women under the age of 35. Iona's 35th birthday was rapidly looming in August! We had raised this with the gynaecologist at the end of 2009, stressing the urgency of the situation but she had failed to mention that the clock was ticking in this respect.

Fact number two: the NHS would not offer IVF to women with an FSH level over approximately 12, deeming them to be effectively post-menopausal.

Er…what?

This second fact came as a total kick in the guts. How could this possibly be? Iona had been first identified with elevated FSH in October 2008, fifteen months previously yet neither our doctor nor the gynaecologist had raised this as an issue. Surely something had to be wrong and surely it could not be two independent medical experts?

Oh yes it could!

Iona's results, while varied, had been consistently high and certainly significantly higher than the twelve that seemed to be the point of concern. Our doctor had missed it which in some respects was to be forgiven though on the results there was clearly a "normal" range given that the result was outside of.

As with our vet, if Dr Armstrong didn't know what the implication of high FSH was she should have looked it up.

The gynaecologist, on the other hand, should have spotted it instantly.

We went back to see the gynaecologist but found ourselves in front of someone new, our "regular" being busy so we raised the issue and finally he agreed that yes it was pretty high, though he did not go as far as specifying whether it was an issue or not and, as seemed to be our lot, he ordered...you guessed it...yet another test to check it yet again.

The experience of hindsight has shown me that even though medical practitioners take copious notes, if you get handed from one to another they have a very annoying tendency to disregard a lot of what their predecessors have done and order tests of their own as if they need to be seen to be doing something.

He must have caught us in a generous mood as we gave him the benefit of the doubt and agreed to the test but we did push him on the matter of IVF and were told that it might be something we would have to consider but no more than that.

When the results came through and Iona phoned to make yet another appointment she was told that the head of the clinic wanted to see her which was ominous. Rather than wait for the appointment she pushed and the nurse grudgingly gave the FSH results out over the phone.

Dawn had already given us some guidance on FSH levels which were again in the high thirties and when Iona emailed her to relate the latest result who replied. "I'm sorry to tell you this on an e-mail, but no IVF clinic will take you on with FSH levels that high. You might want to consider donor eggs."

We remembered back to when we had been told that Iona's FSH levels were "fine". I'm sorry but I cannot find in my dictionary any definition of fine that would cover the latest bombshell that this delivered. Iona was far from fine, she was, by all the literature we could find, nearly post-menopausal!

It was a case of be careful what you wish for. We had wished for answers and by God were we getting them, just not the ones we had expected.

For Iona the situation was reaching breaking point. I

heard her crying as she updated her mother that evening but I felt helpless and frustrated.

As with all our other appointments it was followed up with the inevitable trip to Dr Armstrong for her words of dubious wisdom. One thing I have not mentioned so far is that our doctor's surgery was about as depressing as the local hospital. The reception staff always managed to give you the impression that you were disturbing something terribly important and that your mere presence was an unbearable distraction.

Signing in for your appointment was always a process of annoyed looks, sighs and waiting while the woman the other side of the desk fiddled with paperwork, accessed something important on the computer screen and rearranged her paperclips in case she was caught with them in the incorrect pattern, something her very existence clearly depended on. You would crawl to your seat in the waiting room feeling ashamed for having the audacity to even speak to her.

The surgery ran a simple system by which each general practitioner had a coloured light which corresponded to the colour on your number. Thus, if, as you were in our case, you were waiting for Dr Armstrong you would wait for the blue light and you would know when it was your turn by the fact that all the previous patients would hang their numbers on a peg before going in.

Woe betide if you forgot to hang your number on the peg – the receptionist would fly at you as if you were trying to steal the silver and in her most condescending tone explain loudly and clearly so that the whole waiting room could hear what the correct system was.

I hoped that she did not have a second job at the Samaritans.

Our experience that day at the surgery was no different from those that preceded it. We tried our best to be polite as we signed in but the receptionist ignored us for a whole two minutes while she achieved nothing of any significance before gruffly taking our names, scanning her computer in the vain hope that we had made a mistake and, when she disappointedly realised that we were correct thrust the next numbered tag in my hand.

When I glanced at the peg board and saw how many people were ahead of us I realised that Dr Armstrong was running at her seemingly regular half-hour delay.

It was frustrating to know that the one day we turned up late in anticipation of the delay she would be running on time and we would lose our slot.

I doubt it ever dawned on our doctor that the reason all her patients were always in such a bad mood was the fact that they had to run the gauntlet of her obnoxious receptionists and then face the inevitable delay in the waiting room while their car park tickets ticked over the hour and cost an extra pound fifty.

My mood was not good when we were finally called in.

Iona raised the last FSH levels with Dr Armstrong but even then and even when we told her that this meant Iona was indicated as being in early menopause, her response was to pretty much throw up her hands and say we were not to worry, it wasn't important and everything would be okay. She was pushing mindless optimism to incredible lengths.

In hindsight I should have threatened her with malpractice there and then. She was completely and utterly wrong!

We then came onto the subject of my last sperm test results. The count, motility and morphology had not improved. The embolization had been a complete and utter waste of time and resources.

By this time my blood pressure was simmering a few

degrees off of boiling point and I challenged her about the fact that my previous results had been measured five hours after they had been submitted. She didn't even flinch and certainly did not question this as being of any relevance whatsoever.

I was at breaking point and the tone of my voice reflected this. I demanded to know at what time the lab had received my latest sample but that information was mysteriously not on the report so I insisted that she find out and call me back. I cannot remember whether I was shouting but I suspect I was slightly foaming at the mouth.

It was probably dawning on our doctor by this point that I might not be the happiest person on the planet. The fact that my face was going purple could have been a clue.

When we left that surgery, it was in the knowledge that our GP had pretty much utterly failed us. While I am sure any other doctor would have put us through some of the same tests, our doctor was oblivious of the warning signs that the results were indicating and had offered us neither constructive advice nor any form of counselling whatsoever for our situation. If it had not been for Dawn and Andrew we would have still been running up the same blind alleys.

The call came the next day and she told me the results had been measured at two in the afternoon. I exploded (almost literally) and stared shouting at her down the phone, ranting about how totally unacceptable it was that the lab could be so careless. She then discovered that she had been reading the wrong results and had in fact been reading the time from the previous one. I calmed down a bit but felt no remorse for my shouting match. It was not my fault she was computer illiterate and given how upset I obviously was on the subject, she should have taken it far more seriously than she had and been careful about the information she sent me.

When I finally got the time that the lab claimed to have received the sample it told me exactly what I needed to know.

According to the official report from the hospital, the laboratory received my sperm sample at 8:44am. This is quite remarkable as at that time they were still swimming around in my testicles. I had arrived at the gents just before 9:00am and it was not until 9:10am, give or take a few seconds that I even handed the pot over, let alone them logging it in.

The lab was blatantly lying, either that or there was some strange time-warp operating in that particular part of the hospital! I doubted very much that they were delivering the samples to the lab by TARDIS. What was our doctor's response to this harsh revelation? Yes, I think you are ahead of me, absolutely nothing. This also simply reinforced the sad realisation that we had already come to. We had totally wasted our time with our GP.

This was of course bad news for me but the indications were that I at least had some sperm and they were swimming around a bit, even if they were inherently lazy like their producer. For Iona, the situation was far worse. Her FSH levels, by all indications were way too high and if the literature on the internet was to be believed (and we had no doubt that it was as Dawn confirmed their conclusions from her own experience) then Iona's eggs were basically no good.

In the cold light of hindsight, we realised that Iona had experienced a few particularly heavy and strange periods and we wondered now if that had been a failed attempt by her body to conceive, that perhaps my sperm had managed to reach the egg but that the egg had not been viable enough to implant properly. In the absence of any sound medical opinion, what else could we do but speculate, especially as we are both scientists so both take a very analytical view on life?

Emotionally, we were now in very deep and murky seas. I will not even begin to attempt to tell you what Iona was feeling at this time as that would not be appropriate but for my part I was suddenly face to face with that fundamental dilemma, that of the death of the gene. Once again I was far in uncharted waters.

# Chapter 9:
## A death in the family...

Fundamental to the process of child-birth is the perpetuation of the genetic line. It is a drive that powers the engine of all life on this small but beautiful planet. For billions of years, nature has used genetic diversity to create new species, allow species to adapt to new environmental pressures and ensured that redundant species become appropriately extinct.

Then along came Man. "Stuff all that evolution nonsense!" he said with the arrogance of intelligence and proceeded to develop genetic techniques that allowed the species to effectively by-pass some of Nature's more tricky problems. Not able to conceive naturally? No problem, we'll just do it in a test-tube for you.

The development of in-vitro fertilisation is no doubt one of the most miraculous achievements of the modern human species and has allowed for hundreds of thousands of couples to have babies where Nature would otherwise have denied them. More recent developments have opened up the possibilities for even more couples to carry children to term, even if the eggs and or sperm are not genetically their own.

Science can do some wonderful things but, as with all bargains, there is always a price to pay. I'd already found that out with my foolish bargain with God.

I was generally aware of IVF in that detached way that someone can be who watches television and finds out all sorts of fascinating things about subjects that does not involve them in the least.

Many a time I had watched programmes about war but I had never taken up arms. I often sat down to a documentary about drug abuse but have never even smoked grass. IVF found itself in that category of "things that happen to someone else" in my mental encyclopaedia, or at least it had until now.

Having regarded the subject so dispassionately in the past I had never really considered the ethical or moral dilemmas that lurked beneath the surface. Mankind was messing with the natural order of things, riding roughshod over billions of years of evolution and this raised many questions.

For me, whether assisted fertilisation was right was not in question. Normal IVF I had no problem whatsoever with. They would still be her eggs and my sperm and the fact that they got a prod in the right direction by some person in a lab-coat I had no issue with at all. Medical science has allowed us to cure diseases and repair physical damage that Nature had never intended us to do so the process of IVF was, in my mind, no different.

However, we were now heading far beyond this simple fix. I am not going to get into the spiritual world on this subject as while I have some form of faith it is not a strong and burning belief and I don't personally feel as if we would have offended God or anything like that by using IVF. I did canvas the opinion of my closest friend who is much more a man of the church but he had the same feelings as me.

The problem was we were not facing straight IVF anymore. We were facing donor treatment, almost certainly for Iona and still possibly for me as well.

On a purely logistical side, this was bad news for us in terms of getting treatment in the UK. The first issue was that the waiting list for treatment ran into years rather than months and we were basically not prepared to wait that long. I was by now galloping towards forty and Iona as I have said earlier nearing her mid-thirties. All along we had felt like we were being penalised for behaving in a socially-responsible manner, not trying to have children until we were married and it was not our fault that we had met at the ages we did.

The second issue was that of parentage. Having donor treatment also raised the huge issue of biological parentage. In the UK we would always have the lurking fact that our children would be able to trace their "real" parents.

You may think this is a good thing and that the child should have the right to know who their genetic parent or parents were but it is a huge decision to make, especially when you are already at an emotional low. I was so far out of my depth I really had no idea what I thought.

First, however, we had to face what can only be described as a death in the family. While it had not been confirmed by reliable medical opinion, all the indications were that whatever happened we were not going to be conceiving with Iona's eggs. This was quite simply devastating and to me it felt as if a part of our family had simply died there and then but without a funeral or any of the other trappings of death that allow us to emotionally cope.

I spent a lot of time in silent contemplation about this and about the other equally dark possibility. There was still no guarantee that my sperm was sufficiently viable to use and my genetics might be going the same way as Iona's.

Iona, of course, was utterly crushed by now but even then she was resolved to have a child, whatever it took.

Inside, I was in panic mode. Nothing had prepared us for the emotional shock of having to let go of our most precious commodity, our genetic makeup. I cannot describe to you what this feels like, it is something you really have to experience to understand and I would wish it on nobody.

Men, it has already been observed on many occasions, can be very insensitive and I learned this the hard way one evening. We were lying in bed and I was as was common then deep in thought, struggling to come to terms with how I felt about donor treatment. My initial reaction had been to shy away from any thought of it but to do so would have been to slam the door in Iona's face of any possibility of us having kids and that I could not do. Somehow I had to rationalise things in my own mind so that I would be happy to proceed with whatever we decided to do.

She sensed that I was very hesitant about donor treatment and I could see in her face that her dreams of having children hung by a thread and that I was holding the pair of scissors potentially ready to cut it.

Our friend Andrew had been very open and on the face of it content that his children were products of someone else's sperm but I could not find the strength within me to feel the same way. Just as we were about to go to sleep I foolishly made the casual statement to Iona that I did not think I would feel happy about donor sperm.

I should, in hindsight, have either kept my big gob shut or at least been a bit more considerate. I had already made it clear in earlier conversations that I was not keen on adoption and in one stupid comment I had in Iona's mind crushed one of the two remaining options left to us.

Oops!

Sadly, I don't think she slept very well that night but the damage was done. Let this be a lesson to you men out there about to face the same problems, beware of idle comments like this. Foot-in-mouth disease can be rather painful!

Adoption, while we are vaguely on the subject, was something I really had not seen as being in the picture but mostly due to personal experience. I have known people who have adopted. One particular couple who are probably the nicest, most decent and most suitable for being parents, people I have ever met were dragged through hell by the adoption service for years in order to get the two children they now have.

Observing their experience I had vowed long before meeting Iona that I never wanted to go through that process.

I have also met a number of children who were adopted and they have often had emotional issues due to the knowledge of their original rejection and I did not want any child of mine growing up knowing that their biological parents had in effect thrown them out.

This was one thing to be said for donor treatment. The children that would be produced would be born and brought up from a basis of love, not rejection. The eggs and sperm that were donated would not be rejected by their biological donors but given in the hope that new life which would otherwise not have occurred could be created.

If we were going to have children, I wanted them to come from Iona's womb. This also, of course, meant that surrogacy was also out of the question though, to be honest, I don't think for us it ever really came into the picture. I am sure that it works for some people but I just didn't want to go there.

While I do have a long-standing failing (one of many)

that I tend to hugely over-analyse any given situation, the thought process above did give me some kind of substance to grab hold of with respect to my own rationale for things.

Iona's own internal justification was always going to be different to mine. Without wishing to be sexist women will always have different natural instincts with respect to children than men. However she had come to terms with the probable loss of her own eggs I did not know but outwardly she was still clearly ready to run with donor treatment, with or without my sperm.

This was not that she was trying to cut me out of the loop but I think she felt that being a parent was more than simply being a gene-bank.

For her it was nurture versus nature, if she could still carry the child then she would be inputting physically to their development. Although the genetics would not be hers the physical building blocks of the child, the tissues, nutrients and everything else would.

It did get me thinking. If we could not provide the genetic material, we could at least provide the love and upbringing. For Iona, this was much more definite than for me. Even if it were not her eggs that were implanted, she would still be physically growing the baby within her womb so the actual biological material needed to construct the embryo would be provided by her body.

It was a compromise I could come to terms with. If I provided the sperm, she built the baby; even though it was someone else's eggs at least we both had a part to play.

You have to understand that while I have expressed these thoughts in words here, that is not how they went through my mind. Normally my thoughts run in the form of a dialogue with my inner self (who is usually a rather unhelpful and sarcastic little sod). I add pictures when I am reading fiction and tend to run the film in my head as I am going along which is fun.

With this, however, there were very few words and the mental process was, for want of a better explanation, mainly constructed out of basic emotions, gut feelings and colours. It was almost as if my unconscious self was banging on the wall from his house next door, trying to attract everyone's attention with his point of view.

I guess it is like that game you play as children when you are trying to locate a hidden object and the person who has secreted it shouts "hot" or "cold" depending on which direction you walk. I would throw a fact in and simply see whether I felt anxious or calm and gradually worked towards a place where I was content.

Donor sperm was another matter but one I still could not face as yet. I knew that the only way I was going to be able to make a rational or even emotional decision on that was when someone stared me in the face and told me my sperm were useless and that there was no other choice. Until then I was going to be terribly British and bury my head in the sand and hope the problem would go away.

This is the strange thing about these sorts of circumstances. You simply cannot plan for every contingency as you truly do not know how you are going to feel until those possibilities become realities. I think we are hard-wired not to kill ourselves worrying about things until it is absolutely necessary.

We had the next meeting with the gynaecologist but now it was time to demand some straight answers. With no help from anybody in the official medical services Iona and I had been through the emotional mill and come out the other side. We were shattered, heartbroken but still alive and still determined.

One thing I have not really touched on until this time

was the fact that the gynaecology clinic also played host to the other child-related departments which effectively meant that every time we went there we had to see pregnant women walking around glowing with happiness which was mildly insensitive, at least we thought so until we appeared for our next appointment.

Nobody had felt it appropriate to mention that the clinic had moved to the other end of the corridor, accessible by a different staircase and that the one we had always used in the past led straight into the post-natal clinic. We had to walk all the way through the rooms emblazoned with baby pictures and children's drawings, not to mention the happy pregnant couples, to get to the drab waiting room at the other end.

They may as well have stuck a knife in each of our hearts just for good measure. I could see Iona staring ahead as if her head was locked in a neck-brace, fighting the tears that threatened to pour down her face.

Our turn came and we were led into the office – only to see a complete stranger sat on the other side of the desk and not head of the clinic as we were expecting.

We had gone in with the hope of getting some form of decision but that seemed unlikely now. In that respect we were not disappointed. He reviewed the latest data and concluded that we would probably have to consider IVF. He did state that the FSH levels were high but once again failed to state clearly what this meant or the consequences of what we would need to do. He also, like his predecessor, failed to offer anything in the way of counselling or emotional support.

Packing us out of the door we still had no clear direction except for the fact that we were clearly looking at IVF, we knew from our own research that this was going to require donor treatment and that we were not going to get that anytime soon on the NHS and if we did it would come with baggage.

Every indication was now that we were going to have to go it alone.

One of the dangers of the Internet is that it allows free access to a wealth of information to pretty much everyone with access to a computer and a modem. When it comes to self-diagnosis this is probably like what happened when the Reader's Digest first issued its Family Health Guide and everyone eagerly went through it and decided they had rabies or leprosy or whatever just because they thought they had all the symptoms.

In this case, I would have loved to have been proven wrong, for someone to come up to us and tell us we were just being silly and that everything was going to be okay. The trouble was we knew it wasn't.

Dawn and Andrew had been to a fertility clinic in Barcelona and spoke very highly about it, although there were several other clinics we could choose from. Spain was appealing as they both had a good donor network and also the legal situation that allowed donors to remain anonymous so that there would be no possibility of the child ever tracing its biological parents.

This meant a lot to us. It was not that we wished to deny our child this right; we just felt that from the point that we decided to conceive that we wanted the child to be and to feel that it was ours and ours alone, regardless of the genetics. The donation of the egg would be the catalyst we would require to conceive but after that the child would be in all other ways entirely ours.

I hoped that in the future our longed-for offspring would understand this decision for it is not one that was made lightly.

We made our plans, did our homework and realised

that the clinic in Barcelona was probably the way to go. This would, of course, mean that we would be paying ourselves and a simple "back of a fag packet" calculation gave a bottom-line figure in the region of £10,000 for one round of treatment. Gulp! It was very fortunate that we had squirreled away some of my redundancy but I knew that long-term I would have to get a real job.

It was for us very fortunate that we had the money as there must be many people out there to whom this amount would simply be unachievable. I was very conscious, however, that this would knock a large dent in our savings and with me on an unreliable income our financial future was still shaky at best.

Iona then got another call from the clinic saying that the gynaecologist wished to see us. Not either of the ones who we had seen in the past but the head honcho whose name appeared at the top of the letters. Evidently our results had finally triggered something in the system that meant we were now an important case. In the past the process of getting an appointment had been a slow one but suddenly we were being requested to attend the clinic the very next day.

It was obvious from the start that Miss Dawes was not a happy bunny and with good reason. We briefly outlined the information that her colleagues had given us, as well as the timeline of events and the fact that they had completely missed the significance of the FSH levels. She went rather pale and looking back in hindsight she was crapping herself.

It was clearly embarrassing for her and also worrying as I had my "grumpy old git" face on again. Whilst I did not actually say I was going to make a formal complaint there was a clear atmosphere of threat in the air. She also knew that we had more than enough grounds to make her life *very* difficult.

She was, to be fair, open and honest. My guess is that having worked out just how badly her team had screwed up her only option was to be totally frank and she had done her homework.

Yes, the FSH levels were exceptionally high, yes, we would need donor egg treatment, possibly with ICSI (intracytoplasmic sperm injection) if my little swimmers were still half-asleep as they seemed to be and no, we were not going to get it on the NHS in any great hurry.

I bloody wish you lot had told us that a year ago! She admitted that had she seen the results when they were first taken she would have given us a clear idea what they meant and we were fuming that the others on her team had not.

Miss Dawes did spontaneously recommend the same clinic in Barcelona by sheer coincidence so this only reinforced our own conclusions. At least we were barking up the right tree. The final thing she did offer was that inevitably the Spanish clinic would request a whole series of blood tests which would need to be mostly less than six months old and she said she would write to our GP and request that she help us by getting these at least paid for by the NHS. It would be a small contribution but every little helps as they say and for this we were grateful.

My guess is that if we had filed a formal complaint they would have been paying for a lot more than that!

Oddly enough, after all that, we did not need a referral or anything like that, we simply had to contact the Spanish clinic directly ourselves to arrange treatment.

Again, I wish they could have said that when the first FSH results had come out, we could have spared a year of spinning our wheels and wasting time (not to mention my becoming a regular client of the hospital gentleman's lavatory appreciation society).

There was only one benefit that we could see from the time wasted and, in fact, it could have been a vital one.

Emotionally we were barely prepared for the idea of donor treatment as it was but a year ago it would have possibly been too much. With the utter lack of counselling or support that the NHS offered, the time we had spent chasing our tails had allowed us a well needed period of adjustment to come to terms with the harsh reality of the situation by ourselves.

In addition we had met Dawn and Andrew as well as by now a number of other unfortunate couples who had so generously shared their experiences and helped us along the way. If we had been told bluntly a year ago what the situation was without all that help and adjustment I have no idea how we would have reacted.

Badly, I suspect!

Still, despite everything that had passed, we had finally been officially discharged by the gynaecologist and it meant that for the first time in eighteen months we had a plan. It was time to go and make a baby!

The light at the end of the tunnel which, until now, had been completely dark now had the faintest glimmer of hope.

# Chapter 10:
## The story so far...

It was scary how quickly eighteen months had flown by but something had fundamentally changed. I tried to look at myself in the mirror to see if I recognised the person staring back at me but the innocent lover of good food, fine wine and science fiction was gone.

The first grey hairs now flecked my hair and if I made the mistake of not shaving for more than two days the promise of much more white would adorn my chin.

Life as a bachelor had been hard, the years of loneliness had taken their toll but now I was still recovering from the fact that the dream I had longed for was fundamentally flawed through no fault of mine or, for that matter, my beloved wife.

We had by now become close friends with the Litten-Brown's. They were going through fertility treatment of their own, though their situation was somewhat different to ours but we had become close as we seemed to have a lot in common.

Colin was by trade a chemist who had fallen into the

same industry as I but in his case as a formulation scientist. We had lots of war stories to trade and it even transpired that we had attended the same conference once, though we had never bumped into each other, not a great surprise as there were nearly a thousand attendees.

When I found out his hobby was writing science fiction novels and that we shared the same interests in this genre we were well away. I have been fortunate to be the recipient of a few pre-publication copies of his books and have become one of his unofficial proof-readers.

Jennie was a university lecturer so it was uncanny that she also mirrored Iona's profession.

It was inevitable therefore that we would hit it off and they provided more than one anecdote that found its way into this tale.

When we had first met, however, the significance as to what it would start never dawned on me and it was only a chance occurrence that sparked a major thought in my mind.

Colin had written a brief article for an NCT newsletter which was basically a bloke's perspective to IVF. He was in the process of writing a similar submission for the Infertility Network UK magazine having observed that almost everything written on the subject was done so by women.

This is not a criticism but a clear observation that men find it very difficult to talk about such matters. While Colin's main interest was science fiction he was from time to time driven to write such small articles in the hope that he could impart a few pearls of what he hoped were wisdom.

I had found his comments nearly as helpful as the advice that Andrew had provided and in some cases more so as we were far more on the same wavelength, sometimes scarily so.

We were visiting them one weekend (Colin is an

enthusiastic cook and you will never leave his table hungry) and the subject of his latest article came up. We had been very open with Colin and Jennie regarding our situation and while they could not advise us on everything they were always forthcoming with as much help as they could and were a great sounding board for helping us shape our own thoughts.

It was a passing comment in the article I was reading. Colin was speculating on the death of the gene and the various combinations it could take, sperm donation, egg donation, double donor treatment or even mitochondrial DNA donation.

The issue he was trying to raise was how you approach the subject of discussing your children's origins when they were old enough to understand.

The thought had not even crossed my mind but I went cold as I remembered my own opinions on adoption and my rejection of it as an option based on the emotional baggage it would potentially bring.

Iona and I had spent so much time rationalising how we were going to create the baby we so wished for that we had not even remotely thought about what that child might think about it.

While donor treatment has been around for years it has not been around so long that there are all that many children resulting from such procedures who have grown up to adult life and thus the advice on how to handle that all important discussion was scant.

I remember brooding on the problem as we drove home from our weekend with our friends and that night we talked long into the night.

What should we do? Luckily, up until now the circle of people who knew the truth was very small indeed and entirely made up of trusted people which meant that so far we had rumour control in hand.

This was just as well as it dawned on me that if we had told the world we would now be facing the fact that the information was out of our control. Not knowing how we were going to tell our virtual child in the future we could have been facing an inadvertent slip by some well-meaning family member.

I could not think of a bigger disaster than our child finding out the truth of its existence second hand. The implications of the emotional effect it would have on them, the lack of trust it would generate with us made me shudder. Potentially it could be far worse than finding out you were adopted.

This was a situation to be avoided at all costs but what to do?

Colin had inadvertently provided the answer as one of the things he had said was that he had spoken to a number of other couples going through various forms of treatment and the best piece of advice he had heard was to keep a record of events.

It made a lot of sense to me, especially as by the time we got around to discussing the whole matter with our child it was likely to be something between fifteen and twenty years in the future.

I can barely remember what I did fifteen days ago!

Whether it is true or not I am not sure but I recall reading somewhere that the cells in the human body more or less replace themselves every seven years or so. If that is the case then by the time we got around to having "the chat" with our child I would have replaced this rather flabby body twice and be onto a third.

It was also an interesting exercise to cast my mind back fifteen years and try and remember the person I was then.

That, for me was roughly a third of a lifetime and most of my adult life and I had to confess that the person I was then would simply not have recognised the person I am now.

No doubt life was going to throw a plethora of curve balls towards Iona and I over the next fifteen years and I realised that by then we would be completely different people, emotionally as well as biologically and the pain and frustration we were experiencing would be but a distant memory, lost in the fog of time.

How could we possibly explain to our child what we went through if we ourselves could not truly remember it?

Even worse, I know from experience that the mind can play tricks and create memories that do not exist. My father, a far too experienced alcoholic is a prime example of this. I will not go into details but certain things occurred while he was still married to my long-suffering mother but the events in his mind are different to those that the rest of us remember.

The reason for this distortion is simple. Whether he was drunk and had only vague recollection or deep down realised what horrible things he was doing, he created a fiction with which he justified his actions to his friends and family but repeated the tale so many times that it became real for him. Today he truly believes that his version of events is what really happened.

As you may have gathered by now, this whole process was affecting me deeply on an emotional level, anger and frustration mixing with depression and despair and I could not in all honesty pretend to be thinking rationally. In fifteen years time my take on events would inevitably be distorted.

The answer, of course, was obvious. If in fifteen years I wanted to know what I was thinking and feeling now, the only way I could do that would be to ask the 'me' of now but in the absence of a time machine it would have to be a one-way conversation.

I would write it down!

When I mooted this idea to Iona she jumped at it. The same thoughts had been nagging at her but the idea that we could not only document the events around the creation of our child but also write down our thoughts and feelings filled her with hope, as if the very act of writing it down would inspire nature to provide a child to read it.

Part of me realised that writing it down would be a form of therapy for us both and if that was the case then it was an even more sensible idea.

The question was how we were going to do it? We had not as yet resolved the issue of how and when we were going to explain to our hoped-for child the circumstances of its origin but by keeping the key details secret to all but the trusted few and documenting everything in a volume we would keep our options open.

Iona then raised the darkest of possibilities. What if by some unforeseen disaster we were to die before the child reached an age where it could understand? Who would really know what we were feeling enough to explain it to them?

Late night turned into early morning as we talked and formed our plan.

We would write a book. It would be a book for which there would only ever be one copy and aimed for an audience of one. It would be the story of the journey which Iona and I had gone through both physically and emotionally to create that most beloved of results, our audience, our child.

The book would be titled "The Journey of Love and Hope" for that is what it was.

When we finally drifted into sleep I felt that we both slept better than we had for a very long time.

My mind had obviously been chewing over the proposition as I slept as in the morning it was raring to go.

Looking back over the last eighteen months or so, it is incredible how quickly the memory of events blurs but I am also very conscious that our emotional state has changed beyond recognition since the beginning. I was very glad that I had kept some sketchy notes but even looking through these there were parts that were becoming vague.

It would have been impossible to write this book from the outset, simply because at that time we did not see this as a journey of love and hope, more a quick nip down to the shops. We had no idea that there would be any sort of laborious process and thus the need to write about it was negated.

As you will have read, even through a lot of the past events, we were in a state of denial and to an extent largely ignorant of the journey we were really on. I am sure this is true for a lot of people in this situation.

It did leave me with a dilemma though. At what point should the journey start? Was it from the point that we realised we had a problem, should it have been earlier?

Following quickly on the heels of this was an even greater issue. I had never in my life written much more than a short e-mail and certainly never tackled any form of creative writing. Now I was proposing to belly-flop into the deep end of what was basically going to be a novel-sized tome.

I did not have the faintest idea where to start but fortunately I knew an author who was just at the other end of the telephone.

My first question to Colin was probably ill-advised as when I asked where I should ask he somewhat sarcastically replied "the beginning is usually a good place". This was not, of course, very helpful as the matter of where the beginning was happened to be my most fundamental problem.

Arrangements were made for another dinner party, mostly I think as he had a recipe he wanted to experiment with and we left it at that.

Iona had felt strongly that I should write the bulk of the book, mostly as I had been more organised in terms of record keeping but, from a practical side, as I had more time on my hands being technically unemployed. I had no problem with this and we agreed that I would prepare the basic factual framework of the book laced with my own thoughts and emotions and she would add her parts throughout where she felt she had more to add or personal comments to make.

The dinner party arrived, an interesting affair with some sort of garlic lemon chicken dish that I have tried in vain to reproduce. We stayed over so that I could have a drink and Iona was not required to drive us home late.

Colin tried to explain how he went about writing but it sounded more like water-divining to me. My impression of writing was that the author would find a subject, research it deeply and then prepare a basic synopsis of the story, adding more and more detail so that by the time they actually wrote the novel they were simply putting meat on the bones.

He seemed to skip a lot of this and simply start on page one with pretty much no idea where he was going which he tried to describe as if it were "channelling" or that the story simply flowed from somewhere inside him. Jennie backed this up, claiming that sometimes he would get really excited as he wrote, claiming to be getting to a "good bit" even though he actually didn't know what was going to happen next.

This did not help me much in either respect. I could not take the disciplined author approach as I really did not know what was going to happen next but at the same time channelling was not for me either. When I sat in front of the computer my response was more akin to the flat-line on a heart monitor when the patient kicks the bucket.

The evening was not totally wasted however as we compared notes on our favourite authors and Colin mentioned that one of his was Bill Bryson and that I should look at what I was trying to do as something like a travelogue but in diary form.

Finally I had something I could grab hold of and in hindsight it could not be anything else. Iona and I wanted to capture the emotion of the moment and the only way we could do this was to write down our thoughts and feelings as they happened.

Of course, we were already technically a year and a half down the road but up to this point as I have explained before we simply had not realised the path we were on and certainly would not have seen the need to keep such a record.

The beginning of the journey was already long in the past and my first task was going to be trying to piece together everything that had happened up to this date. I then realised that to do this I would have to go back even further to put everything in context and explain who Iona and I were and the circumstances of our meeting.

There could be no doubt from this just how important having a child was to us both.

It was only when I was going to bed, head swimming with good wine and breath reeking of garlic that I realised I suddenly had a lot of work to do!

Now was a good time to start as we had broken free of the endless holding pattern of the NHS but had not officially come under the care of the IVF clinic. Emotionally, it was a major junction in our long road but was that the sight of traffic cones up ahead..?

Not for the first time I was mightily glad I had put together the purple file as it captured all the major dates when things had happened and the notes I had taken to supplement my dubious memory really filled in the gaps. Even so, it was a mammoth task to recall the previous eighteen months in a way that not only made sense but would also not bore the poor reader to death.

I started the book with an apology but a well-meant one. The apology was to our as yet unrealised child who would eventually be the recipient of the book and the apology was a simple one. While I was addressing the book to that child, I did not know its name or even its gender. I dared not think that the child might not even ever exist.

This was a very strange moment as by the time our child would read our tale we would know very well who they were but part of me felt as if we were reaching out across the gulf of future time to speak to that person with the innocence of who we were now. I wondered how it would come across to our child, hearing a voice from the past of a version of their parents who were long gone.

It gave me a thrill as if we were filling a time capsule, a snapshot of our lives as they were in the early twenty-first century. I realised that it would be fascinating for Iona and I to also read the book years in the future and see how much was familiar and what memories it raised. I knew then that once it was finished the book would be put away to gather dust until the time was right.

The format of the book inevitably changed. While I had key dates of all our appointments our thoughts and feelings were general, flowing around the routine events like a river of hope whereas from this point onwards I could keep it more in diary form, revealing our innermost emotions as and when they happened.

Ultimately, the structure really did not matter. I was

not trying to create a bestseller but an honest record of the journey in the hope that our child would understand not only what we had to go through but also our reasons for why we did, that everything that occurred was driven by our undying passion to have a child. I wanted that underlying love to come through so that there could be no doubt that whatever happened we saw the child as totally ours.

So, dear reader, you know now the circumstance as to why I felt inspired to write a book but the story is by no means over at this point.

I availed myself of a sturdy pocket-sized notebook that travelled everywhere with us and became the repository of every small detail as events unfolded. Religiously, I would then transcribe those notes into the book, embellishing them with our thoughts and feelings as I went along.

There was only one rule that I imposed on the book. Once we had written something, unless it was factually incorrect we did not go back and edit anything. Both Iona and I felt it was very important that the book was honest and that our emotions were captured as we experienced them for good or ill. We were not going to sanitise it in any way. It would be the real journey whether the road was smooth or riddled with potholes.

Keep this in mind from this point in as we return to April 2009.

# Chapter 11:
## A fork in the road…

Our destiny was finally back in our hands so it was with more than a little excitement that I jumped onto the Spanish clinic's website to fill in my registration details and request an appointment. At last, we were taking positive action and I eagerly sat by the e-mail, waiting for the response. We had decided that we would try and go for a Friday appointment so that we could combine it with a weekend in Barcelona, somewhere that although we had been to before we were more than happy to visit again.

It was partly the fact that we had spent a weekend in the beautiful city a couple of years previously that had sealed our decision. We could have gone to any one of many fabulous European destinations but as we had no idea what the fertility treatment was going to entail we decided that even remotely familiar surroundings would be a good thing so that we at least had some idea of the layout of the city.

Okay, the truth was we really liked Barcelona so any excuse to go back was more than welcome. With all the recent stress, a couple of days break was just what we needed.

I had already looked into flights and a good hotel and was just itching to start booking things.

My impatience was to be tested as after a week we had received no response from the clinic.

Frustrating is not the word, after everything that had happened I guess I had expected that when we were in the hands of the real professionals and especially in the hands of a private clinic that things would be quicker. I appreciated that my desire for things to happen instantly was probably unreasonable but I was done waiting.

I could not help myself sending a polite reminder with the age-old "I'm just re-sending this as I have had some email problems so might not have got your reply" which everyone knows means "You haven't replied to me so this is a less than subtle way of reminding you." Iona also sent a note with the same subtle hint and eventually we got a message.

Having sent them some proposed dates I was rather deflated that the appointment time they suggested was on none of them. The cynic in me began to jump up and down and throw his hands up. Was this going to be the NHS all over again? I knew there must be a whole bunch of people out there in a similar situation to us but it was very difficult not to expect to be the centre of attention.

It is at times like this when being a total control freak does nothing but lose me sleep. Someone should have probably put me on mild sedation to stop me clock-watching!

Needing something to do, I called to make an appointment with the doctor to discuss the blood tests that would be needed. Despite not having an agreed appointment date with the clinic, they had sent through all the other details regarding our first meeting, including all the information that they would need prior to our visit. This basically amounted to a complete medical history of our case so far, confirmation of the list of blood tests needed as well as a general medical questionnaire, psychological questionnaire and a general personal information sheet.

I am a cynic on the whole and despite the fact that our gynaecologist had promised to write to our GP and request that she help with the blood tests, I was not about to wait for that to happen. Whilst I was sure that she would be true to her word, I was leaving nothing to chance. This was probably unwarranted, mostly as she had clearly realised how much her colleagues had screwed up and there was a decidedly litigious look on my face so appeasing us was most definitely in her best interests at that particular moment.

Of course, when I got through to make an appointment the best they could offer me with our own GP was a week away. I should not have been surprised! At any other time you can usually get in within a day or two but now I was Captain Impatient, it was going to be a week. Someone up on high was trying to teach me a lesson, I fear.

The receptionist at the surgery then threw me a lifeline, I could see a different GP within a couple of days and I jumped at the offer. It was a bit of a gamble, either a new GP would require us to explain the entire story yet again and we would get nowhere or they would simply take our word for it and do what we asked. I was itching for a fight so while I prayed for the latter I was in a secret and perverse way relishing the idea of the former.

The fact was they could not possibly be any worse than Dr Armstrong!

I then entered into a lengthy e-mail exchange with the Spanish clinic but came out of it with a date! We were booked to see them on the 4th June at five in the evening! The sense of relief was indescribable and I am sure Iona was delighted that I was no longer bouncing off the walls. That then allowed me to do one of my favourite things, getting on the internet and booking flights and hotels.

On paper I already had the trip planned and had undertaken a whole load of research into places to stay and things to do. One of the residual aspects of my previous jobs was that I had a huge collection of air miles with British Airways. Years of business travel had allowed me to accumulate them but apart from a few small trips I had never found any reason to cash them in. Now, it was perfect and we could pay for the flights over to Spain.

Typically, just as we got the appointment date from the clinic, the hotel I had my eye on managed to get itself fully booked for the time we were over and most of the air miles seats on the flights we wanted disappeared leaving us only a few rubbish options, effectively knocking half a day from our planned romantic break.

It was just typical! The clinic had sent a list of recommended accommodation through but they were all booked or did not have facilities we were looking for (okay, I will admit it, a swimming pool!). We had decided that given the stress of the whole thing that we would splash out on comfortable flights and a nice hotel.

I had been busy over the previous months selling off a load of my old stuff on e-bay and had managed to raise enough money to allow us a nice weekend break so we booked business class seats with air miles (mainly so we could go and raid the lounges) and I eventually found a nice alternative hotel with a rooftop pool that seemed to fit the bill.

The key now was to send the clinic all the required information prior to our visit and although we had a few weeks, they wanted everything ten days prior to our appointment. While time was not tight, there was not a huge amount of wiggle-room.

The basic medical information sheet was standard and thus easy to fill in, as was the general information sheet.

The psychological ones were odd and either something was lost in translation or they clearly expected to get a series of manic depressives turning up at their doorstep. I did finish my questionnaire feeling really optimistic and full of the joys of life having managed to honestly answer most of the questions with a resounding negative.

That was encouraging. It was lucky the form didn't ask about my state of anger or frustration with the process so far but at least I recognised it for what it was. It really hit home that despite the way the whole process had gone so far we were still facing the future with a true sense of hope rather than depression and desperation. I realised just how many of their clients must be grasping at the thinnest of straws and that counselling would play a heavy part in the process from beginning to end.

With the forms completed, I scanned the test results we had and e-mailed the whole lot to the clinic with the promise that there was more to follow.

On the day I had booked the appointment with the doctor we arrived at the surgery early which was just as well as the doctor we were due to see was also running early. To be honest, he gave the impression that he had been sat around waiting for someone to come and see him.

Our surgery is one where the resident GP (our doctor, Dr Armstrong) is semi-retired and starting to hand over to a series of junior doctors but they seem to be on some sort of time-share basis. They certainly don't get the benefit of a light to show when they are free and a number system like the other permanent doctors, they have to wander out into the waiting room and ask for their patients in person! Oh, to be in a job where you aspire to a small blue light next to your name.

I had a sense of anticipation as we walked towards his consulting room, bristling as I was for the fight to come.

Iona had suggested that I did all the talking so I clutched the list of blood tests in my hand and got down to it. He listened quietly and professionally as I briefly outlined the situation and Iona noticed that when I got to the bit about us going for IVF, he diplomatically wiggled his computer mouse so that his screensaver – a picture of his kids – disappeared which was very thoughtful of him.

I already liked him a lot more than Dr Armstrong.

I explained that our gynaecologist had said she would write a letter but when he checked the records, no letter had yet arrived. This in itself was annoying as there had been plenty enough time for the communication to have been sent and we had really felt that our gynaecologist had come across with a sense of urgency on the matter. Like with everything else, we had once again been let down.

Fortune was on our side that day as he proved to be a very amiable sort of chap, either that or he simply regarded it as not his problem but either way he signed the blood tests off no problem. It was only then that he mentioned that one of the required tests we had been asked to supply, the HIV test, would forever appear on our medical records and could be accessed in the future for insurance purposes.

This was one of those little moments that you realise make the world an unfair place. We had no choice but to take the test, despite the fact that we knew neither of us had HIV but we would forever be potentially penalised by insurers just because of the fact that we had taken a test, regardless of the result. I filed this one away in the "potential fights to have in the future" drawer in the bureau in my brain. Woe betide any insurance company that refused to give me a policy on this basis, they would find themselves immediately at the end of a discriminatory law suit!

We also requested a complete print-out of all the historical test results which he gladly agreed to arrange with the women on reception so it was in a state of slight shock at how easy the process had been that we found ourselves back in the waiting room while the printer regurgitated our data. It was only when I casually asked the receptionist to confirm the phlebotomist times at the local hospital that Iona pointed out that one of the tests was fasting glucose – if we intended to go first thing in the morning we had to starve for fourteen hours prior to blood-letting. As we planned to be there on opening time at 8:30 the next morning, that left us only an hour to get home and have dinner!

Needless to say we walked quickly.

Iona had a 10:00 lesson at school so we got to phlebotomists an hour and a half early in order to ensure we were served promptly. Despite this, we were *still* numbers 3 & 4 in queue due to a row of old wrinklies who must have camped there overnight.

Iona had sensibly brought some marking to do but I had nothing so faced the prospect of another hour's wait with only the posters on the wall and people-watching to keep me busy. I even resorted to reading our blood test request forms and only then found that I didn't need to fast as I wasn't down for fasting glucose! Iona found this rather amusing, though I would have starved anyway to keep her company. I found it equally amusing that she was down for a blood alcohol test where she has only had one glass of Baileys in the last few months!

By the time the phlebotomist arrived, promptly at 8:30 the incoming patients were taking numbers in the early teens and by the time our turns came around twenty minutes or so later they were in the early twenties. It therefore didn't really matter when you turned up you were going to be sitting around for well over an hour.

Iona went first as she had the greater number of tests to do (there was logic in that decision somewhere but I don't quite recall it now) and had nine vacutainers of blood taken. She hates giving blood at the best of times so this was a hell of a lot in one go for her. When I went in, he was still trying to stuff them into the laboratory sample bag. I was more fortunate as I had to give only four.

I had the obligatory chocolate waiting in the car for her so she couldn't eat it before her blood was taken.

At least then our bit was done. The phlebotomist had approximated five to ten days to get the results back which would be fine as it would still allow plenty of time to get them back and send them over to the clinic.

Finally, we started to relax. Everything we could do had been done. Flights and hotel were booked (and Iona's Mum to dog-sit and play taxi), blood was given and all the other information sent. I scanned the missing historical data and e-mailed it off that evening just to complete their set. All the paperwork went into the purple file (now pretty full) and that was that.

We both slept a lot better that night.

A copy of the letter from our gynaecologist finally arrived (better late than never). It justified my cynicism! In the letter, she had indeed asked our doctor to help us but had stopped short of staying exactly what she had promised us. The letter, while asking our doctor to help, was a bit vague on details and did not directly ask her to authorise the blood tests and get them paid for on the NHS. I was at that moment extremely glad that we had simply gone ahead and done it. Had we been visiting the doctor now, we would have no doubt been facing more of a fight to justify why the NHS should pick up the tab.

It was the final let-down for me from a service that had failed us throughout and I was really glad that we were no longer under their care. In the face of her colleague's poor diagnoses I had really hoped that she would have taken a clearer stance but those hopes were evidently in vain. Still, the tests were done now and we had done them in good faith from what she had said so it was far too late for them to do anything about it now.

She also wrote that there was still the chance of natural conception and that we should keep trying at the correct time of the month but, to be honest, I was more than a little sceptical about this. After all the tests, all the examinations it was clear that she really didn't have much grasp of what was really possible for us and I really did not value her professional opinion much in return. That will sound harsh but with the number of mistakes made, there had been nothing that had given me any confidence that the information we were being given was correct so I was not about to start trusting her now. What faith I had left was being centred entirely in Barcelona.

Life suddenly took an interesting turn. Having had my curriculum vitae with many recruitment agencies since the previous February there had not been even the sniff of a potential position.

This is not to say that I had not been approached with a number of offers but in all cases the agency had clearly not read either the job description or my skills and the types of job I was looking for. Five times I had my hopes built up when a call came from one recruiter or another only for them to be dashed when I read the job description only to find it was nothing even remotely suitable.

Things changed with the sixth such call and when the description came through it looked perfect. Enthusiastically, I contacted the agency and voiced my strong desire to be considered for the position. Things moved quickly, more so than I had anticipated and within a few days I found myself heading for a job interview.

This particular position, at a FTSE 100 company, was

very much within my skills base but I was not sure whether I was punching above my weight. Although I approached it with the same preparation I would have put into any position, the pessimist in me was already gearing up for failure.

I arrived in London early so that I could sneak down to Fortnum & Mason on Piccadilly to get Iona some nice expensive chocolates to take to Barcelona as a surprise. It was unlikely that I was going to be in town again prior to our trip so while not ideal it at least took my mind off of the real purpose of my trip.

The interview (more of a sort of pre-chat) went well and I left with at least the knowledge that I had done as much as I could. It was certainly not for want of preparation, the previous few days had been a frantic process of researching my prospective new employer as much as possible as well as swatting up on my own supposed expertise.

I had been given a list of possible questions that I might be asked, mostly general ones but even so I spent a lot of time preparing model answers which was just as well as I needed most of them on the day! The recruiter phoned me on the train and I told her how I thought it had gone.

I heard in the morning that I had made it through to a second interview! It was incredible news. For the first time in a year there was a glimmer of hope that I might actually be back in a position to support my wife and, hopefully, family! I tried not to get too excited but this was near-enough impossible under the circumstances. A whole new wave of optimism gripped me. If I got the job we could move house, Iona could leave work and spend time raising the family we hoped to produce. Everything we prayed for was within reach.

The nagging thought had been brewing in me for some time that our circumstance was going to mean that I would be the house-husband and do the actual raising of our child while Iona went out to work to be the bread-winner.

I am not a male chauvinist so fundamentally do not have a problem with this although my preference would always be to support my family. The concern which we both felt was that the truth was I was probably not suited to be the one raising the baby.

There was also, of course, the matter of Iona potentially not being the genetic mother of the baby. Undertaking the raising process was very important to her so in my mind it was vital that I landed a job before she hit the point of maternity leave.

No pressure!

Still, for the first time in as long as I could remember my optimism was strong. The interview had gone well, the potential job had come at probably the most perfect time and there was now a very real possibility that our lives were at a turning point.

Could we be that lucky?

# Chapter 12:
## Erupting volcanoes and flaring strikes...

As you may remember, this was the period where the volcano under the Eyjafjallajökull glacier in Iceland (yes, I had to look that up for the spelling) was causing all sorts of fun and games across Europe. The news over the weekend had included the fact that a cloud of ash had closed a number of airports in southern Spain which had given me just a twinge of doubt, especially as the doom-mongers on the Internet were pointing out that eruptions under Eyjafjallajökull historically preceded the larger eruption of Mount Katla which would effectively ground European air travel for months. Oh deep joy! Still, this was only a possibility and there was no sense in worrying about it until it became a problem.

I didn't need to worry about the volcano; fate was brewing something far more unpleasant up. It was right then that breaking news came through that the Unite union had decided to announce a punitive series of British Airways cabin crew strikes, twenty days in all and covering both the 3rd and 6th June when we were due to travel!

I will not commit to paper what I actually said on discovering this but trust me it was not complementary either to BA or Unite and certainly questioned their parentage. It seems incredible to me that under the direst economic conditions some unions think that destroying the company that their members work for will help the situation and that punishing poor members of the public will get them support. I am not taking sides but there must be a better way than this?

It has got to be said that I have a fundamental problem with striking where it is the innocent public who bear the brunt of the pain and, as now, usually those who could least afford it and at times when it would create the maximum inconvenience.

At the time I really didn't give a crap whose fault it was, I held BA and Unite with equal contempt as, I am sure, tens of thousands of people around the country did also. My initial instinct therefore was to stick two fingers up at BA. We could not trust them to actually have a plane for us and this was too important to risk being held to ransom by Unite so I dumped the flights and looked for an alternative.

Iberia were the only other option so I selected appropriate flights but realised at the last minute that they were code-share flights on planes operated by, you guessed it, British Airways! I had been one click away from getting non-refundable flights on an airline I really don't like (they have let me down more in the past than any other airline) using planes that probably were not going to fly anyway for more money than the company actually running the flight in the first place.

Hastily, until I could find a better option, I jumped back onto the BA website and re-booked the original seats (fully refundable again). It did not cost me any money but at least it would cost BA some administrative hassle. It was just as well that I did as shortly afterwards BA closed all flight booking for the strike period until they could sort out their schedules!

Calming down a bit, I got back on the internet and looked for alternatives, discovering that the only other real option was Easy Jet out of Luton, Gatwick or Stansted. Not my favourite option and if we went that way we were going to get lumbered with either non-refundable tickets or at least tickets that would cost us to turn in should we decide to change again. That and the fact that I have a general dislike and distrust of no-frills airlines through bad previous experiences.

We decided to wait for a few days and see how the strike talks panned out. The first strike was set for a week's time so we could see what the effect on flights, especially to Barcelona where BA seemed to have the monopoly in terms of mainstream carriers, was.

It was an object lesson for me in terms of not acting on the spur of the moment when fuelled by emotion. After a few days of relaxation, however, I was at full stress levels again, facing as we were an uncertain trip thanks now not only to the forces of nature but also the petty feuding of the airline and its employees.

What to do? On the one hand, bite the bullet and go no-frills to at least guarantee as best we could that we would get there but 'cattle class' or hold out for BA and Unite to sort out their differences and hope for the best. Why is nothing in life ever simple? I found myself rationalising things in my head. BA were confident that they would run some flights but I knew that they would concentrate on long-haul (i.e. the money-makers) but on the other hand, with a monopoly on the Barcelona flights and therefore no alternatives to dump passengers on as would be the case with, for example, Paris or Amsterdam, they might give preferential treatment to that leg, especially given their code-share with Iberia. Or was that all just wishful thinking?

My fingernails were well and truly mauled.

Our dog (actually Iona's dog) decided this precise moment to start having epileptic fits and not knowing what they were the first was a scary thing to live through. It was as if someone had wired her up to the mains and thrown the switch. Bella was, for a Labrador, not a bad age, galloping as she was towards ten and we found ourselves faced with the agonising decision whether or not to have her put to sleep or to try and get the fits treated.

It was not Bella's fault but just at that moment I really did not need any more stress. Luckily, emotion did not drive us into a hasty decision and so it was she had a stay of execution.

Time was ticking by so I called the surgery to find that our blood test results were back! This was great news as it meant we could go down to collect them and wrap up everything we needed to send to the clinic. I also received a call from the recruiters to say that the second interview in London would be sometime on June 8th, right after we got back from Barcelona (so no pressure or anything!). That was going to be a busy week.

The trip to the surgery was the usual pantomime. Something you could not say about the staff on reception was that they were efficient. When we turned up to request our blood results we caused all sorts of chaos as they hunted through in-trays and files to find them when it was blatantly obvious they simply had not printed them off in the first place. Eventually, someone had the presence of mind to simply send another set to the printer. Certainly by the thick ream of sheets that were eventually handed over, we seemed to have everything we needed.

At the time we were in a hurry to get to a friend's place for dinner so it was not until later that we actually checked the results only to find that after all that the lab had either forgotten to do Iona's HIV test or the sheet with the results had been lost in the earlier confusion. The HIV screen should have been part of what was called a TORCH test which also looked at several other conditions but on the sheet for that particular test the HIV result was spectacularly absent.

It was a trifling nuisance but yet another minor mistake to add to the many that the NHS were racking up.

I scanned everything else and all looked in order, the results either normal or negative for anything adverse so I e-mailed them over to clinic, not drawing too much attention to the missing HIV results in the hope that we could resolve the matter quickly and quietly. We still had plenty of time, after all!

Iona called the surgery to try and track down the missing HIV results. She may as well have been asking for the location of the Holy Grail for what good it did her! Without hearing the other end of the conversation it was obvious that the now familiar confusion reigned in the surgery reception. With no results found, Iona asked whether she would need to go for another blood test and, if so, could the doctor simply prepare a request form that she could pick up from reception rather than having to make an appointment.

That request completely overloaded the capacity of the receptionist and Iona spent another couple of minutes trying to explain the situation all over again. Finally, clearly baffled by the whole thing, the receptionist copped out by saying she would get the doctor to call Iona back that morning.

British Airways announced the revised flight schedule

for the first part of the strike action. While these did not cover the actual dates we were travelling on they would give a pretty clear indication as to which particular flights they were intending to cancel, the logic being that whatever they canned this time round would likely to be so during the subsequent industrial action.

There were at this time seven flights each way to Barcelona on BA's daily schedule and they were going to cancel three of them. Inevitably, our outward and inward flight numbers were among the casualties. I really should have gone down the betting office and put money on this eventuality, I would have made a fortune. What was worse for the remaining flights was that they were not going to be BA planes but operated by a string of charter airlines so the quality of the service was going to be uncertain at best.

We would potentially be paying BA prices for what could end up no-frills service and then I would have to moan to get a "downgrade refund". Sod that!

With the sinking feeling that I was wasting my time, I called the customer service number to make the enquiry as to whether the cancellations were indicative of what they planned to do throughout the entire strike period. I got through to an automated message after which the phone was rudely and bluntly cut off. I then tried the website but was unable to change the flights there either.

Although my recent career had been somewhat locally-based I had throughout the rest of my working life travelled extensively. It is true to say of most multi-national companies that they are very free with their travel budgets, or at least they were prior to the credit crunch. It was not unusual for me to be heading to exotic places in Europe or beyond at the drop of a hat for this meeting or that conference.

My record was flying to New York one day for a one-hour meeting just to fly back the next.

While international travel is seen as a perk of the job in many companies it is nowhere near as exotic as it sounds. My friends used to be very jealous that my career involved so much jet-setting but the fact was as I said before that I became intimately familiar with airports, the back of taxis, nasty business hotels and offices (many of which were in the more industrial areas of the cities I visited so even the scenery was crap).

Where there were perks were in such things as good dinners (with great wines that I could never have otherwise afforded) but critically the air miles.

The company for which I worked did not have any particular contract with one airline or another and we were at liberty to book whatever we fancied (oh, what wonderfully carefree times they were). I, like many, ended up enslaved to one airline as we joined their loyalty scheme and built up the air miles. In my case it was British Airways and I had for years been a member of their executive club, mostly at silver and for a short while even at gold tier status.

I felt that after seventeen years of unswerving membership they could have at least taken my call. I had already suffered an object lesson in loyalty having been made redundant and now BA was doing effectively the same.

My mind was thus well and truly made up. All the indications were that our flights were going to be cancelled and I could not speak to anyone at BA to clarify the situation. I found myself examining the end of my tether and realised that we really only had one option.

Easy Jet here we come! Fortunately, there was still availability on the dates we wanted though it did mean going out of Gatwick rather than Heathrow and it also meant we would have to drive ourselves. The bonus was that we were on a later flight on the Sunday so could at least enjoy a lazy morning before skipping back to the airport.

Having previous bad experiences with no-frills carriers, I was somewhat reserved about this especially as once booked we were committed. There were no refunds to be had so if the BA strike was cancelled there was no going back.

Still, at least we had flights that, volcanic ash aside, had a pretty good chance of getting where we wanted to go and when we wanted to be there. With any luck it would also mean that I would stop worrying about it for a while.

Inevitably, the doctor did *not* call back that morning. Why was I ever expecting that they would?

Iona called back but was put on hold and after a few moments of lift music was cut off. When she rang back to say that the call had been cut off she received the curt response from the receptionist that it was impossible for them to cut an internal call off! I could see from her expression that Iona was very glad it was not me making the phone call. She knew that at that point I would have said something extremely rude.

When Iona did eventually speak to the doctor she really helpfully suggested that the reception staff could sort it out. Oh great!

There was only one thing I could suggest, that we head back to the surgery after work and plant ourselves in front of the reception desk and make a complete nuisance until we got resolution which is precisely what we did. I was really angry at how they had spoken to my wife on the phone so I was now up for a fight and if they didn't come up with the goods then I would be terribly British and write a letter!

The first receptionist got into a complete tizzy over what it was we were asking her and was only saved by her colleague who had taken the call earlier that day. Needless to say, the HIV test had not been done so we "requested" (in that "we are not going to budge from this spot until we get it" sort of way) another blood test form.

To her credit (or to the fact that they were understandably trying to get rid of us), she did go and see the doctor who was hiding out back and returned a few minutes later with the appropriate request form, This would mean that Iona could go first thing on the Monday and at least get that in the system.

There was still time to get the results to the clinic in the time frame they had requested. Just!

BA announced that they were going to take Unite to court to declare the strike illegal – we had clearly made the right decision to jump ship as that decision was unlikely to endear the BA management to Unite and the feud seemed set to rumble on and on. Ominously, another ash cloud from the Icelandic volcano drifted towards UK air space.

We arrived at the phlebotomist at 7:30 but once again she was number four in the queue behind the resident oldies. I began to wonder what time you would actually have to arrive in order to be number one and suspected that it was long before the sun came up.

The phlebotomist was very nicely early (by half an hour indeed) which meant we were out of there promptly. Finally with the job done I e-mailed the clinic to apologise for the omission (not that they had picked up on it yet) and to promise that the info would follow in the hope that I could buy us time should we need it.

BA and Unite were still squabbling but BA had managed to get a court injunction rendering the strike illegal, not that this mattered to us anymore but more ominously the ash cloud had closed UK airspace the night before. It seemed that the summer was going to be a lottery when it came to flights.

A few days later the strike was back on – Unite got the court ruling overturned on appeal. We were very justified jumping ship! I don't know, on, off, on, off, it is like some naughty child who has found the light switch! BA also reported record losses for the financial year which I doubt surprised anybody.

It dawned on me that we were not the only ones planning such important trips abroad and my heart went out to all the other people caught up in the same anxiety as us.

In the height of all this we had arranged to go and stay with my family, something we rarely did as, to be honest, they are a bit of an odd bunch and usually contrive to find more and more elaborate ways of embarrassing me whenever we see them.

We had made the decision as we were going to be with my family to tell them at least part of the story. Whilst we did not want to freely share the information that we were going for donor treatment I did tell my sister and my Mum that we were about to embark on IVF and were going privately. It was sort of a double-bluff in that we felt better that we had told the family but by not sharing all the details we had not lost control of the information. My family had enough that they would probably not question further.

As it was, they took the information with a polite but mildly disinterested "oh." That's my family for you! Still, they would have been justifiably annoyed if they had found out after the fact, especially if they had discovered that Iona's family had been told earlier. I do so love family politics! I bet if I turned up one day to say I had won the lottery or something they would be a bit more interested.

Looking back it is difficult to see where the distancing between me and my family happened. For many years I had supported them through various troubles, both emotionally and financially to an extent but from the point that I was made redundant it was clear that such support was not reciprocal. Not that I was expecting them to shower me with cash or sympathy but the odd phone call once in a while would have been nice. As it was, they only ever called when they had news to tell us (mostly regarding babies coincidentally) so it never sat well with me to include them on our private lives. I guess the failing was on both sides but I did feel a pang of regret that my family were nowhere near as supportive to Iona as hers was to me.

On the way back from my family we dropped in on my cousin Angie. She had a young son and for reasons that are not relevant here I tackled my first solo dirty nappy change (which I managed to achieve without making a total fool of myself despite his best attempts to grab at the crappy nappy before I was able to whisk it out of reach).

Looking down on that tiny bundle was heart-melting! What fears I might have had about the physical process of looking after kids had totally evaporated now. Whilst I was fully aware we were getting a very easy ride that weekend, being able to play with baby but hand it back when it howled too loudly, it did finally dawn on me that like all things in life, it was just a matter of experience, practice and listening to your instincts.

The human race had managed to survive this long without having to look everything up on the internet so I was pretty sure that between us Iona and I would manage.

It transpired that Angie was in a bit of a tricky position in that her husband was in China and she had been called to an important conference but her parents were also travelling. She was stuck for a babysitter.

I hope the way I leapt to volunteer our services did not come across as too enthusiastic and even as I made the offer I knew I should have consulted Iona first. Fortunately for me, she also found baby Oscar adorable and was fully behind me on the idea.

Thus it was that a few days later we found ourselves

being handed a tiny baby and a huge pile of nappies, wipes, bottles, milk, change bag, Moses basket, pram….

For two wonderful days we were playing at parents.

When we handed Oscar back it was with some regret. The experience went very well and a good time was had by all. It is odd, I am sure not many prospective parents get the chance to "borrow" a child for a few days but with Oscar still in the stinky nappy stage it was surprisingly a great experience.

It sort of got me thinking, while nature has us all geared up to reproduce in this modern age where everything is done for us to such an extent that people can no longer think for themselves, my observation of the world (for what it is worth) tells me that there are a hell of a lot of people out there who make remarkably bad parents.

To an extent, a lot of this seems to be the fact that the desire to have a child is sometimes for the wrong reasons; their friends have one, it is a fashion accessory, etc. etc. The harsh reality of dirty nappies, sleepless nights and constant screaming do seem to come as a shock to some parents.

Somewhere along the line in our disposable labour-saving hi-tech society we have dulled our own instincts to the point of atrophy.

Not that I am condoning this but it has to be said that our short experience of actually being responsible for a little person taught me a lot, mostly about myself I might add. I have never doubted Iona's desire for children but any doubts as to how I would feel myself when our own situation becomes real were dispelled by that small bundle of energy we cared for over the space of forty-eight hours.

It was a strange distraction from our troubles but soon we were back on the journey.

Iona was able to go and pick up her HIV results from the surgery but not before running the gauntlet of the rude, unhelpful and permanently confused reception staff. While she came out clutching the sheet of results (in two pieces as they could not work out how to print it on one page so had screen dumped it onto two sheets) she also had the determination that we were going to get the hell out of that surgery!

Once home, I scanned and e-mailed the results and finally could relax that everything from our part was sorted. I was able to turn my attention to nicer things such as booking dinner for us the night of the consultation. After all that, I thought we deserved something nice!

We caught up with Dawn and Andrew and split into "girls" and "boys". The girls stayed in while the boys went out to the local pub for a drink (beer in Andrew's case, orange juice and lemonade for the designated driver i.e. yours truly).

Once again it was so good to have a chat with someone who had been through the process and could give me some idea as to what to expect (though for my part this largely involved the fact that the room in which I was to produce my sperm sample, while liberally supplied with ample multimedia stimulus had very thin walls, something to keep in mind).

As Andrew worked his way up through the beers in order of strength I was able to bounce a number of thoughts and fears off him and he threw in a lot of stuff that I really would not have considered before. The first and most important thing was that he felt that rather than wait to tell our kids at some later stage about their history to get them used to the idea from day one.

This was not something that had really occurred to me but the logic was sound. This did not lessen the fact that later in life there would still be questions about their origins but it did put a whole new slant on things for me. I told

Andrew about the book and he thought it was a great idea and said that in his experience there would still be a strong desire on the part of our offspring to understand the process and that putting it in words would be invaluable.

I hoped this was true!

By the end of the evening I knew we were ready. It was not that we could not have gone through with the whole process without their help, quite the opposite. Both Iona and I are more than capable of facing most situations but it helped so much having some of the uncertainty taken away and also having the benefit of experience to enlighten us to questions that would simply not have occurred to us.

At the risk of banging on about it I cannot stress how helpful the advice of normal people was and how useless the medical profession had been. Even now when IVF had been advised and we had been effectively cut loose to follow our own destiny, the NHS had never offered any form of counselling, even to suggest that we approach one of the many charitable organisations who were there to help people like us. To anyone out there reading this that might be facing the same situation my advice is this. If you are not getting answers to your questions, forget the NHS, go find someone to talk to in one of the charities or help groups. There is probably someone in your area and they are really nice people.

Part of me felt I should demand a partial refund of my National Insurance.

As May passed quickly by, the latest BA strike had kicked off and it was confirmed that our ex-flight was one of the casualties. With both sides locked in their "cock measuring competition" as my brother-in-law so eloquently put it I now felt totally justified in the decision to jump ship when we did. Availability on the Easy Jet flights was suddenly becoming scarce as those more loyal (or misguided) BA passengers suddenly faced the reality that they were not going to be flying from Heathrow after all.

It suddenly occurred to me that we were less than a week away from the consultation. With everything else that had been going on it had suddenly crept up on us!

It was only Tuesday and we were not leaving until Thursday but that did not stop us from beginning the process of packing because let's be honest, it takes two days to pack for a three day trip! Well, okay, it doesn't at all but when there was nothing else to do, all we could think of to keep us occupied was making sure we had everything we would need (which would inevitably mean we would take far more than we would need). I made the huge mistake of reading reviews about the service levels of Easy Jet which were not good, especially regarding the speedy boarding we had booked. I am not sure why I was surprised, it is supposed to be a "no-frills" airline, after all. Just as long as we got on the plane, that would be fine!

# Chapter 13:
## Viva Espania..!

In the grand scheme of things there were going to be two pivotal moments in our treatment and this was the first one, the initial consultation. It would be some months before we would return and that would be for (hopefully) the actual implantation itself! Funny how after so many months so much hinged on such a brief period of time.

The day had arrived when we were to fly to Spain.

The morning dragged like you would not believe. This is a pretty normal time dilation phenomenon that everyone who is waiting for something to happen has experienced. My grandmother would say "a watched pot never boils" which while physically impossible does seem to have an ounce of truth about it. Despite the fact that a pot of water on the stove will take precisely the same amount of time to boil whether you are staring at it or not does not alter the fact that the act of staring alters your perception of time. I have tried it, staring at a saucepan of water to see what would happen. It always boiled. I always looked away before it did so. Not the crowning achievement of my scientific career!

I am a horrible clock-watcher when I am nervous and as I am also a total control freak (which has been pointed out before) it was clear that I was not going to relax until we were actually at the hotel in Barcelona.

It was going to be a very long day for me. I tried to tell myself that whatever happened I should keep my pent-up angst inside and not bug the hell out of Iona which I would inevitably do.

The dog sitter arrived in the form of Iona's Mum and as we had eaten and packed it was a case of sit around the house or sit around Gatwick. Given that a significant stretch of the M40 and the M25 separated us from our goal and that was unpredictable at best we opted for the latter.

It was nice to know that we had plenty of time and although we did see three police cars tearing past us on the motorway, blues and twos on the go they were fortunately not attending any form of pile-up that stopped us, though for a moment we did have one of those "oh no!" sort of moments.

It is horrible when you are in that sort of situation when you are in a hurry for something and there is an accident (sorry, an *incident* as you cannot apparently have accidents these days). While part of you is clearly concerned that the people involved are okay there is also that dark side that is glad that their misfortune has not buggered up your own plans. I do hope that whatever it was that nobody was hurt.

As it was, the roads were kind and we gained the long term car park with plenty of wiggle-room on the timetable and were bussed to the terminal comfortably ahead of schedule.

Of course, by being early we could not check in immediately. Easy Jet have a policy of opening check-in two and a half hours prior to departure and that meant we had a forty-minute period with nothing better to do than hang around and people-watch. We had booked speedy boarding which the internet forums had mixed views on but it did mean that the second the clock showed that boarding was open we could nip up and check in.

I have always been a bit of an airline snob so was, I admit, looking to find fault with the no-frills system. Up to that point, I had been disappointed and I remained so as the girl on the check-in desk sorted us out efficiently and very politely, in stark contrast to some of the miserable sods I have been served by with flag-carrying airlines in the past. My probably unfair attitude towards Easy Jet was in serious danger of being overturned at this rate.

Other books have tackled the subject of airports so I will not embark on a huge rant about them here other than to say that I have spent far too much of my life hanging around the depressing buildings.

I've never really thought about the amount of time I have had to endure the dubious pleasures of airports around the world though one of my colleagues did once and was quite depressed to realise that he had actually wasted five whole weeks of his life in one airport or another if you put all the time together.

Rueing the fact that we were missing out on lounge access and as we had loads of time to kill we ate before going through security at the conveniently-located (and relatively empty) American-style restaurant. This turned out to be a remarkably sensible decision as when we had finished and made our way past the x-ray machines the eateries on the other side were all packed.

We still had ages before boarding so I bought Iona a new watch so she could obsessively stare at it as efficiently as I (actually she had broken the last watch I had bought her a year or two before that so it was a good opportunity to get her something nice). Beyond that, we bought a few supplies to graze on while on the plane and had the pleasure of watching the cultural differences between Germans and Brits in the queue at W. H. Smiths before getting into some serious loitering until the flight was called.

Speedy boarding continued to work for us. At the gate we were, along with the other SB's, corralled into a separate area right by the doors and thankfully the plane was on the gate rather than at the end of a scenic bus ride (which, if you believe the online forums, is where speedy boarding seems to fall apart).

The flight boarded on time and while not first on the plane thanks to the spectacular show of bad manners by the other SB passengers, we did get the second row so it felt like being in business class and Iona got the window seat she wanted.

We were a few minutes late as the poor co-pilot legged it across Gatwick having just got off a different positioning flight but all in all we got out of Dodge without a hitch.

Actually, I was impressed at the condition of the plane which seemed to be relatively new and in pretty good nick. Some of the flag-carrying airplanes I have flown in during my long travelling career have been total rust-buckets (well, not quite) and although I have never actually been involved in a major incident I am sure that it was only a matter of time for some of the old crates.

The worst trip I was on was typically a long-haul to Los Angeles on a Boeing 747 where the toilet on the upper deck was leaking and dripping foul liquid through the ceiling in cattle-class. Remarkably, none of the crew seemed all that bothered by the fact and I tried not to think of all the very important wiring that must have been running through that trickle of yellow water.

I have never been so glad to be on the ground again as after *that* particular flight.

There was also a time (coincidentally on a return flight from the USA) where we came down rather hard, bouncing off the runway at Heathrow and back into the air in what I presume was an aborted landing but one which had enough force to pop open most of the overhead baggage compartments in a mildly comical Hollywood way but also leaving us wondering whether or not the pilot had left the landing gear behind or, at least, irreparably bent.

We came around again and this time the pilot managed to pull off one of the smoothest landings I have ever experienced (which in hindsight did lead me to wonder whether he was also worried that the wheels might be a bit shagged after his first attempt).

Friends of mine have had closer brushes with death at the hands of major airlines. One was sitting on a flight to Amsterdam and was casually staring out of her window as a very large bird was sucked into the starboard engine causing it to flare out on take-off. I can see how this might put the wind up you.

Another had the dubious pleasure of being severely delayed in Madrid after taxiing to the runway but then rather than accelerating to take-off speed, trundling down the tarmac at a sedate twenty miles an hour. It was only as they reached the other end and came to a grinding halt that the pilot announced that at the moment they were about to give it the beans the plane had decided to suffer a major fault and deposit its entire stock of hydraulic fluid on the runway.

Had the fault developed a minute later the plane would have come down like a concrete slab! Needless to say, when the airline in question got the passengers back to the terminal and announced they were going to fix the plane, everyone decided to re-book on a different flight.

Our flight to Spain was uneventful but comfortable and as we arrived at Barcelona I was forced to concede that, at least for now, the airline had done us proud, especially when our luggage arrived in one piece and promptly on the conveyor, something that is quite often hit or miss with some of the "full-frills" airlines.

I used to play a game with my colleagues when travelling to see whose bag would come out last. There was a chap called Kevin who always lost, no matter when he checked in and even if we checked in together, which we frequently did, his bag would always come out ages after everyone else's. It didn't even matter which case he checked in, the result was always the same.

Iona and I had even gone as far as packing half our clothes in each other's case so that if we lost one we both still had enough in the other to see us through. This is actually good advice if you are travelling abroad. There is nothing worse than being the only one in a party wearing seventy-two hour old underpants.

We had a bit of a strange time getting through the airport. We were singled out to apparently trial a new iris and fingerprint scanner by some Spanish security officer who did not speak English so therefore could not explain what was going on. The equipment was slow and inefficient and it was pretty clear that if they intended to replace human immigration officials with these devices they were going to have some pretty huge queues! Mine eventually worked with some cajoling but Iona's flatly refused so we were hustled through anyway in a state of mild bewilderment.

It was only when we were outside that we realised that nobody had actually looked at her passport!

Terminal 2 at Barcelona was, at this time, a bit of a ghost

town. They had moved a lot of stuff to the new Terminal 1 and were in the process of refurbishment. The problem is that the arriving flights all came in at one end but the exit was at the other, meaning you had to walk for about half a mile through closed shops and construction areas to escape. It all felt very weird and very quiet.

A short taxi-ride later and we were at the hotel which was allegedly five-star (but by which star rating I am not entirely sure) but did look nice. We checked in and found our room, beating off the bell boy who was trying to take the suitcase from me. While small, the room was comfortable and I started off by doing my usual prowl around, looking in all the drawers and cupboards and checking out the bathroom.

I discovered that there were no large bath towels, something to be rectified in the morning.

We were very conscious that it was going to be hot and rather than drink the water out of the mini-bar (at the extortionate prices that these things are usually charged at) we nipped out to find an open pharmacy or other type of shop to grab a couple of bottles before turning in for the night. It was useful that we had visited the city before and knew that pharmacies sold water rather than blindly wandering into the nearest bar.

It is a good travel tip if you are ever over in Spain. Water in the pharmacies is dirt cheap but if you are unwary and go to a bar or one of the corner shops you could end up paying four or five times as much for the same bottle!

My worries about the mechanics of the trip were over. My worries about the pending consultation rose back to the surface. Not for the first time, I slept badly!

D-Day had arrived! A voice in the back of my head was constantly trying to reassure me that everything was going to work out and, whatever happened, at least I was going to be able to have a drink that night.

One of the many actions I had agreed to prior to our consultation was to abstain from booze as we had read in many of the guides that alcohol would have a detrimental effect on sperm production.

Don't get me wrong, I am not a raving alcoholic (I can handle it, really....) but I am fond of the odd glass or three here and there, especially at the weekends and when things get particularly stressful while it is not a total crutch I do find a glass of wine or a good gin and tonic somewhat soothing.

I'd been on the wagon for weeks now and was particularly grouchy as a result but tried to kerb my enthusiasm towards the promised evening tipple in case Iona got the wrong impression.

We were both on edge. With the appointment not until late in the afternoon we had pretty much all of the next day to kill, although we had slept in for a long while which was nice.

First things first, before setting out we ate a hearty breakfast. Like hotels all over the world, this one operated a breakfast buffet and we hit this with some enthusiasm, sampling the pastries, cooked breakfast and fruits on offer, as well as a generous helping of cheese and cold meats. We were not sure what we would do for lunch so tucked into one of those breakfasts you could work on all day if necessary.

It was a "when in Rome" sort of moment. Although we had been to Barcelona before we knew that rather than sit around the hotel we should strike out and at least attempt to enjoy ourselves. The hotel was not far from Gaudi's fantastical Sagrada Familia which we had both enjoyed wandering around so we decided to head back there.

On our last visit it had been popular but the crowds

reasonable. Not today! The queue just to get in the place stretched about halfway around its perimeter and the whole area was sheer bedlam. It did not take us long to come to the conclusion "bugger that!"

We had passed a nice-looking market on the way out so headed back via there to get some supplies for breakfasts and picnics, as well as a few nibbles for the evening before retreating to the hotel. It was furnished with a roof-top swimming pool which we had decided to try but which now felt even more appealing.

It lived up to expectations. The first thing that struck us was the fact that they had *huge* towels on offer there and the two that we nabbed were destined to stay with us and replace the face-flannels we had been otherwise expected to dry ourselves with in the room. I wondered how many other guests grabbed them for similar reasons. Given the small supply on offer, I guessed that it was common practice.

The second thing that struck us was that it was quite cold at least when you first got in but after that it was lovely! We wallowed in some luxury for an hour or so, chilling out (literally) and passing the time.

As we were approaching the advanced wrinkly stage we decided it was time to head back to the room for the traditional siesta. It also gave us time to start seriously getting our heads around what we were about to do and what we should be asking.

With the appointment time approaching I packed all our paperwork into our rucksack and we headed off towards the clinic, via a small park nearby where we sat for a few minutes to make up for the fact that once again we were unfashionably early.

Eventually, still early, we could bear it no more and made our way to the clinic. It was everything I had expected, all white, chrome and glass and the receptionists were all young and efficient. The walls had huge plasma screens showing videos of various procedures in gleaming operating theatres, staffed by young, virile doctors and all ended with glowing parents showing off their bundles of joy.

Part of the reception desk had a sign with "International Reception" hanging from chains and was blatantly only put there when foreigners like us were coming and then in the correct language.

We were greeted and immediately handed consent forms to read and sign, as well as having our passports checked and being given complementary bottles of water. Not that we knew it then but this was the start of a long and very formal legal process. We had our own private cubicle to sit in which was very nice and even decent pens with which to fill in the forms.

Just as we were settling down having completed the consent forms to wait for the next step I was called over and given the first bombshell of the day, namely that my hepatitis B blood test was missing!

Confused, I looked through my file for the tests produced but sure enough it was not there. The bloody NHS had done it again! What was particularly annoying in this case, however, was that I had sent all the results to the clinic in advance and requested with the specific question that if anything was missing they were to tell me so that I could rectify it (as we had already done with Iona's missing HIV result).

This really put me on the back foot. Once again, we had been let down by the system but now I was in the embarrassing position of having to sort it out. Luckily the clinic was geared up to do it on the spot so without a second glance I was whisked away to have a blood sample taken.

The corridor heading towards room to which I was led had loads of pictures on the walls of babies, obviously many of the successful results of treatment at the clinic. While the nurse unlocked the door to the side room I glanced around, noting the particularly high proportion of twins in the pictures. Gulp!

In the whole "I hadn't thought of that" vein I had not even considered the fact that the treatment might land us with instant family and that multiple pregnancies were common. At least it took my mind off the moment when the needle when in and she nearly hit the bone.

Blood was drawn but rather than being led back to reception I was shown into the next room where I was going to be providing the semen sample. I had not considered that they would do this so was totally unprepared. Okay, to all you women out there scoffing at this, trust me, these things need careful thought!

I had been warned that the room had paper-thin walls and was that ever the truth. In size it was little bigger than the toilet cubicle I had so often frequented at the hospital in England but this chamber of shame contained a sink, a chair, a rack of magazines and a television on the wall. There was barely room to move even with the door shut.

I was handed a second consent form to fill in (to say that I was producing my own sperm etc. etc. etc.) and concise instructions as to what to do next. Before you start thinking, no, not like that. It was more about how to clean myself before producing the sample so that the sperm was as fresh and contaminant-free as possible.

What was even more disconcerting was the fact that the nurse did not speak English so that all the instructions were being passed on through an interpreter. I presume there was some rule about the fact that the nurse had to actually give the instructions but as all she was basically doing was handing me a sample pot, a clipboard with a form to fill out and a laminated set of instructions, I wondered why the interpreter couldn't just do it herself.

The door was closed and there was a button to push once I was finished that would summon the nurse to collect my sample and form. I listened as they walked down the corridor, the sounds of their shoes distressingly clear and looked around. I was on my own!

Looking back, I think I had formed a mental image of what I was going to encounter at this stage but the tiny cubicle I was in simply did not fit. I'm not sure what I was expecting but certainly something with a bit more space and that felt a lot less clinical than this. All I could think was that it had been designed by a woman, not a man. It was definitely not an area to put you at ease, especially when people walked past outside as a reminder of how utterly non-soundproof the room was.

For the first couple of minutes, I simply stood there trying to collect myself. With resignation, I picked up the instructions and read them carefully. There were sponges, paper towels and liquid soap for the purpose of cleansing so the first thing to do was give the old feller a bit of a wash.

I picked up one of the cellophane-wrapped sponges and stared at it miserably. Without going into graphic detail, I have a relatively fertile imagination when it comes to sexual fantasies (eighteen years on your own will do that for you) but none of them started with giving my knob a polish with a small yellow sponge.

It was only then that I discovered that the sink was about three inches higher than groin level. Oh brilliant! I was thus faced with two choices, get the floor wet or stand on tip-toes. Stupidly I opted for the latter, juggling the instructions in one hand and a soapy sponge in the other as my wedding tackle dangled precariously over the edge of the sink.

By the time I had finished I was clean, the floor was wet anyway and I had lost any inspiration I might have had.

It has been mentioned before that I have spent time in Amsterdam and had visited the red-light district a few times, purely as a tourist you understand. It was odd, though that this scenario reminded me of my impression of what it must have been like to pay for sex with one of the rouge-illuminated girls - clinical and emotionless.

As decorative as some of the girls were, in that slightly used way, their faces all held that same expression that the men meant absolutely nothing to them. Although I was alone in the room, I had that same odd belittling feeling that those girls would have roused in me had I ever stepped across their threshold into the ruddy glow.

Time was ticking by so I knew I had to simply get on with it and grabbed a handful of gentleman's literature. The selection was restricted to two publications, both on the soft-side of pornography and both extremely limited in their choice of decorative ladies.

Just wanting to get the job over and done with I opted for a kind of Russian roulette approach, selected one particular magazine and opened it to a page at random... and saw the grinning face of Sir Richard Branson staring back at me! Argh!

This was *not* what I expected. It was an interview, I hasten to add, not a centrefold (they were that sort of publications that intersperse interviews with important people around the naked girls). This was *not* going well. I admire Branson as an entrepreneur but certainly not in that sort of way.

I chose another magazine and opened it to find a buxom blonde called Mandy staring back at me with bucolic eyes. I guessed her IQ to be in the low thirties and this copy also found itself on the discard pile.

Again, this is a bit of a guy thing but it should be

understood that men have fantasies and fetishes and given the number of blokes going through that room, all tastes should be catered for. While my tastes are mainstream what I am looking for in a fantasy girl may not be the same as other chaps.

As I flicked through the pages of the different magazines I was presented with a wide selection of blond, full-bosomed, white-skinned girls. No redheads, no brunettes, no Africans or Asians, just blonds. You were pretty well catered for if you liked well-endowed blonds. Sadly, they are not my favourite. It really didn't help that they all had that complete air-head look about them: sluts or sophisticates perhaps but not stupid, not for me.

This was the second piece of evidence that made me suspect that males had provided very limited input into the furnishing of this room. Any chap that I know if asked to recommend a variety of classical magazines to stock the shelves with would have come up with a very different list of titles and certainly a lot more in the way of variety.

The room itself would have also been designed in such a way as to create a more "relaxed ambience" for what the chap had to do. There was nothing relaxed about this experience.

It didn't help that the publications were all in Spanish – I couldn't even read the stories.

This was not working out the way I had envisioned so it really came down to the fact that I was in the hospital toilet all over again, just this time with a bit more sanitation. Feeling somewhat dejected, I got on with the task in hand.

The oddest part of the whole procedure, once I had produced the sample and cleaned myself up was pressing the bell to wait for the nurse. In the few moments I had before she arrived I practiced the grin I was going to have on my face when she appeared. I think, judging by the look on her face, I wore the wrong one.

When I was delivered back to Iona she was holding a thick wad of paperwork that she had been given. We sat, watching people coming and going and playing the game of trying to spot who were patients, who were staff and who were donors.

It was only a short wait until we were called to another waiting room behind the reception desk. The chairs here were noticeably more comfortable than those in the lobby, better clearly for paying patients than casual visitors though I did notice the drinks were in a vending machine that you had to pay for. Evidently several thousand pounds worth of payments didn't extend to the provision of free coffee.

There were two other couples clutching similar paperwork and we smiled, realising that they were at the same stage of the journey as us.

Finally, we were led through to our consultant in her nice shiny black, chrome and glass office. The room was devoid of any personal items or clutter and spoke of a "hot-desk" policy. No doubt this was a room that whatever consultant happened to be on duty at the time would use rather than it being her room specifically. Doctors, like scientists, tend, in my experience, to thrive on clutter.

She was very nice, clearly knew what she was talking about and very efficient. My sperm results were already up on the screen and in that much they were infinitely superior to the NHS. While the count and motility were both poor (and morphology results not available until the next day) she said there was enough to work with though they would have to use ICSI.

For those of you who don't know what ICSI is, it is the classical picture of IVF you see on the news with the needle puncturing the wall of the egg.

The reality is that they only use it when the sperm is a bit sluggish as was the case for me. However, that was fine in my book as the underlying message was that they could use my genetic material. I would have a function after all and all my sessions pleasuring myself in toilets were not wasted.

I had very mixed emotions about this. Selfishly, I now did not have to face the problem of what to say next if she had turned round and said we needed sperm donor treatment as well as egg donor. On the other hand, it was rubbing it in with Iona that it would be my genetics that would be used. There was the other consideration that she knew I was reticent about donor sperm so that question had been avoided and whatever the situation, we were now all-systems go!

Feeling like a rat, I knew I had just dodged a very large bullet.

We discussed my other sperm results and I explained to her the situation regarding timings of samples. The consultant listened carefully but you could see it in her face that she was not impressed in the least by our health service. I felt pretty stupid just telling her the catalogue of cock-ups we had been subjected to as if it had been our fault.

She then looked at Iona's results, explaining again that the elevated FSH indicated early menopause but that she was not there yet, however it did mean as we had been told that we would need donor egg treatment. I was at the same time both impressed and depressed at the casual way she said this, as if it were blindingly obvious and tried not to think of the eighteen months on the merry-go-round we had been with our own doctors.

In an anteroom to the office was an examination room with a shiny new ultrasound scanner and she indicated that she needed to give Iona an internal exam. Iona had worked herself up that she had started her period and was on day two but as it happens, this turned out to be perfect as there would be no activity in the ovaries and it was coincidentally the best time to do the scan.

It was again a pity that nobody had mentioned this before as it would have spared my wife from yet more stress!

I got to watch which was fascinating if a bit odd and saw a side (or at least internal parts) of my wife I never expected to see! The scan showed nothing unusual, the cervix was a good shape and the ovaries still showed follicles so menopause was still a way away.

The consultant then took a look at the blood test results. We had read Iona's to indicate that she had high thyroid but this was wrong, her thyroid was underactive, not overactive! Our doctor had utterly failed to look at the results and spot this, yet another cock-up on the part of the NHS and bombshell number 2 that day. Underactive thyroid could have serious impact on pregnancy and it was something we would need to get sorted as a matter of priority!

We were then taken through the rest of the procedure which was pretty much what we expected, though we now had a proper timetable and list of drugs that Iona would have to take and further tests that we both needed to get sorted on our return to the UK (in my case, cystic fibrosis as there is a high rate of carriers in Spain and if I was a carrier it would be potentially bad news). She explained the success rates and percentages and it suddenly felt like we were getting the sales pitch as well as the medical explanation. I realised that this was because we had not signed for the procedure yet so they still wanted our money!

What was advantageous about Iona being on day 2 of her period was that the scan she had could count as the first scan on the treatment and that she could start taking the pill that very day. The consultant wrote out a separate prescription for the required tablets. This was great, we could start the process immediately rather than having to wait until we got back to the UK and Iona was at the right time. It also meant one less trip to a clinic in the UK (and one less thing to pay for there).

With our medical instructions complete it was time to be handed over to our coordinator. I felt as if we were on a clock as it certainly reached that point where we were being ushered onto the next part of the consultation. Note to anyone following us down this route: get your questions in fast!

The consultant was replaced by Maria; a more businesslike lady who I guessed was in her mid-thirties in that way you really cannot tell with some attractive Spanish women.

She was to be our coordinator and primary contact. The tone of the meeting changed somewhat as she was handling the paperwork side of things. She gave us instructions as to when to contact her (day 18 of taking the pill) and then got down to putting together our patient file. This consisted of many things but the details we were not exactly sure of and had not thought to check were our exact height and weight (so they had to get a nurse in to quickly weigh us and measure us both). Oops.

She then wrote down our physical features – at least, she got us to do this and I noticed again that she would not write anything down or suggest anything herself. It was the lawyer coming out again and it was obvious now that they were sticklers for their legal position. Every form had to be signed on every page and you could not move without signing a disclaimer. I guessed that they had been stung in the past and were now ultra-cautious.

The key point for us was eye colour. I have blue eyes (rarer in Spain) but Iona's are somewhere between hazel, blue and green, a combination that was not on their list. Matching brown eyes would be easy, blue would take longer so we said that we were not desperate to hold out for blue. Iona suspected that there were brown eyes in her family and the hope was always there that my genes would dominate anyway.

Our fear was that by holding out for blue the process would take longer and that might bump the critical part just when Iona was starting the new term at school! This was a big dilemma as the perfect timing would be for it all to happen in late August thus keeping it relatively invisible to her work but holding out for precise colouring might prevent this. At the same time, the clinic were insisting that there was nothing we could do to influence timing, it was all down to when they could find a suitable donor and while we appreciated this they did get a bit like a scratched record on the subject.

This is something you just have to get used to with any form of IVF. It is such a difficult area legally that you will be bombarded with disclaimers and cautious statements as the clinics will do everything in their power to ensure they are not in any way liable. I hadn't really thought about it but after a while it was getting pretty annoying.

Eventually, we signed the forms, committing ourselves to the process but the good news was that due to the credit crunch and the poor condition of the Euro they were doing a twenty-percent discount for foreign patients. Bonus!

I did not tell them that we would have paid the full fee quite happily but simply signed the paperwork, handing over to Iona to do the same before were led back downstairs to a third room where we were politely requested for payment for the day's session as well as the scan and blood tests. Nearly €300 lighter and laden down with paperwork, we realised that we had reached the end of our session and, earlier than expected, we found ourselves back out on the warm streets of Barcelona.

I felt very odd. It had all been a bit of a blur, especially coming out with the knowledge that not only had we signed up for the procedure but the clock was already ticking. We walked back looking for the green cross that indicated an open pharmacy so that Iona could get her prescription for the pill.

For my part I also wanted an open bar...I needed a beer!

Iona asked me what I would have said if the consultant had turned round and said that with my sperm the chances were low but with donor sperm the chances would have been higher. It was a difficult question to answer now that it was only hypothetical but I was honest as far as I could with my answer. Had this been the case then I think (and I will never know) that my gut reaction would have been to try with mine initially and roll the dice. Would this have been selfish of me? Probably but I had already thrown a double-six and dodged this one.

All I wanted to do was sit down, have a nice dinner and try and absorb everything that had been said.

An open chemist presented itself and we got the appropriate prescription, heading back to the hotel safe in the knowledge that we were all systems go. We talked a lot about the whole thing but I will be honest that a lot of it is a bit of a blur now.

I had booked a table in the rooftop terrace restaurant, not fancying the idea of heading out too far after the consultation and now I was very glad of that decision. We had a quick freshen-up and change and soon found ourselves in the cool evening breeze overlooking the surrounding streets.

The food was good. The wine was excellent! I think the

waitress must have been empathic as I asked for a glass of wine, intending to behave myself but when it came to the second glass she brought a bottle and simply left it there. Oh well, it would have been rude not to!

We had nibbles back in the room including the Fortnum and Mason's chocolates that I had secretly bought for Iona as a nice surprise for the weekend so we sat back and enjoyed some of those for a while.

That night, we went to bed deep in our own thoughts. At the back of mine, lurking as it had been for the last few days was the next impending crisis, my job interview! As I drifted out of consciousness I wondered why life could not be less complicated.

Breakfast in bed was nice and relaxing, especially as I really did not sleep all that well. My brain had not switched off which meant I had stared at the ceiling for hours. The chocolate pastries we had bought from the market were excellent, even though we scoffed the entire pack that had been intended to last two days! With a lack of tea or coffee, we washed them down with diet Coke to get the caffeine-fix!

It felt very strange that morning. With the consultation over we now had a whole day in Barcelona with nothing to do but enjoy ourselves. I could not shake the strange feeling from yesterday or the dread of what was to come in three days time.

On our previous visit we had not wandered as far as the Park Güell so this was top of our priority list. It was a good walk to the north and what I had neglected to mention to Iona was that there was also a not insignificant vertical portion to the trip, the park being perched on the hills overlooking the city.

It was hot that day, the temperature for the weekend having even caught the locals out by being several degrees above the seasonal norm. For us two pasty white-skinned Brits it was way above our normal expectations of June. Typical English mad-dogs then we went walking just before midday!

There is a good reason why most people take the bus up to Park Güell!

One thing I know we were both doing by now was serious people watching, especially when it came to the women. Somewhere out there was the donor who would provide the egg and it was impossible not to be curious as to what she might look like. I for my part was probably lucky not to get arrested or slapped by my wife as I eyed up the ladies trying to see if there were recognisable local characteristics.

Park Güell was probably not the best place to look as it was mostly full of Brits, Germans and Americans (you could tell the latter as you could hear them right across the park!). It was a good place, however, to walk and talk as by now we were both feeling a bit weird and it had not really sunk in that we were all systems go! Somehow we were again in a limbo-state before getting back to the UK and putting everything else into place.

Returning to the hotel and having another dip in the pool and a siesta we took a trip down to the Cathedral in the evening to light a couple of candles in the cloister. There are a number of saints there and we had thought we had identified one on our previous visit that was the saint of pregnant mothers but that turned out to be a bit of a mis-translation on our part. As it was she was the patron saint of electricians and plumbers! Still, she was holding a baby and the sentiment was the same so it was with her that we left our offering and prayers of hope.

We found somewhere for dinner embarrassingly early but I have never been any good at adjusting to the

Mediterranean way of life when it comes to eating. I am usually ravenous by about five in the afternoon so holding out until ten would be torture for me. The good thing was that this meant that the tapas bar we found off La Ramblas was pretty close to deserted so the service was quick.

By the time the city was coming alive we were about ready for bed.

Despite being knackered, we both had little sleep that night. I'm not sure how much of that was mulling over the consultation at the clinic and how much was worrying about getting home and thus not missing my interview. We had grabbed more supplies from the market so enjoyed another picnic in bed when we awoke.

It was horrible outside and we were very glad that we had already done the outdoor sights. Borrowing a couple of brollies from the hotel we took a hike down to the waterfront to visit the Aquarium (mostly to kill time before heading back to the airport). It was surprisingly good and did take my mind off of things for a while.

As we were waiting in the queue we took a couple of pictures of each other to send to Maria so she had a visual record of our characteristics.

Eventually, we reached that "we may as well get out of here" stage and grabbed a cab back to the airport.

Once again we arrived stupidly early for the flight but when I asked the lady behind the speedy boarding desk what time we could check in, she made a phone call and said "now if you like". Bonus! I was really starting to like Easy Jet by this stage. Other airlines of my experience would have curtly told me the time that check-in opened and politely invited me to bugger off until then.

Check-in we therefore did as at least we could lose the suitcase and get through security.

As with our inward trip, the terminal looked as if there

had been a bomb-scare it was so deserted in places and we ended up walking miles back to the habited parts. Restaurants and other facilities were scant indeed so we simply grabbed a baguette and waited. I hovered, watching the other Easy Jet flights board to see what the procedure was – not the official one but the one created by the passengers themselves.

Like all free-for-all situations there is a constant tension between the people involved, not wanting to be first in the queue but the moment someone blinked too quickly they would line up quicker than iron filings on a magnet.

Sensing the situation correctly, Iona and I casually loitered near the desk as the previous flight was closing which was a wise choice. The moment the doors closed, someone else who was clearly on our flight marched up to the desk and other people reached for their bags. We were about third in the queue and within thirty seconds it was about a hundred people deep!

There then came the second sorting. At this stage there was just one queue but we all knew that they would soon separate us out into speedy boarders and "the rest". Again, this was a matter of skill and judgement (otherwise known as the fact that when the Easy Jet representative put her hand on the speedy boarding sign to move it to the queue we had all nipped out and formed the second queue automatically before she had a chance to open her mouth).

The flight next to us was running late which made me a bit anxious, especially as come boarding time there was no plane on the gate. I should not have worried. Like busses, we stood waiting for our planes and they both came in at the same time. Passengers were hustled off in no time and apart from a short wait to allow a couple of other planes to empty (the arriving passengers having for some reason to walk past our gates on the way into the terminal which showed what a rubbish design Barcelona airport is) we were soon on the plane.

We had exactly the same seats as the way out!

Our experience with Easy Jet ended as it had started. The flight took off no problem, got home a bit late but nothing disastrous and our luggage arrived safely and promptly at the other end.

Before we knew it, we were back in the car and on our way home.

We had made it!

It was only when we got back home that Iona spotted that the hotel had over-charged us for a breakfast we never had! Bugger.

# Chapter 14:
## The ghost of idiots past...

Now while I hope you will appreciate that this story is by design being told from my perspective, before I continue the story I think it is only fair if I allow Iona a few words as it gives a good reflection on her state of mind at this particular moment in time which I would like to start this chapter with (the calm before the storm, if you like).

*I've learnt a lot about myself and my desires for a family through this process to IVF but I have also learnt a lot about my husband. I have always known him to be a kind, considerate and loving person both to me and to others he cares about but some of the things he has done to get us on this road have not been pleasant to say the least. Whilst I know he has had to deal with his own thoughts and emotions along the way he has always thought of me as well when he makes decisions.*

*I have always known that if we have a successful pregnancy my body will not be my own as the doctors will prod and poke in all the areas you would rather not and after all we women regularly have smears but it is not like that for men usually.*

*I often still think about the others who have "easy conception" and the "pigeon pair" but I also know that I have my perfect husband. This process has drawn us closer together and helped us see each other in a very different light. It is possible we are being tested by some higher consciousness but in all honesty I think we should pass that test. I hope and pray every day that we will end this journey of love and hope on a positive test.*

Gulp! No pressure then!

I was off work allegedly preparing for my interview but by this time I was so wound up I was pretty much fit for nothing.

I was very keen to get everything we had on our "to do" list sorted so sent the images & a whole series of questions to Maria. One of the things Iona was keen to make the point was that if there was any way we could get the treatment before October, even if this meant not being fussy with eye colour then we would appreciate it.

Needing a walk, I went to bank to arrange payment of the deposit to the clinic. Having done an international money transfer in the past I knew it involved a bit of paperwork so had brought ID and everything else needed from my side.

It was fortunate I was not in a hurry as it took over half an hour to process the request! Luckily I had already decided due to the not insignificant bank charges that I would send the entire amount in one go rather than just the deposit. I was also speculating a bit on the Euro price which seemed about to change and not in our favour so by paying now I would potentially save us tens of pounds in exchange rate as well.

I left the bank very glad of my decision and of the fact that I was not going to have to go through all that nonsense again!

Feeling somewhat pleased with myself I went back home and sent an e-mail to the hotel to point out their error on the invoice. I tried to be polite and hopefully my tension did not come through in the e-mail.

With everything I could do complete, there was nothing to do now but lurk around the house getting ready for the interview.

The company had asked me to prepare a short presentation on a particular aspect of packaging but I had decided to go one step further and prepared actual mock-ups of several examples of designs to illustrate my talk. I've always been good with my hands but was especially pleased with the results which, if I do say so myself, looked pretty impressive.

I wrote the presentation, embellishing it with suitable imagery and ensuring that the information was as current as possible and eventually reached a point where I actually began to think I was ready for stage two.

After another restless night – how many in a row now I was beginning to lose track – I got a robotic answer back from Maria. She had completely missed the point about timing, either through lack of understanding or her adherence to the legal position. Iona sent her a note back to explain what she meant.

It finally was time for me to head off for the interview and I made my way, suited and booted, back up to London. Once again I found myself in their plush offices and the chap who had interviewed me the first time around appeared to greet me with two other figures in tow. One I knew was his boss, though I had not met him previously but the other was unexpected as the recruiter had only told me there would be two people.

My heart sank as I realised the third man was familiar!

One thing you should understand about the packaged goods industry is that it is very incestuous. Most people working for one company will have spent some time with at least one of their competitors or suppliers and it is not uncommon for people to jump around most of the major players during their career.

An old boss of mine once gave me the sage advice "don't piss anybody off in this industry, you never know when they will come back to haunt you!" This advice I had diligently adhered to and passed on to junior staff and students as often as I could...apart from once.

His name was Howard and he was a total asshole. The problem was, I have a tendency not to tolerate idiots and Howard was the grand master of idiots but the kind that, despite having hidden talents that were so well hidden nobody could find them, always seemed to survive in any environment.

I cannot tell you one single achievement that he has made over a lengthy career, other than not being fired. Partly, I think he was sensible enough to move before he was pushed, greasing his way up the ladder through slick presentation rather than actual performance. He had only recently joined the company himself so they had not as yet had enough time to see through his bullshit.

We had never actually clashed swords but I knew that I was one of a number of people around whom Howard felt threatened, basically as, without sounding arrogant, I could out-perform him in my sleep. If we were to work together it would not take those around us long to realise what a total waste of space he was and that he had delusions of adequacy, not grandeur.

I knew at that point I had probably lost the job. The afternoon was spent in the most gruelling cross examination I have had before or since though the mock-ups went down very well. Having met the other four candidates before the interviews (they had made us have lunch together) I knew my skill set was most matched to the position. Inevitably we had probed each other to see what the competition was like.

For sure, none of the others seemed to have pushed the boat out as much as I in terms of preparation. Even so, I was no longer confident but I gave it my best shot and was told I would hear either way in a week.

By the time I came home I was totally frazzled and really coming down to earth with a crash. Not that I realised it immediately but with the combination of the consultation and the interview I had managed to give myself a bit of a burn-out. Facing the grinning visage of Howard in the process had just about been the final straw.

It was only then did I appreciate the emotions that had been simmering under the surface and again in hindsight the timing of the interview, while unavoidable, was really bad. Note to anyone reading this, if there is anything else in your life likely to involve stress such as moving house, taking a driving test, etc. etc. etc., avoid it like the plague if you can. My brain, torn between devoting stress energy between two separate crises had simply given up and gone into partial shut-down.

The sad thing was that I was so self-centred at this point that I realised I was not considering Iona's feelings very much but in my defence it was largely self-preservation. Not that I was particularly close to cracking but there was too much building up inside me and something was going to give sooner or later.

I was still recovering from the emotional rollercoaster of the last few days but we took some positive action. Given how utterly useless our doctor had been we had decided to change and to register at another local surgery so we took the new patient paperwork down to register and were greeted by the nicest receptionist I have ever met.

The fact that she smiled at us as we approached the desk made me realise we were on to a winner. It was such a stark contrast to the frosty reception we always received at the previous surgery and a breath of fresh air.

Our friendly new surgery felt even rarer when we returned home to find an email from Maria. She had responded to Iona in her usual blunt, legal way and was still clearly missing the point about timing or deliberately ignoring it so we dropped it, not wishing to annoy her and frankly too tired to argue any more.

Being the impatient person that I am, I decided to contact a nearby private fertility clinic to find out how to be registered so that we could get all the scans and other tests the Spanish clinic needed done, not that we had confirmation of the actual timetable at that stage although we had a pretty good idea.

Iona was away all of the following week on a school trip so I was aware it was going to be difficult to timetable an appointment. Not thinking much of it, I sent them an e-mail enquiring as to what we needed to do. I also tried to get an appointment to see our new doctor before Iona left but there were no slots available. No doubt all the patients from our old doctor had become equally fed up and were also jumping ship to the new surgery!

You know when you have a sinking feeling that something's rotten in the state of Denmark as Shakespeare put it? I had one that day. I heard back from the local clinic initially to say they could help us no problem and that when we knew the timetable that we should contact them.

Well, as we pretty much did know the timetable (as we were already on it) I gave them a call only to be told that they could do nothing until they had an official letter from our consultant in Spain. Surely the consultant would have known that a clinic over here would need something official from them…??? I was more than a bit disappointed that once again we seemed about to be running in circles.

This wasn't the iceberg that was about to sink my ship, however. The other thing I investigated online was how to go about ordering the various drugs that Iona was going to need using the Spanish prescription we had been given. The short answer was that we couldn't! Despite England and Spain both part of the big happy European family, Spanish prescriptions are not, apparently, recognised over here and the local clinic had already made it clear on their paperwork that they could not prescribe the drugs as they were not handling the actual treatment.

To all intents and purposes we were well and truly stuffed. Okay, so potentially not as bad as all that but yet another thing we had to sort out. Why they had not made it clear we needed to buy the drugs before getting back on the plane I do not know, especially as they had written out a separate prescription for the pill at the time.

The only reason we had not done so was that we were going to be spending a couple of hundred quid on drugs and didn't want them to be taken from us at airport security. Had I known the hassle it was going to cause I would have taken the chance!

My blood pressure hit the roof! An e-mail was sent back to Maria asking her to send a letter to the local clinic and to clarify what we were supposed to do about the drugs. It was all I could do to keep it polite.

In the meantime, deciding not to wait for Iona to come back from her week of trips I booked an appointment for myself with our new doctor. At the very least I could ask the question about the prescription as there was always the chance they would write out a private prescription so I could get them.

Suddenly, we didn't seem to be getting much in the

way of good service for our €8000! This was supposed to be the good bit, we were out of the hands of the NHS and the Spanish experts were going to wave a magic wand and everything was going to be okay, wasn't that the deal? Apparently not it seems. This all felt like the same annoying issues that we had endured for so many months previously.

Perhaps it was because I was still emotionally tired after the hellish week past, perhaps I was beginning to reach the end of my tether and patience when it came to medical staff but I sat there in a state of some despair. The Spanish clinic was not, at present, living up to expectations. I knew something was not up when I found myself at the point of tears about it, I was that frustrated.

Somewhere, I had expected to be handed the "idiot's guide" to IVF with all the steps nicely laid out but it was now becoming clear that the Spanish were washing their hands of anything that happened on this side of the equation.

We ended the week with more questions than answers and while I had hopes that they could be solved, I really did not feel in the right emotional condition to face them.

It was really good that we had planned to do very little at the weekend!

I was finally on the mend, despite a few scars where Iona had found a couple of empty wine bottles and some beer in the shed. I'd completely forgotten about them, the residue of stress earlier in the year that I had foolishly tried to deal with on my own. Men, if you are going to have a sneaky session *never* forget to hide the evidence!

Disappointingly Maria did not come back with an immediate answer to quell my fears about the next steps. I hoped that this was simply because she was in the process of gathering the appropriate information for the local clinic prior to responding to me (but a "don't worry, I'm on the case" would have been nice).

The more we dealt with Maria the more it continued surprise me that she was less considerate of the emotional side of things when it came to supporting us. In the paperwork supplied by the clinic there was information about someone to contact for emotional support but interestingly they provided neither a telephone number nor e-mail for that individual, despite admitting that it can be an anxious process especially for people living abroad! If that's the case, why not start by providing more supportive coordinators?

Something began to really dawn on me – I was starting to rant a lot! I am sure you reached this conclusion several chapters ago!

Again I realised that emotionally I was still totally swamped by the whole situation such that what were probably small things appeared to be huge crises. It would, I knew, be interesting in the future to read this part of the book again to see how I felt about it in the cold light of day or with the benefit of hindsight. Apologies reader if I am going on a bit. Hopefully it will give you some idea as to how high emotions can run under these circumstances.

The one thing I had continued to do was to diligently document everything that happened, in many cases probably too much but having made the choice to write the book it was difficult on a daily basis to sieve out what was relevant and what was not. Even so, I stuck to my guns in that whatever went down would not be edited, apart from the many parts where Microsoft Word stuck a wiggly red, green or blue line under the text to smugly point out how rotten my English was.

Whether the book was having the intended effect was difficult to say but it was already proving to be an invaluable reference guide to events and on several occasions I had already consulted it to check details that were more readily available than sifting through the purple file.

The few parts I did read again were charged with emotion and in that respect I knew it was going to be priceless. This was the kind of language that I would simply not be able to express in however many years time it was going to be.

Periodically Iona penned her thoughts, adding details where I was not present or putting her own take on events though never did she question my own thoughts or in any way try to contradict me. She felt as strongly as I that the document should be honest and should give a true account of what we both were going through.

We kept in touch with our friends and they kept us going but I still felt that the system was woefully inadequate in terms of professional guidance.

I can see now why this process often leads to the breakup of marriages. I doubt if many people enter into it fully aware of what they are about to face, at least the first time round and most will try and attempt it with woefully inadequate emotional support.

Okay, you ask, why am I not getting support myself now? It is a good question and frankly I don't have a good answer which does make me a bit of a hypocrite ("do as I say don't do as I do" and all that kind of thing).

In the absence of a response from Maria I did have a plan. First thing was to chat with our new doctor tomorrow and see if he could sort out the prescription issue primarily. If he could write out a private prescription for the drugs that would at least raise that barrier to moving forward.

Secondly, get Iona back in to see the doc on her return and, if needed, get her re-referred to her gynaecologist so she could try and unblock the clinic issue.

Finally, as Iona had to inform the Spanish in a week that she was on day 18 of the pill, if they had not responded by then it would be time to play them at their own game. Either answer the question or face the legal repercussions if things go wrong! Okay, now I was *really* starting to rant. Perhaps I was not on the mend quite as much as I thought.

There was an article in the paper about a couple who had conceived on their thirteenth attempt at IVF and it put our own plight into sharp perspective. Reading the story further, however, it seemed that they had spent less than £20,000 in total which I found quite unbelievable until I realised that they had at least three rounds on the NHS and another five or six for free in Scandinavia. They had been going at it for nearly a decade and the thought of that made me go cold.

We had already discussed that we were going to give it one go, possibly a second with frozen embryos if the first attempt failed although we had left that decision up in the air to be faced when required. I had to admire the tenacity of a couple and the deep desire to have children to willingly put themselves through all that. I'm not sure in all honesty that I could.

I was on my own that night, Iona being away on an overnight trip up north to see an old friend so I had plenty of time to sit and fume about things. Luckily, I was possessed of sufficient willpower not to spend the entire evening wallowing in unauthorised food or booze to nurse my woes!

Okay, so there was nothing in the house and as it was raining I couldn't be bothered to go out for supplies! The sad thing was that she probably assumed I was having a sneaky beer when in fact I was for once being well-behaved.

We were now heading for the middle of June and if the old saying is right that patience is a virtue, well, I am clearly not a virtuous sort of chap. When I checked e-mail that morning I found the note from Maria with the letter we would need to send to the UK clinic by way of introduction. Did I feel guilty; did I feel like I had over-reacted? Yes, of course I did, for all of ten seconds until I realised that she had actually forgotten to attach the letter itself!

By now it was just funny and at least I knew that the letter existed. Let's face it, this sort of thing happens to us all, we get busy, distracted or generally wrapped up in other things and make trivial mistakes like this all the time.

I sent her a friendly note back thanking her but pointing out that she had forgotten to attach the letter and that was that. She sent the letter later in the day but there was nothing else on the e-mail. Now, I wasn't expecting a gushing apology or anything like that but if it had been me I would have put a short "whoops, sorry!" or something similar. Maria put nothing, not even her name – she simply sent the letter.

Perhaps Maria was in fact a robot! She certainly had the personality of one.

Now I am not sure whether this is a cultural thing or whether I have already managed to work my way to the front of the "pain in the arse" folder on her desk but I was beginning to really struggle with this. I am used to building relationships with people professionally, nothing major but at least keeping things light and chatty. There are occasions when a more formal approach is required but even then you keep it polite.

Her abrupt nature was bordering on Germanic in its cold efficiency. Not what I expected from a coordinator, especially dealing with something as emotionally sensitive as IVF.

The attachment appeared to suit our needs but on second glance was obviously a stock-letter as it discussed the treatment starting when Iona would start the pill and therefore the need for the first scan that we had already had performed in Barcelona. The grumpy old sod in me bristled at this. If it was a stock letter which we would clearly need for contacting the clinic over here, why had they not prepared it for us while we were at the clinic? Even if it had to be modelled to our particular treatment it was a one-page affair made up of what were clearly stock paragraphs and they could have easily knocked it up while we were being processed.

Scanning the letter, I e-mailed it to the UK clinic with the hope that this would be sufficient for their initial requirements.

I remembered that the Spanish had given us a feedback form to complete after our first consultation. It had not been my intention to do anything about that but now I decided that at some point in the next few days I was going to take a look at it. There were things that really needed to be said (anonymously, of course!).

That afternoon I had my first meeting with our new doctor and I was initially impressed that having arrived at the surgery early he was able to see me twenty minutes before my appointed time (evidently it was a quiet time of day).

Sadly, it was obvious from the moment I started talking that I had made a mistake. I had gone to ask his advice about getting the drugs we needed in the hope that he would fill in a private prescription but from the offset it was clear he was very nervous. First of all, there was no way he was going to prescribe drugs to me that I was not going to take which was fair enough and I really should have thought of that.

Secondly, not being an expert in IVF he was unhappy prescribing drugs anyway that he did not know much about.

He did momentarily give me a ray of hope as he suggested that Iona see one of the partners who had experience of IVF so I thanked him and left. It was only when I got back to reception that I was told that the partner in question was unavailable for six weeks. Oh brilliant!

My blood pressure hit the roof again but I didn't take it out on the receptionist as she was very nice and it wasn't her fault. I wondered what sort of long-term effects all this was having on me and how much shorter my life was going to be as a result of all the stress.

One of the side-effects of being so frequently in the doctor's surgery was that I had a regular check of my blood pressure and it was deeply worrying that it was gradually but steadily increasing as time went on, almost certainly attributable to the pressure that job-hunting and the IVF procedure were putting on me.

Not sure what else to do, I made an appointment for Iona with the doctor I had just left as she still needed to get her thyroid issue sorted out and she might have better luck discussing the prescription.

Dejected, I popped into the supermarket across the car park to get some things for dinner as I had planned to cook Iona a nice chicken risotto for when she got back.

When I picked her up from the station, I was depressed that I had not been able to sort all the issues out in her absence and she could see that I was really frustrated. It had not helped that I had hoped also to hear about the job by then but there had been no news. Despite what other people say, I don't subscribe to the whole "no news is good news" rubbish.

Next day it was an early start as I had to get Iona to the station to pick up her connection for Heathrow before heading up north. She was off to a three-day conference in Prague and I was going for a meeting at a packaging company just south of Nottingham.

I had a rare commodity, a paying customer and despite not being in the best frame of mind there was no way I could not take up the day's consulting (with travel expenses!). What made it even harder was that the person I was dealing with had basically invented something that would have been laughed out of the TV show Dragon's Den but having given him my professional advice and having had that rejected I was simply following his request to put him in touch with some packaging manufacturers that might help him.

I had selected the one I felt would treat him with the most sympathy but I could see in the owner's face as my client waxed lyrical about his great product that he was less than impressed at the waste of his time.

It was while I was in the meeting that I felt my phone buzz silently and I did not have to look at it to know what that meant. For anyone out there who has had to go through the rigmarole of job hunting you know the golden rule that when they make a decision, they tell the successful candidate first and only afterwards get around to breaking the bad news to the losers.

The decision had been made the night before – I got the call just before lunchtime the next day so it didn't take a genius to realise what this meant. When the meeting broke up and my client thankfully departed, I picked up the answer phone message my pessimism was proven to be correct.

There was no explanation but the interview panel had decided not to pursue my application. I then had the three hour drive home to contemplate the fact that I was back to square one and not going to provide stable money into the house anytime soon.

It was probably unfair of me to assume that Howard had shafted me, though I will always remain deeply suspicious that this was the case. I may well have fluffed the interview and the candidate who eventually got the position was probably more what they were looking for. I will never know but it felt better for me to blame Howard than face the possibility that I was not as great as I thought I was.

One of my many failings is that I can be a bit in love with myself, especially when it comes to my professional abilities and even in the face of being made redundant and not landing a job for a year I was still hanging on to the probably unfounded belief that I was some kind of rocket scientist.

The truth was I was turning into an angry, frustrated, middle-aged loser. If this constituted the start of a mid-life crisis then the Harley Davidson was not far away.

At that point, I hit rock bottom and the fight seemed to drain out of me. All those weeks of preparation, all that stress and worry, it had all been for nothing. It felt as if everything I tried to do went wrong which, I know is a very blinkered attitude but one easy to fall into at times like this.

It was the old supermarket checkout scenario again. We are most of us generally wired to be pessimistic as some sort of survival trait, I guess.

Needless to say, I was at that moment all out of ideas as to how to proceed. I checked the job websites in the vain hope that something else had appeared but nothing had.

With Iona somewhere in the air over Europe I suddenly felt very alone.

There was at least some good news when I got back, the local clinic had responded positively to the letter and had asked for the timetable of treatment which I scanned and sent to them and also sent a patient questionnaire for us to complete. At least it felt as if I was making progress there.

Iona arrived in Prague fine but frustratingly there was a fault on the landline between the Czech Republic and the UK which meant I was only able to get a brief conversation with her on the mobile (which probably cost us a good portion of the Czech national debt given the extortionate roaming and receiving fees that our network provider charges). I did my best to reassure her that I was okay so that she would not worry, although I knew she would.

The evening was weird, mostly because I had simply run out of steam. Even with permission to have a beer I did not as I just didn't fancy it (which was a *really* bad sign as my natural instinct under this level of pressure is to dive into a bottle). Even food was a struggle, not that I wasn't hungry but I could not decide what I fancied and everything tasted weird.

I think the dog, senile as she was, sensed that I was feeling sad as she was uncharacteristically well-behaved, either that or she sensed I was in a mood and likely to respond badly to any misbehaviour on her part. Either way, we sat there, one man and his dog, the future now a closed book again.

It did give me a chance to reflect on just how I had felt over the last few weeks. Iona's tiredness could possibly be attributed to the thyroid issue and she was under at least the same amount of stress as I, probably a lot more with exam season at work but it was easy to see how relationships could be put severely to the test as frustration took over from logic. I hoped and prayed that things would start to improve as I knew I was being far from supportive at the moment.

# Chapter 15:
## Scoring some drugs...

Something had fundamentally changed when I woke up the next day. I should have felt empty and dejected but I awoke in a remarkably good mood for no apparent reason. I think that the resolution of the whole job thing combined with the progress with the UK clinic had taken away a huge chunk of pressure. There was still the issue of the drugs to face but until Iona got back there was not a lot I could do about it. If the worst came to the worst, we could always jump on a plane to Spain and get them there, as ridiculous as that sounded.

The local clinic replied on the question about the Spanish prescription and said that the larger branches of certain high street chemists might accept it! It was worth a go and if it ended up as simple as that I would laugh, though I was secretly betting that it would not. They were also talking about booking our first appointment so at least we were definitely in with them now!

I called the customer service lines for a few of the main chemist chains but they all responded in the same way, initial confusion as if I had asked them to describe the far side of the Moon in ancient Greek and then a negative response.

"Sorry, no we don't accept foreign prescriptions" sound very much like "I haven't a bloody clue whether we do or not but cannot be bothered to ask my supervisor so am just going to fob you off."

I did in fact discover after the fact that at least one of the chemists *would* take foreign prescriptions but only following extensive background checks and other procedural matters that would have no doubt driven me up the wall.

Not for the first time my only recourse was to phone Andrew and he was most helpful. He and Dawn had sensibly bought their drugs in Spain but he was aware that there were a couple of independent chemists who, he thought, would honour Spanish prescriptions but he did not have the names to hand.

He did suggest a few online forums that I could use where he thought the details of the chemists could be found and, thanking him profusely, I jumped online.

It took me a while to find what I wanted, not because the information was not there but because the chat rooms were full of frustrated patients like Iona and I. My eyes were opened for the first time to the real scale of the problem as I read the hundreds of pleading messages from couples desperately seeking information and advice.

I stopped to reply to a few, putting them onto the charities and other sources of information that had been so useful to us and I felt good that I might be relieving the pressure for others in our situation.

Finally, I came across the details of two chemists, one in London and the other in the Midlands so I found their contact details – just an email in both cases and dropped them a note to explain our general needs. I know the advice on the internet is to shop around but at this stage my attitude was that whoever replied positively first would get the business!

Settling down to watch the news I saw that BA and Unite were still in deadlock and I had to smile. With all the ups and downs of recent events that seemed to be the only constant! It was becoming a race to see who could resolve all their issues first, us and the hassles of the donor-assisted IVF or BA and the cabin-crew dispute. It was a stupid thing to have a mental bet on but bet I did!

Within ten minutes of my e-mails I had a response from both so I e-mailed them back to get quotes. Given that they were both so quick I decided to change my mind and that I might as well use the cheapest, especially as both seemed to have lots of recommendations. Oh, fingers crossed that this worked! It would be so nice to surprise Iona with the news that the drugs were sorted.

Hoping that my luck was changing I bought some lottery tickets. Well, you never know! Actually, you do know. I didn't win.

I got home that evening to find that the dog had eaten her bed, scattering the contents far and wide. Bella proudly presented me with a large blob of polyester filling as a present when I stepped through the door and I realised what had prompted John Grogan to write "Marley & Me". He should have regarded himself lucky he only had a dog to deal with! Bella was so pleased with herself in her old and baffled innocence that I could not be cross with her.

The winds had definitely shifted and this time they seemed to be favourable. I woke again in a good mood which belied my situation. The scientist in me suspected that this was due to biochemistry and I was simply not flooding my body with adrenaline and all those other stress hormones that can cause so much trouble. The pessimist in me wondered if I wasn't actually in a good mood and that it was just relative i.e. I was in less of a bad mood so it *felt* like a good one.

Even waking to the smell of what the dog had deposited on the kitchen floor in the middle of the night did not dampen my good cheer (well, okay, it did a bit when I was actually mopping it up but that was only temporary).

The tiny voice of realism in my head shouted at the scientist and the pessimist to just shut the hell up and enjoy it while it lasted!

Yet another voice in my head began to wonder whether or not I was mildly psychic as I seemed to have quite a feel for what was going to happen.

As you will probably gather by now, there is usually quite a lot going on in my head and most of it really doesn't help the situation at hand. One of my biggest problems is a tendency to over-analyse a problem (something which kept me single for about seventeen years). This plays into my control-freakish nature so that I usually think far too much about any given issue. Oh, and I don't *really* have voices in my head, in case you were wondering.

When I look around and think that everyone else just seems to get on with stuff it is often true, the reason being that they don't think too hard about it, they just do it without question. The fact that most things tend to sort themselves out simply means that everyone else didn't spent the intervening time worrying themselves sick about it like I tend to do.

Today was a classic example of this. Having made a total nuisance of myself for well over a week I opened my e-mail today to find a message solving the problem of the drugs.

I changed my mind yet again and as the other pharmacy had not yet quoted me for the drugs I decided that the one that had should get my business.

Eagerly, I called bang on nine in the morning when the chemist opened only to be told that the chap I needed to speak to wasn't going to be in until ten. Argh! Doesn't he know how impatient I am? Clearly not but I was so close to the goal now that I just wanted to have it sorted. It was exciting to think that I would be able to pick up my tired and travel-weary wife from Heathrow tonight and be able to give her the good news that both clinic and drugs were sorted!

Trust me, chaps, if ever you reach this stage you will realise that there is not an awful lot you can do apart from be supportive but where you can do things to relieve the pressure from your nearest and dearest, it means a lot. This is especially true when you generally feel like a failure in all other aspects of life as I did at that moment. The thought that I could proudly present her with my minor achievement meant that at least I was doing *something* right.

I felt a bit like Bella presenting her mouthful of bed filling and looking for praise.

For those of you out there thinking "why should I bother, the wife can sort out all of that?" take a good, long, hard look in the mirror for if you are not completely committed to this then you will have deeper issues down the road my friend.

Sitting here as I was today feeling pretty damn proud of myself, I could not help but wonder as to why it had been such an issue in the first place. When it had boiled down to it, there were means of getting the drugs but the problem is that the information simply isn't out there in an official capacity. While I understand completely that the clinics and other medical professionals have a deep fear and legal block towards making any form of recommendation surely with all the self-help groups and other charitable organisations someone could put out a fact sheet as to what the procedure is?

The clinics themselves should at least be conscious of the problem, sorry, let me re-phrase that as I am sure they are conscious of the problem. The clinics should be cognisant that as the problem exists that they should draw this to the attention of their paying customers and at least offer some form of advice rather than letting them hit their head against a brick wall for ten days as I had to.

It felt as if I had been sold an Aston Martin but only after I bought it found that it only ran on a special fuel blend that they wouldn't tell me where I could get, even though there were several garages out there that would happily sell it to me if only I knew where to go.

With this in mind I resolved myself to raising the issue both with the clinic and with the infertility charity via our friends. If I could raise the profile of the issue for other people then hopefully it would save them the stress I had to go through.

You may ask why, having made such a big deal of it, I haven't simply put the details down here. That is simple, I am aware that places come and go and what would be even more frustrating than no information would be to have details for a pharmacy that no longer exists.

Take it from me the information is out there on the internet, even if only in the chat rooms. Persevere and you will find it or better still ask one of the infertility help groups, they should know (in hindsight I could have asked them before and had this not worked they would have been my next port of call).

I called the pharmacy back just after ten and spoke to what was probably the most polite and helpful person I have had the pleasure of dealing with for a very long time. At last, someone nice! Extremely helpful and I was able to pay no problem. The drugs would be with us the following Tuesday.

What a relief! Recognising that I was in an uncharacteristically good mood I took the opportunity to update the book so that this part at least would sound positive. I didn't want our unrealised child to think that I was a totally grumpy old git all of the time!

The fact was we were in serious danger of being back on track. More importantly, I could start to get back to some sort of routine that didn't involve stressing about this, that and everything else. I was itching to tell Iona now! The temptation to send her a text was very strong but I wanted to see her face when I broke the news.

The rest of the day inevitably dragged and this was not helped by the fact that once I had packed everything ready to go (we were heading straight from the airport down to her Parent's in Dorset for the weekend) I discovered that the roads were a nightmare and that her flight was delayed.

Both the M40 and the M4 were stuffed so I eventually cut through the back roads to get to the airport. Depressingly, the traffic reports on Radio 2 were equally bleak about the southbound M3 so it was going to be a slow grind home.

Bella dropped the stinkiest fart I have ever encountered just at the point where we were stuck in a line of traffic so I had to put the blowers on full just to drive the smell away!

Despite the traffic, my phobia about being late meant that I arrived at Heathrow just as her plane was landing so grabbed a latte from the coffee shop while I stared at the arrival boards. Her plane seemed to taxi for ages but eventually it arrived and as soon as the "baggage in hall" indication popped up I took my position by the barriers to wait for her.

It was with some difficulty that I tried to put on a look

of love and adoration on my face but not of excitement when she appeared but I was bursting to tell her the news.

We were in the car when I announced that I had spent some more money and she fell into the trap, turning to ask "what now?" in that scornful, teacher way that she can sometimes adopt. When I told her what on she was suitably pleased and I felt all clever and smug having managed to do something not only useful but that meant we could head down to Dorset and, for the first time in weeks, truly relax.

We then sat in a horrendous traffic jam for the next two and a half hours! Luckily I had brought a picnic.

# Chapter 16:
## An attack of optimism...

For the first time in ages we started the week on the back of a relaxing weekend. I had bought a couple of lottery tickets for Iona, one of which won her ten pounds just to prove my earlier theory about good luck to be at least marginally true. Twelve million would have been better but I don't mind starting small.

I was, it has to be said, in a state of some bewilderment. For so long I had been worrying about things, whether they be flights, blood tests, drugs or clinics and suddenly (predictably?) everything was falling back into place.

My natural pessimism was already wondering what was going to go wrong next but then I told myself off. After the last few weeks, it was really about time I just accepted that perhaps things might be moving forward after all.

The night before we had completed all the details for the questionnaire that our local clinic had asked for so the first thing I did when I turned the computer on was to e-mail everything to them and ask what we would need to do next, especially regarding my cystic fibrosis test.

Our day had started with more mess on the kitchen floor – Bella had managed to find a large bag of dog treats that she had then proceeded to empty and was feeling a bit bloated! Iona kindly sorted it all out while I was in the shower so I missed the worst of that episode.

Iona was now on day 18 of the pill, the point at which she had been instructed to contact Maria again so did so, asking for the next set of instructions from her but also enquiring how vital my cystic fibrosis results were. The need to do the test had been vaguely mentioned during the consultation but it was not really clear why and although I had scribbled a note down about it in my notepad I was starting to doubt my own memory.

The chap from the pharmacy e-mailed the tracking number for the parcel containing the drugs which was a very good sign. Everything seemed to be going well and the drugs would be with me in the morning as promised.

What was even better was that the next e-mail was from the local clinic to say that they finally had everything they needed I could call up to make an appointment. I did so immediately and when I got through to the receptionist she was offering slots as quickly as the following day. I had to smile as this was typical – I could not go as I was going to be sitting at home waiting for courier with Iona's drugs. Rather than having to wait weeks for good things to happen they were now coming so fast I was double-booking!

However, this was very encouraging, to know that you could get in there quickly. After a bit of diary consultation (a quick process on my part) we settled on a Friday lunchtime appointment. That was not too bad, so long as the traffic was kind and I would hopefully be back before the weekend crush started.

Maria then e-mailed back with the not unexpected news that they would need the cystic fibrosis results before they could match a donor and asked us to confirm that we were getting it done. This was again mildly annoying and we both questioned why, if the results were so important, they had not taken my blood and run the test while we were in Barcelona. We would have happily paid to save the time. I wrote back to her to give her the timing of my appointment.

What was also obvious was that on none of the official paperwork was it written down that I had to get the test done in the first place and they certainly had not mentioned it in the letter to the local clinic as I have mentioned before. If it had not been for the fact that I had asked and written it down myself, I could have easily missed the significance of the need for it.

It was yet another "room for improvement" in the increasing list I was preparing for the initial feedback form that was in danger of becoming an essay.

Trying not to spiral back into gloom I turned my attention back to the book. What was scary was that without particularly trying I had already written over a hundred pages of A4 and while it was quite a jumble of facts and emotions it made me realise just how much there was and how little I would be in a position to explain years in the future.

I have never been one to keep a diary, mostly as I am a lazy and undisciplined sort of chap and normally if I had started such an endeavour it would have lasted a week or two before falling victim to my short attention-span.

With the book, however, something different was happening. Writing down the day's events was becoming almost an obsession and I wondered if this was the same sort of draw that social networking sites had for the sad, lonely millions out there. The only difference was that I was not waiting for a response or reassurance over the ether that everything was going to be okay. Quite the opposite, I was creating the response to questions that would not be asked for years!

Later that day, Maria responded to instruct Iona to complete the cycle of the pill she was on, wait seven days and then start a second cycle on day eight regardless of her period (and to e-mail for further instructions at that point). The waiting game had well and truly begun but I'm not sure how patient either of us was going to be. Still, I am not sure we had really expected to have a donor quite so soon and perhaps a gentler pace to the whole process was just what we needed.

It was certainly nice to have some good weather for a change. Recently it had been very cold and gusty but now the sun was out, the wind had died and it was really starting to feel like the summer could be a good one. With everything falling into place, perhaps life was not so bad after all.

Bella managed to bring us down to Earth with a bang when, out on her usual evening walk, she had a massive fit. For a moment I thought she had gone as her body went totally rigid and she stopped breathing but I have since realised this is simply part of the terrifying cycle of the attack.

She came out of it, tired but clearly oblivious as to what had just happened and was back to her old jolly self in no time. We, on the other hand, were utterly shaken as we headed home.

Iona spent the evening wondering whether we were being tested by a higher power, that the dog was a way of seeing whether we had it in us to persevere in order to preserve life. I felt really bad as in my book the best thing to do now was to end it peacefully for the old girl.

That was not a good thought to go to sleep on.

I am sure that most of you have experienced the joys of waiting for a delivery at some time in your lives. It still amazes me that in this age of mobile phones, satellite navigation and wireless connections that the courier companies cannot give a better idea of delivery time.

The courier in question is, from my experience, one of the better ones in terms of parcel tracking (some of the couriers I have dealt with have been completely useless in this respect). Even so, as I sat on the computer watching the real-time tracking information with the number I had been given it dawned on me how utterly irrelevant it was.

The tracker told me exactly what time of day the parcel had been picked up, the precise minute it had arrived in the main depot and subsequently the accurate details of when it had left there and arrived at the local depot and then left there on the delivery van.

So what? I knew that the parcel was being picked up yesterday and delivered today so all this told me was that this process had not screwed up. My life was none the better for having a blow-by-blow account of the movements of the parcel.

All I gave a damn about was when the chap was going to walk up to my front door and ring the bell.

Given that the van left the local depot just after nine in the morning, the only advantage I could see of the tracking data was that I knew he could not possibly be with me before nine-thirty given the distance to where we lived so at least I could have a shower and some breakfast before being tied to the house. This I did and felt much better for it before heading downstairs to try and do anything other than lurk.

The van entered that long, murky limbo as it started its rounds. Here is where I think technology is not being utilised properly. Surely they have some system for working out the optimum route for the delivery van – they know what has to be dropped off (and presumably collected if the same van does both)? The sat-nav must therefore be able to at least estimate the arrival and departure time from each location allowing for a standard few minutes of actual delivery time.

Why they cannot have some sort of system by which you are at least told within a wide error factor when the van is likely to arrive I do not know.

For example, in my case the courier rang the bell at two forty-five in the afternoon so surely he would have known that he would not have been with me in the morning and I would have not had to spend over five hours listening out for the doorbell?

The worst thing about these kinds of days is when you need to go to the toilet. You hang on and on, wondering whether the delivery will show up and then, when you cannot wait any longer, sit there trying to go as fast as possible in case the universal law of sod causes the courier to pick that precise moment to arrive (which has happened to me more than once in the past!).

Still, it ultimately did not matter. What was important was that he *did* arrive and with an appropriately-sized parcel which, on opening, contained the drugs I had ordered. Two of them needed to be stored below 25ºC so I chucked them in the fridge as the weather had chosen that precise day to warm up and exceed this exact temperature.

I e-mailed the pharmacy out of courtesy to let them know the parcel had been delivered.

When Iona got home she was pleased that they had arrived safe but we put the refrigerated drugs in a tin so that they were not so obvious – we had my brother coming to stay in a couple of days and it was preferable that he did not see them as we had not given my family too many specific details as to what we were undertaking. Oh, the levels of paranoia you fall into!

Iona had her first trip to our new doctor and she agreed that he was very nice (and she learned that he was coincidentally half-Spanish). He concurred that she needed to get another blood test so that he could double-check what was going on with her thyroid and he gave her a prescription for the pill.

It didn't all go swimmingly for us as their computer system was down which meant that we could not book the nurse or the follow-up appointment with the doctor there and then which was frustrating but just one of those things. I felt like we were some kind of jinx and that wherever we went, chaos would follow like a loyal pet!

Our new surgery was one of those that are co-situated with a supermarket on one of those deals where the retailer buys a plot of land but is only allowed to develop it if they also construct other suitable facilities for the community. Of course, by having a surgery in the car-park and an in-store pharmacy it is not a great leap of imagination to see why they do not object too much to such a deal.

We had to wait for 20 minutes in the supermarket for the prescription and made the mental note to ourselves that next time we came for anything like this that we would be more organised and have some shopping to get. This was, of course, precisely the conclusion the supermarket wanted us to adopt.

The thing was, it suited us fine as this was in fact the supermarket we used all the time and by moving our surgery here we could kill two birds with one stone. I have to say I am guilty of this convenience thinking and am probably in my way contributing to the sad demise of our traditional high-street shops, though in my defence our small town did not really have much of a high street.

When we got home Iona called and managed to book the appointment with the nurse but as the computers were still kaput she could not arrange the appropriate follow-up meeting with the doctor. She did make a big point of commenting how nice the receptionists were compared to the old bunch of witches and I tried to imagine how they would have dealt with a major system crash! Certainly you would not have wanted to speak to them in the middle of it.

It came to the day that I had to go to the local clinic for my test but as Iona needed my car to ferry some colleagues around I took hers instead.

I have not mentioned before but by this stage and through some strange deal with her father that I still do not quite understand she became the proud owner of a classic purple MGB which she thought was the best thing ever.

It was strange that I drove a very boring car and she had the sports car but to me it was just another liability and I cursed the day her father had palmed it off on her. It had supposedly been restored – if this was the case then I would have hated to see it in the original form as the current rust-bucket haemorrhaged oil in a near-terminal way and had a peculiar habit of stalling at the most inconvenient times and speeds.

For my part I knew its days were numbered but the boy racer in me (he is very small and normally hides in dark places) was quite thrilled at the thought of taking her out for a spin as it was a remarkably nice day and I was still riding on a wave on uncharacteristic optimism.

If any of you own an MGB then you have my full sympathies. They are very much an enthusiast's car in that you need to be enthusiastic about auto repair – you will probably be doing a lot of it. I am most certainly not amongst that breed, while I aspire to owning a nice sports car I want one that starts first time and continues to run until you have reached your desired destination without minor parts falling off at random or the services of an RAC lorry being required.

Power steering would be nice. Oh, and a reliably working radio. Oh, and air conditioning please. In fact, any form of comfort-delivering device would be a bonus. What few accessories her wreck of a car once had installed were either missing or broken which again brought into question her father's definition of "restored".

I left early as while I had my choice of routes to get to the clinic they each had their various perils. One took me through Oxford which can be perilous at times and the other down the A34 towards the M4, a notoriously bad way.

It was sods law, therefore, that I made the wrong choice and became stuck in a huge traffic jam on the A34 that had not been indicated on the traffic reports as I was leaving.

Even though I had left with plenty of time I was still five miles from the turning off of the A34 and barely moving when the sat-nav showed that my estimated arrival time, even if the traffic were somehow to miraculously disappear, was now past my appointment time. Unless Iona's Dad had installed vertical take-off capabilities in the MG I was going to be late.

I was also roasting to death. The lack of air conditioning meant that I had two choices, keep the roof down and allow the overhead sun to barbeque me or put the roof up and be cooked by the rapidly overheating engine. I kept the roof down in the hope that we would move and I would get at least a brief flow of air (the blowers in the car were also stuffed, by the way).

The drawback of this, of course, was that I was rapidly being asphyxiated by the surrounding trucks and vans that

I had managed to be corralled in as I hit the back of the queue. This meant that I could not even see the queue ahead to get any idea whether it was moving or not.

Typically, the radio during one of its cooperatively active periods was not forthcoming with any useful traffic information but the worst thing was the car behind was a police patrol car so phoning Iona was totally out of the question.

Although technically I was not driving, the car being resolutely stationary at that point, I didn't want to add a fine to my woes so surreptitiously texted Iona to call the clinic and let them know I was going to be late while staring around in what I hoped was an innocent way. If the police saw me sweating I hoped they would put it down to the heat.

I had already been told that things were quiet at the clinic on a Friday afternoon so was hopeful that they would fit me in. I wasn't so hopeful that the car was going to get me there, it was making that all too familiar asthmatic cough that usually preceded something involving a lot of steam and the bonnet up. Sensibly, I turned the engine off, hoping it would start again when the traffic moved.

Iona texted me back to say that she had spoken to another very nice person at the clinic to explain my predicament. They were okay about me arriving late so the immediate panic was off. As it was, by the time I crawled to the next junction and got back onto free-flowing roads I was set to arrive forty minutes after my appointed time which, under the circumstances, I did not think was too bad.

The receptionists at the clinic were all very nice and understanding, addressing me by name before I had chance to introduce myself (not a great leap of imagination as by then I was the only person they were expecting).

I was sent straight upstairs to await the nurse. She took

a while to get to me but I did not mind as I was the one who had already screwed up the timings. Actually, it was probably only ten minutes but it felt longer as the place was really quiet! They were not kidding that things were slow on a Friday.

The nurse arrived and led me into the typical small room to take my blood, checking all the way that I was okay with needles. As she looked through my notes she started to complain about the lack of information on the sheet until she realised I had typed it in rather than hand-written it (which I had done to make it quicker and easier to e-mail back) and thus saved her a job. She was very pleased at this.

The finance officer had gone home so they agreed to send me an invoice which was fine by me as this meant I could get out quickly. I left with instructions to call in two weeks to check if the results were ready.

Driving back up the A34 was far easier than earlier, the northbound route running well as opposed to the southbound carriageway which was now pretty much blocked from Oxford all the way down to the M4! Suddenly my hour's wait didn't feel quite so bad.

Iona had also called vet to get Bella booked in for blood tests as the vet was running an offer for old dogs. She spoke to her third very nice receptionist of the day which really cheered her up. I thought back to our old surgery, even gladder now that we had jumped ship.

June rapidly headed towards July and not for the first time I was really glad that football holds no interest for me. The previous day had been spent idling around the garden and chilling out on our deck. In the distance we had heard the anguished cries, cheers and groans as England were well and truly stuffed by Germany in the World Cup. Even before the game had finished the distant groups of fans had fallen silent, sullenly staring into their beer cans as their bangers burned on the barbeque.

Iona, Bella and I, on the other hand, had enjoyed a generally lazy day!

The fact of the matter was that we had definitely fallen into a different pace of life again. After all the frantic organising, chasing and worrying preceding our first consultation things were now more structured and sedentary.

Iona was thinking a lot about the thyroid issue and it was clearly worrying her. She had spent time on the Internet and looking through the Family Health book that lurks on our shelves at home and had already boned up on a lot of general information.

It did strike her, however, that as an underactive thyroid can clearly influence fertility why had neither our old GP nor gynaecologist tested for the condition? It was a good and rather worrying question which I tested at the first opportunity.

I typed in something along the lines of "causes of infertility in women" into Google and the very first page on the results listed problems with the thyroid as one of the classic ones.

I'm sorry but if a layman like me can find it that quickly on the Internet, surely a trained medical professional such as a GP and certainly a gynaecologist should have considered that? I checked back through all the tests that had been performed throughout the entire process but sure enough there was no record of it having ever been done.

Once again I found myself despairing at the medical system in the United Kingdom. We had apparently, so we were being told, explored every route that could affect Iona's ability to conceive but clearly we had not. They had tested her blood for just about every hormone in the book and for more major diseases than I care to think about but had missed the bleedin' obvious.

I felt quite angry, especially as it was yet another thing that we could have sorted out ages ago. Even if it had not altered Iona's reproductive capabilities, if there was a problem with her thyroid then she would not have spent the last year or so feeling so tired and struggling with weight loss, two factors that had made this a very difficult process for her.

Our previous medical support seemed to me about as effective as the England football squad. They certainly made me feel about as depressed as I am sure several million soccer fans were feeling today.

Iona finally managed to make an appointment with the doctor, the computer system having recovered sufficiently from its earlier nervous breakdown. She was to see him on Friday which meant at least by the end of the week the thyroid issue would be fully understood and, if not sorted, at least in the process of being fixed.

You have got to hand it to them, when our new surgery got their system back up and running it worked like a dream. There was a touch-screen on the reception desk that you could use to log the fact that you had arrived for your appointment and it even told you how far behind schedule they were running (and what is more, the estimate it gave was even accurate!).

In Iona's case, the nurse was running a minute behind schedule but what was amazing was the fact that she even apologised for the fact! Had that been our previous surgery (if they had a nurse which by the way they don't) we would have been at least twenty minutes late and all the time they would have made us felt like we were really disrupting their day.

More and more I was really getting to like our new

surgery and wished we had swapped ages ago. The flip side was that it was increasingly exposing the sheer negligence on the part of our previous medical advisors. The discussion we had about the fact that they had missed the thyroid issue the day before was eating at us both and when I casually remarked that it was criminal that they could get away with it the seed was sown. Perhaps they *shouldn't* get away with it.

I could feel the grumpy old man in me waving his stick and I knew in my heart that a letter was going to be written. I'm good at that, writing letters. When I used to work for the multinational packaged goods company we had on file a list of "professional complainers". After every new product launch or promotion the same twenty six people would miraculously have ruined their kitchen, bathroom, dog or carpet with whatever product had just hit the shelves.

Whenever a letter from them arrived there was a "special team" assigned to deal with them. I was on that team but so was the company lawyer.

One of my jobs had been debunking such complaints and usually it was a simple job to realise that the damage caused had been the result of a Brillo-pad on a power drill or something equally creative. People like that tend to forget that companies like the one I worked for employ people like me! That piece of paper on my wall with "BSc" written on it kind of implies that I am slightly more intelligent than your average plank of wood.

Along with one of the chemists on the brand and one or two other experts it would not take us long to find out what had *really* happened. It was a bit like teenagers who think they are being awfully clever when they try and pull the wool over their parent's eyes, forgetting that their parents were once teenagers themselves.

It did, however, make me realise that if you were not so

ambitious in your claims that you could make quite a nice living out of companies. There are many companies out there who, rather than get into a petty fight, will send out vouchers or freebies just to keep their customers satisfied. The cost of this in the grand scheme of things is negligible. I still find this somewhat dishonest if the complainer does not have a legitimate problem but at least the mentality of the company is to try and help.

Then there is the other sort of company for whom the customer service department is merely an unanswered phone or a waste-paper bin in an office somewhere. The bank we use fall into this category and without delving into the gory details they managed to screw up massively on our account and after a protracted period of serious letter-writing I managed to get them to admit defeat and even got compensation out of them in the form of good hard cash!

I am one of those people who expects at least some degree of service if I spend money and when things go wrong to have the company concerned at least make an effort to put things right.

When they don't put things right, I start to write! What is really sad is that I have found myself writing more and more frequently in recent years, an indictment to the fact that service levels in this country are dropping severely, not great for a country that relies heavily on the service industry.

For a while I seriously thought I was simply becoming a completely intolerant old fool but having spoken to a number of people who have lived abroad, Colin, for example who spent two years in the USA and another friend Damien who lived in France for a while, I realise that I am not. They all agree that service in the UK is pretty shocking but you really appreciate the fact when you spend time away from the country.

I have never had that pleasure but in many ways I am glad. If I think customer service is this appalling now I'd hate to think what a spell of overseas service would do to my impression when I finally arrived home again!

I had not written a serious complaint for a while and I will admit that deep down (okay, not even that deep) I was relishing the idea of locking horns with the local NHS primary care trust. My kung fu is strong! This time, I was not looking for compensation, all we wanted to happen was that the next poor couple who came along in our situation were given the benefit of correct medical advice and not led the merry dance we had to go through.

However, before I flew off half-cocked we agreed that we would wait for the thyroid results so that we had our facts on this before going to the PCT. That way we could hit them with the failure to spot the significance of the FSH levels, the lax analysis of my semen, and not thinking to test for issues with her thyroid.

Iona was feeling very tired and run down and even a long lie-in didn't seem to help the situation. It was worse now as when she told a few work colleagues that she had issues with her thyroid they all replied to the effect that they thought she had looked like shit for the last few months! Great, if there is one thing guaranteed to make you feel like shit it is being told you look like shit!

Still, she didn't know what I knew. Even as she was mulling over the fact of feeling so run down I was exchanging texts with her brother Paul and cooking up a plan. That meant keeping her at home until ten o'clock the next morning. Fortunately, she did not have any lessons and was able to make an excuse to be late so, with the excuse that her brother was expecting an important delivery but that I was not going to be around, I managed to set the trap.

Iona had been suspicious, that much was evident though

how much she had guessed was not certain. More likely she had assumed that Paul was being his usual disorganised self and had made us stay home for nothing.

I awoke early so I could be up and dressed and have the Bella fed and watered before the courier turned up and this also meant that Iona could have a few extra minutes in bed. I then kept out of sight waiting for Paul to give me the call.

She awoke having decided that she was going to have a bad day, which was not helped by the news that one of her friends had not only moved house but had his second child. She started to grill Paul as to what time he was leaving, assuming it had to be well before ten thus the need for her to be around. At this stage he was still in his dressing gown and clearly in no hurry to leave.

It was just as she had got into the shower that the courier arrived. I saw the van turn up so was able to follow him back to the house. He rang the doorbell and delivered two large, heavy parcels which Paul and I hastily dragged into the Kitchen.

Appearing out of the shower, Iona called down to ask if it had been the courier that she had heard and asked what the parcels were to which she was informed she had to open them to find out.

By now, the penny was dropping that she had been set up, especially as I was still blatantly around and when Paul announced that the parcels were her birthday present from us both she got the picture. It was only after she had opened the second one that she realised what it was: a six-foot diameter inflatable hot tub! That, I thought, should help to de-stress her and Paul and I had split the costs.

This might seem a bit extravagant but from my perspective it was very practical. We had already considered sending her to acupuncture or some other form of physical therapy to try and counter the stress she was under (although we now realised that some of this might be as a result of the thyroid issue). I don't know if you have ever looked into the costs of such sessions but blimey they are not cheap. Even though had paid half of the cost of the hot tub in terms of sessions at a spa it was going to "pay" for itself in about a week!

Something told me it was going to get a lot of use so would be well worth the investment.

Iona spent some time searching the Internet for pages on thyroid disorders. A lot of the information she was pulling up linked the condition with premature ovarian failure which did not sound good.

I was very glad that the spa had arrived as it would hopefully divert her attention from the whole thyroid thing which was clearly gnawing away at her.

We went home via B&Q to get some trellis panels to block off one half of the deck (and thus prevent any accidents with our over-eager dog and her remarkably sharp claws for her age which I was sure would not mix with an expensive inflatable spa).

With military imprecision, we first covered the deck with hardboard sheets (that Paul had kindly gone out and bought) and inflated the spa. The latter was not as easy as it looked as the instructions were of the "written in Mexican and translated into English via Chinese" type. The words were all English; it was just the order they were arranged in that was mildly baffling.

Eventually, it dawned on me that the different sockets and pipes were all not only different sizes but labelled in pairs so the simplest way of erecting the thing was to completely disregard the instructions. Once we had arrived at this point things went a lot faster.

Satisfied that the spa was fully inflated and the pump

and heater connected, the hosepipe was dangled over the side and the process of filling started. It was obvious that at some point in the last few weeks, evidently as a conservation measure, our local water supplier had turned down the pressure in the mains. Consequently, it took about three hours to fill the 1200 litres in the spa, all the while watching the deck nervously as the weight increased.

While it was filling and much to the dismay of the dog, Iona and I built the corral, supplementing the gaps at the ends of the trellis panels with plant pots so that the only access to the spa was via the patio doors in the living room. I could see Bella slowly reaching the point of realisation that the huge new paddling pool was *not* for her use after all.

I hope, by the way, that you appreciate that I have spent a lot of time talking about the spa. This is, of course, a guy thing as anything with power or that involves assembly is of course male domain and something we are far more comfortable talking about.

As the spa filled and I turned the heater on, I could see by the look on her face that it was going to be a winner. I discovered that she had been on Facebook and had left a message to the effect that she was pleased with it. I hoped it would live up to expectations, though there was little doubt that it would.

As July dawned it was time to get the dreaded thyroid results from the doctor. It was with mixed feelings that we went into the surgery. On the one hand, if there was a problem then on the plus side they could probably solve it with tablets and it would explain why Iona had been feeling so rubbish of late. The flip-side, of course, was that she would probably have to take pills for the rest of her life and it would confirm the incompetence of our previous doctor.

The other alternative was, of course, that her thyroid was normal. This would mean no pills on a long-term basis which was great but would leave her tiredness unchecked and would somewhat deflate my ranting on the letter to the PCT (though not completely destroy it as they still should have checked given the symptoms).

It was the latter. Iona's thyroid results were bang in the middle of the normal zone, her previous test having been just a "blip". Well, at least we knew what we were dealing with. As to her tiredness, it was probably due simply to the level of stress she had been under with everything that was going on (which made the arrival of the hot tub even more important).

We e-mailed the result to Maria along with the fact that Iona was now starting the second course of the pill. The instruction back was to contact again on day 18 for further instructions. Hurry up and wait! Something told me we were going to do this a few times before anything happened.

The only thing outstanding for us now was my cystic fibrosis result which was still a week away. There was no reason to suspect it would be positive but if the Spanish clinic were waiting for that before looking for a donor then the process was not going to be quick.

It was just as well we were going away on holiday in a week's time as I am not sure how patient either of us was going to be.

We had both realised that a change of scene was required and somewhere that neither of us had been to so, not wishing to go too far we had booked into a B&B in Chilham, Kent which we had been recommended and which seemed central enough to explore that part of the county.

Iona was pretty keen to go to Canterbury and it

happened to coincide with the Kent County show and I have always been a sucker for agricultural shows so it was an easy choice and one that would not involve too much travelling.

I just hoped that we would both be in a position to enjoy it.

# Chapter 17:
## Final preparations...

With the holiday mere days away I called the clinic for my cystic fibrosis results on the day they had stated. I got through no trouble but was told the results were not in and to call again on Thursday.

I called the clinic again as instructed and the first person I spoke to said that they would have to look up the results but promised that they would call back but typically nobody did. I naïvely sat waiting for the phone to ring for hours and eventually called again and was given the same promise. Yet again there was no call back for ages and then typically when they did phone back we were in the car and strategically driving through a mobile dead-zone so I missed the call whilst out of signal.

I rang back and this time they had the results. The receptionist got flustered about how to get them to me and asked whether I had a fax (they could not e-mail for some reason that still eludes me) but when I said all I needed was a verbal response over the phone she told me it was negative. It seemed an awful lot of effort for such a simple result. I tried to call the Spanish clinic but could not get through so I e-mailed them instead.

Even as I was feeling glad that it was all over I got an e-mail from Maria to say she needed the official cystic fibrosis results sent over. It seemed the saga was not over after all. I asked whether she could proceed without them (I guessed she wanted our legal disclaimer) but while I waited for her response I e-mailed the local clinic to see if they would fax the results directly to Barcelona as I neither had the results in hard copy or access to a fax machine or scanner to send them myself.

Just as I was considering driving to the local clinic to pick up the results in person Maria responded to say that the results were not necessary (in which case, I thought to myself, why was she banging on about them in the first place?) but at the same time I got an e-mail from the local to say they had faxed them directly! They are such nice people.

I was still confused as to whether the Spanish clinic needed them or not but at least with the results spitting out of their fax machine they could do with them as they pleased.

I was just starting to relax again and think about packing for the holiday when one of my friends called to drop the bombshell that they were expecting their third baby and that she was going to be called Anna.

We had spent a fair bit of time considering names and this was the very name we had thought of using if we had a girl! So much for that plan, we thought. Still, we were very happy for James and Fiona and it did make us realise that the whole naming thing was something we would really have to think hard about when the time came and Iona was actually pregnant.

Before any more bad news could dog us I packed the car

and we were off to sunny Kent, via a friend who had kindly offered to look after Bella. We didn't take the MG, despite the fact that the weather was nice and Iona really wanted to have the benefit of the soft top. After my experiences of the previous fortnight I knew the last thing we needed was the worry of that heap of rust breaking down on us.

The B&B was everything it had been built up to be and Chilham was very pretty. Having driven down on the Thursday we decided to stick to the village and ate in one of the local pubs which turned out to be really nice. I supped my fill of Shepherd Neame ales and we had one of the nicest meals out for as long as I could remember.

Something about the atmosphere in Chilham was really calming and we eventually slept deeply in the four-poster bed. Without going into graphic detail, if nature had not been against us, I am pretty sure Iona would have conceived that night!

The next day we headed to the Kent County Show and I was getting set for a trip to the beer tent and getting some hog roast (not that my interest in such shows is entirely based on their culinary delights, I hasten to add).

Judging by the car park, half of Kent had made the same decision that day as we seemed to be parked miles from the entrance in the middle of a field. This did not matter as we were by no means in any form of hurry.

Half-way across the vast sea of cars, my phone rang which was no big deal until I saw that the number was from abroad and more importantly from Spain.

It seemed that the cystic fibrosis result had triggered something as the call was from Maria to say they could use frozen eggs. Having reviewed our data they had managed to find a suitable match in storage rather than waiting for a new donor to present themselves! If we wanted we could start on the 31st August!

Suddenly Iona and I were both excited and terrified as we stood in the car park with Maria waiting patiently on the other end of the phone while we stared at each other.

We had at that moment arrived at the most important decision of our married lives. What we said there and then would decide the fate of the child we so hoped for. There was no guarantee of success, no reassurance that any treatment we attempted would result in viable embryos let alone a healthy baby.

In hindsight we probably should have been more reflective on the decision but as it was, after a matter of seconds we decided and the answer was yes. Shakily, I passed this on to Maria, asking her to confirm everything by e-mail along with timings just in case I had missed something in my half-dazed condition which was more than likely. After that we both walked around the show in a state of complete shell-shock.

I cannot tell you anything about what I saw at the Detling showground as my thoughts were totally absorbed in what was about to come, though for an agricultural show there did seem to be a lot of people trying to sell me double-glazing or brick-effect concrete driveways.

In a similar way, Iona went very quiet, struggling to accept the sudden turn of events.

Why we were so surprised I am not sure, it was inevitable sooner or later that Maria was going to call to say that things were moving ahead. All I can say is that we had spent so long fighting to get to that point that we had really not given much thought about the actual procedure itself or how we would cope.

I probably had a hog roast though I do not remember it. I hope it was nice. I fear it was expensive.

Fortunately I had brought my laptop so once we were done with the show, earlier than would have been the case had we not received the call I suspect in hindsight, we headed into Canterbury to find a coffee shop with Wi-Fi so I could check e-mail.

Maria e-mailed further instructions for Iona as well as a bill for payment which sent my blood pressure up as we had already paid the whole amount. Iona had to continue on the pill which was annoying as she only had supplies up until Thursday.

Worryingly, Maria went on to say that the outstanding bill needed to be paid before we could proceed. The nagging thought loomed that there was some other charge that we had forgotten or not been told about and if so our budget for the treatment was suddenly going to be sharply increased.

I sent a query in reply but knew from experience that Maria would not respond quickly. Foresight had also made me bring the purple file so this fact was easily checked and confirmed when we got back to the bed and breakfast.

It became very clear that our holiday was not going to be as relaxed as we had hoped and was going to be somewhat defined by the coffee shop we knew had internet access.

There was, however, little chance that Maria would be in contact with us over the weekend so at least we felt confident to do things that took us away from any interaction with the World Wide Web. On the Saturday we decided to go for a long walk along the cliffs above Dover and spent a lot of time talking about babies!

It was just like the day I had proposed to her and we had spent the subsequent day planning our wedding and I was filled with the same sense of excitement and anticipation. All I can say is that it was truly magical. For once, fate was looking kindly on us and provided just about the perfect weather to go for a walk, not too hot with a brisk cool breeze coming off the sea.

Despite my usual revulsion towards anything involving

excessive physical exertion we walked for miles and I loved every step. I had been so wrapped up in the process that I had not allowed myself time to indulge in the dream of being a daddy!

What was sad is that I really did not really appreciate the fabulous countryside we were heading through. Even a tour of the Shepherd Neame brewery could not capture my complete attention despite the fact that it was by far the best tour of any kind of brewery or distillery I have been on and I have done several. I have promised Iona that some day we will go back to Kent and do justice to the sights!

By Monday our holiday was effectively over. Even though we still had the rest of the week to kill our hearts were really not in it and although we did see the sights our days were always revolving around our friendly coffee shop, the staff becoming quite accustomed to our appearance.

Maria e-mailed back with further instructions for Iona but also requested her Hepatitis B results. Actually, she said she was 'reminding' us to get it done though we had not been previously told it was outstanding. This was particularly galling after the fiasco I had endured during our consultation and they could have easily done it at the same time as mine in Barcelona.

Once again I said something very rude but not on e-mail. She also confirmed that we had paid 8000 Euro but that there was an outstanding €875 which we could 'pay on the day'. After a lot of "back of a fag packet" calculations I began to suspect that she had her sums wrong and was assuming we only had 10% discount rather than a 20% one so I queried it yet again, really struggling by now to keep calm. She was really starting to annoy me by the fact that she kept getting her facts wrong.

There was one particularly good point about getting frozen eggs was that they already had them in the clinic.

I should explain at this point for those of you who are not familiar with the process that under normal donor treatment the clinic would wait until a suitable match presented themselves, screening them both for physical characteristic matching and for suitability of genetic markers (thus the cystic fibrosis test I had to take).

Once a suitable donor was identified there would then follow an intricate process by which the donor and recipient are synchronised using hormones so that the donor ovulates at the optimum time for the recipient to "receive". It's all very clever and very complicated.

To be frank it is just as well it is the woman who has to undergo that as I have not met a man on the planet who is organised enough to follow the stringent regime required and not forget to take at least half the tablets.

There is one drawback with this whole process as while they can tell you *roughly* when implantation will occur they cannot tell you *precisely*. In fact, you are lucky to get forty eight hours notice that your presence is required at which point you have to drop everything, book last-minute flights (and kiss goodbye to any chance of air miles seats or cheap deals) and head to the clinic.

You will by now have realised that I am a pathological control freak and the thought of being so out of control made me go cold. The best we could do is keep our diaries free for a period of time and hope for the best.

That, of course, was before the clinic threw us the amazing lifeline in the form of frozen eggs. There would be no synchronisation, no last-minute worries and indeed we knew the date almost immediately.

We could also book air miles seats and a nice hotel and get everything planned well in advance which really took the pressure off.

Optimistically, we were attempting to fly BA again but

hoped we were not tempting fate as the dates we were given required us to fly out over the bank holiday and therefore when Unite were likely to pay silly buggers again.

Iona phoned around to try and find some way to get the pill while we were down in Kent. We had found various NHS places on the internet which she started calling. Eventually she got through to one of the hospitals and was told to come to the family planning clinic at 2:30 that day which was good as it meant we could get it all sorted out quickly. We arrived 15 minutes early but were in there a while.

I found out when she emerged that the doctor usually would not prescribe that particular pill to women with a BMI over 30 as it increases risk of thrombosis. It was only after a lot of explaining and negotiation that Iona emerged avec tablets.

Slightly drained we headed back to the coffee shop for yet another email check.

Maria e-mailed back admitting her mistake about the money. We still need to get the Hepatitis B done so that was yet another thing to consider.

I have to admit that I was getting pretty moody at that particular moment in my life and realised that this was the point where our relationship was once again being tested. Men are really not built for this sort of thing. What is strange is that even though I recognised that I was being an arse it didn't snap me out of my mood as if the bullshit filter in my brain had ruptured.

The next day brought another blow to my blood pressure. The papers started talking about a threatened BAA strike over the bank holiday weekend which was just typical. Once again it was the Unite union but a totally unrelated issue to the cabin crew dispute. It seemed that our timing was just awful.

I realised that we had not written to complain to NHS

and were now unlikely to. Somehow I simply didn't have the energy for a fight, despite the fact that I had so much pent-up anger and frustration it was clearly having a detrimental effect on me. I so love reading the news. The bank holiday strike threat was increasing as both sides started to square up to each other. Here we go again!

The rest of the holiday was a bit subdued after that. We tried to do a few more tourist attractions but the excitement of the fact that we now had a date for implantation was tempered with the worry that yet another strike could make the whole thing needlessly stressful meant that we were really not focused on the delights of Kent.

With July rapidly winding up, we arrived home and Iona immediately called the doctor to ask about the Hepatitis B blood test. She was told to go and see the nurse the next day but at least they were going to do it. The results would then be available in about a week.

In the afternoon I sorted out the diary for when she had to take the various drugs. This in itself was a challenge as each day seemed to be different and more confusingly the dosages changing as the weeks went by. In the end I dug out an old clipboard and a pencil and clipped the diary to it. This was going to take some organising.

Whilst putting this together I found that the control scan appeared to be on the wrong day or at least something did not add up.

Again, I should explain that after the regime of pills and potions the control scan was designed to ensure that Iona's uterus was "ready". Don't ask me the ins and outs of it as this was way outside of my comfort zone but for me it was simply another box that had to be ticked and ticked in a timely fashion so that the whole process did not derail at the last minute.

The treatments were due to start on the 13th August and

control scan was stated in the paperwork we had been given from the clinic as being taken ten days after the start date but the date given on the paperwork was the 27th August. If nothing else this was very tight before we were due to fly back out to Barcelona but even in my simple mind that was two weeks not ten days.

With a sickening feeling I also counted the various pills and patches in my usual control freak way. We had plenty enough sprays but lo and behold we were 2 patches short and the Utrogestan we had been sent was, according to the packet, the oral form and not vaginal type which Iona had been expressly instructed to take! Bugger.

Iona went to see the nurse as planned to have her blood taken. The nurse confirmed that the results would be available in a week. I e-mailed the pharmacy to try and swap the Utrogestan from the oral type to the vaginal type and e-mailed a load of questions to Maria along with our take on the drug diary for them to confirm we had it right (again playing them at their own legal game).

As it was, I quickly got a note back from the pharmacy to say the drugs were okay and the correct type which could be used orally or vaginally but licensing laws meant that they could not be sold as being for vaginal use in the UK whereas the overseas instructions had dual use.

It would have been great if we had been told that in the first place, especially when the pharmacist said that I was not the first person to ask that question! I could not help but think that the whole thing was just a bit shoddy but I did wonder how many people simply never read the instructions on the drugs.

It did mean that we basically had no instructions in English for their correct use. Once again I thought that we were paying several thousand pounds for what was rapidly turning into a pretty half-baked service. To be prescribed drugs that we could not even get English instructions for was, to me, incredible.

At some point in the night and I could not tell you the time I was awoken by Iona. I had sensed that something was on her mind the day before. It was one of those occasions where she had a nagging doubt about something but could not quite put her finger on it and it was only when she went to sleep and allowed her brain to work on the problem that it made the connection.

The 27th of August was when she was supposed to be getting the Eurostar back from Paris where she was attending another teaching conference. The tickets had been booked ages ago so she had totally forgotten about it but if that was when she was supposed to be having her control scan then the trip was stuffed. Her not going would cause all sorts of issues with the school as at the time she had really had to fight to justify the trip. We tried to think of a logical solution to this one but there wasn't one. It was the trip or the scan.

For once Maria came up trumps and e-mailed with good news. Having once again put us through needless stress she admitted that she had got the date wrong and that the control scan was to be performed on the 23rd. This meant that Iona could go to the conference as she didn't leave until the 24th! Typically, however, she didn't answer the other question I had asked, about what Iona should or should not do in terms of day to day activities but we decided not to force that issue until later.

Having sorted out the latest set of problems fate decided to throw me another curve ball. Up until this point I had rather stupidly kept all the records and files relating to the treatment and the book on a single USB stick. You can see where this is going, I am sure. I had always meant to back everything up but one thing and another meant that I never quite got around to it.

You can imagine, therefore, the sickening feeling that went through me as I inserted the USB stick into the computer and heard the crack as something inside it snapped. My heart stopped and I simply stared as the computer resolutely refused to recognise there was anything there.

I went cold. Everything was on that stick, scan copies of all the paperwork, all the letters I had written but most importantly the diary and the rolling draft of the book.

Panic gripped me and not wanting to believe what had just happened I bent down to examine the damaged dongle.

One of the contacts which connected the USB socket to the printed circuit board had snapped leaving it hanging at an unserviceable angle but I had a sudden glimmer of hope. If it was just the socket that had broken then the memory should still be intact. The data was theoretically all still there.

I grabbed a pad of sticky notes, a coaster and anything else to hand and began carefully sliding them under the USB stick, raising the body until the board re-engaged with the socket.

With elation I saw the computer respond, recognising that an external drive had been attached to the port and within moments I was back in business. The next two minutes were like a major surgical procedure as I tried to manipulate the track-pad mouse on the laptop to instruct the computer to copy all the files from the USB stick to the hard drive while at the same time trying not to move or vibrate the laptop more than a few angstroms in case the stick shifted and lost connection again.

It was just as well that I did. When I pulled the stick out it left the socket hanging from the port in the side of the laptop and I knew at that point that the stick would never work again.

Still, the data was safe! For good measure I copied it all onto another stick and then burned a DVD copy as well. I was not going to risk another heart-attack again. It is amazing how an incident like this can really focus your mind on being more careful.

I did not tell Iona. Mostly because I felt like a total moron and I knew that while sympathetic with my near miss she would have reproached me for the laziness that had dropped me in the situation in the first place but also she had enough on her plate as it was. Part of me suspected that as much as we talked there were things she held back.

As August kicked in with a typically British lack of enthusiasm weather-wise a new problem appeared in the mix in the form of a job opportunity up in the exotic resort city of Hull but neither of us particularly wanted to move there. In my time I have had cause to experience the delights of Hull and, I had to say, it was not a place that inspired me much.

There have been a number of surveys over recent years that have rated the best and worst places to live in England and it is sad to say that my memory of Hull, beyond the few instantly-forgettable visits, was that it often scored top of the "worst" list.

I apologise to anyone who comes from Hull and regards it with affection, perhaps it is the southerner in me but I really cannot find anything good to say about the place. The prospect of having to actually move there was not, therefore, one that filled me with much enthusiasm.

Annoyingly enough, it was not the sort of opportunity I could turn down. I revised my CV to fit the job description and grudgingly sent it in.

Iona got her Hepatitis B results back from the doctor

and not unsurprisingly they were all negative so I scanned them and sent them to the clinic.

We put all thoughts of jobs and everything else aside. It was time to enter the next phase of the operation for in the morning Iona would commence on the drugs and thus the countdown to implantation.

# Chapter 18:
## 'T' minus 30 and counting...

It was with some trepidation that Iona started on the Synarel spray! She was terrified that she was going to get it wrong so I advised that as we had plenty of the stuff that she did a few practice squirts into the air before shoving it up her hooter. This also meant that as with all spray dispensers she could prime the dip-tube as the first squirt is always a bit rubbish. Sorry, but as a packaging engineer I have had more than a passing acquaintance with trigger packs, pump sprays and all that sort of thing.

This is the point where I really started to realise just how little input I was going to have on the whole process. Here she was embarking on a tight regime of drugs and treatments and all I could do was to provide moral support and I am not sure I was all that good in that respect.

As the line from the TV science fiction show Babylon 5 goes, "And so it begins…!"

Soon after starting on the spray, Iona showed some spotting (we are talking about blood from her girly bits for you blokes who are reading this with a Neanderthal frown) and she was getting worried about whether or not the period would start on time. I was working on the basis that the pill and the sprays would force her body into a predictable sequence but it was not my body and her periods had often in the past been erratic and undefined.

As the days went on, Iona became very worried about her period as she was not sure if it was actually starting or not even though there was some blood. The scan needed to be done during the period and she was scared that her timings were out. I was scared that she was going to worry herself into such a state that her body would be thrown totally out of synch.

On the appropriate day we were booked in for an appointment at the local clinic for her scan. Iona was very agitated on the way there. We left early as is our way so arrived nearly an hour before the appointment and had tea in the local Tesco café before going to the clinic. They were typically running late.

We were summoned into the finance office to pay first of all (all done very nicely, of course but it still felt a bit cold) and then sat in the neat but artistically sterile waiting room for 40 minutes before Iona was finally called. The scan went okay – they confirmed she has slight polycystic ovary syndrome, mostly on the left ovary. Apart from that, everything looked normal and they faxed the results to Barcelona for us. I asked for a copy of my cystic fibrosis result for the file and we left.

On the way back, Maria called to confirm that they had received the fax but wanted to double check that Iona was on day 1 which I said she was (as that was as far as we could tell the truth). This got me worrying now but I didn't want to say anything at the time. She said she would e-mail today or tomorrow to confirm that Iona could go ahead with the patches as soon as she had shown the doctor the scan results. Iona was very relieved that things were normal.

We got home and I was pleased to see that Iona pottered around the house far more her normal self. I did not question her but it was plain to see that whatever her fears were the results of the scan had gone a long way towards reassuring her.

Things were even better the next day as Maria confirmed by e-mail that Iona could proceed with patches as of Friday! I e-mailed her back to ask about dos and don'ts (that she had not responded on before).

We finally received the instructions from Maria as to what Iona could and could not do (she could swim and bathe but not use the whirlpool and she had to avoid cats, raw meat and uncooked vegetables).

In the news, the Unite workers at BAA voted to strike so the threat of Bank Holiday airport closures was now even more likely. My blood pressure was now off the scale when it came to the union action.

Friday arrived and with it another milestone as Iona started on the patches! She was on one at a time initially and the nasal spray dosage reduced down to one morning & evening.

I helped her with the patch as the instruction was to stick it in what, for her, was not the most convenient place to reach (i.e. her buttocks). I was very nervous attaching the first one but it seemed to be well-designed, flexible and waterproof and almost invisible! Once again the packaging scientist in me took over and my professional interest overrode my fear of screwing it up.

It was scary to think that we were now on stage two of the process! Iona was also very relieved that her period had come full-on so there were no issues there.

For the first day she walked around like a robot, afraid to make any actions that would cause the patch to unstick itself but it became quickly apparent that they were so well designed nothing she could do made any impact on its adherence. Indeed, it was only when the time came for the first patch to be removed and replaced with a fresh one that we discovered just how well it was stuck. Iona said something rude as I tore it off and a good number of fine hairs with it!

Although I had forgotten about the latest job application, others had not and after a brief exchange on the telephone with the recruitment agency I reluctantly went to their local office for a chat. Despite my desperation to find a job I had really hoped that this one would, like all the others, fall through but for once it looked like I had a good shot. This was, of course, utterly typical!

As the days went on Iona began to feel odd as the hormones kicked in. Again, as a bloke it was alien to me to try and understand what it must feel like to have your system flooded from the outside with such radical chemicals.

I had more news about the job and it looked like first interview would potentially be on the 25th so the very next week (and just when Iona was heading off to Paris)!

It felt strange, finding myself in a real déjà-vu situation – planning a trip to Barcelona while worrying about airport strikes and job interviews!

Fortunately, Unite& BAA managed to get their act together and it was announced on the ten o'clock news that they had reached an agreement – the strike was off so this time we would be able to go BA business class!

The next day brought about an incident which brings me on to a very tricky subject and one that I had not really considered until it happened. I am probably going to get into a lot of trouble for this one but there is something that all guys know which is that there is a certain time of the month as the hormones are kicking in when transgressions which would normally be ignored become major crises.

In Iona's case, she was artificially flooding her system with hormones and I guess I should have seen it coming. She had been getting snappy for the last few days but really tore my head off for what would normally have been nothing. We were driving somewhere, I do not recall where, when a particularly bad driver overtook me and carved me up so closely that another millimetre and he would have taken the dirt off my bumper.

I shouted my usual and utterly futile expletive at the moron, despite that he could neither hear nor care what I said but even though she does it all the time Iona really had a go at me.

It really had not been all that big a deal but you would have thought by her reaction that it was nearly grounds for divorce.

I realised it was going to be a rocky few weeks!

The situation was not helped by the fact that as the treatment progressed, the dosage increased and she was up to two patches on alternate days now. I had to work out a scheme for moving the patches around different parts of her bum and ended up with a series of areas (upper left, lower right, that sort of thing) around which I regularly cycled the new patches.

As time went on the areas became quite obvious as her skin always held an after-image of where the previous patches had been as her rear end started to look like a parody of the Microsoft Windows logo.

For me the worst thing was that under stressful conditions I would normally reach for a drink but as I was going to have to 'perform' for real when we reached the clinic alcohol was most certainly off the agenda until after I had provided my precious sperm.

Things were really starting to get tense and I really needed a drink. Blokes beware, if you are going to give up the booze (which you should) then be prepared to suffer!

We had various social gatherings around this time and I really needed (so I thought) a drink and was grumpy as I could not. I was even grumpier as it became increasingly difficult to explain why I was not drinking, especially as everyone we were with knew how fond I was of the odd beer or wine here or there. I cannot remember exactly what thin excuses I used but I do recall they sounded rather unconvincing, though quite what they thought was actually going on I cannot imagine.

With the summer rapidly passing and the number of doses crossed off on the drug diary increasing at an alarming rate it was time for her next scan.

I had, as you will have gathered before, been both fortunate and dutiful enough to attend all the major events in her treatment so far but by now it was all becoming somewhat of a blur.

In this latest scan the radiologist cheerfully announced that her endometrium was okay, showing good thickness and three stripes. Apparently this was good but I simply stood there smiling and nodding sagely where in fact I didn't have a clue what they were talking about. The only bit I latched onto was the "okay" part. As long as there wasn't a problem then everything was fine.

Her reputation had preceded her when it came to her crap veins so when it came to taking blood for yet more tests (progesterone, I think but again I was totally lost) they dispensed with the vacutainers completely and simply went for the honking big syringe! Whatever it was they were looking for we would get the results within the day and it was all very routine apart from one crucial fact. It was the last thing we would have to do before leaving for Barcelona…or so I thought.

I should have realised that it had, by now, been some time since we had experienced some form of cock-up so I should have not been surprised when Maria e-mailed to confirm that I was to report for "duty" at the clinic on the following Monday but it was clear from her e-mail that for some reason she assumed that I would be travelling alone. This was apparent by the fact that she also gave instructions for Iona to go for her last scan on that day before she also flew over.

The usual sick feeling came over me as I feared we had totally missed something. I was sure I had checked and triple-checked all the paperwork and instructions and if I had not, Iona had certainly read them a dozen times. How could we both have missed the fact that she needed another scan?

Simple – nobody had told us it was needed. Nowhere in the paperwork was it mentioned that she would need to get this additional scan at that time.

Trying to maintain an air of decorum, I contacted the clinic and politely explained the situation not least the fact that we had already booked our flights and that Iona would be with me when I arrived to do what a man has to do on the Monday morning. Given that she had so recently gone for a scan, was this additional one absolutely necessary?

Of course the answer came back that it was but that it was no problem, they could do it in Barcelona when we were there.

No problem apart from that it was another expense that we had not been accounting for! An undercurrent of anger seethed in me. What other hidden extras were going to emerge before this was all over? The only mild consolation was that the exchange rate with the Euro was favourable at that time so we were going to "save" a few quid by not having it done in England.

We were now mere days away from heading to Spain but as was typical with us, rather than just having a quiet few days to prepare, Iona had to head off to Paris for her conference while I made the journey to Hull and back for my interview. Curiously, neither of us was in the least prepared for our respective trips.

The one thing that did have to be said was that this was probably the best thing that could have happened to us. We were both more than a little tense and, even without the hormones (as I certainly did not have the excuse of them) we were getting rather tetchy with each other. As much as I wanted to support her I suspected that a couple of days apart would do us both the world of good.

As she left for Paris I was left for an evening on my own, a rare enough event these days but being on the wagon as I was in order to give my sperm at least a fighting chance of being in prime condition my usual beer and kebab session was out of the question. To be honest, even had this not been the case my heart was really not in it.

I made a half-hearted attempt to prepare for the interview which mostly amounted to checking out the company on the internet and glancing at their website but again I could not generate the enthusiasm so wound up having an early night as soon as I had the call to say she was settled in at the hotel safe and sound.

You will forgive me if I focus on my part here, I gather that Iona's conference went well, long and mildly tedious as these things tend to be but generally informative if uneventful.

My interview was not until the afternoon so I had plenty of time to make the three hour drive up. It was inevitable that my inherent loathing of being late for anything combined with my general terror at the fact that I was actually going for a job interview meant that I arrived at the outskirts of Hull embarrassingly early.

This was not a huge problem as there lies about twenty minutes west of the city a rather convenient example of a national chain of café eateries where sales reps from around the country gather before making the final push to whatever prospective customer they are calling on.

I stopped here for a well-needed pot of tea, a totally unnecessary "Olympic" breakfast and a general "psyche myself up" session. Even as I was heading towards the car again I realised that the second breakfast had been a terrible mistake. Although I had managed to avoid ketchup and coffee stains on my shirt I could feel my stomach beginning to gurgle as the fatty food hit the acid. As I had spent most of the morning working myself up there was a lot of this. I just hoped I could make it through the interview without making too many embarrassing noises.

By the time I had found where I was heading, parked and obtained a visitors pass I managed to arrive in the reception area at precisely the prescribed time along with the two other hopeful candidates.

As I sat down my stomach made a slight grumbling noise which did not put me at ease though it clearly amused the other two interviewees.

Being politically correct and much to my relief we were interviewed in alphabetical order and while I did not know the names of the other two they clearly started with a letter of the alphabet later than "F".

I was called up by a very serious-looking lady from human resources and led like a lamb to the slaughter to the interview panel, three equally serious-looking and senior members of the department I was applying for.

There is no point giving a lengthy description of the interview here, mostly as it is of no relevance whatsoever to the wider story but suffice to say it only really dawned on me as the first question was fired at me how little I had prepared.

Whether it is a stress response or some strange form of "fight or flight" I do not know but I have a strange talent of being able to sound convincing when put on the spot. This seemed to kick in during the interview as, despite having done no preparation whatsoever, the slated hour-long interview took nearly two and by the time I found myself back in reception the other candidates (who I guessed had either been given the wrong arrival times or had turned up early regardless) were both looking far less relaxed than after my gut gurgle.

They still had the ordeal to face, I was free to go and go I did, as fast as possible to the first service station with a toilet to remedy my earlier gluttony.

Depression sank in during the drive home as the realisation hit me that I should have taken the interview far more seriously. We needed me to be in employment and while Hull was far from desirable it did not mean we had to live there. The surrounding area has some very lovely places and we could have made it work.

It was too late now. I had chuntered on for nearly two hours and probably made a complete idiot of myself so it was all academic. I vowed that the next opportunity that presented itself would be handled with far more respect.

When I spoke to Iona that night I was absolutely desperate for a beer, not that I told her this. She inevitably asked how the interview went and I felt like a charlatan as I gave her a trite non-committal response (also omitting any mention of the trip to Little Chef). I knew she had wanted to be there for me and I really wished at that moment that she *had* been there. Still, the conference would finish in the morning and she would be home.

I had another early night but barely slept as my mind was full of lost opportunities with the job, the prospect that I was therefore still desperate for work and the date for our trip to Barcelona was looming very close now.

Although I had not updated "The Journey" for many days now I was in such a bleak mood that I simply kept notes on a pad of paper. While I wanted the book to be honest it did not feel right to allow such self-absorbed sullenness to contaminate the pages. I would write this part when I had cheered up a bit after Iona had returned.

When I woke I felt absolutely terrible partly through lack of sleep but mostly through having worried myself into a complete state for half the night. Despite this I was up and about at a good time which was just as well as the phone rang even as I was emerging from the shower.

I had passed the first interview and was being progressed to a second.

To be honest I was stunned. I was even more stunned to hear that I was the *only* candidate being progressed. The job was basically mine to win or lose. The company was very keen to fill the vacancy and wanted me back up in Hull the following week…

Once again I panicked. How could I explain that this would not be possible as we would be over in Spain making a baby? I managed through my blustering to communicate that we were on holiday and that the following week would not be possible so a compromise was settled on that I would go the week after. The only problem was that the interview would be the very day after we got back from Spain.

This was the worst possible scenario. All I wanted to do in Barcelona was to leave all our other worries behind and focus on the task at hand but now I had a second interview to plan and this time I had to take it seriously.

It also struck me that there was a far deeper consequence. Assuming the treatment worked okay we had already formed a vague plan as to what Iona would do during the pregnancy and the support she would get from her parents. If we were to move to Hull then all this would change. Life was about to get very complicated.

My head was still buzzing with all of this when Iona arrived back. Before I had even uttered a word she could see that I was troubled and when I told her the news she went through the same emotions as I, elation that I had passed the first interview but then trepidation at the thought that I might actually get the job and the radical change this would mean in our lives.

It was a lot to think about. All we could do was pack for Spain and wait to see how things panned out.

By this time I *really* needed a drink and I hated to think what sort of effect it was having on Iona but it could not be good. The last thing she needed in the build-up to implantation was stress but there was absolutely nothing we could do about it.

Not for the first time I wished I had better timing in life.

# Chapter 19:
## Chocks Away…

If I had thought that job interviews churned my stomach then I was in for a shock. The day finally arrived for us to head back to Barcelona and I awoke feeling really sick, so much that I could not face breakfast (which, for me, is *really* sick not just man-flu sick).

We had packed the night before (and what should have been a simple process had taken around two hours as we were both determined not to forget a single thing and as a result had certainly over-done it with the amount of "useful" stuff we stuffed into our cases).

Iona was as impatient to go as I so once we realised we were ready and just farting around the house looking for things to check we got in the car for the drive to Heathrow. I will not embarrass us by saying how early we were going to be, assuming the traffic was not rubbish, but at least this time the comfort of the British Airways lounge awaited us.

Typically, today of all days when we had all the time in the world the traffic was free-flowing and we found ourselves pulling into the long-term car park stupidly ahead of schedule. There was not even a wait for the shuttle bus. No sooner had we arrived at the bus-stop than it pulled up. At any other time I can guarantee to be standing there for at least five minutes. It is a universal constant that whenever you are in a hurry circumstances will contrive to make you late whereas give yourself all the time in the world and everything will fall in place seamlessly.

I had checked us in on-line the evening before "just in case" so we didn't even have that to do and just made our way to the fast-track in security, reserved for business travellers, first class and holders of higher-tier BA Executive Club cards. Indeed, there seemed to be so many criteria that qualified passengers to use fast track that there were more people queuing there than in the normal line! Still, it was our only delay and then a fleeting one.

Emerging the other side and going through the usual ritual of putting back on shoes, belt, watch and all the other paraphernalia we headed to the lounge. I was shaking with anticipation and it was really hard to sit there and stare at the booze but not be able to imbibe although it was late morning and even I draw the line at that (unlike some who were happily tucking into the hard stuff!). In consolation they were still serving breakfast so a mound of bacon rolls and gallons of cappuccino gave me something to focus my attention on.

It is funny how the sight of the bacon rolls cured my earlier nausea!

Iona took a more modest approach to the free refreshments and had a cup of tea and some fruit.

For those of you not familiar with the joys of airline lounges they are strange animals and vary wildly on what they offer. The BA lounges probably represent the top end of what you can get and on offer is a wide range of refreshments from alcoholic and non-alcoholic beverages to a wide variety of foods.

You can tell those who have money or who are paying business travellers as they use the lounge for its intended purpose, a comfortable place to wait until their flight is called.

Then there are the other types of travellers, those on economy tickets who have lounge access by merit of their BA Executive card, poorer folk who are fortunate to be sent on business by their companies…and fat so and so's like me. These tend to arrive at the lounge as early as possible and scoff as much as they can in the time allowing.

It is incredible how much some people can devour in an hour! I will admit to consuming probably more than my intended "allowance" on the rare occasions I have the luxury of lounge access but I have seen some who spend the time either power drinking or attempting to eat their own bodyweight in cheese.

No wonder the flights are so expensive!

As I have mentioned before my past life has permitted a certain level of business travel and certainly enough to make me an "old hand" at the whole travelling thing and one thing that always seems to ring true when going through Heathrow is that no matter what flight I am on, regardless of airline or destination, when I look at the departure board at least four flights in the list after mine will always be called before the one I am taking.

I am sure it isn't really like this (another supermarket check-out queue scenario) but I forget how often the flights directly before mine are boarding, several flights after mine have "go to gate so and so" while mine simply says "wait in lounge". It is almost like someone notices that I have booked a flight and does it to wind me up, knowing what a control freak I am.

Still, clock-watching and staring at the departure-board probably curbed my grazing.

By the time we were summoned to the gate it was obvious that we were not going to be leaving on schedule, either that or they were going to have to board the plane in record time.

Some of the people who I interviewed when putting together this tale informed me that when they travelled for their foreign treatments they would take a morning flight for an afternoon appointment! That would have driven me completely nuts, especially as our departure time came and went and we were all still loitering in the gate area.

As it was, we were less than an hour delayed which is not an uncommon occurrence in Heathrow but it was still a huge relief to be in the air and on our way to the Iberian Peninsula. For me, I would not be happy until we reached the hotel. Iona I am sure would not relax for the next nine months.

Barcelona airport was just as we remembered it and we felt very jet-set knowing our way to the taxi rank. As is my way I had a slip of paper with the hotel name on it as I am the world's worst when it comes to trying to make myself understood in the local lingo and while most Europeans put us Brits to shame with their linguistic abilities I have found from long experience that this is the simplest way to ensure you get to where you want to be.

He promptly therefore became hideously lost. In his defence it was not entirely his fault as the hotel we had booked into was very new and in a part of the city undergoing a radical redevelopment which meant that many of the roads were closed, operating on diversions or generally screwed up so that it seemed every day there was a new and bewildering layout. It didn't help that the hotel was so new they had not put up the name boards so it was essentially from the outside an anonymous building.

Our driver knew where he was *supposed* to be, he simply could not find how to get there. He was so apologetic he only charged us a small fare though we compromised on what I thought was a fair payment that we had expected to pay. He was not to know that we were not in a hurry, something I had just discovered as I was digging out the reservation paperwork for the hotel only to discover that check-in time was 4PM and it was only 3:15.

Normally this is not a problem. Most hotels while having a check-in time policy will let you take up your room early so long as the cleaners have done their bit. Not this place. There was not even an attempt to call to see if the room was ready. Check in time was not until 4PM so we were to come back at 4PM. They did at least say we could go to the bar by the pool to wait which is what we did.

Anyone who at that moment wanted to set an atomic clock could have done it with me as I returned to the front desk right on the stroke of four.

I was told to wait five minutes. A very small black cloud appeared over my head and I would imagine my hair stood on end as the tiny lightning bolt struck out but I meekly returned to the bar and did as I was told.

Five minutes later I was told to wait another twenty as the room was not ready. The black cloud crackled another small spark of lightning and this time I stood my ground. They had thrown the rules at me so I threw them right back. Check-in time was advertised as 4PM so I wanted my room. Now!

Two minutes later the room was ready and we took possession.

The full scale lightning storm then kicked off. We had booked the room specifically as it came with a kitchenette so we could more easily self-cater. For sure there was a kitchenette but it was sealed behind a locked panel.

The girl on reception was clearly not glad to see me again, especially when she saw the look on my face. After a lot of arguing and an extra payment of 20 Euros on my part (mostly as I was losing the will to live by that point) she finally agreed to send someone up to unlock it. This was probably just as well as the mood I was in I would have happily spent the twenty euros on a serviceable crowbar.

I had a feeling this hotel was not going to be open for very long with this kind of service.

Seeing that I needed to calm down, Iona dragged me out to the local Carrefour to get supplies and by the time I had filled our shopping bag with cold meats, cheeses, nice bread and various other yummy things I was back to my old self.

This lasted about five seconds when we got back to the room. While we had a kitchen we had nothing of any use in it such as pots, pans, utensils or cutlery. It was almost as if they were deliberately going out of their way to wind me up.

Not to be defeated the old British "make do" spirit kicked in and my British Airways Executive Club card was put to good use as a butter knife. The truth of course was that I really could not be bothered to go out again to buy some plastic ones.

By now I really did need to cool off both emotionally and physically so we checked out the pool which was freezing but fabulous. After that we retired to the room to chill out. I had brought our laptop and some DVD's so we had an impromptu movie night as neither of us felt like doing anything else. At the back of our minds was the thought that the process would start for real tomorrow.

Neither of us slept much that night and when we woke

in the morning we were both oddly subdued, eating our breakfast in near silence before heading to the metro.

As I was led back to the familiar little room Iona was taken next door for the futile attempt at giving blood samples. While I fumbled with the pile of magazines I could hear her faint apologies as the nurse dug around to find a vein.

Having prior experience of the little room did not make it any more inspirational, especially as this was the most important "delivery" I had ever made.

The magazines were new, clearly replaced on a regular basis to only have the most recent examples and I took one at random. Given that my last attempt at pot luck had revealed the grinning face of Richard Branson I was sure that things could not get any worse, especially as I headed straight for the centrefold.

Well, I have to say I was expecting something better than Marge Simpson. It was all I could do to suppress a laugh as I am sure that would have not given the right impression to anyone walking past.

Somehow I managed to find enough inspiration to do what I needed to do and once again I was summoning the staff to take my clipboard and sample pot.

By the time I was reunited with Iona in the upstairs waiting room I was shaking, all too aware of the significance of what I had just done. They called her in for her scan and to this day I could not tell you what they were looking for – presumably looking at her endometrium again but whatever it was they seemed happy with the result and that, as they say, was that.

I tried not to think about my sample pot which by now would already be in the lab and about to be introduced to the waiting eggs. We were bustled out of the door with the promise that they would call the next day to let us know how many viable embryos they had.

My part was now over and even the good news that I could now have a drink did not go far to dispelling the trepidation I now felt. What if my sperm had been too bad to use? After everything we had been through and more particularly all the preparations Iona had gone through the thought that it could all go wrong now made me feel quite queasy.

I tried to lighten the situation by suggesting that if we had twins we called them Bog and Off (after BOGOF – buy one get one free). Iona wasn't in the mood for Christmas Cracker jokes so I shut up. We nearly walked out without the latest prescription for more patches and tablets.

Even though we were not expecting a call until the next day I turned my phone on as soon as we were out of the building just in case they needed to contact us for any reason whatsoever.

With nothing else to do we went in search of a chemist to cash in the prescription but when I looked at it the numbers that were written down were not enough to see Iona through to the end of the treatment! We were not desperate for them but it was yet another niggling thing we had to put right and we would have to get a replacement when we went back in for the implantation.

I had a sudden appetite once the tension of the sperm-delivery had passed and we found a nice little park to eat our rolls (hacked apart with our room door-key as it was the only thing we had with a serrated edge) and this reminded us to go shopping for some more reliable cutlery. I also picked up a bottle of local wine to go with dinner and for once Iona did not frown at my intended alcohol consumption.

Don't get me wrong, I am not a raving alcoholic and giving up the booze for the cause was a no-brainer but there does come a point where a bloke needs a good drink and I had long passed mine.

We ambled our way back to the room, the conversation drifting through a multitude of irrelevant topics as we resolutely avoided the one subject that was on both our minds. Although we had not seen the lab we were both trying to visualise the petri-dish of eggs, willing them to succeed.

Once again we stayed in the room that evening, somehow not wanting to be around people and another movie night ensued. Iona fell asleep during the second film but I did not wake her but sat sipping my wine as I watched her slumbering. It felt incredible that within a few days she would potentially be pregnant.

They had been a bit vague as to when they would call but the implication had been that it would not be until after lunch so we headed to the beach to sit and chill. The outside temperature was not bad and there was thin cloud which meant the sun was not beating down on our pasty English skin.

Iona went for a bit of a paddle but I was content to simply sit and watch the world go by until I realised how many topless ladies there were on the beach, regrettably only a few of whom were in the least attractive. I became deeply conscious that I was a married man and window shopping was really not appropriate, especially on a day like this.

Being totally British in my long trousers and shirt (though I had stopped short of the knotted hankie on my head), I turned my attention to the novel I had brought and read that instead.

Having eaten lunch and with the afternoon dragging by, we wondered whether we would get the call at all and at what time we should contact the clinic to find out what was happening. There had not been any kind of contingency plan so we were a bit lost.

At a quarter past three our agony was ended as the

phone went and I recognised the number. Iona could not even look in my direction as, hand trembling I took the call and spoke to Maria.

Eleven eggs had been defrosted out of which ten had matured and seven had developed to embryos. Success! Transfer was set for five in the afternoon on the Friday and she asked us to present ourselves no later than four as Iona would need to drink loads to fill her bladder.

Ending the call I turned to relay the good news to Iona and at that precise moment the sun came out. It was a good sign and we basked in the crepuscular rays of hope.

That evening we went out for dinner for the first time even though we were both still tense. For me, however, I knew that the pressure was off and that it was now all about Iona. My role had fundamentally changed to one of support as the emphasis shifted entirely to my beloved wife.

When we got back to the hotel I finally felt inspired to sit down and write, going through my copious notes and catching up with the book. I was even more determined now that I would record everything for the future. Sperm and eggs were united and had become embryos. The process of making a new life had well and truly started.

It felt strange, while I had not really given it much thought when I actually looked at the evolving document I realised with a shock that I had already written nearly a hundred and fifty pages. The temptation to go back and read sections was incredibly strong but I resisted, knowing that if I did I would no doubt be tempted to start editing and this went against everything Iona and I had intended for the record.

Once I had brought the text up to date I handed the computer over to Iona and let her add her own thoughts and feelings, something I knew was important at this critical juncture. This was not all about me and if, God willing, Iona did carry through a successful pregnancy and the child grew to an age of understanding then it was important that this record of events came from us both.

I did not read what Iona wrote but by the intense look on her face the emotions being committed to virtual paper were strong.

We had been in limbo up until this point and had not been able to plan anything but now we had one full day in which there was nothing we could do which meant that at last we could be tourists again.

In our previous visits we had pretty much done all the sights in the city so we had already decided once we knew what the plan was to head out and visit Monserrat and this we did in the morning.

Wandering around the great religious site was just what we needed. I could see that Iona was lost in her thoughts as we sat down to listen to the choir, no doubt making her own private communion with God. While not especially religious myself I was still moved to make a silent prayer of my own, if not for me but for Iona for whom this while process meant everything.

A day of trampling around – Monserrat is at the top of a small mountain and you cannot get around without negotiating stairs or sloping streets – as well as plenty of fresh air left us somewhat exhausted.

Normally when I travel I like to fit in with local customs but in Spain this includes eating really late, well after nine in the evening. I knew there was no chance that either of us would be even awake by then and could not certainly last so long without eating so, as much as I hated fitting in with all the other tourists, we found ourselves heading to Las Ramblas to find a Tapas bar.

Experience had already shown that unlike the local's eateries which would still be dark and empty at six in the evening, the restaurants catering for tourists would be open, if quiet. The drawback was that the food was rarely the best but we were so foot-weary by now that we really didn't care.

A few small plates of finger food rapidly became an exploration of half the menu, washed down in my case with a couple of very large glasses of the local Estrella Damm beer.

Despite being tired we walked back to the hotel but when we got back, long before the city really came to life in the evening, we were already turning into bed. Tomorrow was going to be a big day.

# Chapter 20:
## "I-Day"

One of the drawbacks of going to bed early was that we were awake the next morning at the crack of dawn. Okay, it was not entirely the fault of retiring before nine and once again our sleep had been broken and poor quality. I tried not to think of all the sleepless nights we would have once the baby was born and how many we had missed before even getting to the stage of Iona becoming pregnant.

For anyone reading this who has managed to just "get on with it" and conceive naturally, do not underestimate how lucky you are. This afternoon was effectively our point of conception and here we were already frazzled with stress.

We had been given a whole list of instructions as to what we had to do that day, one of which was that we had to avoid any heavily-scented products. Typically, therefore, the weather forecast was for it to be hot and humid and as we were not due to arrive at the clinic until 4PM we were going to be ripe by the time we appeared.

It also meant that we had around eight hours to kill and no inclination to do anything so, unable to think of anything else to do, we headed back to the beach with another picnic and the remnants of the books we were reading.

I wondered how many of the seven embryos they would implant and an odd thought occurred to me. For some reason my drifting thoughts compared the embryos to some weird parallel of my own recent life and that they had reached the first interview stage of some strange job offer, having been selected from eleven original candidates.

Somewhere in the clinic they were now being sorted into those that would go in – the second interview from which only the strongest would progress.

I had many strange thoughts like that throughout the morning which plodded along with interminable slowness. The book I had brought was not helping and the few attempts I had made to read had ended with me staring at the same page for five minutes until the realisation that I had not taken in a single word dawned on me. Eventually I gave up all pretence and simply sat and watched the world go by.

Around one in the afternoon we had a call from the clinic to say that the implantation had been brought forward by half an hour so we were to present ourselves at three-thirty. This was good news as anything that shortened the endless wait was music to our ears.

The day was rapidly becoming hotter than the forecast had predicted so we made the decision to arrive unfashionably early mainly as the clinic had a coffee machine and was air conditioned. Better to sit in the waiting room and cool down for half an hour than arrive hot and flustered.

We were both very apprehensive and must have annoyed everyone else there we were fidgeting so much. The other couples were obviously at different stages of the process. Some were clutching their introduction packs, just embarking on their own journeys, others had different folders, no doubt in for scans or other treatments of the type that we had undertaken back in England.

Every now and then a woman would appear but be taken elsewhere and I wondered if they were the donors.

Gradually, however, the place began to thin out. At three-thirty Iona drank the required three glasses of water and then sat quietly trying to think of anything other than the fact that she would need the bathroom which of course only exacerbated her need to pee.

One by one, the other couples were called in and were dealt with, the newcomers heading via the finance office to cough up the required pile of Euros. I also noticed that the number of staff was dwindling rapidly as the afternoon wore on until we were the only ones left and even the receptionist had gone home.

Had they forgotten about us? With nobody to ask, all we could do was sit there until eventually someone came out and said that the lab were running late so that it would be another half an hour. I sensed more than heard Iona groan as the pressure of her bladder became nearly critical.

Five minutes later we were told there was another delay but much to her relief Iona was told to go to the ladies and then start again with the water. I have never seen her move so fast!

Inevitably they had one more administrative error up their sleeve before the implantation finally began. We were called up, all excited that we were finally going in, only to be taken to the finance office and asked to pay the outstanding thousand Euros on our account.

Frustratingly the person we were dealing with spoke only broken English so it took me quite a while to explain that they had screwed up and that we had paid in full to the point that I ended up having to drag out the purple file, dig through to find all the invoices and wave them under the terrified young man's nose.

Finally realising that it was their mistake he apologised profusely and then announced that we still had to pay another two hundred and fifty Euros for the defrosting of the eggs. Another stealth fee that I am sure had never been mentioned. Interestingly, when he actually processed our account it spat out an invoice for a hundred and sixty Euros as we had somewhere been overcharged by the balance of ninety (which they had mysteriously failed to spot up until that moment).

It was a wonder they stayed in business with accounting like that.

Frankly at that point I would have emptied my wallet and tipped all the money I was carrying on the desk, I could see that Iona was about to burst with anticipation and just wanted to get on with it.

The latest administrative pantomime over, we were sent back out into the waiting room. The clinic had a decidedly "closed" feel about it and it was pretty obvious that we were the only patients still there. I was beginning to wonder if it was all yet another mistake when we were finally called up to the laboratory level (it was now nearly six in the evening).

As had been explained to us before we were entering a clean room environment so we would have to wear surgical scrubs and remove most of our own clothes. Iona was provided with one of those fashionable rear-opening gowns and matching slippers while I had a more conventional ensemble consisting of blue trousers and short-sleeved top, again coordinated tastefully with blue slippers.

Now, as I have explained before I do not possess the most athletic of physiques but the fact of the matter was I had been at the clinic a sufficient amount of time for them to know my general proportions. Why, therefore, they felt the need to give me a pair of trousers that were at least six sizes too small I will never know.

I had no way of asking anyone for something more suitable but fortunately I had worn sensible underwear that day (and of a colour and style that were not too "revealing") so I had no choice but to strut around with my fly agape. Regrettably the top was not long enough to cover my embarrassment.

When they came for us, despite the fact that I was clearly suffering a major wardrobe malfunction nobody thought to try and find something more appropriate. I have to say the whole experience was quite belittling and nearly spoiled the whole thing for me.

They were taking the clean room thing very seriously. Having passed what was essentially an airlock and walked over a huge sticky pad taped to the floor to remove any foreign matter from the soles of our slippers, we were then presented with hair nets to wear and even little bags to slip over our feet to cover the slippers.

Apparently the fact that my fly was agape did not seem to matter in the otherwise sterile conditions.

Thus prepared (I was very glad there were no mirrors around as I must have looked a proper berk) we were then led through the final door and into the treatment room. Beyond I could just make out through the small round windows in the next doors the lab beyond where the real magic must have happened but we were not to go that far.

Iona was told to get on the bed while I was ushered into a chair by her head so that I would be facing the consultant (who, incidentally would also be staring at my underpants and I hoped that would not be too off-putting for her).

When the familiar figure of our consultant came in she did not seem in the least bothered by my attire and pretty soon I had forgotten all about it as well.

While the news was promising things were getting tighter. Out of the seven embryos that had matured five were of good quality and the plan was to implant two and freeze three. This left two other embryos which they were not sure about and they were going to allow them to develop for another two days before they made the decision whether or not to keep and freeze them.

We barely registered this fact at the time as our consultant put the petri dish containing the two embryos on a projector and the enlarged image appeared on the wall. There they were, no more than clusters of seven to eight cells but the sight was magical.

The procedure itself was depressingly simple. After everything that had happened, all the stress, the worry, all the niggling things that had gone wrong, it was over in a few moments.

I could see what she was doing on the ultrasound scan monitor but to be honest it did not make a lot of sense to me. I was more interested in the fact that she seemed happy with what she had done.

It was as simple as that. The consultant wished us well, gave us a replacement prescription (I only just remembered to explain the earlier error) as well as instructions for what Iona should do next.

As she was not allowed to move they wheeled her back to the room we had changed in and we were alone.

By now Iona was busting for a wee again! I was as well and I have to admit that rather than be a gentleman and suffer with her I made use of the en-suite facilities before changing out of my comical costume.

They had told her to stay still for fifteen to twenty minutes but she was absolutely paranoid that if she coughed, sneezed, farted or even spoke too loudly that she would dislodge her precious cargo so it was nearly half an hour before she felt confident to get up and relieve herself. We passed the time comparing notes on the experience, both realising that it was one of those times that would just become a blur in our memories. I took out my notepad and hastily scribbled down as many details as I could no matter how small and even as I was doing so I realised that the memory was already becoming vague.

Iona eventually dressed but when I poked my head out of the door there was nobody around. We had not been told what to do next and as we had her prescription and all the instructions we assumed that was it.

We gave it another five minutes to see if anyone would appear but as nobody did, with a sense of anti-climax, we eventually let ourselves out.

I could see that Iona was walking very carefully, still afraid that any sudden move would send the embryos flying out of place so I steered her to the nearby taxi rank and splashed out for a cab back to the hotel. I could see by the look on her face she was grateful.

Our last night in Barcelona was another quiet one for now was starting what would possibly be the most difficult part of the whole process.

Despite the money, despite the incredible medical science that had been brought to bear and regardless of the months of stress and heartache we had been through, there was no guarantee that the procedure would be a success and that the embryos would take. It would be two weeks before we knew whether Iona was truly pregnant when we went for her official test.

For sure she could do the whole "wee on a stick" thing before but even that was not a hundred percent reliable and we had already decided to wait for the doctors to confirm it for sure.

Two weeks we would have to wait, two agonising weeks.

What made it even worse was the fact that almost nobody knew what we were up to. Aside from her mother, who Iona phoned that evening to give a thorough update, we had not told a soul so we would now have to live for the next fortnight with such a huge secret, both on edge awaiting the outcome.

This is one of the really tough parts of IVF treatment. If, like us, you decide to keep the procedure confidential then it is really hard to behave normally around friends, family and work colleagues as you go through the rollercoaster of emotions that come with it. However, if you are going to keep some semblance of control over the information then this is the price you have to pay.

For us we wanted to be able to tell our child in our own way about their origin and our motivations for doing what we did. I cannot imagine the repercussions and lack of trust that would ensue if a well-meaning (or otherwise) relative let slip in conversation some crucial fact that we had not ourselves shared.

I had already I knew been acting, as far as those who knew me, very out of character and I could only begin to guess what reason they ascribed to my strange behaviour though in all honesty I doubted they came all that close to the truth. With any luck they would put it down to an early mid-life crisis.

Now, however, it would feel as if there was a huge neon sign pointing at us wherever we went and I knew with dread that we would both be on tenterhooks until the day of the test.

The next morning as we headed back to England, I knew we had to do something.

# Chapter 21:
## Run away...

We barely had time to get home and unpack our bags when the call came through from the clinic that the other two embryos had not made it. The three on ice were all that remained.

This put us instantly on a downer for reasons that I really cannot explain but something we had discussed as a distant possibility for the future was that if this pregnancy was successful that a sibling for our dearest creation would be on the cards and, if that were the case, then we felt it was important for it to have the same genetic background so that they had something in common.

That, however, is an entirely different story and one that, God willing, will no doubt form the sequel to this tale.

It did bring home the sense of mortality and the fragility of what we were doing. Out of eleven eggs we were now effectively down to five embryos, the two that Iona carried inside her and the three residing in the deep freeze in Barcelona. To put it another way within a week we already had an over fifty percent failure rate and I know it worried me so I am sure it worried her.

There was some good news however as my interview had been delayed due to one of the key people I was supposed to meet having been called on a business trip. My elation at not having to go through that ordeal so soon after the stress of Barcelona was sadly short-lived. The re-scheduled interview was now to be the day after Iona's pregnancy test and, as it was to be first thing in the morning, I would have to go up the night before.

We had sensibly booked time off on our return so as to avoid being around too many people but I realised we had to go further than that so I suggested that we go away for a few days and she agreed immediately.

Oh, the joys of the internet! What did we do before it? Within ten minutes of making the decision I had made a last-minute booking for the Isle of Wight as once again neither of us had ever been there. Unpacking the suitcases turned into a swift re-pack as we were due to leave again that very afternoon.

There was just time for me to contact our friendly chemist and arrange for the final supply of patches and drugs that Iona would need, scanning the prescription for him as before. Iona called the local clinic to confirm the time for the pregnancy test and as I had feared it was going to be an afternoon appointment. I would be able to go with her but would pretty much have to keep going up to Hull afterwards.

It was with a sense of relief that we found ourselves on the ferry heading for the island. Neither of us was feeling very sociable and the only company we could stand was each other's and only then as we were in the same boat emotionally.

The one thing I had not done was any particular research

on the island. I had booked us into a hotel in Newport so that we would have access to pubs and restaurants but beyond that I had very little idea as to what there was to do on the island.

Iona was not up to anything too strenuous, she was still paranoid that any exertion on her part would screw up the bonding of the embryos so we spent a lot of time driving around visiting numerous small attractions.

It was, to be honest, incredibly relaxing. We did not have a plan or much of a care; we simply headed out and went wherever the road took us. It felt like a metaphor for our lives (apart from having a care, that is). Had we planned the trip I would have prepared an itinerary for each day and the whole thing would have been structured and regimented whereas now, for the first time in as long as I can remember, we were drifting without a heading and I did not mind one bit.

The trip was what my Mother would describe as "soul refreshing". The beer was good as well!

Inevitably we had to head home and back to the normal routine of life. We had actually been off for less than two weeks but there came a point where the world had to go on and we had to go with it.

It still felt weird and that everyone was looking at us when in truth they did not have the faintest clue what we were going through.

Iona seemed to change. Somewhere on the Isle of Wight she had accepted that she could not spend the next week and a half treading as if she were walking on eggshells and for the first time in ages became more of her normal self. I turned my attention to the not insignificant challenge of trying to get a job as the stark realisation dawned that if Iona was pregnant we would need all the money we could get.

Basically, the week dragged.

When the day of the test finally arrived our stress levels were back up in the danger zone again. I had to really be careful as I packed for my overnight stay in Hull as my mind was really not on the interview.

Not unsurprisingly we arrived disgustingly early at the clinic which meant we had to again head for the local supermarket café for a hot drink and another bacon roll. I think I will forever more associate bacon rolls with our experiences with IVF!

There was a ruthless efficiency about the clinic as we were first taken to the finance office to pay the £40 for the blood test but then they dropped some bad news. Up until this point they had led us to believe that we would get the results that very day but now it was not going to be until the following afternoon and that we should call after one. Once again the agony would be prolonged.

The temptation to head back over to the supermarket and get a home pregnancy test kit was enormous.

As per usual Iona's veins seemed to vanish when the nurse tried to get the sample and she ended up having to send us to a different part of the clinic where of all people an anaesthetist had a go (he was apparently very good at this sort of thing). Even so he also had a good jab around before the blood flowed and then only after Iona had, at his request, pumped her hand vigorously.

I did like his instructions which were something along the line of "make a quick grabbing action like you are at the pick 'n mix counter at Woolworth's." It was obviously a phrase he had often used in the past but I did feel like pointing out that he might have to update it, the famous high-street chain having so recently gone bankrupt.

As we were heading back to the cars and saying our goodbyes, I had a phone call from the recruitment agency, all very flustered and apologetic but to say that my interview had to be changed yet again.

I had very mixed feelings about this. On the one hand I just wanted to get it over and done with but on the other it did mean that I would now be around when Iona got the call, even if we had wasted the extra petrol for driving both cars to the clinic.

With unexpected time on our hands we headed for a nearby park for a long walk. Iona called her Mum to give her an update, not that there was much she could say.

Yet again we had another sleepless night.

Iona had various things she had to do in the morning which kept her busy but I had the day free now that I was not going to my interview so rattled around the house trying to find jobs that needed doing.

By the time she came home and we had eaten lunch I was completely stir-crazy and at the stroke of one we made the call, both full of anticipation.

We were, of course, instantly deflated. The test results had not come back but they would chase them and call us as soon as they heard.

Had I known this was going to be an hour and a half I would not have hovered so much by the phone but finally the call did come and with it the result…552 picomoles of ßhCG.

Okay and that means what precisely?

The receptionist was very apologetic as she had only been told to phone us with the result but she neither knew nor was allowed to discuss with us what the result actually meant, the nurse would have to call us to go through that. The problem was that the nurse was now busy with other patients and would not be able to call until after four.

We knew nurses well enough that it was very unlikely that she would be finished on the dot at four, she would no doubt be running over and either way it did not matter as Iona was going to be in a meeting from four until six at the school. The nurse would have to tell me and then I would have to pass the news on to my wife.

This did not go down well with Iona and she was instantly on the internet to see what the numbers meant but the websites she found were not very helpful and really did not explain it well. She gave up and in near silence headed out for her meeting leaving me staring at the phone which lurked in the corner of the living room.

To pass the time I e-mailed the result to the clinic in Barcelona just so they had a record. I would have called but as luck would have it we were on the very day of the week that I knew they closed in the afternoon so there would be nobody there to speak to.

The clock struck four (well, it didn't actually strike as it is a battery powered cheap thing) but the phone remained quiet. I started considering what time I should leave it to before chasing them and decided on five. I knew the clinic closed at five thirty so it was a good compromise.

Two minutes to five the phone rang and the familiar voice of the nurse rang through. She did not beat around the bush and simply came out with the good news that Iona was pregnant! She wished us all the best and rang off.

My heart was pounding with excitement. *Iona was pregnant!* It was agonising that she was still in the meeting and it would be another hour before I could tell her. A vision of her sitting in the meeting trying to engage with whatever the subject matter was filled my thoughts and I wondered if her colleagues noticed how distant she was.

The school was not far away, less than half an hour by foot so I grabbed my coat and headed out. I wanted to be with her when I gave the news and I knew that if she phoned, which she would almost inevitably do, I would not be able to contain myself.

It was only when I was half-way there that I realised that the way she would drive home was a different route than the one I was taking by foot. If the meeting ended early we would miss each other!

I pressed on; increasing my speed and when the school came into view I could see her car still in the car park.

It was rare that I met her at work as I really did not like loitering around the place, especially when the kids were around. I was always afraid that someone would get the wrong idea and take me for some kind of paedophile or something.

By arriving early I now had the dilemma that I could be hanging around for nearly half an hour which, while the school was empty apart from the teachers attending the meeting, might still attract unwanted attention.

There was a corner shop nearby and nipping in for a packet of crisps did kill a few minutes. Eating them took rather less time but all-told I managed to burn five minutes in the endeavour and it was shortly after that when the school doors opened and the teachers emerged, the meeting indeed having finished ahead of schedule.

My phone, set to silent, buzzed and I could see in the distance that Iona had hers to her ear.

Answering, I explained that I was standing across the street and she glanced over to where I was loitering, her face full of anticipation. She hurried over, not needing to ask the question as I was already drawing breath to tell her.

I cannot even begin to describe the expression that appeared on her face at that moment, the combination of relief, joy, excitement and a hundred other emotions. Above all, she began to cry but in a nice way.

Some of the other teachers were approaching so I pulled

her into the corner shop and bought her some chocolate to celebrate with and so that her work mates would not see her tears of joy and ask awkward questions.

As soon as the coast was clear we made our way back to the car and then back home so we could have a proper cuddle as the reality of the situation sank in.

While I cooked a celebratory dinner she had a long chat with her Mum. As I stirred the pasta sauce I did reflect on our attitude as we had clearly both feared the worst but secretly praying that we did not have to face that eventuality, as many I know do. It was probably just as well that we did not.

Speaking for myself, I had not even begun to entertain the possibility that Iona would not fall pregnant and had the implantation not taken I cannot tell you how I would have reacted. As to what she was thinking, again I sense that she had feared the worst but not in a way that she had actually prepared herself for it.

Either way, we had been spared so far.

Part of me felt a little cheated in that by planning the pregnancy in this way, we had not experienced that moment of excitement that comes with natural conception when after making merry the woman misses her period, goes through that private period of uncertainty before weeing on a stick to get that wonderful positive result.

I mentioned this to Iona and she had felt the same so I nipped out and bought a home test kit that she then peed on just for the laugh of it. Needless to say the result was a resounding positive but it was fun to do.

That night we cuddled up and I knew that for the first time in ages we would both sleep well. Whether she realised it or not Iona went to sleep with her hands cradling her belly.

# Chapter 22:
## Meanwhile in Hull...

We were so desperate for life to get back to some kind of normality that it came as a disappointment when we heard from the Spanish clinic to give Iona her next set of instructions. They were not finished with her yet!

First of all she had to book a scan at the local clinic for a week after the date of the pregnancy test and another two weeks after that. She also had to carry on with the pills and patches while they maintained her hormone levels throughout the early stages of the pregnancy.

It felt as if we would never be really free of all the medical attention.

Iona called and made the appropriate appointments while I checked her stock of medications against the new diary I had created for when she had to take what. We were still short so yet another e-mail exchange with the chemist resolved that.

A book appeared – when she had bought it I had no idea but it was one of those "what to expect when you are expecting" type of things (indeed, that may well have been the title but I do not recall precisely). At every waking moment when she was not otherwise occupied I found her with her head buried in this helpful publication.

I have not been a great one for seeking external advice but the help we had received during the early stages of the IVF treatment had stuck with me so when she popped out to get some shopping I took a look myself.

The first thing I read was that Iona would possibly experience flatulence. Terrific, I would be living with Farticus! The other thing that the book did touch on was cravings which probably explained the enormous bag of ready salted crisps that she appeared with on her return and which she had certainly not gone out for.

I wondered what other strange things her body would demand over the next nine months. I do remember one of my friends many years ago who had gone to a local pizza delivery place and persuaded them to add an entire bag of jelly babies to a large Quattro Formaggi thin-crust pizza as his expectant wife was demanding. She ate it as well!

The recruitment agency finally got back to me with the rearranged date for my interview. You guessed it; the appointment was for first thing in the morning of the day after her scan. Déjà vu!

At least this time we both would be more prepared and relaxed about the whole thing. Well, this is what I told myself at the time.

For those of you who have read that immortal classic "Marley and Me" you will know that one of the joys of dog ownership is that they will find the most inconvenient times to do the most inappropriate things. Bella was no exception to this rule, especially now that her health was deteriorating noticeably.

Things came to a head the day we were preparing to head back to the clinic. As before, I had packed an overnight bag so that I could carry straight on to Hull and we had both cars out. Unlike previous trips we were not planning to leave ridiculously early and, while we had left a sensible amount of "wiggle room" in the timings there was not a lot of slack.

It was at that precise point that Bella decided to have a fit. Fitting in dogs is not uncommon but it is terrifying to watch. She went totally rigid, dropped to the floor and began thrashing around with her teeth bared and her eyes staring wildly. The other unfortunate side effect was that she lost control of all bodily functions and, as she had not been walked by that point, everything came out and by her thrashings was suitably spread around.

She came out of it quite quickly, exhausted but seemingly unaware that anything had happened (apart from the fact that she now seemed to be covered in wee and poo which you could see in her eyes was a little disconcerting as she had no memory of rolling in anything).

While I cleaned her and the kitchen up as best I could, Iona called the vet. It was just down the road (fortunately) and as luck would have it they could see us immediately so we bundled Bella into the back of the big car and headed straight there, conscious of the ticking clock.

Of course, the vet needed to take blood samples and do various tests and I sat there trying not to fidget nervously. It was without question important that Bella was sorted but at the same time the control freak in me was screaming that we were going to be late.

Finally, armed with a prescription for some tablets and a sheet of lifestyle advice, we were freed and took Bella home, at least I did, Iona went on to the clinic as she still had a fighting chance of arriving on time and I could at least catch up with her afterwards before carrying on to Hull.

I needn't have worried. The clinic was running horribly

late and by the time I got there not only had Iona not gone in but there were still two other ladies ahead of her waiting their turn.

As it was we had to wait another half an hour and I was mightily glad we had not been our usual early, though I would have preferred a different reason for us being late.

I had not really clicked that the scan was going to be an internal one and had just presumed it would have been like the ones you see on the telly where they smear your tummy with gel and then take a look with the ultrasound probe.

We explained our situation to the nurse and by the timing were told that Iona was the equivalent of five weeks pregnant (though I am not sure how this works as five weeks had not elapsed since implantation but there you go).

Something else that had been on both of our minds was the fact that Iona had been implanted with two embryos. All we knew at this point was that she was pregnant, what we did not know was whether both embryos had taken and therefore whether we were looking at a single child or twins.

In the clinic in Barcelona there were pictures all around sent in by previous patients and it had been noteworthy that in a significant number of these images the proud parents were clutching two babies.

This was the moment of truth and we both stared at the screen eagerly as the probe went in. Not sure why we bothered, we could have been looking at the insides of a hot water bottle for all the sense it made to me.

Fortunately as with the previous scans the nurse seemed to know what she was looking for and reported her findings.

There was only one sac. We did not have twins and more importantly another of the eleven original eggs had now failed.

This was not as harsh a blow as the previous reductions in numbers. While twins would have been very convenient, instant family and all that, we were both very aware from all the reading up we had done that Iona stood a better chance of going full term with a single baby rather than two. There was also, of course, the fact that we would have two screaming mouths to deal with in nine months' time whereas now there would be just the one.

Then the nurse gave us the slightly more worrying news. The embryo was smaller than she would have expected and was more indicative of four weeks rather than five (which still confuses me to this day as it was four weeks give or take since implantation and yet they always seemed to tack and extra week onto the calculations).

At this stage the sac was 8mm x 10mm x 4mm or to put it another way it was about the size of an average watch battery. To me, having only recently seen the microscopic cluster of cells in the petri-dish this sounded huge in comparison!

Whatever the signs she was reading, the nurse was otherwise happy that the tissue around the sac looked normal but she recommended that we had a re-scan in two weeks so we booked it there and then.

She provided a written report that I could email over to the Spanish clinic.

It was hard to go our separate ways as I could see in her eyes that Iona was feeling like me, pleased but at the same time somewhat odd. The loss of one of the embryos meant that everything now rode on the one that was left but that one did not seem to be faring one hundred percent.

I had a long time in the car to think about it though in some respects it did stop me dwelling on the looming job interview.

When I got to the hotel I sent the main details in the

report. Not expecting a response given the hour I was somewhat surprised when Maria pinged back a note a few minutes later.

She was now asking for the re-scan in a week, not two! Also, I had asked her some days previously what drug regime Iona should be on moving forward but she had not answered this and now said that she would provide details after the next scan.

To be honest, I was probably tired and had a lot on my mind but this time I made a decision. The nurse at the local clinic seemed to know her stuff and had been quite insistent at the two week gap before the next scan and as this is what the Spanish had also originally asked for I sent a note back saying that we would stick to the two week appointment. I no longer cared whether she agreed or not, we were not playing this game again. Needless to say, I did not worry Iona by telling her any of this at the time.

I had a lot of time to kill. Hull is not one of those places you go for an evening stroll and there was a lot of catching up to do with the book. Since we had found out Iona was pregnant I had not written anything but now we knew the full story I felt able to sit down at the laptop and bring the account up to date.

As I wrote I sensed a change in my tone. Up until that point the book had been aimed at a theoretical child, nothing more but now it was real. We did not know the sex of the child so for now it remained both an "it" and a nameless one at that but it was real and growing fast.

For the first time I realised that I was writing the book for a real person. I knew at that moment that the journey that Iona and I were on had taken a sudden leap. No longer were we running on hope, we were now protecting a new life, the spark that would hopefully become our much-longed for child.

A shitty hotel in Hull really did not seem the most appropriate place to be having such profound thoughts.

At this stage I must by necessity deviate slightly from the story about our developing baby as I finally arrived at the large red-brick monolith that housed the headquarters of my prospective new employers.

Breakfast was the last thing on my mind, not least as I remembered my previous mistake and had vowed to enter this second interview far more prepared than the first.

Iona called to say that she had made an appointment with her doctor to get a second opinion on the size of the developing embryo and I was glad as she had clearly been brooding over it through the night and a bit of reassurance would be welcome. She wished me good luck and left me to it.

From the hotel the office was only a short drive and I arrived to be slightly early but not too much that I became a nuisance.

When I entered the interview suite I was glad that I had prepared. The room seemed full of suits (in fact there were probably only four or five) which was a lot more than I had been told to expect. The questions were also quite searching and again seemed rather tough given the level of job I was applying for.

Still, having finally collected my thoughts, pulled my socks up and given myself a good kick in the backside over the last couple of days I was about as prepared as I would ever be and fielded their questions well, indeed while it is all a blur I don't think there was a single question that I did not answer with at least reasonable confidence.

I was supposed to be there an hour but it ended up lasting for nearer two before I was released. As my host led me back to the lobby he said that they would not be able to give me an answer for at least two weeks but did not elaborate any further on this.

My heart sank. As the only candidate at the second interview stage I had assumed that once they had seen me that the decision would be pretty quick. Two weeks would be an agony. Still, at least I knew and would not be hanging by the phone.

As the morning galloped towards lunchtime I was heading out of town and riding on an adrenaline high. I have been fortunate enough to have survived for most of my career without the need to attend interviews which made those few I did even scarier. The problem was I had not even considered the implications of them actually offering me the job!

I was exhausted by the time I got home and Iona was out, still at her appointment with the doctor so I sat down to attend to some emails.

You may have had the impression recently that I appeared to have a lot of time on my hands and this is basically true. I was pretty much freelancing and had managed to land a few minor jobs but none that made huge demands on my time. At that present moment in time I did actually have a few minor tasks on the go so it was useful to spend some time progressing them.

By the time Iona returned I had actually managed to achieve something useful which was good as it meant I would actually earn some money that month.

The doctor had been very helpful and had reassured Iona that while the sac was small it was not dangerously so. What neither of the clinics had mentioned was that the critical time was somewhere around the 6-7 week stage where the embryo would develop a heart and it would start beating. This would be detectable by ultrasound and she advised Iona to make an appointment with the midwife.

This was an important psychological step for my wife. Not that we were going to finally hear our baby's heart but that she was going to be seeing a midwife! For Iona, this suddenly made the whole pregnancy real. No longer were we just seeing doctors, consultants, radiologists and nurses, we were now going to see a midwife and midwives only mean babies.

Fate seemed to have another card up his sleeve and as the embryo developed so Bella seemed to decline. What had started as a single fit turned into two, then three, each one more severe than the last. Cleaning up after her became an almost regular occurrence and I would not let Iona get involved. The last thing she needed in her condition was to be around that foulness.

As we waited for the next things to happen life did indeed begin to return to some kind of normality. Iona was still on the pills and patches but this was our only real reminder of what was happening.

Europe was plagued by a wave of strikes which hit Spain and I was extremely glad that they had not coincided with our visit. It also struck me that the pioneer of IVF was awarded the Nobel Prize and we decided to take this as a good omen.

Time ticked by but slowly the date of the next scan grew closer and closer and with it the realisation that this was the cruncher. If the embryo had truly taken and was doing fine we would see it here and for the first time it would begin to look like something recognisable but most importantly we would see the heartbeat!

The prospect was at the same time terrifying and exciting and then the day of the scan arrived.

# Chapter 23:
## I hear you knocking...

Although it was not planned that way, while you have arrived at Chapter 23 in the real version of "The Journey of Love and Hope" I found myself writing this part at the beginning of Chapter 13. I really hoped it was not an omen.

Bella managed to have what was becoming a rare good day and we felt relatively confident to leave her alone as we once again headed to the clinic. The road was becoming far too familiar and I found myself navigating on autopilot rather than listening to the sat nav.

For once they were running early and no sooner had we sat in the waiting room than Iona's name was called. I guessed that as they were ready and we were there they had decided to get ahead of themselves for a change.

My elation in the days prior to this had evaporated and I was now very nervous. Not only was it crunch day for the baby but I also knew that any day I would hear about the job and have all that to sort out.

The nurse came back and got straight down to business with the ultrasound. I was beginning to be familiar enough with their operation to have a vague idea what I was looking at and in the past there had been a lot of repositioning as the operator tried to get the best angle.

None of that this time, she managed to go straight to the egg sac and there, about 10mm long next to the sac was the tiniest form that was beginning to develop and even as we were both taking this in we could see the minute pulse of the heartbeat. I almost melted with joy and a tear trickled down Iona's face.

From what the nurse could see Iona was nicely on track and the scan did not indicate any other problems. She happily predicted a due date at the end of May. What was even more thrilling was that as far as she was concerned this would be the last time we would need to come to the clinic and from this point onwards we would be under the normal care of our GP and the midwife.

She printed out a picture of "blob" as we had already named the tiny shape and I clutched it proudly. Baby's first picture! I only wished I had a snap of the cells in the petri-dish as well.

Iona was still concerned as to what she should avoid and the nurse gave her a list of things to be careful with but especially swimming which was to be avoided for a few weeks. Armed with this good advice we made our final farewell to the clinic that had served our local needs so well.

We left very happy people and when I got home there was an e-mail waiting for me from the recruitment agency to say that while no decision had been made it had been elevated as far as the CEO of the company and this meant there would be another delay before it was resolved and it would not be until the next day that I would hear. This all sounded very odd but there was not much I could do about it.

I had this strange feeling that on so many levels we were at a major turning point in our lives.

You will have noticed that I regard the journey of life as being very much that, a journey along a road that has regular junctions and crossroads. Each of these represents a choice and the direction you take at each junction determines your future fate. It is a common enough way of looking at our life paths but for me most of the major decisions had been made on a whim rather than as a result of careful deliberation.

There are, however, junctions at which you do not seem to have much of a choice. The road you are on naturally takes a direction such as merging with the motorway and you have no choice but to go with it, all the while wondering what would have happened had things turned out differently.

This was one of those moments. So many events had been put into motion that would determine the direction of our destiny that I knew that all the threads were coming together at this time. Where it would take us only time would tell but the one thing I was sure of was that the life we knew was coming to an end.

Bella seemed to be the epitome of this thought. She was losing weight drastically and with each fit part of her never came back as if her very personality was dying piece by piece. It was horrible to watch her slowly leaving us but the day we came back from the clinic we could see in her face that the Bella we knew and loved was gone and all that remained was an old, tired and scared shell.

Her time had come. We both knew it but facing it was almost impossible. Here we were in the process of gaining a new addition to the family but now we would have to lose one as well.

For a while we toyed with the idea of giving her a week but the truth was we would be doing this for our benefit, not hers. It would delay the act for us but in the mean time she would carry on fitting and spend her waking hours scared and confused. Many old dogs become devout members of the eternally baffled, some in a happy way and some in an agitated way. Bella was definitely in the latter category. She would neither enjoy the additional time nor thank us for it.

The only thing we could do was book her in for the very next day.

That night I decided not to update the book. My heart really was not in it and although I wanted to give the old girl a cuddle she no longer had any clue as to who I was so that would have achieved nothing. She had a plate full of sausages for her tea, that she *did* appreciate and she curled up in her favourite bed that night to sleep.

The romantic story teller in me would love at this stage to say she went peacefully during the night but sadly this was not the case. We were awoken in the early hours to another fit and another clean-up session. Fate was not smiling kindly on our poor old dog that day.

You can probably imagine the sort of mood we woke up in the next morning. We were tired and very subdued as the thought of what we would have to do to our poor dog dominated our thoughts.

My temperament was not, therefore, improved when I opened my email to receive the message from Maria with instructions for Iona's final drug treatment, instructions that contradicted everything we had previously been told resulting in us having significant excesses of the very expensive drugs.

She also sent through a form that we would have to have filled in on the day of the birth. Talk about forward planning! I did not reply immediately but instead went off to find something replaceable to break as I vented my anger and frustration. Of course, it didn't really help though it felt good for a moment.

The Spanish clinic had reviewed the data we had sent them and proudly gave Iona her due date – totally different to the one that the local clinic had given and again different from that suggested by our doctor. We decided to go with the one our doctor had written down as this would be the one the hospital would work to.

Our appointment at the vet was not until the evening so it was a very long day made even longer as I remembered I was expecting a job offer. When at five thirty I eventually received the call it was merely to say that no decision had been made as yet.

At this stage I wished the day would just end but we still had the agony of having Bella put down to endure.

I will not describe the event here but when we eventually got home the house felt very empty indeed. Iona cried herself to sleep and I simply lay there staring at the ceiling long into the night.

Both of us were feeling pretty ragged and not for the first time we were glad of the friends we had made through Infertility Network UK and we found solace in some the next day who, hearing of the loss of Bella and secretly wanting an update on the scans invited us round for dinner.

I have to say, after weeks of living what felt like a secret life it was so refreshing to be around people with whom we could speak freely and speak we did. We knew we could not be around our extended families, especially those with kids, as it would feel too weird knowing Iona was pregnant but not being able to make the official announcement for another month or so. If nothing else the last thing we wanted to do was tempt fate at this late stage.

The job offer remained elusive which was becoming worrying as the original start date on the application was a mere three weeks away. I was holding off on two relatively large jobs in anticipation of the offer but would not be able to do so much longer and if I did commit it would render me unavailable until the New Year.

As the day sailed past it became increasingly obvious that this was what I was going to have to do. I set myself a deadline of five-thirty as being a decent amount of time but as this came and went and the phone remained silent I bit the bullet and accepted the two short-term contracts.

In my mind, the job offer was already being prepared for filing in the "lost cause" folder.

Actually, I felt rather good about it. The reality was that if the job had been offered I would have had to move up to Hull temporarily and we had already decided that in that eventuality Iona was not going to follow in the short-term. Now, I would at the very least be around for the next three months or so to help out as her pregnancy progressed. There would also not be any hassle around Christmas which was particularly pleasing.

I dropped a note to the recruiter and explained my position. I felt pretty good that I had given them a reasonable amount of time to come to a decision but life had to go on and I had to earn money so I hoped they would understand.

The recruiter called back sounding somewhat tense. I am not sure what they had expected but while they accepted my reasoning it was clear that they were worried as to how they were going to feed the information back to the company. Frankly, I didn't care. They were the recruiter: that was their problem!

It is amazing how calling someone's bluff gets a result. The offer came in less than an hour later along with the plea that they really wanted me to start at the end of the month.

Considering my position carefully and talking it through

with Iona, I called back and said that I would accept the offer but not the timings. Having already committed my time to my two customers I was not about to renege on a deal and if they wanted me for the job then part of what they were getting was my integrity to see through my commitments.

Grudgingly they agreed and a start date was set for the first working day of January.

Iona and I went out for dinner to celebrate but already the doubt was setting in. By accepting the job I had committed us to a move to Hull and that brought with it a whole new set of complications, not least of which, given that the job came with a car we were suddenly going to be one automobile over what we required.

The choice was obvious and the beloved purple MGB was now surplus to requirements. For Iona I could tell that the thought had already crossed her mind as the MG was not the most practical of cars for putting a baby seat in and given its personality which was quirky at best it did not have the reliability required for the transportation of children.

Typically, of course, with the credit crunch the arse had dropped out of the used car market, especially for "classics" but I did have a couple of interesting experiences on the road to shifting the god-awful thing.

The first was those websites who advertise that they will buy your car regardless of age or condition.

Now, you have I am sure gathered that I am an atrocious cynic and my immediate reaction to these sites was that for sure they would buy any car but at the same time they would do so for rock-bottom prices. Still, knowing of my pathological cynicism I gave it a go and tried three of the biggest sites, comparing what they offered to the sort of prices quoted in the popular used car trading magazines.

All I can say is that my response to the quotes I was given amounted to two words, the second of which was "off" and I encourage you to use your imagination for variations on the first word. I also knew from people who had actually sold cars this way that the actual price you get is always lower once the garage has seen the vehicle and added the depreciation for the three molecules of paint that have been abraded from some obscure part of the bodywork.

I had resisted placing an ad in the usual used car magazines but the response from the online sharks immediately sent me that way.

It was a waste of time, of course. There was not a single nibble which left only two options, the first of which was to put it on the ever popular online auction site (who I will not be giving free advertising to at this point given what happened next).

I listed the car with a reasonable starting price (five quid above what the "we will fleece you for your car" sites had offered). I gave a full and honest description of the car, refraining from using such phrases as "leaks like a sieve" and "probably the most annoying piece of shit on four wheels" but I was reliably informed that any MG enthusiast would see past such trivial matters. Love is blind, as they say. In this case with the shocking purple paint job you would need a lot of love but beauty is in the eye of the bidder.

Very quickly we had a few watchers but no bidders and there were several other similar cars for sale with equal lack of interest so my hopes were not high.

Then the email came through from someone in "Scotland" who really, really wanted the car but was unable to pick it up in person but would buy it if they could use a delivery company they knew. For my trouble they would even pay a lot more than the asking price and would send a cheque for that amount plus three thousand pounds for the transport and all I had to do was to cash the cheque, write a new cheque for the three thousand pounds and take it to the nearest Western Union to wire it to the delivery company who would then come and take the car.

It sounded like an unbelievable offer so I immediately did not believe it. I think it took me about five seconds on the internet to find a hundred people who had been caught in similar scams. The money would vanish, the delivery company never appear and then a few days later the original cheque would bounce. Did you know that there is a time difference from a cheque clearing and the money actually becoming available? I didn't until then and this is what they play on. The banks really should be more responsible in explaining this but I guess the words "bank" and "responsible" really do not go together these days.

Anyway, as you can imagine my response to the enquiry was that all this would happen over my dead, rotting corpse!

The scam was slightly spoiled by the fact that the person involved used pretty bad English and the cynic in me was operating at full strength. It sounded too good to be true ergo it was.

If nothing else, there were plenty of similar cars in the vicinity of the buyer's purported location so to pay over the odds and then three thousand pounds for delivery was simply incredible. Their greed had blown the scam wide open.

I never received a response to the email I sent back but they probably learned a lot more colloquial English than they had before. I also alerted the auction website but nothing came of that. I am willing to bet a lot of money they are still out there trying the same scam and sadly roping enough poor trusting fools in to make it worth their while.

What does this have to do with the book? Nothing, of course but I threw it in to do my good deed of the day. If

I save even one person from falling for the scam then my job is done.

We decided there and then to simply trade it in for the people carrier that Iona would get and stuff whatever price we got for it. After all the assholes I had dealt with I would have rather scrapped it than sell it to someone on the make. At least with the garage we would have some degree of haggling.

The formal job offer arrived in the post and I signed it, committing myself to a start date on the first working day of the New Year.

Despite taking it easy, Iona showed a bit more spotting but a hasty consultation to the oracle of Google convinced her that this was not a major issue and something that could occur. Even so, I would not let her come shopping for the groceries, ordering her to take it easy.

When I came back she was in a total state again but for a while would not explain why. I finally got it out from her but it was a bit of a tricky problem.

I have explained before that we had chosen to keep the nature of our treatment secret from all but her mother which meant that the rest of the immediate family were entirely in the dark with regards to our situation.

Her brother had already started a family but it seemed that the decision had been made that after one child they were not going to have any more. This was indicated by the fact that all of the expensive items that their parents had bought, most notably the pram, car seat and cot, were suddenly about to appear on the same internet auction site we had been trying to sell her car through. He had said something in passing about listing them during a casual phone call which had left her completely torn.

In her mind, Iona had naturally assumed that she would be able to make use of the aforementioned items but it had simply not occurred to her that in not telling anyone, there was no reason at all why they should be expecting to pass them on.

Paul had simply reached a decision with his wife and decided that being bulky items and of no more use to them that they would dispose of them in an appropriate fashion.

Iona desperately wanted them but how could we stop them being sold without giving the game away. What made the situation even worse was that their mother was away on a short holiday and not in communication so Iona had no way of asking her to surreptitiously step in.

The only good thing was that we knew we had a bit of breathing space as Paul was travelling so did not intend to list the items until the weekend and as fortune would have it they were coming to ours for dinner on the Friday evening.

Iona for sure could have done without the stress but one of the side-effects of the fact that her body was full to the brim of hormones was that even the smallest things took on great importance.

The next day she had more spotting and a few aches and pains but everything on the pregnancy websites indicated that this was no cause for concern (she was, therefore, automatically concerned as I am sure I would have been in the same situation).

I was very glad when Friday arrived and her brother showed up with his tribe. Iona and I had discussed it, at least, I had discussed it with her and we had agreed that I would take him aside and by some means as yet undefined convince him not to list the items.

When it came down to it, he took me aside and asked if there was anything wrong. Clearly he had sensed in his sister's tone that something was up. I made a decision there and then and in the most careful tones possible suggested that he did not list the baby things but if he gave me a price I would buy them from him there and then but no questions asked and no mention to his wife of this.

The penny dropped and I could see that he knew he had put her in a difficult position. While he had no idea of the actual circumstances the fact that his timing had pre-empted her announcement was unfortunate.

He agreed and said he could easily delay selling the items until we went public and that we would sort it out then.

When we re-joined the others I simply threw Iona a thumbs-up sign but the relief on her face was priceless. When I told her later what I had done she agreed that it was the only way, trusting her brother to keep the secret until we made the announcement.

She then felt bad that she had not told him but as I pointed out why would she? Had it been a normal pregnancy we would have waited until the proper time and the only reason to tell him earlier would have been if we were going to confide in the rest which we were not.

It was getting cold outside, October being a good way through now but finally we felt where we were in a position that allowed us to relax. The baby was, as far as we could tell, developing well, my employment situation was sorted out and all the stupid little things like the car and her brother had been resolved.

We were truly getting back to some degree of normality.

Of course, the very next day we had both come down with stinking colds. I find this is often the case when you are running on adrenaline. While you keep moving the body seems to find reserves of antibodies and other useful defences that keep all diseases at bay but woe betide the moment you stop and take a breath.

This is precisely what we had done and at that moment everything caught up with us like a landslide.

Typically as is always my way I got the symptoms in linear progression rather than all at once whereas Iona had the full-blown effect in one nasty go. She was terrified of sneezing in case she sneezed "blob" out which was ludicrous but she took it seriously enough to make very strange noises every time she tried to strangle the nasal outburst. She would not be convinced that "blob" was well and truly embedded and it would take more than a good blast from her nostrils to send it flying.

The only good thing for her was that she got over the cold in a couple of days whereas I was still lingering with the runny nose and sore throat stage. This was just as well as she had the next midwife appointment.

While we had given some thought as to where she would give birth, the options being the rat-infested shite-hole I had been obliged to give my sperm samples in (do you get the impression I was not impressed by the facility) or a much more modern unit which was a bit of a drive away but had a great reputation.

There was a third option which was a small maternity unit nearby but they only had midwives so if anything went wrong (the cynic in me assuming the worst) they would have to send Iona in an ambulance to the nearest full unit which would get her back to the same run-down old ruin of a hospital that I loathed so much.

It was simplest to plump for the shiny new place and risk the drive. Of course, we should have been considering Hull but we had no knowledge of the units up there and, to be honest, no inclination to go and have a look. To this day I could not tell you whether they were world-class or worryingly-crap. Iona was going to have her baby down South and that was the end of it.

As this decision was being made almost by default my mind was racing trying to work out the logistics with regards to my job.

While I was thinking this Iona was discussing a couple of optional appointments with the consultant and it was only once she and the midwife had agreed to this that I registered the fact but, realising that I had zoned out, Iona explained that it was something offered as routine for IVF patients. For me it was no problem at all. The NHS had been so poor up to this stage that I felt they owed us some proper care for a change. If it was on offer we would take it!

The midwife brought out "some paperwork" to fill in. This is where I am sure every mother out there will cringe as that heavy booklet hit the desk and we realised that we were going to be there a while. I forget how many times we have had to write down our complete medical history but this one was thorough! Just when we thought it was over, the midwife would turn the page and yet another list of questions would stare up at us menacingly from the form.

Luckily we are very boring from the perspective of any family medical history so most of the responses were "no" but it still took three quarters of an hour to get through it all.

The last form was to book the next scan and the screens for Down's syndrome – it would go back to the hospital and they would write to us with a date…hopefully. We were told that if we had not heard by mid-November (her 12 week date) we should call them. Given our experience with the NHS up to this point I *really* hoped it would not come to this.

With the paperwork over, the midwife felt Iona's tummy to see if there was anything untoward going on but could feel no swelling or anything else suspicious. When asked about the spotting they confirmed that it was normal and nothing to worry about (too late!).

The midwife then took blood and despite being warned that Iona's veins had a tendency to hide managed to fill three vacutainers quite easily for the series of routine blood tests that, despite having already done for the IVF, Iona had to do again.

Iona had also provided a urine sample which was normal and she was given another pot to fill for the subsequent visit.

Ultimately, it was all very routine and indeed a bit dull after the rollercoaster of IVF. Iona was to see the midwife again at 16 weeks (so mid-December) and she was given the programme of "events" so she knew what would be coming up. Sadly for me most of the ante-natal stuff I was going to miss once I had made my way up to Hull.

Finally, armed with the booklet of notes, we were released. I played courier and dropped the blood samples off at reception and we then headed over to the chemist as Iona had been advised to take vitamins as a precautionary measure.

Over the next few days it came to my notice that Iona was acquiring a rapidly increasing pile of samples, vouchers, leaflets and other paraphernalia that the midwife and others had given her. Not only were they appearing from nowhere but they seemed to be self-replicating. Within the myriad of offers were forms to fill in and take to the various chemists and supermarkets which could be redeemed for yet more freebies and leaflets which, in turn, contained forms to fill in to join yet more manufacturer-driven baby clubs and get yet more free samples.

I wondered where it was all going to end and whether our recycling bin was going to be big enough.

One particular incident made me laugh. Bearing in mind

we were still a few weeks away from the "big announcement" when we could *finally* go public with our news, Iona went into a popular chemist chain to redeem her voucher for a suitable carrier-bag full of freebies. Was it discreet? No, the bag was bright pink with "good news" scrawled all across it as well as various endorsements for baby products and publications. Bearing in mind most mothers-to-be are probably given this stuff at the same time and therefore not in the public-announcement realm of things yet, the bag was hardly subtle!

Watching her look through the leaflets the realisation began to dawn that this was getting serious now! According to the books, "blob" would now be pretty much fully defined in terms of physiological features and have functioning internal organs. The next scan, whenever it was going to be, would be revealing indeed!

The realisation also sank in heavily that by moving to Hull I was going to miss a lot of the final stages of the pregnancy. Having struggled all this way to help get us where we were now it seemed as if I were being robbed. Had accepting the job been the right thing to do after all?

I thought back to some of my ex-colleagues in previous companies who had missed chunks of their new baby's development through being off on sales trips and realised that they were totally mad but that they had also made the choice to put career first. I would not say mine was particularly a choice but the timing was abysmal.

My mind was changed very quickly when out of the blue I received a call from my old boss at the packaging consultancy. It had not even begun to occur to me that in my new position I might bump into my old firm once again but it was far better than that. I was about to become their customer! In the intervening time when I had been out of their employment things had changed drastically and they had forged a few new links, one of which as luck would have it being with the company for whom I was now committed to work.

I could imagine the look on my old boss' face when he found out that I had been offered the job. Having so recently made me redundant here I was now in a position to really make his life difficult in one of his biggest new contracts.

Oh, the irony of it!

He was always one for turning on the charm and as my new employers had written seeking a reference it was no shock that he knew so when he called his opening gambit was to congratulate me on landing such a good role. He then went on to suggest that we met up at the consultancy where he would happily give me an update on all the recent industry developments and them perhaps we could go for dinner.

It was clear that he was fishing to see how much of a grudge I was bearing but I have never been one to pass on a free dinner. I accepted, on the caveat that I was in no way representing my new employers, not knowing at that point what their attitude to such a meeting would be and we set a date for just before Christmas. I put the phone down with a big cheesy smile on my face.

It left me with a huge ego-boost, not that I was going to get one over on my old employers (though there was a part of that felt like screwing them over, me being only human after all) but suddenly I felt back in the game. It also gave me a much more positive feeling about the whole Hull job which was good.

# Chapter 24:
## Back to normality…

October was all but at an end when it really sank in that I was moving north in just over two months but was woefully unprepared for the event.

A shopping trip was in order and one place I had always wanted to go was Kingston-upon-Thames (having had a friend from there who constantly raves about the place).

It was a bad move. I should by now have recognised certain expressions on Iona's face but the one she wore as we walked around that fair town (apologies for any residents of Kingston if you have city status) which, by the way, I do agree is a fabulous place to wander around.

I was so engrossed in the lengthy shopping list of miscellany that I was searching for that it took me a while to realise that her gaze was not directed towards clothing stores or chocolate but to the many jewellers that Kingston sports.

Not only was she looking in the window but her gaze was focused on one particular section…eternity rings.

Iona has Celtic blood and symbolism mean a lot to her.

If you think I am superstitious you ought to meet her and her family. You cannot cough, sneeze, and go for a walk or anything without being careful not to say this, tread there or look at that.

The whole process of the pregnancy had become so fundamental to her that she needed to symbolise it in some way and the logical one was the perpetual band of the eternity ring.

Oddly enough, in my own superstitious way I could not help but feel that we were seriously tempting fate if we jumped the gun and bought it early, these things usually being purchased on the birth of the first child to symbolise the circle of life or some other suitable occasion.

However, Iona's belief was far deeper and it did not take me long to realise that we were not going to end that day without the outlay of a sizeable chunk of money on a depressingly small item.

Within half an hour of my realisation of this fact and my subsequent suggestion that we "take a look" a bespoke ring was on order though at least it would not be ready until February.

The other thing I noticed about the Kingston trip was how quickly Iona became tired. On returning home this continued and she kept getting various symptoms that seem to agree with what the guide books say she should be feeling at that moment. We were both a bit on edge with the knowledge that as of a few days time she would start to ramp down on the external medication and that these would end completely in less than two weeks, the assumption being by that point that the placenta will take over and run things okay.

She had been on the patches and vaginal tablets for so long we had simply taken them for granted and their application was now part of our routine daily life. As such, their absence would be missed.

The twelve week scan was sort of becoming a crux point for everything in our lives. First and most important would be the test as to whether "blob" was developing okay and whether Iona's body really did take over fully once the hormone treatment stopped. Secondly, it would of course be the time when we could finally tell everyone that she was pregnant, if not by what means and stop playing the clandestine game we had been forced to play for so many months.

This aside, there was also the twenty week scan to consider where they looked for all sorts of other anomalies.

Of course, I had not factored this in when thinking about the job (once again it was all me, me, me). Something was bothering me about the timing of the twenty week scan and in typical fashion my brain worked out the problem as I was dropping off to sleep one night.

I would start my new job on the first Tuesday of the year...the scan was on the Friday! I would have to ask for a day off before barely even starting! Not going after everything that had happened was simply not an option but again the timing was terrible.

Iona had her own worries as the twelve week scan loomed on the very near horizon which resulted in a bout of terrible insomnia which in turn screwed up my own sleep patterns. It was as if nature was giving us a taste of things to come without the screaming and smelly nappies.

Part of her worry was that we had been warned that the hospital we had elected, who would do the twelve week scan, was very popular and therefore very busy and the chances of getting an appointment on the day we wanted slim.

This seemed to be confirmed when the letter from the hospital arrived and she opened it. The first sheet of paper confirmed her appointment date as being the 3rd December. Instantly I started to do the calculations, realising that this would be week 15 and very late. She was just starting to work herself up and slag off the NHS when I spotted the red stamp at the bottom of the page that said "multiple appointments included".

I turned to the second sheet and spotted our mistake. The 3rd December was the extra appointment we had requested with the consultant. On the next page was the actual scan date…for the 11th November! It was a day before her official twelve week point.

This was absolutely perfect. Not only was the appointment for 8:30 so nicely at the start of the day but it was a whole two days before a big family party on her side which would mean we would have plenty of time to absorb the information before "breaking the news" and that a lot of the people we would want to tell would all be in the same place at the same time, avoiding that whole favouritism bit.

I would have to arrange something to share the news with my family but that was not difficult as they are all in the same area so I arranged a "we happen to be passing so will drop in" kind of thing in the hope that it would not arouse suspicion.

It also meant that I could start organising seeing some friends, arrangements that I had been putting off until I knew the scan date so that I could tell them in person.

As the day of the scan approached the serious ramp-down of the drugs and patches began. This simply gave Iona something new to worry about as she doubted her own body's ability to take over once the external hormones ceased.

I felt very male and while I tried desperately to find

reassuring words I knew that what she was experiencing was something I would never understand.

For me the biggest problem with this stage of the whole procedure is the waiting. I noticed this when I was updating the book as suddenly I found myself with less and less to say as the critical events became more infrequent. Of course, any pregnancy is like this, short flurries of activity joined by weeks of dull routine but when you have spent so long even getting to the start of the process the waiting is agony.

It also felt stranger and stranger writing to someone who was developing rapidly within Iona's womb. We still had no idea whether it was a boy or a girl and had long ago decided not to find out. So much of the process had been engineered that the only thing we had left was that surprise on the day of "It's a ...."

Even so, the book was progressing nicely. By now I had filled nearly two hundred pages meaning that the whole thing was going to be the size of a small to medium novel! When I had started I thought I would end up with a thin sheaf of paper full of dates and key events but without realising it the book had taken a life of its own.

I ached to go back and read some of the early passages, events that as I had suspected were already hazy in my own memory. The logic of writing everything down was even sounder than I had at first allowed for and I suddenly realised that by the time our child reached an age where he or she could understand our reasoning all the crucial facts would have long ago faded into the background mist of my memory.

This again made the book so precious. I wondered what, had it not been for the record I had taken, my recollection of events would be like in ten to fifteen years time and whether erroneous facts would have repeated themselves so many times in my memory to have become, as far as I was concerned, true. I have seen this happen in people so many times when they can quite literally remember things that never happened through repeating the lie in their head enough that it creates a false memory.

There would be no chance of this here, even if I did not recognise the "me" talking through time any more.

Needless to say I resisted the temptation to go back and peek.

Fortunately, I started to find things to write about again. Two days before the scan I put the last patch on Iona's buttocks that now had the appearance of a small quilt thanks to the regular adhesive squares.

The day before the scan she used the last tablet and we put the drug diary through the shredder. Finally she was at the end of the medication. We were both getting a bit nervous about the scan as a lot seemed to be emotionally riding on the result. It was also another NHS Hospital and our experiences up to this point had not been good, though this one did have a good reputation. My main concern in my typical control freak way was getting there and parking, both of which I expected to be rubbish.

It was most gratifying on the day of the scan to rip the last patch off and Iona was so pleased as well she didn't yelp when I did so, not that there were many hairs left to yank out with the adhesive.

We left nice and early (probably far too early for some people) but it did mean that the traffic was okay, though not exactly quiet even at seven in the morning and when we got to the hospital there was plenty of parking, though again I was sure that was soon to change. It was blowing a gale and lashing it down so not the greatest of mornings to be out and about and we were both more than a little nervous.

Despite having building work the hospital felt less tatty and more welcoming than the others of our experience, though that would not be difficult to be honest. The reception was closed but we found a map and worked out where we were supposed to go and then headed for the restaurant on the first floor for breakfast (bacon roll & coffee for me, Bakewell tart and tea for her). We sat there for about half an hour and chilled out in about as non-chilled a way as possible.

At eight, we headed down to the antenatal unit (even though our appointment was not until 8:30). As we opened the door, an alarm went off which made us both jump and in horror we thought it was us until we realised that there was a fault somewhere and the alarm was sounding intermittently, much to the annoyance of the reception staff.

They were all very nice and friendly and asked us to take a seat. I noticed that the reading material included such publications as Heating & Plumbing Weekly. Interesting!

We were seen promptly but it became apparent from the outset that we were not going to be able to do the Down's syndrome screening as one of the bits of information they need to make the prediction was the age of the mother… i.e. the donor. The radiologist said she would contact the screening nurse after the scan and ask her.

The scan was the traditional external one which was far more comfortable for Iona. Immediately we saw a very normal looking baby as well as a heartbeat. As if to make the point the baby moved, giving a twitch of excitement. We had to laugh and inevitably "blob" became "Fidget".

Looking at the scan was truly magical. The nurse, taking a more routine approach measured the crown-to-rump length at 58.5mm giving an estimated duration of 12weeks 2days today and a due date of 24th May. She counted all the bits and we saw the nose, eyes, two hemispheres of the brain, two arms with hands, two legs with feet and the stomach and abdomen, both of which she confidently said were okay. It was a great relief as all looked fine.

Given that the baby was growing normally she said to us that this indicated that the placenta was working fine so Iona had no worries having just come off of the medication.

She gave us four scan pictures to take away which of course we treasured as if they were original da Vinci sketches.

We were then handed over to the screening nurse who explained more about the situation with the Down's syndrome and suggested that we try and get the mother's age from the Spanish clinic. It all depended on whether or not we wanted to know and, if we did, whether we would act on the information if it were bad.

I felt it was a bit rough if we could not get the mother's age that we would be denied the Down's syndrome screening. What was scarier was that even if we did do the screen they would then do the diagnostic testing which itself carried a 1% chance of miscarriage which I didn't like the sound of.

Luckily, we had until 13 weeks 6 days to do the test so a few days to think about it and try and get information and indeed even up to 20 weeks we could do a quadruple test and still get a result.

The nurse then went on about sickle cell and thalassemia testing which depended on ethnic origin – Africa for the sickle cell and the Mediterranean for thalassemia. Given we did not know about the mother it meant I should really be tested as it was one of those where the chances were good if both parents were carriers but if I was clear then it was low risk.

I rolled up my sleeve with a sigh and gave blood for the HPLC test.

Driving away we decided to both think about the whole Down's thing for the day before making a decision.

Back at work, I scanned the report and images and sent them to the Spanish clinic along with a general question regarding how we went about doing the Down's test (if we could at all). I also e-mailed my new company to request the Friday off as vacation and explained the situation to them. Hopefully they will be sympathetic but I will not be that surprised if they said no.

Iona wanted to tell her headmaster the news but he was not in so she had the agony of building herself up for the meeting only for it not to happen.

My company came back to me quite quickly but not with an answer as the girl in HR needed to ask my new boss but she promised to get back to me on Monday. She didn't indicate that there would be a problem but clearly wanted him to be able to make the choice. It would be a good test to see what he is like.

Under other circumstances this would have been annoying but we were in possession of scan photos so took a large mug of hot chocolate each to bed and spent a disgusting amount of time staring lovingly at them. We could now tell people with confidence!

For once the Spanish clinic stepped up to the plate. I had a note back from Maria giving us the age (23) and blood group (O positive) of the donor which was much easier than I thought it was going to be. Iona and I agreed to go ahead with the screening test now we had the info, though we were not sure what we were going to do with the result if it were bad. I wonder how many couples really think this through or whether they all adopt (as I am) the "it won't happen to us" attitude.

Interestingly, although the donor is anonymous, it did mean that we were starting to build up a picture of her. We now knew her age, blood group and general appearance (which should be similar to Iona but with possibly darker skin). It was also likely that she was either local to Barcelona or had been a student there.

I realised that this was a dangerous pastime. The whole point of the donor remaining anonymous was precisely that, so we did not know who she was or would ever have means to trace her. Iona was the child's mother and that was that. The egg, as far as I was concerned, was simply tissue used to facilitate the pregnancy. Iona was carrying it, Iona would nurture it and Iona would raise it.

As I had these thoughts I knew I had to commit them to the record but unlike a lot of the book I spent a lot of time phrasing it carefully.

In hindsight, a lot of what I wrote was probably done in a hurry, on the spur of the moment or whilst not in the best frame of mind. I had accepted this from the outset with the desire to capture the moment at all times, good or bad but I realised that this meant it would potentially be a very strange account to read.

I understand this now that I am writing the version that you, dear reader, have engaged in which has the benefit of editorial review, careful revision and a keen eye towards narrative flow, structure and pace (at least, so I have been told – writing is still a bit of a mystery to me). The real version is probably a mess!

However, whether it was a mess or an engaging account I knew that there were certain points which would need careful explanation and this was one of them.

# Chapter 25:
## Here is the news…

The day we told people about Iona being pregnant started with a lie. Actually, the lie had been delivered some days before but now we were acting it out.

It was Paul's birthday and we had arranged to go out for dinner in the evening but had enlisted his help to shift a load of garden waste and other items to the tip – a job that genuinely needed doing but not on that specific day as we had insisted.

Paul being the helpful chap he is agreed without question not realising that our ulterior motive was to keep him out of the way while his wife and his mother prepared the surprise birthday.

It was one of those milestone birthdays (I will not embarrass him by mentioning which one) and it had been decided that it would be a fancy-dress affair. As it was a surprise party and therefore he was not in on the gag, his costume, a rather fine Darth Vader affair for reasons that I will not go into here, had been chosen and rented for him.

The party boded to be a good one. A lot of their cousins

were young enough to take it seriously (by which I mean they would take the fancy dress seriously unlike the oldies who would do the usual trick of wearing some of their own old clothes and claim to be Jimmy Cagney).

I managed through what I thought was a sterling performance to delay Paul such that as the hour for dinner approached he was still at our place and it was decided that he would use our shower and that his wife would come over with his change of clothes ready to go out.

The look on his face when his "change of clothes" were presented by Wonder Woman, as his wife was now dressed, was a picture.

Iona had gone as a Can-Can girl, mostly because the dress was big and warm while I went for my old fall-back of Sherlock Holmes (who, like most famous people real or fictional, I in no way resemble but the costume is easy).

Realising that we were going to in effect hijack Paul's party we told his wife before heading to the hall we had hired. She was *very* excited and both Paul and I knew that once the news was out the girls would be talking babies all night. This, of course, meant that the boys could prop the bar up talking babies...at least for the first few pints before we resorted to the more traditional bollocks.

We had not discussed how we were going to break the news but once we got there and had the obligatory "Surprise!" for Paul, not that it was one by that time, I headed to the bar to get us some drinks but by the time I got back Iona, in her excitement, had already done the rounds and the news was out.

I have to say I felt a little hurt. I was just as proud as she was and it would have been nice to have seen people's expressions but the deed was done and she was happy. I put a brave face on it and basked in the congratulations while inside I felt just a little deflated. After all the months of stress I should have probably anticipated this so I didn't blame her.

Later on she sensed that I was a bit "distant" so I told her why and then instantly regretted it as she felt very guilty. They always say that honesty between couples is very important but it is at times like this that I question that statement. Iona would have probably been far better off not knowing. I should have hidden it better.

By the next day, Iona was still brooding about the fact that she had told her family without me which now made me feel really guilty as she clearly hadn't done it to annoy me. She finally got to speak to the headmaster and tell him the news. He was very pleased and meant that she was far more relaxed now that the information was "out there", even if she did ask him to keep it to himself for now.

I started sorting more things out for the new job, sending in my company car request and buying myself a sat-nav (as to put one in the car would have meant going over my allowance). They also came back to confirm that I could have the Friday 7th Jan off which was great!

For reasons that I honestly cannot remember we started discussing a second child based on the embryos that the Spanish clinic had frozen so I composed an email to enquire what the "rules" were.

Maria came back to me to say that yes it was very early to be thinking about number two but in principle we could start either after Iona finished breast feeding or a year after she has a caesarean birth (if this is what happens). At least we know! It seems that when we fill in the post-birth questionnaire that they would contact us then and discuss options. Thus, it looks like any sibling will not even be started until early 2012 and therefore not in the world until the end of 2012 (so if the Mayans were right we might just be able to squeeze number 2 in before Dec 21st 2012 when the world is supposed to end…bummer!).

Having decided to go ahead with the Down's test Iona made an appointment to give blood but not before having a near shouting match with the woman at the hospital who initially did not understand the need to get the test performed quickly until Iona spelled it out in that slow, calm voice that normally has me running for cover. Fortunately the message got through before violence occurred and an appointment was set for the next day, still within the time limit we had been given.

We left at normal time and as expected the traffic to the hospital was a lot lumpier than the last time but we still arrived in good time and parking was no issue. The receptionist, as before, was very friendly and we were called not soon after the appointment time. As was always the case, the nurse had problems finding Iona's veins but managed to get one in her arm. She took the blood for the Down's test and also a set for general screening.

The nurse we had seen the previous visit popped in to say hello and told me that I was about to get a letter to say that the blood tests I had for sickle cell etc. had all come out negative so I was in the clear there. I almost shrugged off the result as if it was obvious that it would be negative. What I would have done if she had said positive I do not know but that was not an eventuality I now had to face.

Iona was told that we should get the Down's test results within seven days – a phone call if higher risk and a letter if low risk.

The matter of her telling her family without me was still smouldering away but a good friend of mine had an excellent perspective on the situation. In his words the man at this stage of the process begins to feel like a spare part and our job is to "take the flak". Not sure I entirely agree but I did somewhat see where he was coming from in the former part of the comment (and perhaps a bit of the latter).

Iona was really tired and feeling sick by the time we got home (largely due to a bad migraine she had) but she laughed when I told her what my friend had said and it seemed to clear the air. For sure the matter was not mentioned again.

I left her there in bed while I caught up with the laundry and I realised the time had come when I was really going to have to pull my weight around the house in terms of cleaning etc.

Moving to Hull was really going to be a problem.

A few days later the letter from the hospital arrived about the Down's syndrome. This in itself was a good sign as we had not had a phone call. The news was good, we were low risk. Talking to Iona about it, it became apparent that even if the result had been higher she probably would have not been able to terminate the pregnancy. I was glad the result was low as I am not sure where I would have stood on that issue and it could have become difficult. It felt like yet another bullet dodged and I realised that there were a *lot* of bullets coming our way.

With the stress of the scan over and the excitement of announcing our news in the past we seemed to be settling into some kind of a routine. The pregnancy had really become frighteningly normal but it was everything else in life that was up in the air.

The MG had been festering in the garage since the abortive attempts to sell it but it was now time to buy the big car that Iona would need so we headed out to look at people carriers and tested all the most popular models...and hated every one of them!

While I am not a massive petrol head I could not bring myself to part good money for the selection of metal boxes with nasty plastic dashboards that were on offer and we decided to go for a Land Rover Discovery instead.

Okay, so a slightly different price bracket which meant we were now in the second-hand market but at least the car looked good, came with lots of toys, was safe an above all would drive in weather that was not brilliant sunshine.

Now I had a mission I was back in the second-hand car magazines and online sites searching for a suitable chariot for our child.

One presented itself relatively quickly in a garage near Wheatley so not too far away. It even had a winch, though I doubted I would ever actually use it but it was an extra toy so instantly desirable. For sure the running costs would be high but the MGB burned petrol like a steam engine burns wood and I hated to think what the miles per gallon we were getting were. The Land Rover could only be an improvement.

I called the garage and explained that I wanted to part-exchange an MGB and they said it would be no problem so we arranged an appointment.

Paul came with me but not before spending an hour getting the wretched purple pile started and helping me nurse-maid it to Wheatley.

I will not bore you with the ritual that then ensued of taking the Disco out for a test drive (at which point I had already fallen in love with it) haggling over the price of the Land Rover, the part-ex price of the MGB, the extras that would be thrown in, blah, blah, blah but ultimately I had a figure in mind for all of it and when the dealer came down to something appropriate I handed over the credit card.

To be honest I would have probably sold the MG for less and bought the Lanny for more as I really wasn't in the mood to haggle but the dealer caved in quite easily so that, as they say, was that.

The Disco was ready to go and already cleaned and it was a stark contrast to the MG driving home, especially as I was not in fear of stalling the engine at every roundabout or wondering at what point we would have to call the recovery services. The driving position is also a lot higher so I felt like royalty!

When we got home Iona reminded me that while I had bought it, the Disco was still *her* car!

For me it was a great weight off my mind, knowing that we had resolved at least part of the car problem (we still had my car to shift but that should be easier). The spend was easily justified as it was in our eyes a new pram as much as a new car, chosen largely for its capacity for safely carrying Fidget around as well as pram, change bag, etc. etc. etc.

As winter set in it became more and more apparent that, while she was not showing too many outwards signs Iona was clearly pregnant. The aches and pains were increasing and jobs around the house that normally were routine now became a taboo.

For example, our vacuum cleaner, one of those cheerful red things with a name and a smiley face, while not particularly heavy lived in a relatively inaccessible corner of the under-stairs cupboard requiring it (him) to be physically manhandled out of his hidey-hole whenever his services were required. He also shared the same Achilles heel as Daleks in that he was rather stumped by staircases meaning that he needed a helping hand whenever this task was required.

Okay for all you Whovians out there, I admit that Daleks have sophisticated anti-gravity systems that allow them to hover & fly and there has been more than one occasion where I have wished that Henry was fitted with something similar.

Asking Iona to lug him around was out of the question

so by default vacuuming (or at least getting the damn thing out for vacuuming) was now my job.

When her Dad called and asked if "we" would go and help him move some furniture out of his house – he was having a major clear out and there was a load of old stuff that had to be moved to the garage – he really meant "me" as my good wife was in no condition to assist beyond moral support.

The job was not made any easier by the fact that it decided to snow that day so the concrete between the house and the garage took on the coefficient of friction of polished glass. It was just as well that the furniture was on its way to either the tip or the bonfire as certain parts of it were in no fit condition after we had both practiced our pirouettes on the ice.

Driving back the next day was about as much fun but as Iona was really tired I took the wheel, all the while wondering how she was going to cope once I was up in Hull during the week. I knew that a job rota would have to be established by which all the heavy lifting tasks were saved for the weekend when I would be around.

The snow seemed to abate the next day which was good as it was the day I headed to my old company for the "update". It was actually a very useful day and any dreams I had of being a total git went out of the window, partly as I was actually getting something worthwhile out of the session but mostly as I really am not that sort of chap.

Dinner was good and only marginally spoiled when I got out of the restaurant to find the snow had returned with a vengeance and the motorway was closed due to a particularly creative pile-up. It was depressingly late by the time I arrived home and the roads were all but impassable. Only then did I realised I had neglected to phone home and as my phone had been switched off Iona was unable to reach me to check I was alright.

Oops!

When we woke the next day I realised just how much she had cause to worry as we found a taxi buried in a wall just up the road from us. When it had crashed neither of us knew. For sure it had been after I had arrived home but we had both been so tired we had slept through the fun and games.

The roads were still treacherous when we went to the hospital for Iona's appointment with the consultant and I began to appreciate our timing having made all the earlier trips in relatively kind weather. With all the recent delays resulting from the snow there must have been patients who had been obliged to miss their vital appointments with all the stress that would have carried.

The time of the consultant appointment was at 9:00am but we left early to allow for the icy roads which typically were quiet as most sensible people had stayed at home. This meant we got there at about ten past eight so had time to go to the restaurant for bacon / sausage butties and coffee / tea. The regular intake of bacon rolls was definitely a fringe benefit of the process as far as I was concerned.

I did have to laugh, however, as the walls were covered in the usual posters warning of the dangers of diabetes and heart disease while the cooks served up grease and sugar.

Despite presenting ourselves at the ante-natal dept ten minutes early it was 9:15 by the time we were called up and then it was one of the nurses who started the appointment by taking Iona's blood pressure and checking her notes. It was good to hear that all her recent blood tests had again come back normal.

We then sat there for half an hour before the consultant finally arrived and when she did she was so laid back she was nearly horizontal. I noticed that as she had walked in she left the door open, despite the fact that we were talking about confidential issues. The nurse closed it a few minutes later but I thought it was a bit unprofessional. The consultant was also drenched in perfume which made my eyes sting! At least it would keep the flies down in the room.

I felt as if the whole meeting was a bit of a waste of time and apart from saying that everything was normal she really didn't add anything new or give any new advice (and certainly was not well versed in the difference between donor egg treatments in the UK versus Spain). She gave Iona a cursory examination for the show of it and that was that.

Although my impression had been that it was a wasted journey, Iona had the reassurance of seeing someone and hearing that everything was normal. She also got to ask a few general questions about sleeping on her tummy (which she had avoided but was told she could do), using the electric blanket or car heated seats (both okay) or steroid face cream (again, no problem) so at least these would make her life a bit more comfortable.

We made a follow-up appointment for 40 weeks (on her due day, in fact) and that was that.

On the way back we decided that we would start discussing names on the way down to Dorset for Christmas. When I say "we" I of course meant "she". At what point this thought had crossed her mind I do not know but she announced completely out of the blue that the names would be chosen at this time and place and what could I do but agree.

To be honest I had not even thought about it and suddenly the fact that I would now be required to was really scary. As soon as we had potential names the child would become even more real. The bachelor in me felt rather uncomfortable and not for the first time did I wonder if I was *really* ready for parenthood. In my heart I had no doubt that I wanted the child but the enormity of the responsibility that brought had mostly been lost in the background noise of angst.

The harsh reality of having a pregnant wife really struck home as Christmas loomed. Having sold the MG we were now in a position to empty the loft, get all the boxes down and start the laborious process of sorting through stuff. We knew that at some stage soon we would be moving house and I also needed to find certain items to survive with in the short-term.

The absence of the rust-bucket and the fact that the Disco was perfectly happy out on the street meant that the garage was now empty and waiting to receive junk for sorting. However, in her state there was no way Iona could shift and carry so she stayed in the kitchen making Christmas sweets instead.

I called a couple of friends and with a bribe of wine and dinner they agreed to come and help lug boxes.

As it was, we had a huge list of other jobs to do including chopping the grape vine which was taking over one whole corner of the garden, putting up Xmas decorations etc. etc. but somehow managed to get them all done! I'm not sure who was more exhausted by the end of it, us or her but we were all pretty zonked. The party that ensued was, I must admit, a very drunken one but my friends' assistance was suitably appreciated. I doubt their hangovers the next morning were.

I stuck my old car on the online auction site for a "get rid of it" price and had contact from someone offering slightly more in cash for a quick sale. Done!

The very next day the chap came up laden with cash and after an "everyone was happy" sort of deal drove off cheerfully while I took the money to the bank. Once again

I felt like life was gradually changing from the old ways to what would be our new life up in Hull. The cars were now sorted and the process of thinning out the house had begun. What could possibly go wrong?

Stupid bloody students, that's what! Iona found herself embroiled in an incident at the school in which one of her pupils of, let's say, ethnic origin had stepped quite severely out of line. I apologies profusely if my phrasing is not politically correct but this particular individual was the sort that would be disruptive in class and the minute they were chastised for it pull the race card.

This was precisely what had happened now. Having once again failed to present any homework and being challenged about it on one of the rare occasions she had deigned to show up to school, the pupil in question had immediately flown off the handle, become abusive and started accusing Iona of being racist.

My wife was understandably deeply worried and concerned by this regarding the impact it would have on her career as even in cases such as this where the pupil is clearly a trouble-maker our politically correct society still comes down on the side of the accuser not the accused. I was more concerned on the impact it was going to have on Fidget!

The situation escalated as the letter arrived from the student's parents stating the grounds for her claim and formally accusing Iona of racist behaviour several times. For me it was red rag to a bull and I was in fighting mood.

I took a pencil to a copy of the letter and using my grumpy old man head ticked off all the legal issues that I could see (and there were many – unfounded remarks, contradictory statements and facts that were quite blatantly not true). If they wanted a court case they were going to have one!

Iona checked through her e-mail and other records to

get the supporting evidence which was almost exclusively on her side and we submitted a formal rebuttal to the powers involved with a less than veiled threat that if they wanted to "make something of it" a counter-suit would be swift and harsh. I believe the chant is "come and have a go if you think you're hard enough!"

Despite this, Iona was still deeply concerned. While the school were assuring her that "everything would be alright" their attitude did not seem to be taking it quite as seriously as she was, especially as the headmaster was about as wet as used toilet paper (and about as useful). In my mind I was already plotting litigation against them as well and the fear was there that this would have a very detrimental effect on the pregnancy.

Relief came from an unexpected angle when one of her cousins who had a young daughter just coming out of newborn sized things arrived with a bag of baby clothes and maternity wear for Iona to browse through. This gave them both something to natter about so I took my leave and found some odd jobs to do.

The respite was, sadly, short-lived. Iona went for her middle-of-the-night wee and there was blood in it. She didn't tell me at the time but when I woke up she told me what had happened and said that she wasn't going to go into work but was going to call the midwife early (she had her appointment anyway that afternoon). Although we didn't say it we were clearly both thinking the worst and my dark thoughts towards the student and the school were brewing. If we lost the baby over this I would unleash a shit-storm the likes of which they would never have seen before.

Iona searched on the internet for references to the blood in her urine and thought it could be down to the fact that she had eaten pineapple two days before which some internet site said could bring on a miscarriage.

I had intended to go out and do some work on the residual contracts I had but stayed home as well to be with her and make sure she was okay (and to be on hand for any emergency). In the process I was able to do some of her work and thus take a bit of the pressure off while she stayed in bed but not before she called the hospital and told them the situation (the midwife was engaged). They said that as the blood seemed to be stopping that she should take it easy, stick to her appointment but if the midwife felt there was an issue they could do a scan the next day or Friday.

Iona spent the rest of the morning and early afternoon worrying as she drifted in and out of sleep.

We left for the midwife early (again) as I just wanted to get there and get some answers.

Frustratingly, although the check-in computer claimed that the appointments were running to time we were nearly fifteen minutes late going in. Fortunately, the midwife is mad as a brush but extremely nice and good at her job. From the outset she was reassuring while listening carefully to what Iona had to say.

The fact that the blood was stopping seemed to her to indicate that Iona had a bit of a raw patch on the cervix that had bled but that it was not indicative of a larger problem but to call the GP if it returned. As to the pineapple, she simply laughed and said that in moderation there was no issue (ah, the joys of the scare-mongering internet).

Realising, however, that Iona and I were clearly worried she laid her on the bed and felt for her uterus (which she could and which felt fine) before getting a microphone and speaker and trying to find the baby's heartbeat, though she prefaced this with the fact that there were no guarantees at this stage.

We had nothing to worry about, Fidget's heart was beating loud and clear. One thing we have never had a problem with in the pregnancy is the strength of Fidget's heart which, to me, is a really good sign. We could even hear the sounds of the placenta working. All was well.

She sent us off with the clear advice…keep it simple, keep it boring!

Good advice!

# Chapter 26:
## It's the season to be merry…

We had not seen Dawn and Andrew for some time which we both felt bad about. They had been so helpful at the beginning of the journey and yet we had seemed to abandon them as matters progressed. In some respect I felt that this was due to the fact that we were beginning to stand on our own feet and cope better but it somehow felt wrong not to let them know how things were going.

Dinner was arranged and everyone was very excited that an evening of girly and boy talk was on the cards. They were genuinely pleased to see us and it was so nice to finally be with people with whom we could be open and normal. It felt really nice to share our experiences with them, especially as they mirrored their own so closely with their getting treatment in Barcelona.

Andrew and I swapped stories about the "little room" while the girls compared notes on how it felt to have a baby on board. They also gave us all sorts of great advice that it would not even have occurred to us to ask for and let us borrow a baby name book to mull over.

It was a measure of how relaxed we felt in that before we knew it my watch showed that the time was nearly midnight!

Buoyed on the wave of a good evening the next day had good news. To this day I will not know what happened but all of a sudden the race allegations against Iona were dropped and the pupil involved mysteriously disappeared. There was talk of police involvement and "other factors" but it was clear the school was very keen to brush the whole affair under the carpet and once the pupil had been expelled that, as far as they were concerned, was that.

As December moved on, Iona continued to get tired but restless at night. I ordered her a special pillow (sort of "C" shaped that she could cuddle into that supported her growing tummy) and despite the Christmas rush of parcels it arrived in good time. Rather than wait until the 25th I gave it to her straight away as an early present for her and Fidget so that she could get use of it. It seemed to go down very well, even if she did keep whacking me in the face with it in the middle of the night as she readjusted!

The threat of snow was ever present and Iona was becoming anxious about getting down to Dorset. We had packed the day before to be ready to leave and as she had a doctor's appointment first thing in the morning we decided at that point to simply get out of town and make a break for it.

By now I had wrapped up the last piece of work on the last contract so my rather unsuccessful stint as my own boss came to an end.

It was a strange way to end a job. I had no desk to clear, there were no goodbyes and for sure no leaving party.

As the morning broke we were very glad to be in possession of the Land Rover. The roads were once again treacherous and after she had seen the doctor we made our way slowly down to her parent's place. We shared the driving but the conditions were bad enough that we had to concentrate even harder all the way.

We completely forgot to have the conversation regarding names!

Somewhere along the line Iona must have mentioned our plan as the first thing her Mother wanted to know when we arrived was which names we had settled on. Having discovered we had forgotten to discuss the matter she packed us off to the guest room to "have the chat" under threat that we would not get a hot drink until we did.

Iona had made a list as well so we started with girls and with letters of the alphabet. "Got any 'a's'?". It became clear very quickly that our lists barely coincided with starting letters, let alone actual names.

For the boys, we quickly arrived at idea that we both felt happy with (which did not include "Henry" for obvious reasons) so concentrated on the girls' names. After a few moments of looking gormlessly at each other we started by crossing off those we really hated or which would produce yet another embarrassing link to "Forde". The list was quickly pruned!

I was very keen to have either a Spanish-sounding or an unusual name but realising that we were rapidly approaching an impasse I decided to let Iona have control of the first name and that I would complement it with a second.

She was very keen on Eleanor, a name I was not averse to and it allowed me to use the name I was starting to favour, Athena as a middle name (after the Goddess of wisdom from classical times). If, Fidget, you do turn out to be a girl, you now know who to blame!

I knew that when I made the next update to the book it would forever feel different for now, whichever way things turned out, I knew what the baby would be called.

It was a very momentous day for another reason. We went to Mothercare. Iona had seen some things that she wanted us to take a look at as well as wanting to go shopping with her Mum. However, when there we found a microwave bottle steriliser at half price as well as some other bits and bobs which we therefore bought. It was the first things we had actually bought for Fidget and I realised we had passed a milestone. The baby was real and we were tempting fate by actually buying things.

I think a lot of it was that given Fidget was so well developed neither of us had any doubts that there would be any other outcome than a successful birth.

I hoped we were *not* jumping the gun!

Iona also selected a number of items for her parents to buy her for Christmas, mostly Winnie the Pooh – branded things such as the baby bath & changing set.

It also dawned on me at that precise moment that whilst my opinion was important to her, she was most definitely in charge of the purchase of baby things. She had been promised by a number of people the loan or hand-me-down of various things and we had already secured the pram but suddenly I realised that I had lost track of exactly what we were getting and what we had to buy. I just hoped that Iona was remembering it all.

She was, of course, women are good at that sort of thing.

The day before Christmas Eve I was roped into singing Christmas carols in the village square which for Iona was really an ulterior motive for telling the vicar and all the people she knew about the baby. Oddly, at first they did not seem all that excited but I think we had taken them by shock. The singing seemed to be going well so I decided to do my usual trick of miming the bits I didn't know or were too high for me to reach and mumbling the rest so that my utter lack of singing ability did not spoil the event.

My fear that they had taken the news badly was short-lived as once we got into the village hall after the carols for mulled wine and mince pies they "warmed up" and were all very enthusiastic.

I gave Iona a Christmas card to her and Fidget! She hadn't got me a card so I think I embarrassed her a bit but within a few minutes she had put together one of the ones we had hand-made for our friends and family. Not for the first time I wondered what next Christmas would be like!

We were going to midnight mass at the church and as a result Iona was sent to bed for a couple of hours so that she would go the distance. I, in the mean time, spent a pleasant afternoon helping her Mum to cook all the meaty things (turkey, stuffing, sausages in bacon and all that sort of thing) for Christmas dinner.

December 25th arrived. It felt odd that this would be our last Christmas without the baby. Most of the presents I had bought Iona were not particularly baby related as I knew she was going to get loads now from friends and family and wanted to get her things that were for her. I did, however, get her a baby book that was written in the style of a popular car maintenance manual which I think she liked.

We enjoyed a nice quiet Christmas, church in the morning and then back to her parents' place so I could complete my task of assisting in the preparation the Christmas feast and then in the evening we headed over to her friends to play some games and, in my case, drink a lot.

All the time, at the back of my mind, lurked the uncertainty of where we would be this time next year. For sure life was likely to be completely different.

When Boxing Day had been and gone I started to feel very depressed. All through Christmas I had the knowledge in the background that the New Year would bring a drastic and, to be honest, unwanted change in my life. The control freak in me was screaming as the only arrangement I had with my new company was to turn up on the Tuesday morning for the start of my induction and that they would put me up in a hotel for the first couple of weeks while I sorted myself out with accommodation.

I had no idea what I was getting myself into but I knew what I was going to be missing. I knew it bothered Iona as well. She was really feeling the effects of the pregnancy now and it was only a week before I would effectively vanish.

We went on a tour of other family members but my black mood never quite went away as the end of the year loomed. As we were nipping backwards and forwards I realised that there were some important documents regarding my new job that I had intended to read and complete which were still sitting on the dining table at home. As we were going to be generally in the vicinity I persuaded Iona to let me head back to collect them, though I sensed she would rather that I forgot about the whole subject and chilled out.

As we got home I had a funny incident in that I had a card for a courier to say a parcel had been left but when I checked next door they knew nothing about it. It was only when I checked the card again that I realised they had put the parcel in the wheelie bin...which my neighbours were literally at that moment in the process of putting out for collection. Had I not returned to collect the forgotten paperwork on that day I would have lost it! At least it was reassuring that there were times when fate smiled on me.

We headed back to the peace and quiet of Dorset with a quick side-trip to Bournemouth to get me a new suit for my new job and to drop in on some other old college friends of mine. They were unaware of Iona's condition as my plan had been to tell them face to face and they were suitably pleased and we had a very nice dinner as well as getting loads of baby-related suggestions and comments. They had four kids and knew what they were talking about.

I was becoming quite anxious, knowing that New Year's Eve was our last full day in Dorset before the whole "rest of our lives" thing started. The day was generally quiet as I tend to find it usually is though we did go round to her friends' place for drinks prior to heading to the church to listen to the bell-ringers ring in midnight. Neither of us particularly likes big parties and this is a really nice relaxing way to see off the old year. Also, from the churchyard you get a great view of everyone else's fireworks!

I turned to Iona as soon as the last bell had sounded and said that we were now in the year in which our baby would be born.

And so ended 2010. It had been such a mixed year and looking back it was amazing just how it was wrapping up given how our lives had been twelve months ago. Then we were still mired in the uncertainty around whether or not we could even have kids but I doubt that either of us would have honestly thought that we would in twelve months not only have discovered our situation to be the way it was but also to be so far down the road on actually creating a new life.

For me it had been a rollercoaster of frustration, hard work, despair and hope when it came to the job situation but the result was now creating its own dilemmas.

As I went to bed in the early hours I wondered just what the move to Hull would bring.

# Chapter 27:
## To boldly go…

With the morning came that horrible realisation that the holiday was over and for us it would mean the dawning of a new way of life. 2011 was going to bring a new job for me, the stress of buying and selling houses and the thrill of the birth itself. It was a lot to think about and suddenly we were several levels up on the "real-o-meter". Before I had been able to push things back into the "worry about that in the New Year" folder of my mind but now of course it *was* the New Year.

I really hate going home day after a holiday away. No matter how hard I try I always end up wanting to pack the car and just get home, knowing that we still have to unpack the other end and that there is really little point in delaying. It always means that the last day ends up shorter than it should.

Returning to the house was also very strange, conscious as I was that this was very soon going to cease to be where I lived on a permanent basis. The small nervous shrew-like creature in my distant ancestry that still lurks in the most basic part of my brain ached to simply bury my head in the sand and hide away from the big decisions to be made in life. Why couldn't things stay the way they were?

Then I took a good look around the house and realised that we could do so much better. End of sentiment, now I just wanted to fast-forward to a time when we could get shot of the place and buy our new family home.

It was all getting very stressful, no sooner would I be in the job than we would be looking to start the house selling process.

A plan had been hatched while in Dorset that Iona would move up as soon as she went on maternity leave and we would try and coordinate house selling around this time but that we would then get her Mum to come up and stay during the period when Iona was giving birth. It would at least mean I would be around when the event happened but we would need to find a hospital up there etc. etc. etc...

I packed my pathetically small amount of things, a suitcase and my laptop bag and tried not to make it an emotional day but I was feeling very low, not wanting to go and afraid of the new life I was getting myself into.

The morning passed far too quickly and before I knew it the time had come for Iona to drop me to the train station. Part of me wondered if this was how couples going through a separation felt.

We made our farewells and I headed to the platform, secretly hoping that the trains were cancelled. They were not. My four-coach train to London arrived on time and I found my allotted seat – occupied by someone else who I evicted promptly, not feeling in a particularly charitable mood. With insufficient room to do any work or writing I attempted a crossword but eventually resorted to watching the world go by.

After nearly missing my connection (I think my

subconscious was still secretly plotting against me) I eventually caught the Hull train.

The landscape became steadily bleaker and more industrial and I knew I had entered the North. It was a relatively short taxi run to the hotel but it still cost £45 – so much for the cheaper cost of living up here! The popular inexpensive hotel chain that my less-than-generous soon-to-be employers had stumped up for was deserted and I was practically the only one staying there that night. It had the feel of the morning after a big party and the Christmas decorations were still up which did little to make it feel welcoming under the circumstances.

Having checked in and found my small but functional room, I called Iona to say I was there safe then went down to the bar for a drink. Almost immediately I felt very, very homesick. At least I resisted the temptation to bury my woes in too much alcohol as I was, as I kept reminding myself, starting my new job in the morning.

Of course, it snowed in the night. Despite having booked a taxi for a time that would easily get me into the office he was twenty minutes late which made me equally late on my first day. The only consolation was that my new boss was also snowed in and would end up an hour and a half late, arriving about twenty minutes after I had finished my HR induction.

The first day was pretty much all induction but it was clear from the start that they were really not ready for my arrival, having neither desk, computer, phone or anything else for me. The only thing they did provide was a pool car (as they hadn't even ordered my company car despite my getting the paperwork to them two months in advance). This was going to be a real challenge and while I didn't think I had made a mistake, it was certainly a case of "I was not in Kansas now!"

Life also became that bit more complicated as my new boss, Andy, hinted to the fact that I might not need to relocate permanently but on this he frustratingly did not expand.

All I could think about was Iona at home alone.

Day two of the new job and I was starting to find my feet. The induction process continued which was just as well as I was living off of the meeting table in Andy's office. The chap whose desk I was to take over was supposedly moving downstairs but as his new home was currently an empty room, when that was going to happen suddenly became vague. It seemed just as well that I was going to be pretty much out for the next two days.

It was on day three that a rather startling revelation was made. As I had not actually been given the job I had been originally interviewed for but an expanded role, the scope of my position was now European rather than localised in the UK. Practically this meant that being based in Hull might not be the best option. It also became clear that the company was undergoing a pretty major restructuring, something they had previously neglected to mention.

What this meant for me practically was not expanded on but I was told to hold fire on plans to buy a house in the area.

This of course was not very helpful and I mulled over it in my mind all the way back down the motorway as I gladly headed home.

I had not mentioned any of it on the phone, partly as I was receiving information in dribs and drabs but mostly as it was a conversation I wanted to have face to face as I tried to fathom what the implications were.

Iona, as always, had the sensible answer to the problem. Rather than move almost immediately we would delay the house hunting until Easter, she would remain in the area to have the baby the hospital we had picked (thus avoiding the need to find a new one at the last minute) and I would try and work from home more around that time.

During my first three days it had been discussed that working from home was an option, indeed given the fact that there was no space I almost felt that they were trying to get rid of me from the building and Andy had already said I could work from home on Fridays which was a real bonus and meant that I could come home on Thursday evenings.

It was a good plan, even though it would extend the time I would be running up and down the motorways but if that was the price to pay then so be it. I would still go ahead and rent a place but now I would look closer to work and for something smaller just for me and the occasional visit from Iona or others.

The plan was a weight off of my mind, even if it only delayed some things rather than solved them.

Iona worked from home on the day of her twenty-week scan which meant we could have a lie-in together which was nice and also that she was around all day. I ran around doing various chores while she marked and then in the afternoon we headed over to the hospital.

It was only when we got there that I felt totally useless. Iona was obviously very nervous about the whole thing and I had been so wrapped up in the new job and the move to Hull that I had not had time to even think about let alone get worked up about it myself or, more importantly, support her. This was exactly what I hated about the way life was turning out; when she needed me I was not there for her.

We sat in the waiting room watching all the other expectant mothers and I tried not to think about there being any problem as I was sure that neither of us was in the least prepared for bad news.

Iona was initially called for an MRSA screen, something

they "offered" in that way where they were obviously going to do it anyway unless you really kicked up a fuss. There was no consent form or anything like that. It was just assumed that you were willing.

As it was, we had no problem doing the screening.

While we were waiting we saw one couple who were going in for a scan but had brought a whole gaggle of mothers, mother-in-laws, grannies, aunts or whatever and the nurse was politely trying to tell them that they could not go in en-masse. The mother-to-be simply stared at them aghast, completely failing to see why she couldn't take her entire extended family in with her. What the hell were they expecting? Eventually they seemed to go in on a shift-rotation basis.

On the flip-side, there did seem to be a lot of women attending their appointments alone and I felt even gladder to have been able to get home to support Iona (and, of course, not to miss the event).

Despite the appointment being at three in the afternoon they were not running too horribly late and at about quarter past we were called in.

This time it was a bloke doing the ultrasound but he was very nice. Iona got on the bed while I sat on a chair doing the usual guy thing of being basically surplus to requirements in all ways apart from moral support.

At least I had a telly to watch, hooked up to the scanner so both Iona and I could see it.

As you may or may not know, the 20 week scan is quite detailed where they look for anomalies and all sorts of things. The foetus is sufficiently developed to look like a small person so that any defects would be obvious. It is also the scan in which, if you ask, they attempt to identify the gender of the baby.

We did not want to know the baby's sex so I was terrified that we would inadvertently see a dangly bit and find out.

I shouldn't have worried either about problems or gender.

True to form, the moment the scanner touched Iona's belly we saw Fidget's strong beating heart! This was immediately followed by a comment from the chap doing the scanning to complain that Fidget was lying in a very awkward angle which made his job difficult.

Our fears about finding out the gender were also quickly dispelled. As the scanner moved around we caught glimpses of arms, legs, spine etc. While we were obviously looking at a baby it was very difficult to interpret at any point exactly what was on the screen or even at what part of the body we were seeing.

The sonographer seemed to be happy with what he was looking at and was occasionally heard to say things like "brain developing well", "kidneys looking fine", "yes, that looks okay". All I could see on the screen was an amorphous fuzzy grey lump. For all I knew, he could have been uttering complete cobblers though in truth he came across as very professional and confident.

We were there for several minutes staring at the image on the screen that reminded me of the Alien from the famous science fiction movie. If you have not seen it, look up the artwork of H. R. Giger on the internet and you will see the sort of thing I mean (all exposed spines and stuff like that).

I could see that Iona was very relieved to hear that everything was normal. Fidget at this stage is about 20cm long and all of its dimensions were normal apart from its head which while okay was on the low end of the scale. Iona didn't mind in the least – if that trend kept up it would make the birth easier!

We got a few scan pictures but they were not great. I commented that even though Fidget did not have Iona's genetics it already had her mannerisms i.e. hating having photos taken! It made it even more important that I had been there as I had seen things on the screen that were simply not reproduced in the pictures. Had I missed the scan and only seen the images I would have been quite unimpressed by what I saw.

Heading back via the supermarket we bought a few more baby things (as we had yet another voucher) and for the first time I felt far more comfortable doing so. Passing the 20 week scan and knowing everything was still normal was a psychological milestone for me.

When we got back I scanned and e-mailed the report and pictures to the Spanish clinic just to keep them in the loop while Iona called her Mum to give her an update and run up another huge phone bill.

Perhaps now I could relax a bit and just get on with the new routine of life. I felt a bit odd, as if I had simply been away on a business trip. Not sure how long it is going to take me to settle to the idea that I was now split between two locations but it was very nice being home.

Saturday was a good day. After a relatively lazy morning we headed over to the University of Reading where we had tickets for a talk by Sir David Attenborough. He was suitably entertaining and everyone in the audience (Iona and I included) were totally in awe of him.

We ended the day with a nice meal round at the local curry house – we were booked in for 8PM but we were so hungry we went over just after six thirty! Hopefully Fidget is getting a taste for Indian food. I had heard somewhere that the more varied your diet during pregnancy the better it was for the baby but I was not sure how true that was.

Sunday was even nicer, to start with at least. Iona and I

went over to Kingston to pick up her eternity ring and had a nice chat with the chap in the jewellers. After the successful scan I didn't feel quite so superstitious about it.

She looked in Primark for some comfortable bras as the ones she was wearing were making her sore but could not find anything suitable.

It was, however, really hard to then jump in the car that evening and head north again (not helped by the jacket potato covered in left-over curry that was sitting heavily in my belly). When I got back to the hotel it suddenly felt really sad and depressing.

I resolved to sort a flat out as a matter of priority!

The first thing I did on arriving in work on the Monday morning was to bite the bullet and do a concerted search on the internet for a flat. There were depressingly few around and when I called one of the letting agents to enquire about the availability of furnished rented places was pretty much told that they were about as common as rocking-horse shit.

That said I was put on to someone who had two he could show me that evening.

I hit the lowest point so far at work. Andy had a meeting in his office so I was turfed out and had absolutely nowhere to go for 40 minutes. I ended up in the tiny kitchen pretending that I was there with a purpose but really feeling totally conspicuous and stupid, drinking gallons of machine latte to keep me occupied.

As I stood there I wondered not for the first time how Iona was coping. She had worked from home in the morning to wait for a chest of drawers we had ordered as a changing table but then was going to go to school and finally tell everyone the good news (not that she could have hidden it for much longer).

I finished work early to meet the agent at the first flat.

Typical for me I arrived half an hour early and he was ten minutes late but at least he called to say so.

The flat was perfect – for me (though would be quickly inadequate for us both and baby so I hoped it would not come to that) and was in a nice safe, secure environment. Being as I was totally bored already with flat-hunting I didn't bother going to see the other one.

I called Iona and gave her the good news, especially that I could probably move in the following Tuesday so that this week would be my last in the hotel.

As can only it seems happen to me I had a bit of a strange hiccup with the letting agent in the morning. I phoned them back only to be told they had never heard of the property! Luckily, as the agent had called to say he would be late I had his mobile number and called him. Got through fine but had no idea whatsoever where the other number had come from. To this day it remains a mystery. I had only called one letting agent and did so from the number I had written down which, overnight, had eerily turned into the number for a completely different agent.

Still, confusion or not I was in contact with the right people and finally received the application form which I completed and sent back but as I needed scans of utility bills I had to ask Iona in the evening to get those.

It was only later in the evening when I was going to bed that I realised I had been a bit ratty on the phone, largely as I was struggling to settle in to my new job given the ongoing absence of anything useful that would enable me to do my job properly and the added anxiety of getting the flat sorted, that and the deepening feeling that Iona was a hell of a long way away.

I texted an apology and the speed at which the response came back indicated quite clearly that she was awake and worrying about me.

# Chapter 28:
## ...to Hull and back.

Gradually, as the days passed, the new job began to take on some form of familiarity even if the underlying issues did not resolve themselves. I found myself striding with confidence down the corridor to where the loos were and the count of people for whom I could put a name to a face had passed ten (I am pathologically bad with names).

My boss kindly let me slope off early on the following Thursday so I left at three-thirty. The traffic was totally rubbish and it was nearly eight before I reached home. I entered the house tired and drained with the feeling that this was going to be my life for the next few months. Still, at least this weekend was going to be a long one.

Her cousin Emma was there when I arrived, she had popped over to drop off some cards and she had given us a present in the form of a picture frame for the scan pictures. Iona had mentioned that I had been very ante-posting the pictures on certain popular social networking sites so Emma was paranoid that I would not like it.

Quite the contrary, I thought it was great and not an

issue as we would keep the images private and the frame in our room.

The oak chest of drawers we had ordered to double as a changing table had arrived and it looked very nice and very suitable for the job. All it needed now was a baby.

I was not sure if it was my imagination but Iona seemed to be showing a bit more, as if being able to tell everyone at work had allowed her to relax and get large with confidence. For sure, it must have been that time when Fidget was growing at a sufficient rate to make a difference.

Fortunately Emma had places to be and as we were both very tired we had an early night, though we chatted in bed, mostly about houses as there had been a few more appear on the email alert I had signed up for and regularly received from some of the popular property-finding websites. Iona also mentioned that she had been told by someone of a medical persuasion that she should have been advised early on not to wear under-wired bras so it was no surprise she was getting sore. The good old NHS strikes again!

I felt her tummy – starting to feel what can only be described as a bubbling as Fidget started to move around. It would not be long now before it started to kick! That was totally thrilling!

On the Sunday we really started to take our chances as we ordered a cot online, still at a good price but one with all the bells and whistles we needed. Fortunately, as I had a meeting in London the next day my weekend was extended slightly so I didn't have to dash off.

We joined the NCT and booked a session at an upcoming baby show for pain relief. I still didn't have to leave as I had already decided to drive up first thing in the morning to get the keys to my new rented flat. I wondered how many excuses I could possibly invent for further shortening of my working week up north. So far things were working out pretty well but I knew that had to end soon.

At least this time when I headed up it was to achieve something that would give me at least a modicum of freedom. I arrived at the letting agents early so was able to move into the flat before lunch time. While it was, I am sure, a nice flat it felt a bit cold and sterile, mainly as it had none of our stuff in or more importantly my wife. Even the appeal of being a bachelor for a few days during the week, being able to drink beer, eat what I liked and watch whatever I wanted did not seem to quite step up to the mark. I knew if I did all those things I would feel guilty and the fact was I fundamentally did not want to be there. If alcohol or other vices were brought into the mix it would be a disaster.

While quiet alien to me, I decided there and then that I would not indulge while enjoying my freedom. Somehow it just didn't feel right and I knew that whatever I did would be no substitute for what I really wanted which was simply to give up and head south again.

I do apologise at this point to all northerners, I am not having a pop at your fair land and I even admit that I was probably being somewhat harsh on Hull but the fact of the matter was that my heart really was not in it and you have to go with your heart as I hope you agree.

The weeks began to blur into one as I left on the Sunday night only to return on the Thursday evening. The weekends were all too short and if we did anything with friends or family I began to begrudge the lost time.

At the very least, despite what my company had said we still had to prepare ourselves for the eventuality of moving house and before this could happen there was a spectacular amount of sorting out that had to happen. As most of this involved shifting heavy boxes around and the vast majority of the crap to sort was mine it was not even as if Iona could do much in my absence.

It was probably not the best weekend to start tackling the mammoth task of thinning the house out as it was Iona's mother's birthday and we had a house-full of people over for a "winter barbeque" (one of those traditions started by a now sadly deceased male member of the family but which seems to have carried on regardless). I had not taken into account the fact that everyone would bring overnight bags, presents and other random stuff so that the already-messy house became like the left-baggage office at Waterloo Station.

Still, the benefit of having a barbeque was that we could spread out into the garden. Now, you may question the logic of a winter barbeque but trust me it works. Picture the scene, it is cold and dark outside, everyone is wearing thick winter-woolies and huddled around the barbeque with a sausage and a stiff drink (or, in some cases, a hot cocoa). There is something almost primordial about huddling around the camp fire at night.

I have yet to meet someone who has not enjoyed the experience though the post-barbeque hangover is less appreciated.

It went well and it was another great excuse to talk about babies. Iona's mum had a suitably good time and I managed to at least make a passing resemblance of enjoying myself and not be a grumpy old sod.

Inevitably the Sunday brought back my bleak mood as we cooked the traditional roast lunch but my thoughts were already on the need to pack and make the journey north again that evening. I was only a few weeks into the job and already the loss of my Sunday evenings with Iona was beginning to really irritate.

The flat was starting to become a symbol of everything

that was wrong about the situation and things at work did not help either.

I had naturally assumed that after a relatively short induction period and certainly beyond the point where I could find my way to the gents and back without needing to ask for directions that I would get into some real work but as the days wore on it became increasingly apparent that they were padding out the induction for reasons that were not being shared with me.

Everyone else around me seemed awfully busy and spent their day in the plethora of meetings, conference calls and other activities that normally prevent technical people from doing their real job but here I was sitting at a small table with barely anything on it feeling like one of those temporary wheels you get in modern cars now that can only run at a certain speed for a certain period of time.

The natural induction programme had pretty much finished and yet I was not participating in anything of any significance.

Finally I plucked up the courage to voice my concerns to my boss. I think my comments came as no surprise and while I did not get a straight answer it was clear that something was afoot and that this something was linked to the hints about holding fast on moving house.

Panic gripped me. Had they made a mistake? Had I applied for a job that no longer existed? The thought of being made redundant so quickly made me sick even though every fibre of my being wanted to be anywhere else but Hull.

Full of conflicting emotions, not getting completely plastered in the evenings was becoming more and more difficult. It was made worse by my calls home. Things were starting to happen that I was missing.

At first it was little things. The cot we had ordered had arrived which was no real problem apart from the fact that the box was way too heavy for Iona to move so was sitting where the courier had left it in the middle of the living room and would do so until I got back on the Thursday night.

Then, inevitably, Iona felt her first kick from Fidget. This put me in the blackest mood yet even though it was unlikely that I would have felt anything from the outside but to miss the look of joy on her face was devastating.

I really wished that the company would give me something to do, something challenging to get my teeth into and to take my mind off of Iona and the baby.

Tedium set in and the week dragged indescribably and it was all I could do on the Thursday afternoon to wait until a respectable time before making my escape.

The further south I went the more I felt myself relaxing and the thought of being home filled me with a sense of euphoria. I didn't care what happened I just wanted to be in my own house.

I arrived to find that the boiler had blown up. In the distance just beyond this plane of existence I heard Fate sniggering. It was fortunate that I was there, not that Iona was incapable of coping but it really hit home that if and when things went wrong I was a long way away.

What should have been a relaxing weekend ended up as a series of frustrating phone calls until I eventually convinced the company with whom we had an alleged twenty four hour call out plan that they should in fact send an engineer within the twenty four hours promised. I was not sure which part of this they found complicated, especially as it was their scheme!

I spent the entire weekend (or so it felt) with my hand on Iona's tummy but Fidget had either gone quiet again or knew I was waiting for a kick and had decided to play silly-buggers with me. Needless to say that by the time I had to drive north again my child-to-be had utterly failed to perform on demand.

The new week started in a most interesting way as a chap called Jan from their Amsterdam office suddenly arrived out of the blue and I was informed that he was the chap I would now be working with.

Confused, I sat down with the amiable Dutchman and he explained the situation. During the interview process the company had been going through some changes and, as I had suspected, the original position for which I had applied no longer existed. This was not to say the job itself had gone, rather it had evolved into something quite different.

In the old role I was to be based in Hull and running a number of key projects primarily for the UK but in this new position I would be reporting to a team that had a far more European focus and indeed were scattered across sites in England, the Netherlands, France, Germany and Spain with even some links to the USA and China.

At this my ears pricked up and the more he described the role the more interesting it sounded. Of course, the greater responsibility did not come with more money which I felt was moderately sneaky but it would mean that I would have to do a lot more travelling and wound not, in fact, have much to do with the Hull site specifically.

Strangely, Jan was still of the opinion that I would be Hull based and it was obvious from what he said that my direct report would remain as it currently stood for all things functional such as expenses, appraisals and all that administrative stuff. In my mind I questioned this but that was a conversation for later.

It did leave us in a bit of a quandary. If we were going to move house we would need to decide pretty quickly and indeed we had already set a date for Iona to come up for a visit the week after Valentine's day so that we could look at areas, if not houses. One of my missions when I had first moved to Hull had supposedly been to scope out the surrounding towns and villages to try and find a few places that I could take her to but in this I had utterly failed.

Something in me had resisted starting any form of search. I had not even picked up a copy of the local newspapers to get the property section. Indeed, I had barely any knowledge of Hull city centre itself, my movements being restricted to work, the flat and the local supermarket.

Incredibly I had not even checked out the local pub or chippy although to be honest neither looked appealing. I have certain things I am looking for in a pub but the huge "Sky Sports shown here" banner and the fact that two of the windows had been smashed and boarded up somewhat put me off and as far as the chip shop was concerned, the grease was condensing on every surface and that really did not sell it to me.

We spent hours on the phone discussing what we should do but there was really nothing we could decide until I resolved the work situation once and for all. Until I knew otherwise we had to proceed with the plan.

Despite knowing that one way or another we would have to move house I took great delight the following weekend in putting the cot up "just to check it was okay". There was some logic in this action in that when we came to actually put the house on the market it would make our box room look like a nice spacious nursery as opposed to the pokey single room that it actually was.

Little did I realise that within hours the gleaming new cot was turned by Iona into a storage vessel for all the clothes, toys and other paraphernalia that she had collected for Fidget. I noticed at that point that there was a lot more than I had seen entering the house and clearly friends and family had been donating "hand-me-downs" while I was away.

One thing was for sure, in the early days Fidget was not going to want for things. Among our two families were enough with young girls and boys that I realised that this was only the tip of the iceberg. Everything Iona had gathered so far was the usual unisex stuff for newborns such as white baby-grows and all that sort of thing but as soon as we knew what Fidget was the flood-gates would open and I knew our house would become filled with bag loads of clothes.

Iona had no problem with charity. While we were not poor, the value of everything we had been given even at that point ran into the hundreds and by the time we had enough clothes to keep Fidget warm through its first couple of years the savings would be much higher.

Even so, part of me felt that I wanted to buy *some* things for our child. I had seen what had happened to family members and friends where the well-meaning relatives and chums had all gone on a shopping frenzy and bought so much stuff that they really could not justify spending any of their own money on things for their own children. It was almost as if when you have a baby you instantly lose all control over it.

I found myself updating the book and reflecting on this as I did. It was strange, the book had been intended to be a record of the decisions we had made to go for IVF and the subsequent challenges we faced but now I realised we were into a whole new set of problems.

Fidget was, as far as we could tell, developing normally and everything we were experiencing was probably just as anyone else would find. The peculiarities of our situation with my getting the job and the need for us to move were unusual but again far from unique.

I began to question exactly what I was trying to say in

the book and all of a sudden it became difficult to express just what I was feeling. There were so many conflicting emotions and issues but how they impacted the baby was unclear to me now.

Knowing that I had to resolve the work question quickly I asked for a meeting with my boss but typically that was not going to be possible until at least the following week.

Heading home with the huge question mark did nothing to break the increasing tension.

# Chapter 29:
## And the answer is...

Arriving home that day was probably one of the scariest moments of the whole journey (though little did we suspect at that time that Fate had something even more heart-stopping in store for us at a later date).

No sooner had I stepped through the door than I realised something was terribly wrong. The hallway in our house allows a partial view into the kitchen as you walk through the front door and the first thing I could see were the broken plates all over the floor.

Dropping my bag and not caring if that meant that the laptop was a gonner I ran through to find Iona hunched over a chair clutching her head from which a trickle of blood oozed.

A quick glance showed what had happened. She had reached up to get some plates from the cupboard as she prepared dinner for my arrival but something must have given way as the shelf and all of its contents had fallen on her.

Her sobs of pain and shock turned to relief when she

realised I was there and without question I took a clean tea-towel, ran it under the tap and gave it to her to press against her sore noggin while I gave her a hug.

I don't know much about first aid I am afraid to say and she was in her "I don't want to make a fuss" kind of mood but I didn't want to take any chances so whisked her down to casualty to let an expert take a look. That is what they are there for, if nothing else!

After a suitably long wait we were eventually seen by a nurse who quickly concluded that it looked a lot worse than it was and Iona didn't need stitches and didn't have concussion which was good news. Even though Iona had fallen over, she had a nasty bruise on her arm to show for that, everything also seemed fine with Fidget. After patching Iona up and putting a plaster over the cut she sent us on our way.

She was devastated and afraid that I would be angry that she had smashed the plates but I told her not to be so silly and that I was just glad she was okay. Inside I was screaming as yet again I had just timed perfectly arriving at the point of chaos.

I felt myself trembling and realised that I was also in a state of shock so when we got back I made a large pot of tea before tackling the clean-up job. Typically it was another weekend where we had family around, this time for a christening so I knew I would have to head out to the twenty-four hour supermarket to buy replacement crockery.

Fortunately there was such a place nearby and the set we were currently using was a relatively inexpensive white set and easily matched.

The shelf was also easy to fix even for one with my dubious DIY skills and by early evening all signs of the disaster aside from the plaster on Iona's forehead were gone.

She had calmed down a bit but was glad when her family arrived as was I as it gave me an excuse to crack a bottle or two (possibly three) of wine and ease my trembling nerves.

As before, they came laden with yet more baby stuff which was added to the rapidly growing pile in the cot. I saw changing mats, a potty and all kinds of other devices the function of which was beyond me. I knew I had a lot to learn but Iona seemed to be pretty confident as to what they were for.

I know I should have paid more attention but the male chauvinist in me "left all that kind of stuff to the wife". No doubt in the fullness of time I would receive my instructions.

The weekend was slightly better than previous ones as I had a meeting in their head office in Southampton on the Monday which meant I did not need to make the run up north on the Sunday evening. My colleague Jan and my boss were also attending the meeting which was some big "group hug" as someone I knew in my previous job called it.

Every company has these, big update meetings where everyone goes and sits in a large conference room all day being subjected to endless presentations that they really could not give a damn about. For most people it is a day out of the office and an excuse for a free lunch, at least, that's how I normally see them.

For me, however, this one was destined to be far more interesting. As the morning session ended I was called aside by Jan and we went to a side room where my boss and a few others were waiting.

Jan asked me straight how I felt about the move to Hull and I said quite openly that I felt it made no sense and in fact from what I had seen I was going to be spending more time in Southampton and travelling than anywhere else and Hull was just a place to put a desk.

They agreed and within a curiously brief discussion (no more than two minutes) it was proposed that I relocate to Southampton rather than Hull and would I mind if this were the case? I would still need to come to Hull for a day or two a week but my main office would remain down south and therefore I would not need to relocate to the north.

Would I mind? Suddenly here was the solution to all my problems, or at least that is how it felt at the time. I knew I should at least attempt to be professional about it and I did want to discuss it with Iona first so I said I would let them know in the morning but it was probably a yes.

I tried to call Iona from the conference room but she was frustratingly not answering. I was disappointed as I ached to tell her the news but decided that rather than keep trying I would wait until I was home so that I could see as well as hear her reaction.

As you can imagine, the rest of the day dragged. I could not even begin to tell you what was presented in the afternoon session as my thoughts drifted with the implications of this new development.

Given everything that had been said before I knew that I should not have been totally surprised by the new twist of events but I had not dared to hope that the rumblings I was hearing would mean that I would keep my job and at the same time not be required to relocate north.

All things considered it was the best possible outcome.

I had to be really careful not to speed on the way home though the idiots on the roads meant that this would have been all but impossible on most stretches.

When I finally fell through the front door I simply blurted it out but so rapidly that I was almost incomprehensible and had to repeat myself so that Iona understood what it was I was getting at.

To say she was pleased was the understatement of the century. Within a minute she had the Great Britain atlas out and the internet on and one of the popular house-finding sites loaded. I guess that was a "yes" then.

Of course, she was not looking for houses in the Southampton area – her eyes were fixed on a very narrow portion of Dorset – in the same village as her mother! I had no problem with this. I would be absent between Hull and travelling a lot so any support she could get was worth having and being that close to her mother would be perfect.

Logistically, however, this gave me a problem. Rail fares from stations close to where we would live were stupidly high so I realised that the only way to work it would be to drive to Southampton each day (as I would still get a company car and was paying the same for petrol regardless of how far I drove). It would mean early starts but it seemed feasible.

We watched a DVD that had come with the NCT membership which was clearly aimed at blokes who do nothing around the house as it was basically saying that the husbands would have to actually do things like cooking and cleaning. The women were all stay-at-home mum types, no middle-class career ladies in sight. It was interesting but I learned nothing (apart from the fact that the NCT obviously have an assumption as to how most men would react).

What was interesting was the fact that the DVD basically worked on the premise of "now you have started your journey" from the point of discovering that the wife was pregnant. It really brought it home how long we had been on the journey before ever getting to the point of a confirmed pregnancy!

I still had to head back to Hull but had agreed that I

could drive up on the Tuesday morning which, given I was still heading back the Thursday afternoon, made it a short and relatively pointless visit.

As always I was itching to get back but this time with good reason as it was Iona's 25 week check-up with the doctor.

Thankfully, everything seemed normal and although the doctor had some trouble finding Fidget's heartbeat this was mainly because our baby was living up to its nickname by kicking and wriggling constantly. There was no doubt whatsoever that Fidget was alive and well.

We had arranged to meet one of my best friends that evening (mostly as another excuse to get cast-off clothing) and went for a curry. As we were walking into the restaurant I heard a terrible crash behind me and for a moment thought that Iona had fallen over. I was guiltily relieved to see that it was my friend who had slipped on a wet patch on the floor.

Fortunately he was not hurt and the owner of the restaurant was so mortified that we were going to sue him that he gave us free drinks (his second mistake, not mopping the floor being the first). A good night was had by all, well, at least by the boys.

A serious hangover was probably not what I needed to start preparing to move with real purpose. We had already started a major sort of the house, mostly to get rid of the huge pile of stuff that I have been hoarding for years but now we had real enthusiasm. First things first, I took the wheels off of the pram so that I could give them a good wire-brushing down and then paint them with Hammerite as they were a bit rusty from having been stored in a garage. It took a while and by the end of it my hands were aching but it was worth it, the wheels came up very well. Iona was pleased!

I was in a good purging mood so decided that among the other junk I was getting rid of, it was time that the large pile of LP's and singles in the cupboard went. I was about to sell the HiFi and get shot of the record player anyway so I would not be able to play them so there was logically no need to keep hold of them.

Whilst in the cupboard I also went through the MCIU box of paperwork ("might come in useful" for those of you not familiar with the term) that I had collected during my time at my previous job. On reflection, very little of it was in any way useful besides possibly lighting a bonfire so out it went. I also had loads of papers and information relating to my various periods of study that I had kept for reasons now lost so to the recycling they were also relegated.

It was quite therapeutic!

We had also taken the Sunday to be our Valentine's day (as I would be back up north on the 14th) so we exchanged presents, went to collect Iona's flowers (which had been delivered but taken back to the sorting office) and I cooked a yummy meal in my new Le Creuset dish which she had bought me to encourage me to cook more.

I think Iona had realised that the best way to keep me out of a black mood (and stop me boozing) was to keep me busy and when she realised I was becoming more and more interested in cooking, mostly thanks to my various friends who are all great chefs, she saw it as a hobby to be encouraged, even though, bizarrely, she was still trying to discourage me from eating.

I didn't feel anywhere near as sad as I thought I would when I listed all my junk on the internet auction site. It is funny how the prospect of a family changes the habits of a lifetime. For me a lot had to do with that age-old and usually male-related phenomenon of "collecting". In my mind, the records formed part of a "collection" though quite what the theme of the collection was I truly was not sure. The only thing I truly collected among all of it was dust.

The fact remained that I had not played a record for something in the region of six years and many of the discs I had never played. The other brutal fact was that many of these were destined in my hands to never grace a record deck at any point in the future.

Why was I keeping them then? Simple, for the same reason I had hoarded CD's videos, DVD's and the other plethora of junk that formed my existence, they were a substitute for whatever it was that my heart was secretly yearning for. That something had been a wife and family so, without realising it, the collecting bug had deserted me and all that remained were the dry husks of the passion it had once generated.

To put it another way, it was, in my eyes, junk! The only sad thought as I listed it for auction (Iona having kindly performed the boring task of making a list of all the albums, titles, etc.) was that it would be to everyone else nothing but junk so I pretty much listed them as such, putting 7" discs and 12" discs in as two job lots, though I could not bring myself to list some of the "better" ones, planning to either keep a few or list them separately in a burst of optimism.

The good thing was that with them out of the way, the cupboard in the small room now easily housed a great deal of baby things such that the nursery was becoming very functional.

I had a nice Valentine's present from work – they wanted me to go to a sustainable packaging conference in London on the Wednesday which meant I could also work from home on the Thursday and therefore had another short week in Hull! Needless to say I jumped at the chance. We had planned to go to Dorset at the weekend but decided to move our plans and have another weekend of sorting so my being home for longer was going to be a good thing.

It felt strange being home so quickly but nice as this would be the work pattern I would be adopting in the summer.

Fidget was really starting to kick now, not just the faint ripples I had felt before but proper percussive thuds. As I am sure many men do, I wondered what that must have felt like, realising that it would not be an experience I would ever have unless I was infected by an alien (and we all know how *that* ends!).

I had noticed that the rate of "expansion" of Iona's belly was increasing noticeably, not a huge shock now that the little one was entering the final trimester and getting to the "putting on weight" stage.

I felt somewhat out of things in that Iona's mind was obviously buzzing with a multitude of little details concerning the baby, things to buy, things to ask, things to eat, things *not* to eat. All I could boast was "things to eat" and I wondered whether I should be doing more or whether to trust her that she had it all in hand. Looking at the way she seemed to be enjoying the whole nesting process, I decided that it was probably the latter. In truly "hairy hunter" style my role was to go out, earn the money and when around lift heavy things and help as much as possible.

The conference was dull as dishwater but had one particularly redeeming feature. Lunch was catered using M&S food and there was plenty of chocolate on offer! Being good with respect to my diet, I abstained but that did not prevent me from filling my free bag with offerings for Iona. She was suitably pleased when I got back and took them into work as rations for when she had the sugar-urge.

It was another weekend of sorting but again rewarding as we got rid of a load more stuff. What was even better was that I had an offer on the LP's, some chap who wanted to come and see them and would pay cash on the spot!

I invited him over and he duly arrived, sifting through the stack with some interest and at the end offered the grandly sum of fifty pounds (I had been expecting to be hauling them down the charity shop or the dump so that was ideal).

Cheekily, I had also mentioned the other LP's that I had not listed and he sifted through these, offering another £50 for the lot. Sold! A minute later I had sold the singles for £15 and he even took the CD recorder I had listed for another £25. Two trips to his car later I had one happy customer, two happy sellers and a much emptier table!

We had watched another DVD this time entitled "Understanding Childbirth" by Betty Parsons MBE. It was aimed at Mum's and Dad's but had clearly been filmed in the early eighties, judging by the hairstyles and clothes (and the fact that it had obviously been transferred from a very dodgy video at some point) which made it somewhat amusing but beyond that and not trying to be in any way difficult, it was definitely aimed more at the Mum's than the Dad's.

I guess in some respects I am blessed with a relatively well-rounded education and while I am not saying I didn't learn anything, I do have to confess to Mrs Parsons that my mind was somewhat wandering during the hour or so of the DVD that we watched.

After all the recent excitement and two short weeks, the next one was going to be a normal affair at Hull, my transfer to Southampton not being due to kick in for a couple of months but for some reason I felt really tired and lethargic (or, as Iona would probably have it, lazy). A lot of it was that I was under the weather, trying to shake off an annoying cough that I had managed to pick up from somewhere.

It was a struggle to make it through the week but at least now the project work was coming in so that I had something to get my teeth into.

On the Friday Iona was able to work from home so that we could make an early dash to Dorset at lunchtime and beat the traffic on the M3. I think both of us needed the break as well as the fact that now we knew we would be moving there it was time to start seriously thinking about where and when.

Iona told her Mum officially what the new plan was. At first she probably assumed we were joking but when it sank in that we were serious she was very excited, though she was constantly checking with me to make sure that I was okay as I would be the one doing even more driving. I told her it was a lifestyle choice and that I would therefore do whatever was necessary!

We went to Mothercare on the Saturday as they had one of their regular sales on and spent loads of her mother's money, getting the mattress for the cot, bedding and other such odds and ends, mostly as they had a ten percent off deal. One of the things we wanted was a "bed in a bag" which was out of stock but could be ordered at the till. I noticed what had happened but said nothing until we left the shop – the assistant had taken the 10% from the order when placing it online but then put the total onto the main order…from which a further 10% was taken! As the bed in a bag was already on a third-off we got it for nearly half price!

Iona and I then went for a drive. She had found a couple of potential houses on the internet and although we had not booked appointments we went to see where they were and also drove around to agree a search area. As we stopped I checked on the satnav to see how long it would take to get to Southampton and Hull but curiously it did not seem to make much difference once we were off of the main roads.

The area bishop had dropped into the church on Sunday morning and stayed afterwards for a cup of tea with the parishioners. We had bought Fidget a small teddy bear which was still in the car so I asked him if he would formally bless the cuddly toy so that we would have it for Fidget. He smiled and told us a story that the Archbishop of Canterbury had told him about a little girl who had brought a ragged toy rabbit up with her and had insisted "and bunny" when he had given the blessing which the gracious Dr Williams had happily done.

The bishop equally kindly blessed our teddy and I somewhat cheekily took a photo of him doing so but it was just one of those moments on this journey that I wanted to capture.

Feeling very blessed and Christian, we headed off for a quick lunch before dashing home as I had booked tickets to take Iona to see James Blunt at Hammersmith. We got there in plenty of time for a quick pizza and the show was excellent. Iona was worried that the loud noise would affect Fidget but there were other pregnant women there who didn't seem worried and anyway we were in the balcony and it wasn't all that loud.

When we got home, I looked back with reflection that it had been one of life's really good days!

I managed to wangle an entire week without having to go north by crafty timetabling of a visit to a supplier and a two-day meeting in Southampton after which it was deemed that heading north for one day was a bit of a waste. This was just as well as one of the water pipes in the house decided to spring a small but annoying leak.

Somehow I could not help feeling that just as we were trying to get the house ready for sale everything was starting to break. Whoever bought it would have all the problems ironed out and would never know the grief we had saved them!

It was also at this time that I passed the two hundred page mark on the book with some surprise. I had never thought that I would pen more than about fifty pages but now it was reaching epic proportions. Even the word count was rapidly spiralling towards the hundred and forty thousand mark which was incredible.

Inevitably I broke my cardinal rule and flipped back a few chapters to read what had happened over the most recent few months and at that point I felt quite sick. With harsh realisation I discovered that pretty much everything I had written was a self-absorbed rant about the job, the house and a whole bunch of other irritations (which I have deliberately tried to reproduce in the last few chapters here just to make your blood boil) and almost nothing about Iona.

Here was I griping about having to drive north and sit in an empty flat while she was the one left at home, gradually getting bigger as Fidget developed which meant she could physically do less and less as each day went by. Not only that but she was carrying the brunt of the emotional pressure as it was her womb in which Fidget was growing.

I could get in the car and drive away from the stress but Iona had to live with it each waking (and even sleeping) moment. Everything she did had consequences down to the food she ate and the things she exposed herself to.

There is no doubt in my mind that I was not unique in this and I am sure many if not most men have the same detached attitude towards pregnancy. We cannot conceive what it must be like and therefore do not try.

Those devices you can get which are essentially strap-on pregnancies might give you the feel of what a baby on board feels like but only in the same way as putting a rucksack full of beer on your back makes you feel what a camel must experience with its hump. You look a bit silly but it is all rather artificial.

If the life or death of the strap-on water bag relied on every movement you made then I think we might approach the situation differently rather than just looking like a self-congratulating plonker.

Of course, there was one other factor that I had not considered when I confessed all this to Iona, women have the instinctive sense to know that men will behave in this way and I had simply performed to expectations. It didn't make it right but at least her emotional make-up had prepared her for it.

I don't think that getting it all out in the open made much difference in the end as in truth there was not much I could do beyond be as helpful as possible when around the place. Fidget was ultimately Iona's physical burden to bear and to a large extent her emotional one as well. I could do nothing to help Fidget, all I could do was to help Iona and do all the "heavy lifting".

Just when we were really starting to plan the last stages of the pregnancy someone at work noticed that I was not all that busy and before I could say "corrugated cartons" I had been seconded onto another project and it was apparent that this was going to get me travelling briefly across Europe towards the end of March / early April.

On the one hand it was good as it meant I would get around a bit and get my face seen in the right places but on the personal front I knew I would have to plan it carefully if I wanted to be around for the latter-stage appointments.

February rolled into March and the list of minor disasters continued. The Disco was poorly (leaking oil) so we took it down to the garage and while it did not seem to be a huge problem they were not able to get the part and fix it until the following Monday. Not for the first time I was struck by the fact that I was not around all the time but luckily I was there at that moment so at least she could use my car while I worked from home.

So far I had managed to be around to fix (or mostly arrange to be fixed) all the things that had gone wrong but sooner or later I would not and this continued to bother me. The sooner we could sort out the move to Dorset and be near her family the better.

When Iona had her 28 week appointment with the midwife I realised that before we knew it the baby would be out in the big wide world and we had not even put our place on the market as yet. With the credit crunch in full swing and the house market as depressed as Marvin the Paranoid Android there was no guarantee whatsoever that we would buy and sell quickly, indeed the process could take months.

I cannot remember exactly when I had that epiphany but it made me go cold as we only had three months to go before the due date! Even if we shook hands now we would be moving exactly when Fidget was due to be born. I made a mental note to *really* work on my sense of timing.

The midwife appointment was the usual affair. She was running a half hour late which was annoying as we showed up our usual twenty minutes early and thus sat around for nearly an hour. She took some blood, something Iona had fortunately not been aware of so hadn't had time to work herself up over and again checked the baby. The heartbeat was strong as always though the baby was lying upright, not down. Either way the midwife did not come across as particularly bothered by that at this stage.

We asked her about the baby grants, the £190 of free cash that the government handed out to all pregnant women and the midwife confirmed that these had all dried up at the beginning of the year. Once again, due to timing, we were losing out through no fault of our own. It reinforced my resolve to never vote bloody Labour ever again as it was, in my personal opinion, their fault the country was in this mess in the first place.

We celebrated the fact that Fidget was still doing well with a ceremonial "burn-up" that evening. As a wedding present we had been given a metal fire-pit which we had used extensively in the back garden but was now suffering from a few years exposed to the elements. To put it another way, the whole thing was little more than rust held together by the encrusted soggy ashes from previous burns.

There was a lot of old paperwork that I had sorted but which had not been recycled as well as various "MCIU" (I am not explaining that again so if you were not paying attention earlier on then tough) pieces of wood that had been lying around the house, garden, shed and garage but which there was no point in moving.

It was great as we had no worries about over-cooking the poor thing and had a roaring blaze going. As the flames died down so did the fire pit, slowly unfolding like an origami model as the layers of ash burned away. It was a fitting end for it and in the morning there was little more than a pile of twisted rust that was laid to rest in the local recycling site.

Iona had an open day at work at the weekend and it meant I had the place to myself so plenty of time to quietly get on with the process of humping boxes around and sorting out the last bits of crap that could be chucked / recycled / sold or given to a jumble sale.

We were it became obvious, becoming dangerously close to being ready to sell the house! There were still a few things to do around the place but they were minor and as the jobs ran out so did the excuses.

Iona was getting very large now and less and less able

to do any major jobs, which was no problem as far as I was concerned, I was glad to do my bit as little as it was.

I should explain at this stage that some months previously we had contacted a few estate agents in the area to make initial enquiries about selling our house. The reaction was mixed, I have to say. Initially it was like putting my arm in a Brazilian rain forest river and very quickly becoming covered in leaches.

With even the sniff of a client they were all over us like a rash and, in most cases, about as welcome.

They came in varying degrees of cheap shiny suit and as per the stereotype drenched in nasty after-shave but all but one clearly had about as much training in estate agency as I had in Paraguayan contemporary art.

As quickly as it became clear that we were not at that stage ready to sell, despite the insane amount of heavy sales pitch they used, they evaporated like a strawberry Mivvi in a blast furnace.

There was one exception, a chap called David who turned up in actually quite a nice suit, had a very subtle preference of after-shave brand and was not in the least pushy. He did not mind in the least that we were only looking speculatively at the time and left us too it but with the occasional and pre-arranged courtesy call to see if our situation had changed.

Now that we were finally at the point of actually wanting to sell it was a no-brainer as to who we would contact. All the other agencies had instantly ruled themselves out by their lack of professionalism and aggressive attitude (and their appearance and eye-stinging aroma) and when we invited David back in our opinion was well-founded.

He proposed that rather than simply advertise and hope for viewings he would arrange an open-house and get it all done in one go. Nice!

Without hesitation we signed up and got the process moving, mostly as through the secondment I was now on at work, a sudden and unexpected trip to China was looming for me and I was determined that the house sale would not be delayed by my absence.

It was only at that point that I realised that I really ought to also go and talk to the bank to arrange a mortgage conversation and that with everything else going on we were really not as organised as we thought with the whole house move thing. It would, after all, be a good idea to know what we could afford before we started actually falling in love with places.

This did not, of course, stop Iona from scouring the property sites on the internet for suitable candidates. One of the benefits of relocating to Hull would have been that we could potentially have pooled all our resources, set our sights moderate and through a bit of financial jiggery-pokery allowed ourselves to be mortgage-free.

Moving to Dorset meant that this was now spectacularly out of the question and I had a nasty suspicion that the gulf between our resources and our requirements was going to be a large one. I wondered just what I would come back from China to find as I knew Iona well enough that she went mostly with her heart. There would no doubt be some shortbread-tin cottage out there that she would utterly fall for that would lumber us with a hideous monthly payment.

Okay, that is probably a bit unfair but I did dread returning from the trip to be presented with a picture and the loaded words "what do you think?"

The other option under consideration was to get a "fixer-upper" or something with potential to be extended so that we could add value to the property at some later date and extend it as and when we needed / could afford it. Here I had the scary thought that we would buy a pre-barn-conversion (i.e. a barn) and be living at her folks place for ever while we slowly died under the oppressive planning permission system.

To at least calm my thoughts a bit before heading to China I took a sneaky look myself to see what was on the market. While there were a few places that could be suitable, none of them looked in particularly poor condition or were stupidly over-priced and none were drop-dead gorgeous. I was, for now, safe.

With this in mind I gave Iona the challenge of marking out a search area and lining up some viewings for my return. With our place about to go on the market we really needed to sort the other end out, whatever that might entail.

Fidget was very active now but I realised that I was lapsing into a sense of routine. With all the initial stress of the pregnancy over we had now entered a period where it was all normal but for me being away so much I was beginning to feel somewhat disconnected from the whole process. I guess this would always been the case in that Iona was the one actually carrying the baby but it continued to feel wrong that I was not around to help her on a day to day basis.

I also realised that this was a lull before the oncoming storm. We had not been to the hospital to check out the maternity unit or anything like that but time was galloping on. In my mind, Iona was still somewhere in that "mid-pregnancy" stage but the truth was that her due date was rapidly approaching and the date where an early delivery was possible even closer.

We had known several people who had dropped their babies six weeks early and if Iona did that then we were only a short few weeks away from possibility being parents.

Just before I headed off to the airport the estate agent came as planned and we went through the deal to sell the house. As he treated us as "returning customers" to thank us for giving him the business he had already dropped his fee from 2.5% to 1.8% which was less than the others were offering.

We agreed to take the package from him (conveyancing etc.) more to make life easy for us than anything else.

As I was going to be back on the Friday, we booked the energy survey and the measuring appointment for then (around my mortgage appointment which I also managed to fit in).

It felt exciting to know that we were actually going to be selling!

Iona headed off to Dorset for the weekend and left me to make my own way to Heathrow. While there she sorted out the fact that if we did not sell and buy at exactly the same time we could stay at her Mum's place until we got something more permanent which was good as it took the pressure off.

With little else to do I headed off to Heathrow early so that I could abuse the lounge again prior to the flight to China.

# Chapter 30:
## Land of the rising smog.

Being away felt odd and I was glad that Iona was not further forward in her pregnancy as I realised it would take a lot of time to get home in the case of emergency. My work phone, while set on "rest of world" kept being blocked, I presume by China Telecom for reasons best known to themselves. This was a pain as it meant I was not able to get through on some occasions and had instead to listen to some pre-recorded voice in Mandarin who for all I knew was telling me to run as the end of the world was nigh (but was more likely saying that my call could not be connected at that time).

Her Mum had come back to the house with her to "daughter-sit" while I was away and little did I realise at the time that she was also blitzing the house and doing all sorts of jobs: painting, silicone sealant on the windows, fixing things etc. She is pretty handy to have around, my mother-in-law!

China was depressing. The direct flight from Heathrow to Hong Kong is over eleven hours and I was bored after about two (and nearly comatose by the time we made our final approach). It was one of those tedious trips that you waste an entire day getting there and what is more an entire weekend in this case.

The factory was in Zhongshan which is just up the Pearl River Delta or, to put it another way, an easy ferry ride from Hong Kong. Easy, that is, if you know what you are doing which I did not.

Having a factory is like saying you have a sand dune in the Sahara. There are a *lot* of factories in Zhongshan!

I speak as much Chinese as I do Martian and the written language is about as baffling as you can get if you don't know even the basics. Trying, therefore, to book a ticket to Zhongshan and, what is more, find out which boat to get on was a major challenge but the intrepid traveller in me won through. Okay, that is a total lie. After standing for five minutes with a look of obvious despair on my face I was pointed in the right direction by a very kind ex-pat called Keith.

The ferry ride to the mainland was terrifying. Hong Kong harbour is probably one of the busiest waterways in the world and the water itself is covered in garbage, floating plant debris, the occasional misplaced container and a million and one other things that could easily have sank our twin-hulled ferry, not to mention the immense container ships that plied these waters.

It did not help that it was foggy as anything. If there had been a band on this boat my guess is they would not have carried on playing as we sank after hitting whatever shit-berg would inevitably hole us.

By the same miracle that must bless these ferries every day we arrived at Zhongshan remarkably on schedule and I saw the most joyous sight, my contact with a board on which my name was (incorrectly) written waiting for me.

I am no Alan Whicker and once I am in a place that

does not speak English my colonial roots show through. There is a reason that England conquered more than half of the world, it was to avoid having to speak the local language or engage in the local customs. Even today you can go to any one of a hundred Mediterranean resorts and find fish and chip shops and pubs, acknowledgement that it is not just the Americans who expect to find something familiar wherever they go in the world.

The first thing I saw in Zhongshan was a branch of Pizza Hut, rapidly followed by KFC. Had I come to the wrong place?

I will not bore you with the details of the trip but suffice to say after four days of breathing in smog, driving through mile after mile of industrial estate and eating the parts of animals that even Bella would have turned her nose up at, I was mightily glad to be back on the ferry on the Thursday evening and heading back home. In the entire week I had not been able to speak to Iona even once which was by far the longest we had gone without speaking since we had met, let alone since she had become pregnant.

If I had any doubts that the bachelor in me was long gone they were dispelled now. I could barely function properly without hearing her voice and it was as if I had travelled six thousand miles but left my soul behind in the process.

Even though the flight back was thirteen hours (into the wind that blew us over on the way out) and didn't start until nearly midnight local time I did not mind. Every second brought me that much closer to home and to Iona and Fidget.

When I got back to the house in the early hours of Friday morning I was amazed by the work that had been done. Other family members had made impromptu visits and everyone had been really busy. The house looked really good. There was still work to be done but the kitchen had been de-cluttered and the bulk of the sorting done!

I put the kettle on and took a cup of tea up to Iona.

Once I had freshened up and knowing that the best thing to do after a long-haul flight is to simply struggle through and resist taking a nap, the day was one of sorting house things. As planned, the chap came at nine to do the energy rating and then I headed down to the bank to see what the story would be in terms of mortgage.

The good news was that the bank still did the offset flexible mortgage that we had used before and which meant we could pay overpayments, keep some of the money in the bank rather than on the mortgage (but still counting towards the interest), etc. The shock was how much they would potentially lend me. Given I had not even been in my job for three months they were willing to lend me nearly five times my salary! Did I just dream the last three years or had the credit crunch never happened? I thought the days of silly mortgages were over but clearly not.

Then, of course, I realised that this was just the mortgage broker pushing buttons on a theoretical model. The real decision would come when the application went in and the back-room accountants sucked in air in that way once reserved for car mechanics and said "not a chance".

Luckily, I had no intention of taking that much and was in fact seeking a far more moderate sum. Still, it indicated that the chances were very good that we would get the money without too much question.

The estate agent and his team came at three and measured the house though I put them off taking the photos as we were still in a mess but he was fine with that. It did, however, mean that we would have to go through the entire place and tidy up so that they could return in a few days and take the shots. As these were what was going to help sell the place it was important that they were right.

I remembered from when I had bought the house in the first place and had rejected so many options on the basis of the nasty pictures. It was a good lesson learned that we did not make the same mistake.

That in mind Iona and I blitzed the whole place including the garden and put it ready for the photos. We also sorted the greenhouse out, a part of the garden that we had both seldom entered and did a tip run will loads of junk. She wrote a list of jobs that needed to be done in anticipation of the photos so we started going around the house doing what we could to prepare ourselves.

I noticed that she was flagging even earlier in the evenings and was usually asleep on the sofa by about eight thirty. Once again it brought it home that she was a long way towards the big day! When Fidget kicked now it was very visible.

Iona had inflated a large ball that she had been given so that she could start the process of getting on her hands and knees regularly to encourage the baby to adopt the correct position in the womb. I was glad we no longer had Bella as she would have seen it as a great new toy!

I contacted the estate agent again and arranged the photos to be taken on Saturday afternoon. At least that would give us a target to get the house ready for even if the list of jobs was still huge.

It was only then that a strange problem occurred. Through careful financial management we had contrived to pay off the small mortgage on our current place but when I had done so it had not occurred to me to enquire where the actual deeds were. The bank denied all knowledge of them and it took a lot of phoning around to discover that they were with my original solicitors, buried deep in their antique safe. It was a heart-stopping few hours when I thought they might be lost forever.

The pace of things at work really began to pick up as I realised that the project I had been seconded to was vast and needed urgent attention. This was good as it did take my attention from all the bureaucracy of house selling though in turn this meant that poor old Iona had to pick up the reins.

What was not so clear was when I would actually get around to doing the job for which I had been employed and this worried me deeply. I confronted my boss with my concerns but the answer was not all that reassuring and I had the distinct impression that the team in which I was to work was not as stable as I had been led to believe.

It was while I was mulling this over that I got a text from Iona. She had been surfing various baby sites to get an idea of Fidget's development and according to the ones she had read the foetus should be something in the region of three and a half pounds and sixteen inches by all accounts. Blimey!

It put me in a better mood so I went back to my boss and mooted the idea of bringing my official transfer to Southampton earlier than originally agreed and to the beginning of May. That would mean that there was little chance of my being "up north" when the baby was due.

Thankfully it seemed to cause no issues and was pretty much agreed on the spot. I was put in touch with the office manager at the southern headquarters to arrange a desk, computer, phone etc.

The evening I was due back Iona had a massage booked, something a friend had bought her. I really wanted to go with her so tore down the motorway at probably unhealthy speeds and literally bounced onto the drive just as she was leaving the house. I doubt there is a taxi firm in the country who could have timed it better.

Suitably chauffeured she arrived for her session fashionably early.

As it was, the address was just around the corner so we would easily have made it on foot in plenty of time. Thus, I had driven for over three hours to drive her less than a mile!

The session was one that was aimed at pregnant women which shows what I know, I thought a massage was a massage but as I sat there I gaped at the posters and adverts describing all the different techniques available.

The woman gave her a 20-minute back rub and then a 10 minute foot and ankle session. It looked like Iona was enjoying it and the woman did seem to do some good. I was more fascinated by the pack of ear candles I could see on the table! Yes, they were seriously proposing that you lie down on your side, they put one in your ear and then set light to the candle!!!

I wondered if this was a massage therapy or in fact a subtle form of blackmail (pay up or we post the video on the internet).

It was Iona's 31 week appointment with the doctor and we sadly found out it would be her last as the doctor was leaving (having only been a locum covering for maternity leave). This was a real shame as she was very nice indeed. Baby was fine though there was still the question of how it was lying but as the doctor said, it was too early at this stage to be worried about it (but it would not be long therefore before it would be time to worry!).

It was still nice to have such routine appointments and find that everything was progressing okay. The only thing we had realised was that we had not heard from the hospital to go and see the maternity unit so the doctor suggested that we call them directly to arrange something.

Iona tried to make her 34 week appointment with the midwife but she was already fully booked however the surgery agreed to contact her and call back.

While I was home they called to say that the midwife had kindly agreed to come in early on the appropriate day to see Iona so an appointment was made. I thought that was really nice of her but I guessed given how busy she was that this was not an uncommon occurrence.

I spent the rest of the day preparing some information for a patent that was being filed at work but also at the same time casting half an eye around the house. I was conscious that the estate agent photographer was coming to take photos the next day so I would be busy getting the place spick and span in preparation.

That Saturday was a very busy day! Iona had to go into work for another open day which meant that I was going to get the house ready on my own. This was not a problem but I optimistically judged how long it was going to take and dragged her into town early to do some shopping before she had to head over to the school.

Of course, by the time we got back I looked at the clock and still thought that I had hours to go so that I would spend a couple sorting the place out and then put my feet up!

By the time I had a shower at 3:30 I was totally knackered but when I looked out of the window I realised I had not removed all the grubby CD's on strings that kept the birds off of the garden so had to hastily sort all that out. I was ready with ten minutes to spare! I took the opportunity to take my own photos and take a video of the house while it was looking so good.

The photographer arrived with a crappy little digital camera, took a few cursory snaps and then was gone! It seemed like all that effort had been for nothing but in reality I knew the house was now ready for viewing and that it would be a much easier job to keep it that way than to start from scratch again.

It felt really exciting that the house was all but ready to go.

That evening I updated the book again and realised that while it was a bit of a dead part in the tale as far as Fidget was concerned, this would soon change. I wondered how the book would read in twenty years time and whether Fidget would read all the nonsense about jobs and house moves with a bit of a frown.

One thing that was clear, at least to me, was that I was secretly glad of the distraction that the job and house brought. I still felt a bit of a fish out of water when it came to the pregnancy. Somehow, it still felt important as part of the wider story to let Fidget know not only our reasoning around taking the choices we had made to go through donor IVF treatment but also the events that unfolded around its gestation.

For me, securing a good future for Fidget was under the circumstances even more vital than had the pregnancy been "normal" and I know that for Iona her maternal instincts were about as strong as they could be.

Fidget was totally precious to us for so many different reasons. I just hoped the book explained this.

After a quiet week at work not helped by the fact that the woman in human resources who was sorting my new contract out had just been made redundant, I left early on the Thursday and took the Friday off so we could head down to Dorset that evening. Iona had booked some house viewings for us the following day so we could start the whole process of shifting to the south coast.

We made it down in good time which was nice as we

were both somewhat tired. It was noticeable each time I got home how much bigger Iona was getting though she still seemed to be having a really good pregnancy which was nice.

We saw three potential homes and of the options each had features we liked but at the same time things that would need doing so there was nothing we immediately fell in love with.

That evening we took her Mum out for Mothering Sunday to a local pub for a nice meal.

With house-hunting over and lovely weather we took her Mum's dogs to the beach so they could have a good splash which everyone enjoyed. It was nice to chill out for a bit, though we did not walk far as Iona was more up for sitting on the beach than roaming up and down it.

The dogs on the other hand had other ideas and kept me busy with a ball for well over an hour. I was knackered by the end of it but noticed that Iona was equally as tired and all she had done was sit and watch. I could catch my breath and recover but she had to carry her burden all day.

Mothering Sunday came and Fidget had bought Iona a card and a Venetian glass heart pendant (with a little help from Daddy who had actually bought it on the plane back from Hong Kong). We went to church for the traditional service after which the vicar blessed Iona's eternity ring and a titanium band she had bought me in return that we had bought and we started wearing them which was nice.

The evening was a bit more relaxed as I was not heading up to Hull but over to Europe on the Monday.

Iona had a list of jobs to do with regard to the house-hunting (one of them we needed to check with a builder to see if we could extend one of the places as the way it stood it was inadequate for our needs).

When we arrived home I discovered that Iona had

started to sort out the hospital bag and once again I realised the gulf between what I was feeling and thinking and what she was. Here was I worrying about work and other selfish things while she was being practical and making ready for the birth. I am not sure if this just means I am totally useless or whether it is just a girl-boy thing that the girl instinctively gets on with it while the boy just gets in the way?

I headed off to Europe and while not boring you with the details, spent the next four days on endless trains going to our factories that are in the butt-end of nowhere. I did spend time in Brussels where I bought Iona lots of Belgian chocolate.

If I thought the house was clean when I left it was manicured by the time I returned from Europe. Another group effort on the part of her family had ensured that the place was spotless for the open house session at the weekend.

I did what I hoped was my bit doing the last bits of cleaning and tackled the oven and the patio doors which were the two most obvious things and by the time we had all finished the placed was about as clean as it had ever been. All we had to do in the morning was to clean the bathroom after our showers and basically get out of the way as by this stage my mere presence made the place look untidy.

By now we had decided that all three houses we had initially viewed in Dorset were not for us and communicated that back to the respective agents.

The chaps from the estate agent arrived just before 10:15 and put their open house flags up! It was time for the big push. We were really excited but at the same time nervous but the first viewer arrived early which was a good sign. We took ourselves out of the way and kept our fingers crossed. The sun was shining the blossom on the cherry tree out and it could not have been a better day.

We headed back to arrive at the end of the open house but as I was walking down the road I could see the flags were already gone and the chaps had packed up five minutes early. It transpired that the early-bird was the ONLY viewer and that three others they had booked in had all cancelled.

We both felt really deflated. After all the hard work and everything it seemed as if we had wasted our time, especially as the estate agents were showing our only prospective buyer another house later that day.

Sullenly, I walked around to the bookies to get some horses for the Grand National, smelling the scent of barbeques as I did. Suddenly, I realised that the day was too perfect and it was not a great surprise that most people had bagged house hunting for chilling out and watching the horse racing.

Note to self. Don't try and sell a house on Grand National day, especially if it is also good barbeque weather!

In some respects it was not so bad, it was to be fair only the start of the house selling and we did not have a place to go to but there had been so much build-up to the event that the anticlimax was devastating.

Of the horses in the national, Iona had picked one and I picked three. All four made it round (unlike two that sadly died on the course) but only hers made any money coming in second as it did!

We were still feeling low but had an NCT baby fair at the local hotel to go to which took our mind off things. A friend of ours was manning the reception so we saw her a bit and had a really good session on pain relief. It was meant to be a workshop but as we were the only attendees it became a one-on-one session!

It became apparent during the session that we had, as we had suspected, missed out on a lot of classes and other information from the hospital. Somehow we had slipped between the cracks and not been told or offered things that we probably should have. Whose fault this was I could not tell. Should we have been asking, should we have been told and who should have told us?

Once again it left me feeling that we had been let down somewhere along the line but it was too late to make a fuss about it now. Fortunately, the woman running the pain relief course, a mother herself, was able to answer a lot of questions for us so the session really filled a lot of gaps in.

We had planned to go to the hospital for a look around after the show but time ran out and we were both, to be frank, really tired so we decided to do it the following weekend. It began to dawn on me that when it came down to it, things would probably just work out naturally.

I had probably the lowest point in my new career. During my train jaunt around Europe the previous week I had been e-mailed by my boss to say that I was being moved out of my temporary office in Hull but when I arrived I found all my stuff dumped in a pile on the floor and utter confusion as to where I was going to do. What was more, my boss was no longer my boss but nobody had bothered to tell me that.

I pretty much snapped and voiced my total displeasure at the situation to the group director who, in her usual manner, did nothing about it. She had it in mind that I was going to move into the office with her but as my computer had been moved into the packaging office with the other engineers and designers I made the executive decision to go and join them so grabbed my stuff and made myself at home.

That was that but I sat there for the rest of the day really feeling that I had made a huge mistake taking the job on. Nothing was going to plan and it seemed that I was getting no support and feeling more and more isolated.

It dawned on me that I was probably having a mid-life crisis but that it was being masked by everything else that was going on. For sure, this new job that was supposed to have removed the anxiety of being unemployed was proving to be even more stressful. I was struggling with my weight, having trouble sleeping or keeping focused and generally feeling lost and confused. I had also been thinking about Aston Martin's a lot, a sure sign of a mid-life crisis!

The truth was that things were actually starting to settle down, moving to the new desk would be the start of this process and it was just the fact that it had taken so long to reach this point that was the trouble. At least, that is what I kept telling myself.

Typically, after such a rubbish day, I had my first evening out in Hull, meeting an old work friend who was up for a meeting in town the next day. We went out and spent a long time trying to find somewhere decent to eat but eventually gave up, found a pub and then had a particularly dodgy kebab afterwards. It tasted wonderful!

Being tired did not help my mood and I struggled through the following day. Iona, back at home, was arranging viewings for our place at the weekend so at least things were starting to move again.

On the Friday we went for the next midwife appointment which was meant to have been at 08:45 but ended up over a half-hour late and when the midwife did arrive she was not our usual one who we were expecting.

This threw us a bit. The new midwife was nice enough but quiet (partly as she was a bit flustered I think). She checked Iona over, doing the usual urine test and measuring her weight (how much!?) before feeling for baby. Although Fidget had turned to be head down, its back was the wrong side, facing left not right so Iona was told to keep on her left side, do a lot of exercises on her hands and knees and all that sort of thing to coax baby to flip around.

For me it was encouraging but scary to know that the baby had turned downwards. From here on in, there was only one way to go – out!!! On the back of the pain relief classes it was now clear that the launch was imminent.

From what she was saying it reinforced the fact that we had missed out on a lot of information and classes from the hospital which was increasingly annoying to say the least but there was nothing we could do about it.

Iona's next appointment was due in two weeks but the royal family had frustratingly decided to have a wedding on that day so the clinic would be closed and we already knew that all the bookings that week were already taken but she managed to add a slot for us so we could come on the 27th in the afternoon.

It was a bit of a shame as it would mean we would not stay in Dorset between the Easter and Royal Wedding weekends but good that we had an appointment close to the appropriate time. I was, however, not entirely convinced that she had entered the appointment correctly.

The following day we had lunch with an old friend of mine which was very nice – a six-hour lunch involving much wine (good hair of the dog for me as I had drunk two bottles of wine the night before) and great food. While we were there we had a derisory offer on the house - £190K – which we refused. This was followed up by a subsequent offer - £195 – also refused, mostly at the urging of the rest of the lunch party who were egging us on to hold out for more (and we were inclined to agree).

On the Sunday we were finally going for the 4pm tour of the maternity unit, though we were still not sure that they were still available. The literature on the subject was very contradictory, some leaflets claimed that tours were available while other sources stated that they had ceased in favour of an "online virtual tour". Since the latter was not to be found I was working on the principle that the real thing was still active.

Arriving at the hospital, the first thing that struck me was that directions to maternity from reception were somewhat lacking. Fortunately a friendly porter just happened to be wheeling a trolley past and he put us on the right track.

Maternity was upstairs and once you got to the stairs there was a nice sign for it. I was glad that we had checked first and not arrived in a panic!

There were a couple of mums with bumps already there which was a good sign that the tours were still on and sure enough, by the time the nurse came out to meet us at four there was a sizeable crowd of expectant couples.

We had a quick look around the maternity unit (reassuringly behind very secure doors) and saw one of the private rooms (at £100 per night) but beyond that there was not a huge amount to see. They gave us some useful information and then took us to the delivery suite (which was back towards the stairs and we had completely missed it so it was just as well we were shown where it was).

The nurse who showed us around was mad as a brush but in a nice way and we were shown the options of birthing rooms, one where you sat on bean bags and one with a more conventional bed. We couldn't see the birthing pool as it was in use but to be honest with our inflatable hot tub I had a fairly good idea what we would have seen.

I liked the idea of the first room with the bean bags as it looked a lot more relaxed. The hospital appeared to be very progressive with new birthing techniques and that came through with their facilities (which included a CD player – note to self to find some suitable music).

While the tour was brief, we did come away feeling a

lot more confident that we knew what we were doing on the day and I was far more chilled but still scared about the whole thing.

The only annoying thing was that Dads cannot stay over and whatever happened I would have to leave outside of the extended visiting hours. In some respect I would have to anyway with the house to sort out (as I was going to discover like most new Dads that the vacuum fairy doesn't exist and the pixies that operate the washing machine are but a myth). I was sad as it would have been nice to have been asleep in a chair by their bed the first night.

I drove back up to Hull that night feeling a lot more ready for the big event yet at the same time less and less ready to be back in bloody Hull.

After a relatively busy week sorting work stuff out I left early so I could get back in time for us to carry on to Dorset again. Despite a lot of chasing my new contract was not as yet finalised which was frustrating but there was not a lot I could do about it.

It was nice to get back to her folks place in good time as it meant we could really enjoy the Easter weekend and relax.

We had another couple of house-viewings but we ruled both out for various reasons. Then, fate delivered what could only be called an absolute blinder but in this instance a good one.

At church, where by now I was on good speaking terms with all the "regulars" in the congregation, we got talking to one couple about our plight to find the perfect home, only to find that they were in the process of preparing their place for sale and did we want to come and have a look.

We followed them back from Church and checked it out there and then. While it was not perfect it ticked more boxes than any of the others and what was more because they had not engaged an estate agent we could do a private sale.

Not wanting to dive into it, we agreed to give it some serious thought and in return they agreed to do nothing further until after the Easter break.

I could sense straight away that Iona was interested and I had to admit that the place had potential. What was most appealing to her, of course, was the fact that it was only a short distance from her mother. For me, the fact that there was a particularly good pub a reasonable walk (or at least, stagger) away was great.

Alcohol was somewhat on my mind that weekend. Please do not get the wrong idea as I am not a raving alcoholic even if I do give that impression. Yes, I like a drink and yes, sometimes I do tend to over-do it but when I need to I can be sensible.

This was one of those times. We had agreed that as Iona reached the stage where it was possible that there could be complications or an early birth that I would go on the wagon again so that I could be on call to make the dash to the hospital if required. Easter Sunday was therefore my last day of boozing until the baby was born. Okay, so I did make the most of it!

Before heading back home we had another look at the potential house, this time with the eye of what improvements we could make (and therefore what we would need to budget in terms of building work and all that sort of thing). Depending on how grand our designs were there was potential for not only an extension but also a conservatory and a considerable remodelling of the garden.

A nagging voice in the back of my mind pointed out that having already put ourselves through a new job / new house / new baby situation that taking on an extension so early was probably crazy.

The house had real possibilities and as we left we both realised it was a highly potential option. True it was not perfect but we had already decided that at this stage we were not holding out for perfection but for a sensible compromise which would be workable. This seemed to be it.

Rather than making a snap decision we decided to sleep on it for a few days and make our minds up once and for all when we came back the following weekend which they were okay with.

We still had a couple of other house viewings but these were quickly rejected for one reason or another until we reached a point where the short-list of houses was *very* short. It was an important decision as it would be the place where baby would grow up so we had to get it right.

Having taken some time off after Easter we headed back via the doctors where Iona had her 4pm appointment with the midwife but when we got to the clinic there was no appointment! My suspicions had been confirmed, the fill-in midwife had cocked up!

Luckily, as we were in such a nice surgery the lady on reception merely added us in to our regular one's list thus we were still booked in for 4pm but actually were called up a few minutes early.

It was quite sad as we realised it was probably the last time we would see her. She checked Iona out – all well and heart beating strongly as before. The baby had turned around, it's back now facing the other way but was still head down and one fifth engaged (i.e. in the right place but not ready to go yet).

When we got home I had a phone call from the estate agent to say we had another offer on the house - £195. Iona had spent the previous week feeling guilty that she had forced me to reject the original offer (I would have been inclined to take £195 from the start) and we had already discussed that we would accept this if it came up again.

The estate agent was just drawing breath to convince me that it was a good offer when I cut him short and said "okay!" and accepted the offer. Hooray!

Although off the booze I was allowed a bottle of beer to celebrate. We then got the call that the couple wanted to come back on Monday to look at the garage and the offer on our place suddenly turned into a half-offer. Boo!

As the weekend ended my new contract from work arrived which helped to ease my nerves a bit. Buying and selling houses is a stressful task at the best of times and with Fidget so imminent we were both on tenterhooks. Indeed, it was only when we both found ourselves snapping at each other for the smallest of things that it dawned on us just how tense we both were.

Whilst updating the "Journey of Love and Hope" I also realised that it had now been a year since I had started keeping the official record. It was scary how quickly the time had flown by and just how much had happened within that twelve months. Undoubtedly Iona and I were both very different people now compared to then and it even more made sense that I had written everything down. So much had changed in a year so what would happen after a decade or two I could not imagine.

Our friends from whom we were looking to buy the house were away until the weekend which was annoying as we had decided to put in an offer.

From my part, I just wanted to get job done. Fidget was now very developed and kicking like crazy (Iona was more and more reaching for my hand to put on her tummy as it was moving so I could feel) so there was a lot going on.

I knew I was feeling very tense as a result of the imminent baby, house move and the job and just wanted things to get back into some form of routine. With the career side of things settling down it was now just baby and house to sort and baby was not going to be long!

It was the royal wedding so we spent a much-needed distraction around another friend's place with their family and a few others around. We watched the televised coverage on their big projection TV before having a very nice barbeque.

That took up most of the day and took our mind off things, at least partly.

The day after, it was time to talk business. It is strange, when buying from a complete stranger you have no compunction about haggling, talking tough and all the other buying tactics but when it is people you know it can be quite embarrassing talking about money.

They were in a similar situation and we spent nearly an hour talking about anything other than the house while we both waited for the other side to broach the subject.

Finally it was down to me to break the ice and through a blustered set of negotiations we eventually came down to a compromise price. Our inclination was to go for it but it still needed careful thought and I had to go back and work the numbers to see where it would leave us in terms of mortgage and money for renovations and extensions.

This we did in the evening (I wished it could have been over a bottle of wine but had to settle for lemonade) and the good news was that we could make it work...just!

We went back the next day and accepted the deal for the house with some relief. Our friends were clearly pleased as it meant they could start looking for a place so it was a really nice happy time. They wanted to crack a bottle of champagne but we had to defer as neither Iona nor I could partake so it was agreed to celebrate after we had exchanged and Fidget was around to join us.

We headed back home and I felt a lot more relaxed knowing that at least the Dorset end of things was hopefully sorted. It would not matter if we did not immediately sell our house as we could get a mortgage for the place in Dorset and pay off the bulk as soon as our old place sold.

Iona was already heavily planning what we would do with the place and I knew at that point that there would be no respite to the chaos once we had moved in. Still, in some respects it would get all the pain over and done with in one go and hopefully after that we could revert so some sense of normality in a house that was everything we wanted.

After a session cutting the grass and hedges, we hosted our prospective buyers, a very nice Russian couple who came for a second viewing. I was able to show them around properly and really do the sales pitch and they seemed to be very happy with the place. They left saying they would firm up their offer with the estate agent so it seemed like we had a deal!

If that were true then the house move was really on and we could be in Dorset before the end of June! They were renting and wanted to move quickly and as we had broken the chain and had the option of putting our stuff in storage & staying with Iona's folks it meant we could be flexible.

I still felt tense, while a sale in principle was agreed I would still be happier once it had all gone through but at least things seemed to be moving and they were a very nice couple.

We did get the feeling that we had been charitable to both our buyers and the sellers of our next place but such is life! It would be good to no longer have to keep the house in show-room condition for viewings.

As well as not drinking I had promised Iona that I would not make any overseas trips during the last weeks of the pregnancy in case there was a problem but work had other ideas and at the beginning of May I was sent over to Amsterdam for two days. This, of course, got me into loads of trouble with Iona but there was little I could do about it.

Fortunately her mum was available to come and stay with her though in truth there were no signs that anything was wrong or that she was imminently heading into labour, even though she was now only a few weeks away from being due.

I did vow, however, that any further trips were to be avoided like the plague. Typically my flight back was late but fortunately nothing had happened and I had gotten away with it!

I headed into Southampton to get my pass etc. for Head Office. It felt good that this part of my life was really starting. With my new desk and with a fob to get through the doors and a pass (at least, a photo as the pass making machine was buggered so I would have to wait until Tuesday to get the real thing) I felt like it was real.

Fidget was kicking & moving so much now you could see Iona's tummy moving clear across the room! It also had the curious habit of sticking what we presumed was its bum out so that every now and then a large bulge would slowly appear and then fade again.

We had dinner at Dawn & Andrew's place which was really nice, especially as they were desperate for an update on Iona's condition. They gave us a load of baby stuff as well as a really nice monitor with a broken power supply but I was confident I could find a suitable replacement.

We talked babies late into the evening.

The day after we went to the NCT nearly new sale at the local hotel and I have never been to a bigger bun-fight! It was like the January sale at Harrods, when the doors open there was an avalanche of people tearing at the stalls to get the best bargains.

Luckily, with so many things already donated to our cause there were only a few things we were looking for specifically so I was able to run and find those while Iona waddled in with the other pregnant ladies. We also found a load of other useful things including some nice wooden toys and Mega Blocks!

I had to head north again that evening which felt weird, especially as I was coming back the next day but it was the shape of things to come as this is what my life was going to be like.

Once in Hull I started to pack the flat up and that felt great. It was possibly the last day I would be in Hull before the birth but it was one full of meetings and there was more than a little impatience on my part to get back down South.

Iona was heading out in the evening for dinner with Aunty Paula so when I got back I had time to unpack quietly and chill out.

When she got back it seemed that Iona was starting to get Braxton Hicks contractions, those uterine contractions that happen prior to labour (or so I am told). Whatever it was, between Fidget kicking like crazy and the spasms that she was feeling, her stomach would go really tight. It was the first real signs that events were reaching a conclusion and we were both excited and at the same time terrified.

# Chapter 31:
## Hurry up and wait...

I was now fully ensconced in Southampton which was good as it meant I would be on easier call and around in the evenings. I even got settled in my new desk. I got a call from the people we were buying from to say that they had found a house and that we were on for the move and that they had spoken to an estate agent with two solicitors – they could use one and we could use the other to speed things up if I were interested. I said absolutely. At this stage anything that shaved time from the process was welcome.

We also got confirmation that the couple were indeed interested in our house so I agreed to send off the deeds. As I was already in "house" mode I made an appointment to see the bank for the following week to arrange the mortgage and also called around a few removals companies to come and quote on moving everything.

The house move was really happening! The "For Sale" sign outside the house changed to "Sold" which was an absolutely beautiful sight.

I popped into London in the morning for a meeting

with a potential supplier and then came home (via Harrods so I could get some nice celebratory wine) so we could go to see the doctor.

Despite our arriving early for our appointment she was running 39 minutes late which was apparently not uncommon. We had not seen this doctor before so that was not a great start but as it was, another GP stepped in and saw us to take some of her workload.

Once again, baby was fine and the heartbeat strong. He judged that the head was two-fifths engaged so getting ready!

Scarily, our next scheduled appointment was at the hospital with the consultant – on her due date in two weeks!

It was Iona's last official day at work and Pru the cleaner had given her a whole load of baby stuff as a present which was really sweet. She did, however, seem glad to be finished even though there were a few residual issues to resolve.

I was also glad that she could stay at home and, theoretically, relax.

In the evening we tested the baby monitor we had bought to make sure it all worked okay and had much merriment playing around with it like eight year olds. Without even doing so consciously we were spending most of our time fussing around making sure everything was ready for the arrival.

The cot, the pram, changing table and pretty much everything else we would need were built, cleaned and ready. I had sorted all the stuff I had brought back from Hull, Iona had her hospital bag packed and ready and now, without anything else useful that we could do the waiting game began.

It was, of course, absolute agony and it was not long before we were both looking for things to distract us. A pile of DVD's were bought, watched and then watched again because neither of us had been paying attention the first time around. I sorted out my wardrobe of clothes for no other reason than it was something I had not messed around with for a while.

There was, of course, plenty to do with the house move but in some respects we had to keep the place habitable until after baby was born. We could not live in an empty shell full of boxes.

I lapsed into a new routine with my trips to Southampton and became acquainted with the whole new set of Southern idiots on the roads. In my experience, Northerners are no better drivers but have different bad habits. In the north, drivers seem to have the universal lack of lane discipline but tend to drive quite slowly.

This is something I had seen in China where drivers are generally very slow and very appalling such that they cruise gradually into trouble.

Down in the south, of course, the pace of life is much higher, people are on the whole more unfriendly and average speeds (roads allowing) much higher. Lane discipline is just as terrible as everywhere else but you tend to get far more people trying to drive into your boot or undertake you than you would in Yorkshire.

Either way, it made for an irritating commute.

Iona, on the other hand, was coming to terms with daytime television which she normally hates with a vengeance but in her condition she was not up for much else most of the time. Fidget was still active (phew) and occasionally got hiccups which was funny.

Later in the week we headed to the bank in the morning to sort the mortgage out but after sitting there for half an hour it transpired that their system had crashed so we were unsuccessful. Despite being told I would have no problem getting an offset flexible mortgage when the adviser punched the numbers we were really close – we had to put down 25% deposit and the sum we were suggesting amounted to about 25.1%. it was cutting it rather fine.

We left with it still unresolved and I had my hair cut instead.

In the afternoon, the chap from the removals firm came and this was more successful. He surveyed the house and went off to give us a quote. We were both really starting to think that things were moving.

Thanks to the previous computer crash I had to go back to the bank the next day to sort the mortgage out but this time the system was up and running so hopefully all was well.

I had managed to wangle some working from home days which was good as I was able to camp out in the kitchen and work while Iona vegetated in the living room but it did mean I could keep her supplied with drinks and nibbles and generally stop her from doing jobs. I knew her well enough that even though she was barely capable her naturally tidy instincts would drive her to start vacuuming or trying to clean something.

A week before Fidget's due date we had a very strange occurrence. For some odd reason we both had the strong feeling that Fidget was going to arrive that day. It didn't happen but it was strange that we both felt the same way.

We then discovered in conversation that we were both having very vivid and generally unpleasant dreams. It was clear that we were both so incredibly on edge that everything else in life was coming to a grinding halt. Until Fidget was born we would both be good for nothing.

Things were so desperate that on the Saturday I even dragged the lawn mower out and gave the garden a much-needed haircut!

That evening we wrote the contact list of people I would call, text, e-mail and social network when the event happened! That was the very last outstanding job to do so we were, in my mind, ready!

I was glad I had done the garden the day before partly as it was windy and grotty but mostly as I had a panicked phone call from Jan. There was a major crisis brewing at work and I had to be in Hull for first thing the following morning.

This was not welcome news but there was little I could do about it. That put paid do our chilled day.

It was strange to leave and I felt very tense. With Iona so close to her due date the chances of my having to do the mad dash down the motorway was suddenly now very strong.

At least her Mum was free and came up to "fat-sit" as it was now being called while I was away, again hopefully for the last time.

Typically, after all that, my morning meeting was cancelled so I had the day relatively free to get on with stuff but I could not leave as the meeting was re-scheduled for the following day. I ended up phoning Iona several times to make sure she was okay to the point that I was probably starting to be a pest!

That evening I was very restless, waiting for the phone to call and had a slight panic when I did phone when she didn't answer. As it was she was in the garden where her Mum was kindly doing some weeding so there was no problem but it did give me a momentary heart attack!

I had an early night but little sleep as I was constantly listening out for the phone.

I was really glad when lunchtime came and I could jump in the car to head home. Even if I got the call now I was already on the way back.

By the time I arrived home and nothing had happened I

was mightily relieved as it meant I was spared the long dash from Hull. Whatever happened now I would stay south until Fidget was around even if it meant getting into a fight with my employer.

Her mum was still there and had done several loads of laundry, helped with the shopping and generally done her motherly things for which I was most grateful.

Everything for the house seemed to have stalled and the anticipated mortgage offer, quote from the removals and information from our solicitors were nowhere to be seen. I was really not in the mood for spending the late afternoon making endless phone calls but there was nothing for it. The house had to be sorted and there is no getting away from the tedious bureaucracy in this process.

Finally, with steam coming out of my ears, it was all sorted. I knew we were really into the house move as it seemed to be endless paperwork and petty details now!

Fidget kept moving to one side which made Iona's tummy very lop-sided which was at the same time strange but funny. More seriously, she seemed to think she might have had a bit of "issue" i.e. potentially the start of the mucus plug coming out but wasn't sure.

Finally, due date eve arrived and I went into work with some trepidation. I was still two hours from home here but as I had a meeting with Jan that was important I could not really stay at home again. He was late for the meeting and it went on so it was nearly quarter to six before I left and not much before eight by the time I got back home. Fortunately, Fidget was not in a hurry to arrive.

Indeed, as the due date dawned we now knew that Fidget was destined to be late and that we were going to keep the appointment with the consultant after all. We got up early so we could try a different route to the hospital. The plan was to leave early so we could get breakfast there and thus we arrived in plenty of time. I had the obligatory bacon butty and Iona uncharacteristically had a sausage one.

When we arrived at the clinic (20 minutes early) it was already busy and thanks to one of the doctors being in theatre everyone was running late. We didn't get called in for our 9:00am appointment until well past 9:30! We seemed to have a knack for picking days when the medical team was being called to emergencies (either that or it was a common occurrence).

The midwife who saw us was accompanied by a trainee (who was very nice) and it was the latter that started the evaluation. Fidget's heartbeat was again strong though the place where they could hear it was now very low on Iona's anatomy.

Given that the room was very warm and they were making Iona hop up and down from the bed, it was not a great surprise that her blood pressure was high.

The consensus was that the baby was still only 2-3 fifths engaged but they wanted to get the consultant to take a look.

We were left waiting for a few minutes while the consultant dealt with another patient. When she came in she got Iona back on the bed and repeated the examination though in her opinion, the baby was not "engaged" so we were a bit confused as to what that was all about.

She then told us that in her opinion we should give nature 10-12 days to get on with it and if not then to induce labour. It was not a great surprise that after all this when they took Iona's blood pressure again it was even higher!

They booked a date for induction should labour not happen naturally so at least we had a cut-off point, not that either of us wanted to get to that stage. She also advised that we saw the midwife earlier rather than later to re-check

Iona's blood pressure etc. and also do a stretch and sweep, whatever that was (it sounded horrible to me).

We finally got out of there at 10:15 and made our way home resigned to the fact that our lives were still on hold. Iona booked the midwife appointment so that was all done. Scary stuff! As I said to Iona, if things panned out that Fidget did have to be induced, it would prove to be the most organised pregnancy on record, especially given that with donor eggs we'd had plenty of time to plan the trip for implantation in the first place and now we would be possibly spared the mad dash to the hospital!

Still, there was time yet for her to go into labour naturally but I already had a sneaking suspicion that this was not going to go according to plan.

The following day Fidget was now officially late but with no sign of coming any time soon. There were one or two house things to sort out (a few bits for the bank and sending our acceptance to the removals firm) so I did those, in the process I found out from the bank that the valuation survey on our new place had been done and was all okay.

I then spent the rest of the day doing various jobs, partly as they needed to be done but mostly to kill time while we waited.

Out of curiosity and also to make sure I knew what to expect I looked up "stretch and sweep" on the internet and found that usually, a membrane sweep will be carried out by your doctor or midwife either while you're at home or in the doctors surgery itself.

They are performed during an internal examination and involve your midwife inserting a finger into your cervix (to stretch it a little) and then making a firm, circular, sweeping movement around the neck of your womb. This movement helps to separate your cervix from the membranes of the sac that is currently housing your baby, and is a procedure that helps to stimulate the release of prostaglandins - the hormones that signal to your brain that it's time to start labour.

It was at that point that I realised that Fidget being late was probably going to involve some unpleasant procedures for Iona to try and hustle things on. The worst thing was that there was no guarantee that a) the midwife Iona trusted would be able to do the stretch and sweep and b) if she did that it would work. The indications in the various internet chat rooms were that if it did have an effect that Iona would go into labour within a few hours.

Iona was getting quite worried, especially given her recent elevated blood pressure and I could see she was either seeking reassurance that all was still okay or for Fidget to simply get on with it and make an appearance.

That evening despite neither of us having the slightest interest in football we watched the back half of the Champions League Final on the telly, Manchester United versus Barcelona mainly because of Fidget's origin. We were rooting for Barcelona and they stuffed Man U 3:1. It felt odd that I could tell you the score in the football and yet I had no idea what was going on in the world at large.

There could have been an alien invasion and we would have been none the wiser.

The following day we took Fidget shopping to pick up some supplies on the logic that if it was going to be late we had to get on with our lives. There was also that whole "let's try and jiggle things about and encourage labour" kind of old wives tale. I could, however, see that Iona was getting very worried and she was mulling over the idea of going back to the hospital early for a blood pressure check.

I scanned her baby notes in just for the record though in doing so I had my first good look through the booklet and realised just how much had not been filled in, mostly due to the fact that she had not had complications, any record of ante-natal classes but also that there were several pages for the record of induction that I feared we might be using. Like Iona, I felt as if the deep water was just ahead of us.

As with many nights previously, Iona snored a lot and was snuffly though she didn't check to see where my nose was in the middle of the night as she had been prone to doing recently and which she had clearly realised she was doing as she asked me if she had prodded my nose the night before. I hadn't mentioned it before as I didn't want to worry her and it really didn't matter.

Iona is one of those people whose brains remain very active when she is asleep. Half conversations in the early hours of the morning are common and were at first very disconcerting. She would ask me a question in a perfectly lucid voice but when I would answer and get no response I would only then realise she was still asleep.

Sleep walking was rarer but even stranger if you have never been with someone who is prone to that sort of activity. For Iona it tends to become most prevalent when she is undergoing deep emotional stress as she was now so most nights I would find her wandering around the bedroom, muttering to herself or prodding various parts of my anatomy for reasons best known to her subconscious.

The trouble is that my response to stress is to not sleep at all or at least to sleep lightly so the combination for me was terrible. The slightest noise or movement would wake me up so when she was in full swing I would get very little rest.

The waiting game really set in and with both of us knackered through broken sleep the days began to drag.

Three days past her due date and still no sign of movement. Iona was still worried though she was probably making herself feel bad partly because she was worrying about it.

We had both had headaches over the last few days as the weather was very thundery and the pressure quite high so it was difficult to tell whether her symptoms were baby or weather related.

Due date + 4 days and Fidget still in absolutely no hurry. We were starting to get a lot of phone calls from well-meaning family and friends, mostly on the "just phoning to see if anything had happened" vein. It was funny as we can go days without the phone ringing at all. I tried to reassure them that we would call around when things began to move in the politest way possible without encouraging them to all bugger off and stop phoning. As if we would have had the baby and not told anybody…..!

Despite the rising tension I had a very productive day doing some design work while Iona relaxed (a bit too much as she had an afternoon nap in the middle of the DVD of "Love Story" which she had borrowed from a friend).

When we went to bed it was in the knowledge that Fidget was not destined to be a May baby although it was still going to be a Gemini, ironic given that it was so nearly one of twins!

Wednesday 1$^{st}$ June or due date + 5 days arrived and once again I was working (lurking) from home while Iona sat around in a state of some limbo eating Frazzles and killing her brain cells watching daytime telly.

We had the appointment with the midwife to do the dreaded stretch and sweep at 4pm so we were both conscious that this could well be the calm before the storm.

Do I need to tell you that we were half an hour early? We were joking that the midwife would be late so we would probably have a bit of a wait. However, when we got there Iona's appointment came up on the check-in computer as 3:45 and that there was no wait.

We assumed this meant that the system couldn't cope

with the extra 4pm appointment so was simply stuck on the last time available but as it was we were called in before four.

It was not our usual one sadly but another new Midwife which immediately rang alarm bells in me for some reason and my fears were quickly proven to be correct.

While she was very nice, as soon as Iona explained the situation she quickly replied that she was not prepared to do a stretch and sweep and that they would not do that sort of thing at the surgery unless by a doctor. I immediately went into foul-temper mood and sulked, wondering why yet again we were being told one thing by one medical practitioner (the consultant at the hospital, by the way) but yet another by the midwife.

It was a major anti-climax as I am sure Iona had, like me, built up that something was going to happen, indeed, even more so as it was to her that it was going to happen, me being just a spectator. We had even put the hospital bags in the car, just in case!

The midwife examined Iona and said that her urine was okay but her blood pressure was still high…big surprise… but otherwise the baby seemed fine and its head was engaged and wedged in the pelvis. Instead of the stretch and sweep she said that we would need to go to the foetal assessment unit at the hospital for the three days before the day that Iona would be induced which in my diary would be the 5th, 6th and 7th but she then phoned to book an appointment for …the 3rd…?

At least having passed the buck she did that much and had a 10am appointment to speak to someone who hopefully would know what the hell they were talking about.

We came out of there and I had to admit I was both angry and disappointed and therefore not a lot of help to Iona which I know was wrong of me. I just wish that the

NHS would get its act together and read from one hymn sheet! The same words would be okay even if the music was different but at the moment we were not even in the same language!

T + 6 days. I had decided to go to work today, partly on the logic that if I did so it would probably set things going (on the "a watched pot never boils" kind of thinking). I didn't head off too early but I was also conscious that I had a few things to do and showing my face would not be a bad thing.

I got into work just before 11am. It was 1:30pm when Iona called to say that she was getting stomach pains and full tightening. She wasn't sure what it meant but it did sound like things were kicking off. Incredibly it sounded as if my superstitious logic was sound!

Having planned to leave at 3pm anyway there was no question that it was time to go home. I alerted my boss to the situation and legged it.

By the time I got home, it was pretty much over – no baby, just that the signs had pretty much stopped. False alarm! Actually, it was probably a precursor of things to come so I was not downhearted and I still felt it was the right thing to do to head back home. At least I had felt the experience of the emergency call and the dash back home, even if the emergency had subsequently gone away.

Iona and I went for a walk to try and get things moving but once again Fidget was in no rush.

I had spoken to our estate agents and had a conversation that things were moving. Our buyers were looking to move in at the beginning of July or, failing that, towards the end. I said I would check with our side to see how things were going that end so gave them a call.

It was a bombshell. The house they had put an offer on had fallen through a couple of weeks ago. They had been gazumped but had failed to tell us this fact so we had been happily moving forward thinking everything was fine when in fact they were going nowhere.

They had put an offer on a new place and were going to hear tomorrow whether or not it had been accepted but suddenly I felt like the house of cards was really beginning to fall down.

After the disappointment of the previous day it was a real blow and I again reacted more than I probably should have. Apparently it had been spotted by the family that I had been "a bit stressed" – if that were the case then it was probably a good thing that they were not around today. I knew it had all been going too well.

Hopefully tomorrow would bring better news.

Fidget was now officially one week late. The day did *not* start well. I was not sleeping well as it was doing my usual pondering over things but at 1:30am the sickening smell of cold shit wafted from downstairs. The toilet had not only backed up but somehow backfired and left a quite remarkable mess and a stench that can only be imagined.

Shovelling shit in the early hours of the morning is, as I am sure I have mentioned before, not my favourite pastime but it had to be done and there was no way I could even begin to consider letting Iona do it.

This did not improve my mood.

After more restless sleep we finally awoke and had breakfast before heading off to the Day Assessment Unit (the "DAU" as I will call it mostly as I am too lazy to keep writing it in full).

The car park at the hospital was very busy as visiting hours had just started but we still found a spot with relative ease, though I was glad I had taken the small car and not the Discovery as it was a tight fit.

The DAU was housed in the same wing as the maternity

unit but when we pressed the buzzer, nobody answered. Finally, a passing nurse took pity on us and let us in. There was someone on the reception desk but she was on the phone which is why she had not responded.

There were four adjustable chairs in the DAU like big versions of Laz-ee-Boy chairs and Iona was put in one with her feet up. I was on a normal chair slightly to one side. It all seemed very comfortable and friendly until the student midwife (with the odd name of Bubbles) came up and as soon as Iona explained the situation and asked for the stretch and sweep she said they didn't do them there but we should ask our community midwife…!

I would imagine at this stage that my face turned an interesting shade of purple. All I could think at that precise moment was "for f**s sake!" Iona was slightly more controlled as I was bouncing off the walls and explained that we had been sent by the consultant to the midwife who had refused and referred us back to the hospital.

The student midwife explained that she wasn't being difficult but they could not do it practically in the chairs and that it needed to be done on a bed. She then proceeded to pull a curtain around Iona – shutting me out in the process as if I was not there – so she could attach the electrodes of a monitor that would track the baby's heartbeat over about twenty minutes and where Iona could, via a control, indicate every time the baby moved.

I, on the other hand, sat on the other side of the curtain seething both at the fact that once again we had been misinformed but also that the midwife had shut me out as if I wasn't there.

At least I could hear the heartbeat which, as always, was fine. Iona's blood pressure was still high (not as high as mine, I was willing to bet) but after a while Fidget went to sleep.

After some time on the chair, Iona felt faint so they put her on her side. I was finally given a job to do, probably to stop me looking so sulky, holding the blood monitor sensor in place on her tummy while they took her blood pressure again. She was by this time getting very hot so I stood and used her mini-fan to try and cool her down.

There seemed to be a lot of sitting around with not much happening as the machine took its measurements but eventually the other midwife announced that they would take a blood sample to make sure Iona was okay. Her urine test had been clear of protein but they were still worried about her high blood pressure but it was also becoming increasingly obvious that nobody wanted to make any diagnosis and that they would defer to a doctor to do that.

As per usual, Iona's veins did a vanishing act at the first sight of a needle so the midwife eventually had to go in through the side of her hand. By the look on Iona's face, it hurt like hell (as it had done in the clinic), especially on the way out.

By now it was about a quarter to eleven and as the results were not going to be available until noon we were released to go for a walk.

We headed straight for the restaurant and Iona had a sausage buttie and a sticky bun while I had TWO bacon butties! We got there ten minutes before they stopped serving breakfast which was good as I could see that Iona needed some food and I was by that time dying for a bacon roll. I also bought an emergency chocolate bar for her for later.

With time still to kill we went for a quick wander and a tactical pee before heading back to the DAU.

When we arrived it was obvious that the results were back but that the midwife was using them to give Bubbles a quick lesson, though Bubbles didn't seem to know the answers to most of the questions she was being asked which was worrying.

The excellent news was that the blood tests were all negative so Iona did not have pre-eclampsia (which in my bloke way I knew was a bad thing to have but did not have the slightest clue what it was)! The midwife told us that the registrar had just gone into theatre so she was going to call down to the ante-natal clinic to see if the consultant could see us. As it happened, it was she who answered the phone and agreed so we were bundled downstairs back to the clinic where we had started a week previously!

It was just after twelve when we got there. It was not busy and got quieter as the time passed, leaving at the end just us and a young couple having a quite spectacular domestic. It was nearly 1pm by the time we were called in by the same student midwife (Karen, I think her name was) we had seen the week previously but at least she was really nice along with the other midwife we had also seen who seemed to know her stuff.

They told us that the consultant was in the other room but would be with us soon so when there was a knock on the door and some chap walked in we were both a bit surprised.

He was a registrar and being yet another new face we had to explain our situation all over again! When we said that it had been suggested earlier that Iona might be induced he asked us why (you're the f\*\*ing doctor, you tell us!).

Once again I bristled as it seemed that he was going to do nothing but I think his survival instincts kicked in. Whether it was the body language we both adopted or something else I am not sure but he seemed to back down and started to explain that inducing early gave a greater risk of problem and that Iona's blood pressure was at the top end of normal which is why they were being hesitant even though her blood work and biochemistry were all okay.

He did also say that we should see our midwife for another blood pressure check on Monday.

Another midwife then came back in to do a sweep and once again the curtain was drawn with me on the outside. I cannot therefore add any comments about the procedure here as I was not privy to it.

All I could tell after the grunting and other strange noises was that things were not going well and afterwards the midwife told me could not reach the cervix (baby's head was high) and that Iona was therefore not ready and the sweep could not be done.

By now they had also noticed that Iona's legs were swelling up (probably due to the fact that we had been sitting around for about four hours by this time and the room was again hot!).

The midwife asked if the baby moved more than ten times a day. Iona replied that while it had moved she was not counting. I do not recall us ever being told to count the movements but now the midwife was insisting that we did and that they wanted at least ten movements a day – any less and we should be on the phone immediately. Nice of them to tell us this before!

She also said that our local surgeries often refused to perform procedures for patients at that particular hospital as they saw it as "out of their area" and didn't want to take responsibility. There seemed to be a lot of buck-passing going on. Evidently the "National Health Service" was not as national as the name implies.

Then, to really add to the confusion, they started to doubt whether the baby was even engaged and dragged a portable scanner in and the registrar to take a look. We hastily told him that we didn't know the gender of the baby but as it was he was only interested in the head.

They needn't have worried. It seemed that the head was in the right position after all.

Finally, the consultant appeared, gliding into the room like royalty, and said that we should come back in tomorrow to get her blood pressure checked and then again on Monday to the DAU where she would meet us (she would be on the ward that day). Finally, the registrar made an appointment for us for 11am and we were allowed to go.

We decided to get a 7-day car park ticket!

By the time we left it was past two in the afternoon. When I got back I communicated to work that effective immediately I was on holiday as in all fairness I could not reasonably say I was working from home if we were going to be back and forth to the hospital. It would mean that I would not get lots of time with Fidget when born (as I did not qualify for paternity leave having not been at the company long enough) but it was important that I supported Iona up to the birth so that was that.

We got home to find that the toilet had covered the bathroom floor with liquid shit yet again. By this time I was at the end of my tether with the house. The sooner we moved the better.

Iona fell asleep in the room furthest from the pong and while she dozed, our friends called to say their offer on the new house had been accepted and that they had a timescale of around eight weeks to move so hopefully the house was back on.

With some sort of plan for the next few days mapped out we went to the supermarket to stock up.

I put a Star Trek movie on the DVD player that evening so I could veg in front of something mindless while Iona chilled out.

Back we go tomorrow!

T + 8 days. Typically the main road down to the hospital was closed for resurfacing, something that they had failed to give advanced warning of, so we had to take a circuitous route that had more roundabouts (and, thanks to the works, more traffic). Luckily as always we left early and still arrived in plenty of time.

The hospital was very quiet it being a Saturday morning, I guess due to a lack of routine clinics, blood tests and all the other appointments that go on during the week. It did mean we could park easily!

We got to the DAU and immediately the midwife gave Iona a grilling about her urine sample, interrogating her as to whether she had used a clean (not washed) pot. One of the other midwives had a laugh about how much she was going on about it. I was not so amused.

Iona was hooked up to the monitor again (and I was left outside the curtain again – is this some sort of secret ritual that men are not allowed to witness?) while the midwife checked the urine sample but all was well and she said that the swelling in Iona's legs was just one of those things, not helped by the fact that it was very humid that morning.

We found out that the second trace on the instrument was in effect measuring Iona's stomach muscles as she had a tightening which showed up as a hump on the graph. The sensor had a pressure switch that the muscles could push against.

Iona's blood pressure was lower and certainly not giving cause for concern. The only problem was that once Iona had made herself comfortable in the chair, Fidget went to sleep again! Iona had a couple of white chocolate cookies and as soon as the sugar rush hit, Fidget woke up again, its heart rate soared and it became very active. The trouble now was that the midwife wanted Fidget's baseline heart rate to be around 150-ish but with all the sugar it was well over 160.

Iona had another tightening which showed up on the trace just before she switched it off.

It took Fidget about half an hour to calm down but we definitely had a sugar junkie on our hands!

The midwife booked us in for a follow-up on Monday at 8am so that we could coincide with another appointment that the consultant had with another lady at 8:30 – the logic being that Iona's trace and urine would have been measured by then so that the consultant could comment and we could get out of there in good time

We got out of there and headed home but it was still after noon by the time we got back!

Fidget settled back down and made no further attempt to make an appearance that day.

Part of me wondered what was happening in the rest of the world as for sure our universe had shrunk to encompass just our house, the hospital and the road in between.

T + 9 days. Guess what, no Fidget! It rained for most of the day so we had a very lazy one watching telly for most of it. Iona did so with a kind of glazed, distant look. The clock was well and truly ticking now and her body was resolutely refusing to do anything constructive like go into labour.

T + 10 days. As we had an 8am appointment we decided to leave around 7am so I got up at 6am to make bagels for breakfast to eat in the car.

OMG! If I thought the traffic was bad on Saturday it was absolutely horrendous today. They had resurfaced the road at the weekend but the implication of the signs which had eventually appeared had been that the work would be completed by then. As it was the road was down to one lane and the open surface covered in gravel!

What should have been a twenty minute journey took

just under two and a half hours. We had worked out early on that we were going to be late so phoned through to the DAU to say we were stuck.

We finally arrived at 9:30 after a tactical wee and a tactical cookie for Iona. Karen was up in the DAU which was nice and the consultant was also there but by the time Iona had been hooked up to the monitor she had vanished again. Karen had a feel but it seemed that Fidget's head was still high.

Iona's blood pressure was still elevated but slightly lower than Saturday which was good news but as with Saturday, no sooner had Iona sat in the chair than Fidget went to sleep so eventually Iona had another cookie to try and wake it up.

I began to learn that just before Iona pushed the button to indicate Fidget had moved its heart rate would suddenly go up so I could predict when it would move! We also realised that the sensor that monitored movement was knackered so eventually Karen replaced it with one that actually gave a credible reading.

The midwives were happy with the sensor data and switched the monitor off at around ten thirty but it was a quarter past eleven before the consultant arrived. She diagnosed gestational hypertension and then said that she had studied under the professor who was the world expert in the subject and who claimed that it was normal and would lead to normal labour even though he always seemed to induce his patients! I'm to this day not sure what message we were supposed to take from this.

She took us into a side room and gave Iona an examination (external and internal) and said that we needed to decide a cut-off date. She realised that Iona's cervix was closed and baby's head remained high (two fifths palpable above the pelvis) so it still had a long way to go.

The consultant was of the opinion that we should not mess around with several rounds of induction and simply go for the one planned round on Wednesday but if that did not work go straight to a caesarean afterwards. It was not the news we wanted to hear but if that was the medical advice then so be it.

It would mean that when we went in on Wednesday Iona would be staying in so at least we could plan. The consultant also told us that she would be around Wednesday afternoon and if the people we were dealing with started to make other decisions to page her and she would put a line under the whole thing and overrule them.

Finally, someone actually making decisions and not only that but agreeing to be around to reinforce them!

Tuesday was Iona's last chance to go into natural labour but we both had the same impression of inevitability that this was not going to happen from the outset.

It didn't.

Even as we were going to bed I knew we would not be making the mad dash in the middle of the night. Iona was very quiet.

# Chapter 32:
## Journey's End.

Finally it was T + 12 days and hopefully D-day.

We both woke in a very reflective mood. Nature had been given every chance to get on with things but at every turn she had failed. Now it was once again time for science to give a helping hand and unless Iona went into labour on the way to the hospital the medics would take charge.

I think we were both a little disappointed at this. So much of the process had been artificial we had both hoped that at the end things would be normal but in this we were to be disappointed.

The night before I had updated the book as much as I can and it felt as if I had left the story at a cliff-hanger which, in some sense, I had. When I next put finger to keyboard the deed would have been done and my anonymous audience of one would have a name.

While we had both been aware that our lives had been on hold it was only now that I realised just how much this was true. My thoughts had imploded more and more inwards until now when there was nothing but the baby. Post sat unopened, phone calls unanswered.

I looked in the mirror and a total stranger stared back and I was quite shocked at how much I had changed. We had been so deeply involved in the frustrating process that IVF had been that I at least had really not come to terms with the glaring fact that by the end of the day we were likely to be parents. I wasn't ready!

Well, that is probably not true and I am sure that I was far more prepared than I felt and I have no doubt that the jitters I was feeling were perfectly normal. Iona, on the other hand, was totally prepared physically but mentally she was terrified. It was all down to her now and she was torn between elation and sheer terror. Although I had not heard her I am sure she had spent most of the sleepless night praying.

Everything we had suffered, all the heartache, frustration, anger, annoyance but at the same time all the hopes and dreams had led us to this point.

I felt mildly sick.

Once again we left early, heading out at seven and arriving at the hospital at 7:35 so that we could have breakfast in the restaurant. Rather than my customary bacon butty I went for the full breakfast – six items but as bacon and hash browns came in pairs it was actually eight! To be truthful I was eating out of habit rather than appetite.

Despite the fact that our appointment was not until 9:30 we got to the ward at 9am precisely. The buzzer was really crackly but one of the midwives let us in. The ward with the beds was very clean and very modern (I since found out that the place had been refurbished a few years previously and very well kept). It was nice that it was also clean and quiet.

As Iona was examined we made the point of repeating

the consultant's plan i.e. to try just one round of induction and then go for the caesarean section. Part of me was also name-dropping as the staff were obviously terrified of the consultant and if the fear of wrath made them move then so much the better. Although I had not watched those TV medical dramas I had seen enough to learn this much!

The plan was to go with something called Propest, the slower form of induction and wait the full 24 hours before surgery rather than the prostyn gel. The midwife confirmed this with the consultant before proceeding so already we knew that if induction did not work it would be tomorrow before the caesarean.

I listened to the discussion as if they were talking in ancient Greek. In the rush of, well, hanging around waiting (which I know is a contradiction in terms) I had stupidly not read up on induction and had no idea how it worked, let alone that there were different forms. I presumed it was something drug-related and not someone standing behind her with an inflated bag poised between their hands ready to burst it but when it really came down to the moment I was not really on top of the situation.

Iona, on the other hand, had clearly boned up on the procedure as she held a lengthy and intelligent conversation with the medical team. Not for the first time I felt somewhat unrequired.

They offered that Iona could elect to stay in or go home during this period but that their preference was for her to stay so they could monitor her. She filled in the selection forms for the next three meals – she was staying! We both thought that would be best and made a note to get her bag of things from the car once the induction had been performed and she was sent to walk around.

The idea of the Propest I finally discovered was to open the cervix to 2cm and to allow them to break her waters;

at least that was what someone said in the sort of tone they would normally reserve for ninety-year-olds with terminal dementia. I didn't mind as I had given up all pretence of intelligence.

They strapped Iona to the monitor again and left her for 20 minutes to get a trace of baby's heart rate and movements. While we were waiting, someone came around checking the cleanliness of the ward, even as far as the top of the curtain rails and underneath the seats of the chairs! It was very impressive and you had to admire their diligence. I guess with all the MRSA and other bug scares they have to be ultra-cautious, especially in high-risk areas such as maternity.

They measured Iona's blood pressure but changed cuffs as one of them seemed to read high. I got the distinct impression that the equipment had seen better days or at least had seen rather too much use. Her blood pressure was still high despite this. Regardless of the fact that Iona had recently eaten breakfast, Fidget had done the usual thing and gone to sleep for the monitor.

The midwife gave an excellent explanation as to the procedures and then left us too it.

It was truly exciting. Within a matter of minutes they were going to induce Iona and as far as Fidget was concerned it was a case of ready or not you are on the way!

What could possibly go wrong now? Bugger, did I just say that?

We were sitting there all calm and quiet when every alarm on the monitor went off and it lit up like a Christmas tree. Fidget's heart rate had plummeted from around 165bmp to nearer 65 in a matter of two seconds! We looked at each other for a moment and I am sure the blood drained from both of our faces. My heart rate went through the roof as panic set in.

Nobody reacted and certainly nobody came running. Iona screamed at me to do something which broke my paralysis and I ran out of the ward to grab the midwife, noting that the alarms were clearly audible by the desk and that she *was* ignoring them. She came hurrying in and I could see from the look on her face that something was terribly wrong. She made Iona turn on her side and the heart rate came back up but it had been down for nearly two minutes.

I am not a doctor but even I could see that this was not normal.

The midwife hurried to get the doctor to check and we both were suddenly very concerned and feeling very sick. Whatever had just happened was clearly not run of the mill. The duty doctor came back and his expression was also worrying.

The midwife was explaining to him the situation as they approached and I clearly heard her say that she had spotted the problem which was a blatant lie! She had done absolutely nothing and would not have budged an inch had I not alerted her but I let it drop. Now was not the time for a fight even though my blood was boiling and emotions were riding high. After all the cock-ups that we had suffered with the NHS this was the most insidious.

I could see the absolute terror on Iona's face and she needed me to be focused at this point.

Although Fidget's heart rate had come back to the 160's it was very regular and he wanted to see variability in the trace. He explained that the umbilical cord could be around the baby's neck and did not want to start contractions in case it made the situation worse.

Terrific, so we cannot induce the baby for fear of hanging it!

He went off to find our consultant but came back soon

after with another one and they formed a huddle to discuss tactics.

Fidget's heart rate plummeted again while they were talking and as they had not noticed (so the combined medical experience of a midwife, doctor and consultant were happily ignoring the fact that our baby was in the process of strangling) I shouted at them, probably louder than I had intended, and they made Iona move and sit up to try and resolve the problem (which it did).

On the unimpressed meter my needle was now thoroughly buried in the red and I think it showed. I have a particular knack of facial expressions and at this particular point I think the "screw this up and I will sue you to oblivion" face was glaring at them.

Suddenly it was clear the situation had become critical. The consultant was under no illusion that things were rapidly getting out of control and made the choice. Iona was going into surgery and she was going immediately.

I am sure at this point that if my face was already white it would have gone transparent. Iona's certainly did and I could see in her eyes that she was thinking the worst. This is where being a scientist is really not helpful and I kept trying to tell myself that Fidget's heart had not stopped so oxygen starvation to the brain should not have happened but our combined imaginations were running wild.

Whatever was going on, Fidget was in foetal distress and I was quite definitely now surplus to requirements. I was whisked into a side room and given a pair of hospital scrubs to change into.

My state of panic was then heightened to another level, if that was at all possible under the circumstances. The scrubs were a medium and far too small for me! I was left in the side room feeling helpless and frantic while they prepped Iona for surgery. They were certainly not going to wait for me and I would not want them to do so but within a few seconds I was going to be on my own while Iona and Fidget where whisked off to an uncertain fate.

I am afraid it was not a time to be subtle. I stuck my head out of the door and almost screamed at one of the other midwives who luckily took pity on me and found a pair of large ones that fitted fine. I had just enough presence of mind to put my camera in my pocket. It was terrible, the situation was critical as it was but the staff in the hospital seemed to be doing everything in their power to make it more stressful.

My clothes were hurled in all directions in the side room – I did not care about them now. My eyes were focused on the small window in the door so that I could see if the porters went rushing by with Iona. Whatever state of dress I was in I was going to follow them, even if I was subsequently arrested for indecent exposure.

Fortunately, I was just changed when they were ready.

I remember obsessing about the form that the Spanish clinic had sent us to get filled in when the baby was due and stuffed it in my pocket as well. It was something that would continue to obsess me throughout the delivery and knew I was starting to blabber. In hindsight I was not in a normal state of mind and I apologise most profusely to everyone around me for both my behaviour and language should I have said or done something inappropriate. I have never before or after experienced madness but at that precise moment I was bordering on the edge of sanity and in this I am not joking.

The truth is had it not been for the notes I took straight after the event I would not be able to tell you what really happened. Such was the shock that Iona and I found ourselves in that both of us have pretty much blanked the experience. I guess this is some kind of post-traumatic stress response but I suspect my memory of the next hour is based more on the image I have formed having told the story several times rather than a true recollection of events.

Iona is no help as she was pretty much in la-la land for most of it. Oh, the benefit of really good drugs!

As I got back to Iona they had just about finished the explanation of the procedure so I had missed all of that which was frustrating as even if she needed confirmation of what had been said I could not help her now.

I appreciate it was all a bit of a rush but had it not been for the stupid cock-up with the scrubs I would have done a quick-change that would have made Superman proud and been back for the explanation. Now I was about as much use as a sore throat to a sergeant major.

One of the doctors was trying to put a drip line in but was almost shoved aside as the alarms went again and another medic made it quite clear we were moving right there and then! The doctor could either get out of the way or be run over. Fortunately for him he chose the former as Iona's trolley did a standing start that would have made a Bugatti Veyron proud.

We were a category 2 emergency which sounded serious enough but when Fidget's heart rate crashed for this third time we were upgraded to category 1. I had enough sense left in me to understand what that would mean – a general anaesthetic and myself stood in the corridor in my scrubs looking even more stupid than I usually do.

I have often seen in medical dramas the bit where they go tearing down the corridor, nearly smashing doors off their hinges in the process but I never actually thought I would not only see it for real but be literally running after the bed myself. Iona seemed oblivious to the impacts as the two porters hurtled her towards the operating theatre.

Hospital staff, patients and visitors dove for cover as we ran headlong towards the theatre.

Someone on the team realised we were an IVF pregnancy and as soon as we arrived they checked Fidget's heart rate and found it had recovered again so downgraded us to category 2 so that I could be present and Iona could be awake. I could have kissed them (luckily I didn't as it was a bloke)!

It was ten past eleven, we were in theatre, everyone was bustling about in a hurry, and I was shell-shocked and just in the way. Eventually I was ordered into a chair (but still in the way as it happened but as that was where they had put me I didn't have enough clarity of mind to realise that at the time). The only moment in which I had a part to play before the kick-off was to hold the sensor on Iona's tummy that was monitoring Fidget but that would not happen for a few minutes so at first I felt really self-conscious.

It only took one glance at Iona to make me feel really guilty. I was worrying about how I felt but she looked dreadful as if she had already been told the baby was dead. The problem was, while they worked on her I could not even hold her hand and from where I sat I could barely even catch her eye though I did enough to see the tears flowing.

Time was moving on and I tried to remember how long it had been since Fidget's heart rate had first dropped. Then, with horror, I realised that it could have been happening for much longer, we had only found out about it when the monitor had been hooked up nearly two hours previously.

What damage had been done?

The drip was put in, Iona was wired up to the monitors and then they finally relieved me of my duties as they prepared her for surgery. They had a very cold spray that went on her back before the epidural went in and then they laid her down for ten minutes to let it take effect.

Ten.....long....minutes. It was like the eye of a hurricane.

All of a sudden everyone relaxed. There was absolutely nothing they could do now until the drugs took effect.

To check how she was doing they used the same spray on her legs. She didn't even realise they had done it!

The moment they were happy the anaesthetic was sufficient they went for it and everything became frantic again. There was a screen up just below Iona's chin and we were that side while they worked on the business end.

All I could do was stroke Iona's forehead until they cut through. At 11:39 the head was exposed and at 11:45 the baby was out. They let me peek but I only caught a fleeting glimpse of it as it was whisked away and did not catch the gender or even whether it was alive or not. I did have a look at Iona's insides just so say I had done so. Well, how often do you get a chance like that?

Looking back it was a very strange thing to do but I was terrified to look into the corner where our baby had been taken for fear of what I might see there.

One of the midwives took my camera and took a couple of pictures before I was called over to cut the umbilical cord from…my new daughter!!!! She was alive, she was well and she was staring up at me with big, dark eyes.

My heart melted. I had harboured a secret wish to have a baby girl but had not said so to Iona as I knew that it would have put even more pressure on her had she not delivered what she felt I wanted. The truth was that I would have been equally happy whatever it was and especially that at first glance she was breathing and had all the right numbers of things in the right places.

The fact that it was a little girl was, however, the icing on the cake and such sweet icing it was.

Hello Eleanor Athena Forde. The picture of me after cutting the cord says it all. I am grinning so much it is a wonder the top of my head didn't fall off Monty Python style. For what felt like an age but was probably only a few seconds I stared down with immense pride at baby Eleanor and she stared back up at me with her big, deep eyes.

She was also covered in meconium thanks to the foetal distress and they had not cleaned her at that stage. She emerged into the world head to toe in shit. It seemed like a fitting start if her life was to be confronted with the same epidemic of rubbish customer service that seemed to dog Iona and I.

She had come out covered in poo and had another big one while they were sorting her out but I didn't care. She was our daughter and nothing else mattered. Apart from putting a nappy on her they did very little in the way of cleaning her up of the meconium and just let it dry on. Apparently it is good for their skin but I cannot see people rushing to the spa for that kind of treatment.

Once I saw past the yellow gunk on her I realised that not only did she have incredible eyes but also long dark hair and long slender fingers with beautifully formed fingernails. In fact, the more I looked the more I realised just what a pretty baby she was and it was not just that she was ours!

Only then did I remember Iona! Whoops. The midwife took Eleanor back and put her with Iona so she could see her for the first time and I took the first of many photos. Finally, they sat me down and let me hold her while they sewed Iona back up. In the process Iona became nauseous and although I alerted the theatre staff to it they gave her an injection too late and put the sick bowl too far away from her and she vomited down the side of her face and shoulder.

After that she was sort of out of it while I was in a daze. They took Eleanor back off of me so they could weigh her – 7lb 7oz and give her a vitamin K jab which she took without a fuss.

I remembered the form that the clinic had asked us

to fill out and thrust it into someone's hand, mumbling something about it needing to be completed.

Finally, by just after noon we were done and we were wheeled out, slower than we had been wheeled in, thankfully, to the recovery ward. It had pictures of Peter Rabbit and friends on the walls. Iona and baby were both checked out but were both recovering well. Eleanor was put on Iona skin to skin to start the bonding process. We would have been moved relatively quickly but there was some sort of argument over the fact that while the other patients were being served lunch they were not accepting any transfers from recovery so we were sort of stuck there in limbo for a while.

This was a slight problem for me as there was nowhere to sit so I perched precariously on the edge of her bed but to be honest I really did not care anymore. My world had just changed forever.

Iona had a slightly artificial grin on her face and a dreamy look in her eyes but beyond that she was completely out of it. They were *really* good drugs.

Eventually they moved us to the post-operative ward in Maternity where our stuff (minus my shoes that I had left in the side room where I had changed) was waiting.

They put Iona on a saline and oxytocin drip and left us too it.

Iona could barely move, still being numb for most of her body but it was the first time we could enjoy Eleanor together.

It was only then that we talked about what had happened and we took stock of the situation. In the space of about three hours we had gone from preparing for a routine induction to having a baby under the most stressful circumstances! It then occurred to me that Iona and I had probably saved Eleanor's life, possibly twice. It was a sobering thought and made me go cold with the thought as to what could have been. It also made me very angry that we had been put in that situation in the first place.

Weeks after the fact we were to read about an almost identical situation in the papers but in that instance the monitor was taken away from the pregnant mother as it was "needed elsewhere". The baby died and all the legal proceedings in the world would not bring it back. That could so easily have been us but I was very glad that I had not read that at the time.

I did not realise it but we were now in the ward "quiet time" when partners were normally kicked out but when they came to see us and suggested we put her in a baby-grow I had to repeat (as I had mentioned it before but could not remember when) that we had left the bag of stuff in the car not expecting to have a child so soon!

One of the midwives took me to find my shoes but then abandoned me and I was so turned about I struggled to find my way back to the ward, only realising which one it was due to the proximity to the toilets and the words "Post-op Ward" on the door (a bit of a give-away).

I changed in the visitor's loo and then headed out to the car, remembering to grab my phone on the way as I now had proud daddy duties to do!

My first call was to her Mum but the phone cut off as someone pressed the wrong button. I called again and got through. She thought I was calling to give an update on the plan and was quite flustered when I said "Er...it's a girl!" She was totally flustered as they were on a day trip at that time having, like us, not expected things to move so quickly or dramatically. She wanted to know when she could come in (later I was able to text her to say to come in at visiting time at seven).

Next I called her Dad and I then spoke to my Mum

and left a message for my Dad before moving onto siblings. It is very difficult getting the political correctness of who to call when and whose nose would be put out of joint if they found out after so and so. This was not, of course, helped when key people were not at the end of a phone.

Sorry to say at that point my attitude was along the lines of "bollocks to them". I had made the effort and was not going to wait and let news travel around uncontrolled just because they happened to be out.

I did my best and then grabbing the bag and heading back to the ward.

When I got back it was still "quiet time" and although only ten to three (when visiting re-started) they would not let me back in.

Iona was still pretty exhausted and feeling manky but she had to lie there all day, though she did have a catheter in to provide for her biological needs. I could see that all she wanted was a shower and to go home.

She tried Eleanor to the breast and she took to it well (nose-to-nipple, open wide and then clamp on!). At one point the student midwife Karen popped in which was really nice and it was good to see her. She had a chat and a cuddle (with Eleanor, of course).

The afternoon was a bit of a blur with most of it spent with Eleanor skin to skin with Iona.

They brought her supper at six but being recently post-op it was reduced rations even though she was starving. I asked the midwife for some cotton pads (which we had forgotten to pack) so I could clean Eleanor up a bit and change her nappy if needed. She of course went away, became distracted and forgot.

A very proud Granny and Granddad arrived at seven at which point I tried again with the cotton pads, this time with success and gave Eleanor as good a clean as I could (which was not much – meconium is like road tar to get off!) but changed her nappy and put her in a baby-grow without causing her bodily harm for which I was most impressed.

They left at eight and as I was exhausted by this time I was away soon after, even though daddy visiting hours extended to nine. Iona was understandably worried about my ability to drive home (as, secretly, was I).

When I got back I raised a glass or three of wine and I do recall chatting with a few people on the phone but probably talking a load of nonsense. I was on such a high I stayed up late as I knew I needed to wind down before sleeping.

It was then, memory already beginning to blur, that I grabbed the computer and wrote the account of what the day had brought. I had started the book with an apology as at that point it was aimed at a virtual person, the mere suggestion of a child but now she had a name. Being able to speak to her for the first time was an incredible feeling and so overpowering that I nearly succumbed to writer's block. Still, I knew if I did not write it down that night I would regret it so write I did, a tear in the corner of my eye all the time that I did.

I woke up feeling very strange. Whatever position I had gone to bed in was the one I awoke in and my body ached like crazy. No sooner had I got out of the shower than I broke out into a cold sweat and my muscles began to shake. I made a cup of tea but I promptly threw it back up in the sink. This was no hangover and it dawned on me that I was suffering delayed shock.

Some years previously I had experienced a minor road accident when stuck in traffic on the M3. It had been a really terrible evening with rain lashing down and the motorway was down to two lanes due to road works. Inevitably, through the rain I had seen the red brake lights of the car ahead as I joined the back of the queue.

Unfortunately, the car behind me had been far too busy on his mobile phone and was totally oblivious to the standing traffic until the very last minute when, wide eyed, he hit the anchors.

I had see this unfolding in my rear-view mirror but there was nothing at all I could do but brace myself as he ploughed headlong into the rear of my car. My seat collapsed and I was thrown backwards which probably saved me from any form of injury beyond the slightly bruised thumb as my hand struck the steering wheel.

The driver of the car behind who had also miraculously survived unscathed had seen me disappear and had thought my head had fallen off – evident by the sheet white face that peered through my window when he came to investigate only to find me staring up at the stained roof of my elderly car wondering what the damage was like.

His car was totalled and indeed we never did find his left headlight whereas when the police arrived (and one of them jammed a screwdriver into the seat mechanism to hold it up) they realised that as my rear lights were miraculously intact even though the boot would never open again I was allowed to drive away once the investigation was complete.

It was only some hours afterwards that the shock had hit me and I was violently sick and it was this precise feeling that was overcoming me now.

My legs ached from all the standing I had done the in the wards on the previous day and all in all I was in a pretty poor shape.

As I drove to the hospital I felt terrible with the thought that I might not be well enough to go and see Iona and Eleanor. The traffic was awful as there had been a five-car shunt on the road but fortunately coming the other way so

I got through it and arrived at the hospital in time to go to the restaurant for a well-needed bacon butty (or two) and a cup of coffee, all of which settled my stomach and after which I felt much better. By the time I got to the Maternity ward I was feeling far more human.

Iona looked terrible as Eleanor had cried for most of the night and kept most of the ward awake. I changed a sticky nappy but the good news was that Eleanor was feeding well. Her life was so simple, suckle, shit and sleep.

There was a bit of a yellowish tinge to Eleanor as jaundice was beginning to set in. Having changed her I had a bit of a cuddle and eventually put her in her cot while Iona (who no longer had the catheter or IV drips in) went for a well-needed shower.

While she was away, the midwives came and moved us to "C" ward next door so that when Iona came back we were settled in our new "home".

The morning was a blur of cuddles, feeding and chatting but I think Iona was glad I was there to help out, give her foot rubs and generally do what I could. There could have been an alien invasion outside but we would have been none the wiser. As far as I was concerned there was Iona and Eleanor and nothing else.

Lunch arrived – not what she had ordered so she had to send it back and get the correct meal despite having filled in the menu cards the previous day. Food seemed to be a random lottery in this place.

At 1pm I was kicked out for "quiet time" so grabbed a sandwich and went to the car to do all the other texts, e-mails etcetera to put the news out about Eleanor's birth.

On the stroke of 3pm I was back in the ward for more "Eleanor time". Granny and Granddad appeared soon after, coming in for the 3-5pm visiting slot. During the afternoon, the staff were becoming concerned about Eleanor's colour so did a heel-prick test to collect some blood for analysis. Eleanor took the needle well but didn't care for having her foot squeezed and said so with her particularly well-formed set of lungs!

It amazes me how such a loud noise can come from such a small child.

The result came back just before I left for the night. Her bilirubin levels were just below the level where light therapy would be used but very close to the line so more tests were planned to monitor her situation.

I left just before nine and headed back for a late supper of pizza and wine. I started to really feel the pride about being a Dad! It was also the first time I had really stopped all day so I opened the laptop and began to write.

Even though it had only been a day since I had last updated the book so much had changed since that point.

Writing about the birth had been very hard. As I have said before the memory is now a distant blur and even at that stage details were becoming shaky. I had to really concentrate to put the facts down as accurately as possible while at the same time reliving the shock of when Eleanor's heart rate collapsed. Now, I found myself describing silly details about things that Eleanor had done. She was barely a day old and her every waking moment was being documented.

I realised then that I was getting to the end of the book and with the birth of Eleanor both Iona and I were coming to the end of the journey we had been on for so long.

The book had been not only an escape but almost an obsession on my part. Some people bottle things up inside, more recently there are those that pour their hearts out in social networking sites but for me the book was the epitome of the journey. I had no idea how Eleanor would view it or even if she would understand it but I now knew that if she did not then I would.

The journey had been all-absorbing as our lives had fallen down a constantly narrowing funnel until nothing else mattered. Our awareness of events around us had become less and less until we were pretty much oblivious of the world around us.

Now, for me at least, reality had snapped back. It is rather disgusting but the only analogy I can think of is if you have ever had to have your ears syringed. You do not notice the gradual loss of hearing as the wax builds up in your ear canal but gradually the world becomes muffled. Then, suddenly, the blockage is removed and hearing returns in a shock of clarity. You also tend to have balance issues for a few minutes which was pretty much how I felt.

Normality had been restored and with it the knowledge that there were so many parts of my life, the new job and moving house for a start, that were on hold but now needed urgent attention. There was also the small matter of a new baby and wife both still in hospital.

The journey had, in one respect come to an end but life carried on regardless. I could have carried on writing for ever now but that was not the purpose of the account. Eleanor was alive and well and while life would bring many new challenges for us all, it was no longer appropriate to carry on writing.

With that thought in mind, I began to bring the book to an end.

# Chapter 33:
## The show that never ends...

I woke up feeling miles better but still tired. I went into the hospital for breakfast and to the ward where Eleanor was settled & asleep. Having taken more blood samples they had decided to supplement her breast feeding with formula – 15ml from a plastic cup which she apparently lapped up. This had settled her down and she had slept much better during the night.

I was shown how to give Iona the intramuscular injection that would prevent blood clotting and deep vein thrombosis, something I would have to do for the next three days which was a bit nerve-wracking to say the least!

The midwives started making moves that implied we were soon to be discharged and the lady from Bounty came to give us our next packs of freebies but then the paediatrician came and delivered the bad news. Although Eleanor's results were below the line they were close enough to cause concern so they were going to recommend light therapy to break down the bilirubin in her skin.

The device was in the form of a UV lamp which fed

an umbilical of optical fibres that in turn fed a flexible mat that she could lie on and which could be wrapped around her as she was swaddled in a blanket. She even had a pair of soft shades to protect her eyes. It meant that she could be placed in her cot or picked up and that the cot could stay by Iona's bed!

We fed and changed her so she would be comfortable and then they wrapped her up and switched her on. Robo-baby was born!

Once again I left at lunchtime but on the way out was nearly run over on the pedestrian crossing to the car park by some stupid woman who was not watching what she was doing.

I got back to find both mother and baby asleep which was cute! Eleanor looked very odd under the photo-therapy but between feeds she settled well and the umbilical allowed us to cuddle her when needed.

We could see the therapy taking effect as she was visibly less yellow as the hours went by.

I carried on trying to be as helpful as possible focusing more on supporting Iona than Eleanor though I did my fair share of feeding (formula, of course, my moobs being of little use in that department) as well as nappy-changing. It was becoming apparent that with every shift change there was a new batch of midwives and we never seemed to get the same ones back which proved to be very confusing!

What was annoying was that with each one came a new opinion as to what we should be doing, contradicting all previous advice whether it be breast feeding techniques, the interpretation of blood test results or whatever. I really could not understand why patient-facing members of staff could not give a consistent message. Surely they should realise just how confusing this is to people who are only in hospital because something stressful is happening.

We also felt as if we were being judged at every moment when the midwives watched what we did which we felt very uncomfortable with.

I asked again about the form that I had provided from the clinic requesting the record of birth but as I had suspected they seemed to have lost it. I had a look in Iona's notes to see if the information was in there but there was no sign of it.

In some respects I should not have been surprised as in my dazed blur I could have given it to the cleaner for all I knew. No doubt it had been lost in a file somewhere and the importance of it understandably lost among the more pressing needs of getting Eleanor out of Iona safely.

Of course, what I should have done is ask someone after the fact when the dust had settled but in my defence I was not thinking straight.

Granny and Granddad came for the 7-8pm visiting slot mainly as Iona wanted some fresh pyjamas and a small pot of olive oil to rub into Eleanor's hands which had some peeling skin.

Again I left around 8:30 feeling very tired and came home via the kebab van (my diet was not the best but I really did not have the energy to cook). I had been taking loads of photos but was conscious that they only existed on the camera so made a point of backing them up on the computer, just in case. It would have been just typical that the camera would have found some creative way of deleting everything and I had tempted fate enough over the last two years.

These were memories we could not replace! While I was there I e-mailed a few to our friends and colleagues as part of the wider announcement.

The next day I woke up full of anticipation that we would be going home today. I had even gone as far as asking her

Mum to get some "Welcome Home" banners and balloons the previous day which I quickly put up.

I got to the hospital and it was quiet being the weekend. I had the customary bacon roll before heading to the ward. Eleanor was asleep and Iona seemed in good spirits, even after I gave her the intramuscular jab.

Iona had already texted earlier to say that they had tested Eleanor overnight and that the results were good enough for them to stop the light therapy but the paediatrician still needed to see her before she could be released. Of more concern was Iona's blood pressure which was still high and they wanted to take more readings to see if it was going down before letting her go.

She started getting weepy which was not a huge surprise under the circumstances especially as she was due the "baby blues" by now, the hormonal problems that usually kick in on day three-ish.

Iona was starting to express milk but Eleanor had by now become lazy and preferred the bottled formula that required far less effort on her part. She had also started to poo normally, having passed all of the meconium.

The paediatrician came and as Eleanor was still a bit yellow requested yet another heel prick test! I headed out with the midwife to do this as they came to read Iona's blood pressure again.

The midwife was a real know-it-all and where others had taken blood while Eleanor was in the cot, she insisted on laying her flat over her lap face down while she squeezed her heel. Eleanor screamed and then vomited down the midwife's leg. I don't think I helped the situation by saying out loud "Good girl, Eleanor!" After all the officious medical types we had encountered there was a certain satisfaction in watching one of them be proven wrong.

By now it was 1pm and obvious we were not going to

be discharged before I was kicked out for the afternoon quiet time.

While I was out, Iona texted to say that Eleanor's test results were fine so all we were waiting for were her own blood pressure readings so fingers crossed!

When I got back it was more of what was becoming the routine – waiting for people to come and do tests and every midwife disagreeing with the previous one and not coming back to do anything when they said they would.

One student midwife came and stupidly started asking Iona about home and instantly triggered floods of tears! All Iona wanted to do at that stage was go home and the constant promise of this just for yet another problem to arise was driving her around the twist. The midwife knew she had made a mistake but I could have screamed at her. I am sure the growing frustration in both our faces was clear.

Iona's blood pressure was still high so going home was out of the question now and they prescribed tablets to try and get it under control.

What was obvious to even someone like me was that just being there was keeping her blood pressure high – white coat syndrome I believe it is called - and one of the student midwives offered to see if there was a private side room clear which we gratefully accepted. The thought of a bit of privacy and quiet to allow Iona to have some chance of a good night's sleep was worth a go, especially as a new mother had arrived with her baby in the next bed and the baby was clearly going to scream throughout the night.

A room was free – side room 7 and we were quickly moved…and then told that it would cost us £100 per night! Months ago on the tour we had been told that side rooms were available on request at this cost but would be offered for free if you had twins or other medical reasons. As we had been offered the room for *medical* reasons, I felt pretty cheated but again kept my mouth shut as if we had to pay, for Iona and Eleanor's benefit it was worth it.

Iona's blood pressure was still sky high so they tried a different cuff on the monitor again and got a different result. They then spent a while experimenting with cuffs and found that Iona almost exactly sat between two sizes so the results were at best spurious. The one that was most reliable was, unfortunately, the higher reading.

I left just before the ward closed for the evening and drove home in a sullen mood. This was not the way it was meant to work out. I had to remind myself that only a couple of days ago we were in the middle of a life-threatening crisis but it had always been my expectation that the baby would come, we would all merrily head home and would then live happily ever after.

Still too tired to cook I stopped off at the local Chinese for something in batter and sweet and sour sauce (if it was chicken then it was a part of the chicken I would rather not know about). I had bought the traditional cigar and a nice bottle of wine to celebrate the birth but in the heat of the moment had totally forgotten about both.

The evening was warm so I went out onto the deck and had my own private party.

To be honest, with Iona and Eleanor still in the hospital it was a bit hollow but we had heard that even the tobacco smoke on clothes and skin could greatly increase the chance of cot death so it was good that I got it out of my system while they were away.

Iona had called and put me on standby in terms of coming in just in case she wanted anything but when she had not called by 8:40 I realised that it might be because her phone had died! I texted to say I was coming in and she called, speaking quickly as indeed her battery was almost dead and gave me a list to bring in.

There was still no news either way but they had increased her tablets for the blood pressure as it was simply not coming down.

We had planned a small party with a few family members in the understandable expectation that we would be home but as this was clearly not going to be the case I did some hasty phoning around to put them off before heading back to the hospital.

The doctor came and queried why Iona had changed the timing of her drugs but it transpired that a midwife had changed it after talking to the doctor on duty which it also then transpired was none other than him! We were both getting really fed up with the constant change of opinion, overruling of other people's instructions and general screw ups that seemed to be going on. To have someone disagreeing with himself was just too much. He didn't seem to understand our frustration.

At lunchtime I went to the supermarket to get some more bits and bobs for Eleanor and called my Mum and Dad, offering them the 3pm slot to come and visit which they jumped at. They came bearing cake and loads of presents including a lot of knitted clothes that my Mum had made.

They had a nice cuddle and it was good that they had seen Eleanor so small.

At hot drinks time I was offered a coffee! It was the first thing I had been offered since we had arrived on Wednesday. Even better, when it came to dinner time they again brought the wrong one for Iona and when she asked for a replacement, they left the incorrect one for me!

While in general the maternity unit was really good the one huge failing from my perspective was the utter lack of any catering facilities for the fathers. I was not expecting to be fed but to have somewhere to make a cuppa would have been nice. As it was, to be simply treated as if I wasn't there when Iona was getting a drink was just silly.

I learned fast and my rucksack was usually well stocked with drinks and snacks when I arrived in the morning (the chocolate never being destined to pass my lips!).

We did have some good news before I left. Iona had requested to be moved back to the ward as the private room, as nice as it was, had not worked in terms of bringing the blood pressure down and she felt we could not afford a further stay (I would have gladly left her there and stumped up despite my anger at the fact we had been charged in the first place). However, the midwife on duty took pity on us and allowed her to stay at no additional cost. As grateful as I was I made sure she put a statement to that effect on Iona's notes.

Dinner that night was from the local curry house and I knew I was rapidly running out of fast-food outlets. Much more of this and I would be forced to cook for myself again!

Okay, I will admit it, part of me was revelling in the fact that I could indulge in junk food at will and I knew I would pay for it later. It was as if the very last vestige of bachelor life was gasping its last breath.

The difference that night was that I didn't have a drink. That much of my self-indulgence was over. I was now a father (which was still something that hadn't sunk in) and had even more responsibilities than being a husband. The fact that I also had a mortgage meant that I probably needed to invest in a pair of slippers and a pipe soon.

The next day I undertook my Groundhog Day trip to the hospital. I had worked out that I could see into her side room from the window by the door to maternity and spotted Iona & Eleanor. We waved to each other before I was allowed in.

They came to measure Iona's blood pressure but it was *still* high so the doctor came to say they were going to up the dosage of her drugs but that she would be in for another night until they were sure her blood pressure was both down and stable.

They had to take yet more blood from Eleanor but cocked up the first time after causing her considerable distress so had to come back and do it a second time.

A midwife confirmed that Iona could stay in the side room for the rest of her time and we would only be charged for the first night.

I got another coffee and free lunch which was good as at lunchtime I had to go for more nappies and tights for Eleanor.

By the time I got back the car park was rammed full! I spoke to work and gave them an update and my boss was very understanding. In the background while I spoke a lorry was reversing which my boss thought was a medial monitor which added to the impression of crisis! I have to say, it was an impression I did not correct which was somewhat naughty of me.

It was another day of waiting, tests, waiting, lack of information but as the day wore on it did look more and more promising that we would finally get a result in the morning.

It was a psychological day for us both as if we could get out at any time she would not have been in for a calendar week. Iona was less than optimistic and told me not to bring the big car but to come in the small one. I put the seat in the car anyway, just in case.

Overnight her blood pressure had been coming down but she was still borderline and the doctor who was supposed to have come the night before still had not shown up and by the time I had to leave while they had taken more readings there was no news. I am sure he was busy but it was still frustrating.

I drove home to pick Iona's Mum up with the idea that she would sit around the hospital café during the visiting slots but when we got back to Iona's room she had a stern face and told me not to get settled.

She had already started packing – the doctor had released her!

Quick as a flash and not waiting for someone to change their minds, her Mum and I took as much as we could carry back to the car and brought the seat back.

We sat around for a frustrating hour before they finally completed the discharge process and I got Eleanor in the car seat but even on the way out we were stopped as if we were stealing the child. They needed to check Eleanor's leg bands to prove it was our baby and to check the car seat which they clearly should have done in the room but like a lot of the check-out process they had forgotten. This was probably the moment that I came closest to swearing at them. It was their fault the check had been overlooked but rather than apologise we were being treated almost like criminals.

I understand and fully appreciate the need for security but does it really take that much effort to read the check points on a clip-board?

Finally, just after four in the afternoon, we were free!

I was a very proud and relieved Daddy carrying our daughter out of the hospital for the first time.

Epilogue: Back to reality.

In fact the title of the previous chapter still applies here. Life is the show that never ends. Iona and I were both exhausted. From start to finish the journey had been over two years and in the process we had both changed so much it was a miracle we still recognised each other.

The blessing was that the result was a healthy bouncing baby (with a spectacular pair of lungs as we discovered in the dead of night when it was feeding time).

It is strange how the mind can programme itself into pattern recognition. Say, for example, you see a VW Camper Van on the television in some prominent place which is not difficult as the BBC seem to have bought one that they use on pretty much every country-based documentary at the moment.

Anyway, once you have the image ingrained in your mind from that point onwards everywhere you look you will see VW Camper Vans. This is, of course, not the case and they were always there but now your brain is noticing them whereas before they were filed in the "ignore" bracket along with party political broadcasts.

The same was true of IVF. Two years ago I would have paid no attention to anything on the subject in the newspapers or on television but now the papers seemed to have stories on a daily basis.

Reading them I realised we had been extremely lucky! The stories mostly had the same general theme in that the couples involved had tried for years, been through multiple failed attempts and heartache but had finally had success. The others, however, were the horror stories, the mistakes and malpractice that had cost lives.

I thought back to our own case and to how close we potentially came to being yet another column in the Daily Mail.

It was humbling that for all my moaning we had the result we had hoped for, that our emotional investment had paid off. I doubt that either of us had the strength to have coped had things gone wrong.

At this stage I should also pause and give thought to all of those who have not been as fortunate as us. As good as the science of IVF is the procedure comes with no guarantees and the failure rate is still significant.

This story had a happy ending but I am conscious that there are so many out there for which their own journey led them to heartache and to those you have my sympathies and my hope that you found the strength to try again and not give up hope.

The days after getting Eleanor home were strange as we came to terms with normality, something we simply had not enjoyed for two years. The house move was still imminent, my job was still new and I had a lot of settling in to do and, above all, we suddenly had Eleanor to care for.

Surprisingly, fatherhood came easy, mostly because I steered clear of any helpful books or internet advice and just got on with it.

Inevitably, we worked our way through the endless conveyor belt of visitors to get around to friends and for me this was in some way the part I was most looking forward to. Most people had no idea of the true nature of Eleanor's creation and it had been incredibly difficult especially throughout the latter stages not to let slip in a moment of distraction.

This is something you will find if you end up in a similar position and want to keep some or all details secret. It is like any form of distortion of the truth, the simpler you keep the cover story the easier it is to uphold. In our case we managed to keep the full facts to all but a very select few. Iona's parents knew but the only others were the tight band of friends we had who had experienced IVF first-hand and had been instrumental in guiding us along our own journey.

Speaking to these friends now was a true pleasure, especially as we really compared notes as to our overall experiences.

As I have said many times throughout this, had it

not been for their sage advice we would have struggled to overcome those small problems that could so easily have spiralled out of all control.

What I found incredible, however, was when I mentioned about the general level of medical advice and care we had experienced and they came back with similar stories with some variation (and with some anecdotes which have worked their way into this tale of woe).

It was clear that the system was fundamentally flawed. I had no experience of undertaking IVF through the normal British system but it did seem that the moment you went private in any way the wheels of the medical bus would fall off.

There was, in hindsight, so much in the way of advice, information and other things that Iona and I had missed out on purely as her pregnancy was out of the ordinary. We were not, however, the only ones in this respect.

Bob Litten-Brown had written articles on the general subject of IVF from a bloke's perspective but as a father himself what little time he had for writing was devoted to his first passion of Science Fiction. He had, however, penned his own message to his daughter and as I have mentioned before was the inspiration for me to do likewise.

I had by now all but finished "The Journey of Love and Hope". The only thing that remained was for Iona and I to check it through and write a final personal note from each of us to Eleanor. We had decided to let the hassle of house moving die down and spend a few months with her before doing this. That way we would be emotionally over the stress of the events around her birth and could both take a step back.

The book and our writing would be a time capsule for her, interpreted by our future selves (hopefully) in the best way possible but it was important that what we wrote now would make sense.

Neither of us had read the book all the way through and neither intended to do so and we agreed to keep private the closing "letter" to our daughter.

We met up with Andrew and Dawn and the Litten-Brown's and while it wasn't quite a group therapy sort of thing it did turn into an IVF-centric conversation. It was, for all of us, just so nice to be able to talk about it freely.

As the wine was flowing so was my conversation and I knew I was rapidly descending into "grumpy old man" mode as were the other men present. It was, I guess, inevitable that someone would sooner or later suggest that one of us put out some kind of self-help guide for other blokes in our situation.

It was also, I guess, inevitable that Bob would volunteer me. As a keen writer he was always trying to encourage the bug in others and he could see that even if I lacked the skill I certainly had the passion. Although he had written several science fiction novels and a few articles on IVF he knew in his heart that it was not his destiny to write a book on the subject but suggested that I might rise to the challenge.

Well, I thought, why not?

And so, dear reader, we arrive in the here and now. Twelve months have passed and so much has happened in the intervening time that I could easily write another book on the subject.

Suffice to say, Iona, Eleanor and I now live in Dorset, my job in Southampton is going well, Eleanor is growing up incredibly fast (and most people say she takes after her mother) and life, on the whole, is good.

More importantly, I have finally managed to finish this account of what might have happened had I *really* been called Robert Forde, my wife Iona and my daughter Eleanor and we *really* lived in Dorset. The truth, of course, is somewhere between the cracks in the fiction.

Sadly, everything you have read is based on truth even if all the names, places and dates have been changed to protect not only our privacy but that of others. Embarrassing doctors or pointing the finger of blame is not what I want to achieve and thus none of the details here can link back to anyone real. I probably should of, to be honest but now I simply do not have the energy to take them to task and, to be honest, Eleanor is such a joy to us that I do not want to sully her existence by continuing a protracted campaign against the medical services.

What I hope you will get out of this, however, is a pretty frank idea of the kind of stupid little problems that can thwart you along the way. Please do not let anything you have read put you off as that was most definitely not my intention. Indeed, if anything you have learned from this tale has in any way helped you please, please pass it on. Iona and I gained so much from the kindness of others that I do feel it is our place to help each other.

Do not be afraid to ask but if you do not know where to turn to, I can heartily recommend the infertility charities as a first port of call. Infertility Network UK was of immense help to us but there are plenty of others and they are generally made up of folk who have first-hand experience. There is absolutely nothing wrong with asking for help and they will certainly not preach. They understand your problem far more than you most likely and it is amazing how many feel moved to help others.

If I have one closing message it is this:

After two years of anxious struggle and the final moments of heart-stopping terror, through all the problems, annoyances and frustrations, through all the financial expenditure would I turn around and say hand-on-heart that it had been worth it?

The answer is simple, I would say yes without the slightest hesitation or question and I would do it all again tomorrow, which leads me on to another thing...Iona turned around yesterday and asked me what we were doing about number two?

That, as they say, is another story.

Lightning Source UK Ltd.
Milton Keynes UK
UKHW021158160321
380445UK00008B/1747